ENCHANTED CROSSINGS

'There's magic on every page of *Enchanted Crossings!*''
—*Affaire de Coeur*

In these three unforgettable romance stories, bold heroes and headstrong heroines challenge the magical borders of time and space to fulfill their hearts' desires.

MADELINE BAKER
"Heart of the Hunter"

"The Queen of Indian Romance conquers a new genre!"
—*Romantic Times*

ANNE AVERY
"Dream Seeker"

"Anne Avery opens wonderfully new horizons on the leading edge of romance!"
—*Romantic Times*

KATHLEEN MORGAN
"The Last Gatekeeper"

"Kathleen Morgan grips readers with sizzling passion and inventive plotting."
—*Romantic Times*

ENCHANTED CROSSINGS

ANNE AVERY ◆ MADELINE BAKER
KATHLEEN MORGAN

LOVE SPELL ◆ NEW YORK CITY

LOVE SPELL®

September 1994

Published by

Dorchester Publishing Co., Inc.
276 Fifth Avenue
New York, NY 10001

Printed in the United States of America.

ENCHANTED CROSSINGS

MADELINE BAKER
HEART OF THE HUNTER

*To Adrianne Ross and Gail Link,
two talented friends who know how to let their
fantasies unwind and enjoy "The Music Of The Night."*

Prologue

Indian Territory, 1877

The two men glared at the Indian who stood between their freedom and a king's ransom in gold.

The Indian was tall, his skin the color of dark bronze, his eyes as black as the bowels of hell. His voice was like slow thunder as he ordered them to get out of the cave and leave the gold behind.

Charlie McBride was willing. Life was more precious than gold. Any fool knew that.

Any fool except Denver Wilkie.

As soon as they cleared the cave, Denver drew his .44 and fired at the Indian. Denver was a crack shot and the bullet struck the Red Stick in the chest, just left of center. Blood oozed from the wound, spreading like crimson tears over the warrior's buckskin shirt.

The Indian fired back. His first bullet struck Denver in the throat, unleashing a fountain of blood.

The second smashed into Charlie McBride's shoulder. He staggered backward, tripped over a rock, and landed on his rump, hard. More frightened than he'd ever been in his life, Charlie stared up at the Indian, certain he was about to be given a one-way ticket to hell.

For a moment, the two men stared at each other, and Charlie felt as if the warrior were probing deep into his soul, prying into the innermost secrets and desires of his heart.

And then the warrior lowered his rifle. "Take only . . . what you need," he said at last. "If you take . . . one nugget more . . . my spirit will haunt you . . . for as long as you live."

His mouth as dry as the dust of Arizona, Charlie McBride could only nod.

"My body . . ." The Indian was swaying on his feet now. "Do not leave it . . . out here . . ."

Charlie nodded again. "I'll bury you," he said. "You have my word on it."

"Inside the cave," the warrior said, his voice growing faint. "Swear it . . ."

"I promise," Charlie said, but the Indian was past hearing.

Slowly, the life faded from the warrior's eyes, the strength left his legs, and he fell slowly, gracefully to the ground.

Although he was growing a little light-headed from the blood he'd lost, Charlie McBride kept his promise. He jammed his neckerchief over the wound in his shoulder to stop the bleeding, then wrapped the dead warrior in Denver's faded Hudson's Bay blanket and left the Indian's body on a natural shelf deep in the bowels of the cave, across from the treasure he had died to protect.

Then, his saddlebags filled with a fortune in gold, Charlie McBride rode away from the mountain.

His first stop was the land office, where he bought two hundred acres of land, including the Indian's mountain, even though he knew he'd never set foot in that cave again.

Chapter One

Montana, 1994

She felt it again, a warm breath whispering against the side of her neck, and then a chill, as if a cold winter wind had found its way into the cavern.

For a moment, Kelly didn't move, only stood there, her lantern held high, unable to shake the feeling that she was being watched, that unseen eyes were contemplating her with equal parts of curiosity and malice.

But that was ridiculous. There was nothing to be afraid of, she told herself. Nothing at all. If her grandfather was right, no one but members of the family had been in this cave for more than a hundred years.

Taking a deep calming breath, she placed the

lantern on the ground and returned to her study of the body that occupied a narrow shelf along the side of the cave wall. The body, wrapped in a faded Hudson's Bay blanket, was located exactly where her grandfather had said it would be.

In her mind's eye, Kelly could see the ancient remains on display in the local historical museum, along with a small white placard that named her as the contributor.

Kelly shook her head. She had never truly believed her grandfather McBride's ramblings about the riches supposedly hidden in a cave in the mountain behind the ranch. She had thought all his talk about a wealth of Indian gold guarded by the ghost of a savage Lakota warrior to be nothing more than the confused yearnings of an old man's mind, a jumbled mix of old legends and fables handed down from one generation of McBrides to the next.

A long sigh escaped Kelly's lips as she stared down at the blanket-wrapped corpse.

She believed her grandfather now.

Answering some call she didn't understand, Kelly drew a corner of the blanket back, then blinked in surprise. She had expected to find no more than an emaciated corpse, a skeleton clothed in tattered shreds of deer hide; instead, she saw the well-muscled body of a man dressed in a buck-skin clout and fringed leggings. His moccasins were unadorned. He'd been tall, long-legged, and narrow-hipped. His hair was black and straight and fell well past his broad shoulders. His jaw was strong and square, his cheekbones prominent, his forehead wide. His nose was long and blade-straight.

Kelly stared thoughtfully at the dark stain on his shirt front, and then frowned in bewilderment. Why hadn't the body decayed? She had the strangest feeling that the Indian wasn't dead at all, that, like Sleeping Beauty, he was merely sleeping away the centuries, waiting to be awakened by love's first kiss.

With a shake of her head, she put away such fanciful thoughts and then, impulsively, she touched his cheek with her forefinger. His skin was supple and . . . warm.

Warm when it should have been hard and cold. When it shouldn't have been skin at all. After all these years, the body should have returned to the dust from which it had been made.

A shiver of unease skated down Kelly's spine and she glanced around the cave, every instinct warning her to run. Abruptly, she jerked her hand away from his cheek. It was then she saw it, a small buckskin bag resting against his chest.

Curious, she opened the small sack and emptied the contents into her hand. For a moment, she could only stare at the large medallion resting in her palm.

Fashioned in the shape of an eagle with its wings spread wide, the amulet was about two inches in diameter. And it appeared to be made of solid gold. Even in the flickering light of the lantern, the fetish seemed to glow with a life all its own. It felt warm as it nestled in the palm of her hand.

Kelly stared at the eagle for a long moment, and then, almost of their own volition, her fingers folded over it, and her gaze was drawn to the numerous bags of gold dust and nuggets stacked one on top of the other against the far wall. There was enough money there to pay off the mortgage on the ranch, enough to settle her grandfather's hospital bill. Enough to keep her in comfort for the rest of her life.

Her hands were trembling as she pulled the blanket over the face of the dead man. She couldn't put his remains on display. She knew somehow that he wouldn't want that. Tomorrow, she'd bring a shovel and bury the Indian in the furthest corner of the cave where he could rest undisturbed.

Kelly sighed. The body had rested here, undisturbed, for over a hundred years. She wasn't going to bury it so *it* could rest in peace; she was going to bury it for her own peace of mind.

As she stepped away from the narrow shelf, she felt the warm breath against her neck again.

Put it back.

Kelly whirled around, her gaze searching the cavern's dim interior for the source of the deep male voice. But there was no one there.

Suddenly anxious to be gone from this place of death, she slipped the medallion into the pocket of her jeans. Folding her grandfather's map, she stuck it inside her shirt.

For now, she would leave the treasure as she had found it.

For now, she wanted only to go home.

Her boot heels made soft crunching sounds as she hurried toward the entrance of the cavern. The cave was long and narrow, with a high rounded ceiling and a sandy floor.

Extinguishing the lantern, Kelly left it on the ground inside the mouth of the cave. The opening was only a few feet high and barely wide enough for her to fit through. It had taken her over two hours of intense searching to find the cave at all, and then it had been by sheer luck.

Kelly squinted against the sunlight as she crawled out of the cave. For some reason, she had expected it to be dark outside.

Her grandfather's old gelding, Dusty, whickered softly as she stood up. She patted the buckskin's neck, suddenly glad for the presence of another living creature, and then she swung effortlessly into the saddle and reined the horse toward the Triple M.

Riding away from the cave, Kelly slipped her hand into the pocket of her Levi's, her fingertips moving over the golden eagle.

From behind her, she heard a low rumble, like thunder echoing off the mountains, and then she felt it again, that chill that was colder than the north wind.

Seized with a sudden uncontrollable fear, she drummed her heels into the gelding's sides and raced for home.

Chapter Two

Kelly studied the golden eagle as she ate dinner later that night, intrigued by the intricate carving. It was the most beautiful thing she'd ever seen, tempting her touch again and again. She marveled at the rich feel of the gold beneath her fingertips, at the delicate lines that formed the bird's deep-set eyes and sharp beak. The wings were exquisite, the talons honed to fine sharp points.

Rising from the battered kitchen table, she quickly washed up her few dishes, took a long leisurely soak in a bubble bath, then settled into bed, pillows propped behind her back so she could read.

But she couldn't concentrate on the book. She kept thinking of the body in the cave. How long had it been there? A hundred years, at least, she thought, because the Triple M had been in her family at least that long. Why hadn't the body decayed? She stared at the eagle, propped against the table lamp beside her bed. Why had the body of the Indian felt warm to her touch?

Kelly shook her head. Surely that had been a product of her overactive imagination. But she had not imagined that long, lean body. He must have been quite an impressive man in his day, tall and broad-shouldered. She knew somehow that his eyes had been as black as sin, that his teeth had been straight and white, and that when he smiled . . .

She laughed softly, uneasily. What was the matter with her, fantasizing about a man who'd probably been dead for over a hundred years! First thing tomorrow she would bury the body. It made her uncomfortable just knowing it was there.

She was about to switch off her bedside light when she saw a dark shadow at the window. All the air seemed to leave her body and her heart suddenly seemed too big for her chest as she watched the shadow pause, then move on.

For a moment, she was frozen with fear, then she bounded out of bed, ran into the living room, and grabbed the shotgun from the rack over the fireplace, grateful that her grandfather had taught her how to shoot.

Heart pounding, she stood behind the front door, listening, waiting. For the first time, she realized just how alone she was. Her closest neighbor was five miles to the south. She couldn't pick up the phone and dial 911 for help.

Far in the distance, she heard the lonely wail of a coyote, and then there was only silence, a silence as deep and dark as the grave.

She stood there for a quarter of an hour, her whole body tense. And then, gradually, the sounds of the night returned. She heard the frogs croaking in the pond behind the house, the song of a cricket, the soft sighing of the wind, and she knew somehow that whatever had been lurking in the shadows had gone.

It took a long time to fall asleep that night, but when sleep finally came, she dreamed of a tall, dark-skinned warrior with hair as black as midnight and eyes as deep and dark as fathomless pools of liquid ebony . . .

In the morning, her fears of the night before seemed foolish. She'd never been one to be spooked by shadows in the night. She'd lived alone in Los Angeles ever since her father had died five years ago. Lived alone and liked it, but when Grandpa McBride's health started failing, she had tried to convince him to come to L.A. and live with her. But her grandfather had refused to leave the Triple M. Like Kelly, he had cherished his independence. She knew he would have died alone if the hospital in Cedar Flats hadn't called to inform her he was there. She'd taken a two-week leave of absence from her job with Wolfe, Cullman and Chartier and flown to Montana to be with him.

Kelly felt a familiar tug at her heart as she thought of her grandfather. In days past, when she was a little girl, her family had spent their summers at the ranch, and Grandpa had charmed her with tales of the Old West, repeating the colorful tales his great-grandfather Charlie McBride had once told him, tales of Indian fights and buffalo hunts and mountain men.

Her grandfather had been on his death bed when he told her about the gold his great-grandfather Charlie had buried in a cave in the mountain behind the Triple M.

"Gold?" Kelly had said with a grin. "If there was any gold up there, don't you think someone would have found it by now?"

"It's there, girl. My great-grandpappy told me so."

"Why didn't he spend it?"

"He was afraid of it, afraid of the ghost who haunts the mountain."

"Ghost!" Kelly had exclaimed.

"I've seen him, Kelly girl," her grandfather had said, his gnarled hand squeezing hers with surprising strength.

"Really?" Kelly had asked, leaning forward. "When? Where?"

"When I was younger, and braver. I followed my great-grandpappy's map and found the cave. The gold's in there, girl, a fortune, just like he said."

"And you never touched it?"

"Oh, I took a little dust now and then, when I needed it. But something told me not to try and take more than I needed. Now it's yours, Kelly. Use it wisely."

18

Those were the last words her Grandpa Frank had said in this world. He was asleep when she went to visit him the next morning. He'd opened his eyes, smiled at her, and then, with a sigh, he was gone.

And now the ranch, and the gold, belonged to her.

After a quick breakfast, Kelly went out to the barn and saddled Dusty. She had a grave to dig, and it was a long ride to the cave.

Kelly approached the cavern with a growing sense of unease. Chiding herself for her foolishness, she slipped on a pair of heavy work gloves, removed the shovel she'd tied behind the saddle, and ducked into the cave.

She paused near the entrance to light the lantern she'd left the day before, felt her heart begin to pound as shadows came to life on the walls. The cavern was roomy inside, high enough for her to stand erect once she was inside.

Nothing to be afraid of, she told herself. The dead can't hurt you.

Her booted feet made hardly a sound on the soft, sandy earth as she went deeper into the cave. She wouldn't have to dig a very deep hole, she decided, just deep enough to cover the body.

Her heart was pounding like a runaway train as she drew near the ledge, and then her breath caught in her throat.

The ledge was empty.

The body was gone.

Not believing her eyes, Kelly ran her hands over the surface of the earthen shelf, searching for some sign that a body had actually been there, that she wasn't losing her mind. Nothing.

And then she saw it, the colorful Hudson's Bay blanket, crumpled in a heap beneath the ledge.

For a moment, she felt relief. She hadn't imagined it after all. The body had been there, and now it was gone.

Bewildered, she stared at the blanket. Gone, she thought. Gone where?

Lantern in hand, she searched the floor of the cave for some sign that an animal had dragged the remains away, but there was no sign of animal tracks, no footprints other than her own.

She laughed at that. Of course there were no footprints. Ghosts didn't leave footprints.

With a cry, she turned on her heel and ran toward the entrance of the cave, scrambling out of the narrow opening as if Satan himself were snapping at her heels.

She dreamed of the Indian again that night. She was walking in the moonlight when suddenly he was there beside her, his black eyes glowing like dark fires. He gazed at her for a long moment, the awareness growing between them, and then, quite unexpectedly, he brushed his knuckles against her cheek. The touch exploded through her like lightning, and while she was trying to recover, she heard a voice echo in her mind. A voice that was husky with warning. His voice. *Put it back.* And then he was gone.

She woke to find the sheets tangled around her legs, her brow damp with perspiration.

Unconsciously, she reached for the golden eagle she'd placed beneath her pillow, and as her hand closed around its smoothness, she heard the warning again. Only this time it wasn't a dream, and she didn't hear the words echoing in her mind.

She heard the words, spoken clearly, from the shadowed corner of her room.

"Put it back."

On the verge of terror, Kelly scrambled across the bed and switched on the light, her eyes wide as they searched the room.

There was no one there.

Chapter Three

Harry Renford stared at the young woman seated before him with obvious disbelief.

"Pay off the loan?" he said, repeating her words as if he hadn't heard her quite right. "You want to pay off the loan?"

Harry sat back in his chair, his hands folded on the desktop as he studied her face. Kelly McBride was a pretty girl, with long, curly brown hair and large blue eyes. He'd known her grandparents, Frank and Annee, for years. Annee had died almost ten years ago, but Frank had stayed on at the ranch, alone. He'd gotten pretty feeble in his old age, but he'd refused to leave the Triple M, and the ranch, some thirty miles southeast of town, had fallen into a state of disrepair.

Old man McBride had died three weeks ago,

leaving behind a mountain of hospital bills and a sizable mortgage. It had been in Harry's mind to buy the Triple M when it went on the market and discover for himself if the rumors of a hidden gold mine were true. It had seemed a safe investment. If there was no gold, and he doubted there was, Harry planned to turn the Triple M into a guest ranch. But then Frank's granddaughter had shown up to claim the old place. He'd made her what he considered a generous offer for the ranch, an offer she had politely, but firmly, refused, thereby upsetting his carefully thought-out scheme.

Harry shifted in his chair. He wasn't a man who liked to see his plans upset, especially by a young city girl who probably didn't know the difference between a dandy brush and a hoof pick.

"Well, that's fine, Miss McBride," he drawled. "Just fine. But where, if you don't mind my asking, did you get the money?"

"I don't believe the source of my funds is a requisite for paying off the loan, Mr. Renford."

"No, no, of course not. Well, it will take me a day or two to get the necessary papers drawn up. Why don't you come back on, say, Friday afternoon?"

"Fine. Until then, Mr. Renford."

Outside, Kelly drew a deep breath and let it out in a long sigh of relief. She was glad to be out of Harry Renford's sight. She didn't like the man, though she didn't know why. It wasn't his looks, she mused. He was quite a handsome man, with a shock of wavy blond hair that was just turning gray at the temples, a charming smile, when he cared to use it, and light gray eyes. It was his eyes, she decided now; they were cold and unblinking, like the eyes of a snake.

Well, as soon as she paid off the mortgage on the ranch, she wouldn't have to deal with him again. Tomorrow she would drive into Coleville and see about selling some of the smaller nuggets. She didn't dare do it here. Cedar Flats was a small town where everybody knew everybody else's business. She didn't want to have to answer any questions about where the gold came from.

Frowning, she started down the sidewalk to where she'd left her car. In a few days, she'd have to decide what to do about the ranch. When she'd first arrived, it had been in her mind to sell it, but once she'd seen the place again, remembered the good times she'd had there, she'd known she couldn't sell the old place. It had, after all, been in her family for over a century. Still, it was horribly run-down. The house and the barn were in need of repair, the house needed painting inside and out, the corral fences needed new rails, there was no stock to speak of except for Dusty and a couple of aging chickens.

Nevertheless, she was here, and she was here to stay, even though it meant relocating, quitting her secretarial job with Wolfe, Cullman and Chartier, finding other employment . . .

Kelly laughed softly. She didn't need to work anymore. Having access to those nuggets was like having a trust fund. She was set for life.

She was unlocking the door of her car when a man appeared beside her.

"Miss McBride?"

Kelly hesitated a moment before answering. "Yes?"

"I'd like to talk to you."

He was Indian, she thought, noting his dark skin and high cheekbones, though there was nothing particularly sinister about that. There were lots of Indians in Cedar Flats. Most of them lived out on the reservation.

"Talk?" Kelly said. "About what?"

"The Triple M."

Kelly glanced around, reassured by the presence of other people nearby. "What about it?"

"I'd like to buy it."

Kelly glanced at his faded green shirt, the sleeves of which were rolled up to his elbows, exposing bronze forearms thick with muscle. Frayed blue jeans hugged his legs; his feet were encased in a pair of run-down black boots. She doubted if he could afford to buy a cup of coffee.

"I'm sorry," she said politely, "the ranch isn't for sale."

She opened the door and slid behind the wheel, but before she could close the door, the man took a step forward, placing himself between her and the car door.

"Could we go somewhere and discuss it?" he asked.

Kelly shook her head, thinking that his voice was as deep and rich as dark chocolate fudge.

"Please."

The word seemed torn from his throat, and she had the sudden unshakable feeling that this was a man who hadn't done much apologizing in his life.

She looked at him then, really looked at him for the first time, and felt a shiver of apprehension skitter down her spine. He looked remarkably as she had imagined the corpse she'd found in the cave would have looked when he was alive.

Kelly's heart begin to pound as she noted the similarities. Like the body in the cave, this man was tall and dark. His thick black hair fell past his shoulders. His legs were long, his shoulders were unbelievably broad beneath the almost threadbare shirt. He seemed made of solid muscle. His eyes were as black as obsidian, just as she'd imagined those of the dead man would have been. His nose was straight as a knife edge, and his mouth . . . oh my, she had never seen such a sensual mouth on a man in her whole life.

He stared down at her, one black brow arching slightly, as if he knew exactly what she was thinking.

"Are you sure we can't discuss it?" he asked in a voice as seductive as candlelight and champagne. "Maybe grab a cup of coffee in the motel coffee shop?"

"I'm sure," she said, wondering if he was truly suggesting what she was thinking. "Now, if you'll excuse me . . ."

Kelly stared pointedly at his muscular forearm, which was resting along the top edge of the car door.

His dark eyes flashed with anger as he stepped away from the car.

In an instant, Kelly shut the door and locked it. Shoving the key into the ignition, she gave it a twist, put the gearshift in drive, and pulled away from the curb.

But she couldn't resist a look in her rearview mirror. For some reason, she had expected him to have vanished from sight, but he stood in the middle of the narrow two-lane street, staring after her.

Kelly let out a long ragged breath as she turned the corner at the end of the block. Whoever the man was, he intrigued and frightened her as no one ever had.

Lee Roan Horse felt his brows draw together in a frown as he watched the light blue Camaro careen around the corner and disappear from sight.

His first meeting with Miss Kelly McBride hadn't gone quite as planned, he thought wryly. For a moment there, she had looked at him the way most white women did, with a mixture of interest and curiosity, and then, for no reason that he could fathom, she had stared at him as if she were seeing a ghost.

So, he mused, what now?

Hands shoved in the back pockets of his jeans, he crossed the street to where his battered Ford truck was parked and climbed inside, only to sit staring out the windshield, his finger tapping on the steering wheel. She had something he wanted and he had two choices—ask for it, or take it.

He'd tried asking . . .

* * *

Kelly sat up, jerked from a sound sleep by a sudden coldness. She glanced quickly around the room, shivering as a gust of wind blew in through the window across from the bed.

Her mouth went suddenly dry as she stared at the window. She had closed it before she went to bed.

Her heart began to beat triple time as she saw a faint shadow move in the hallway. Instinctively, she reached for the Colt .38 in the drawer of her nightstand. Her hands were shaking as she gripped the gun in both hands. The weapon, small and compact, infused her with a sense of security, though she doubted she had the nerve to actually squeeze the trigger.

A board creaked in the hallway, and then she saw a man outlined in the doorway of her room.

Her heart climbed into her throat as she drew back the hammer on the Colt. The noise seemed very loud in the stillness of the room.

"Don't shoot."

Kelly blinked into the darkness. She'd know that voice anywhere.

Transferring the .38 into her right hand, she reached over and switched on the bedside light with her left.

"What are you doing here?"

The Indian shrugged. "I don't guess you'd believe I came to talk?"

Kelly slid a glance at the clock on the nightstand. "At three a.m.?"

"I couldn't sleep."

"So you decided to crawl in my bedroom window and have a look around?"

He frowned. "I came in the front door. You really should lock it, you know."

"The front door?" Kelly glanced at the curtains fluttering in the faint breeze. "Then how did the window . . . ?"

"What?"

"Nothing. You didn't answer my question. What are you doing here?"

"I want to buy the Triple M."

"I told you this afternoon, it isn't for sale."

"This is Lakota land. My land."

"Excuse me, but I believe this is *my* land. I have the deed to prove it." Or she would have, come Friday afternoon.

"I don't care if you have a trunk full of deeds. This is Lakota land, stolen from my people over a hundred years ago."

Kelly grimaced. "And you expect me to give it back to you, just like that?"

"I said I'd buy it."

Kelly let out a sigh of exasperation, wondering how such a remarkably attractive man could be so obtuse. He'd changed clothes, she noticed, and thought he looked even more handsome, and more dangerous, dressed all in black.

"And I said it's not for sale. Case closed. Now, get out of here before I call the police and have you arrested for . . . for . . ."

"Breaking and entering," he supplied, his voice suddenly as hard as the look in his dark eyes.

"Whatever. Good-bye."

He didn't move, only continued to stare at her from out of eyes as black as the night. The gun wavered in Kelly's hand, and for a moment she had the impression that the Indian in the cave was standing in front of her.

Put it back.

Kelly blinked several times. "Did you say something?"

He frowned. "No, why?"

"I thought . . . I mean . . . Never mind." She shivered as she felt it again, the same cold chill she'd felt in the cave.

"Are you all right?" the Indian asked. "You look like you're about to faint."

"I'm fine," Kelly said. "I've never . . ."

The words died on her lips as she stared past the Indian to the wall behind him. She watched in stunned disbelief as his shadow took on the shape of an eagle, its wings spread in flight . . .

"You've never what?" he asked, frowning.

"Never . . . fainted," Kelly replied, and then everything went dark.

When she came to, she was lying in her bed. The covers had been pulled up to her chin, and there was a cold washcloth over her brow. The Indian—she'd have to ask his name, she thought groggily—was standing beside the bed staring down at her, a frown on his handsome face. He'd taken her gun and shoved it into the waistband of his jeans.

"You okay?" he asked.

Kelly nodded, her gaze fixed on the gun.

He shook his head ruefully. "Would you feel safer if I gave it back to you?"

"Probably, but my hands are shaking so badly I don't think I could hold it. What happened?"

He shrugged. "Beats the hell out of me. One minute we were talking, and the next you turned white as the sheet and keeled over."

Kelly's gaze slid past him to the far wall. "It's gone."

"What's gone?" he asked, glancing over his shoulder.

"Nothing."

He grunted. "I put the coffee on. You want some?"

"Yes, please."

Lee Roan Horse shook his head again. She was some piece of work, he thought. First she pulled a gun on him, then she fainted dead away for no apparent reason, and now she was as polite as you please.

He left the bedroom, returning a short time later with two mismatched mugs of coffee.

Kelly sat up when he entered the room, her gaze fluttering over the gun still nestled in the waistband of his pants.

"You look like the cream and sugar type," he muttered, handing her one of the cups.

Kelly took the mug, her fingertips brushing against his as she did so. The contact, brief as it was, made her suddenly, acutely aware that she was in the house alone with a man. A very virile, very attractive man, who had a gun.

"You're not gonna faint on me again, are you?" he asked.

"No." Quickly, she took a sip of her coffee. Heavy on the milk and light on the sugar, it was exactly the way she liked it.

Lee sat down in the chair beside the bed and looked around. The bedroom was small, containing only a double bed, a mahogany nightstand, a matching chest of drawers, and the overstuffed chair he occupied. The walls were blue, bare except for an old gilt-edged oval mirror and a painting of a desert sunset. A colorful rag rug brightened the wood floor.

Stretching his legs out in front of him, Lee regarded Kelly McBride over the rim of his cup. She was a pretty woman, he thought. Not blatantly beautiful, like Melinda, but pretty nonetheless. She had long curly brown hair. Her cheeks were sunburned, and there was a light sprinkling of freckles across the bridge of her nose. Her brows were slightly arched above soft blue eyes. Her mouth was wide and generous and he wondered how it would look curved in a smile, how it would taste . . .

Kelly felt her cheeks grow hot under his intense scrutiny. "Why did you come here?" she asked, disliking the silence between them almost as much as she disliked the way he was looking at her.

"It's my birthright. My ancestors were born on this land. They fought here. They died here."

It was the truth, Lee mused, or at least as much of it as he was willing to tell her.

Kelly stared at him. She didn't believe one word he said. And then she frowned. Did he know about the gold? But that was impossible. No one knew.

Except her. And the ghost.

Lee straightened in the chair and leaned forward. "Why won't you sell? You don't belong here."

"Oh?"

"You're a city girl, Kelly McBride." McBride, he thought. Why did that name sound so familiar? "A city girl," he repeated, frowning. "Anyone can see that."

"Well, I'm a country girl now." Kelly lifted her chin defiantly, trying not to think how right her name sounded on his lips. "Besides, I like it here."

Lee stared into his empty coffee cup. "I have a feeling you aren't going to change your mind," he muttered ruefully.

"Finally we agree on something."

"Yeah." Setting his mug on the bedside table, he stood up. "Well, good night, Miss McBride."

"Good night, Mr. . . . You never did tell me your name."

"It's Lee," he said as he placed the Colt on the top of the dresser. "Lee Roan Horse."

"Lee Roan Horse." She repeated the name, surprised to find that it conjured images of conical tipis and warriors bedecked with feathers and paint riding across a vast sun-kissed prairie.

Lee turned toward the door, paused, ran a hand through his hair, then turned back to face her again.

"I don't suppose you need any help around here?"

Kelly's brows shot up. "Doing what?"

He shrugged. "Whatever needs doing."

"I'm afraid not."

"I couldn't help noticing the house needs a new roof. And a coat of paint. The barn, too. The corrals could all use some new rails."

Kelly nodded. Everything he said was true, but she couldn't shake the feeling that he didn't really want a job as much as he wanted an excuse to prowl around the ranch. Again, she had the feeling that he knew about the gold.

"The place does need a lot of work," she allowed, "but I'm afraid I can't afford to hire anyone just now."

"That roof on the barn won't hold up much longer."

He couldn't have seen the condition of the roof at night, Kelly thought suspiciously, so how did he know how bad it was, unless he'd been here before, during the day?

"I'd be willing to work cheap. Room and board and whatever you feel you can afford."

It would be a mistake. A big mistake. She didn't trust him, not one bit. But that wasn't what frightened her. It was the attraction she felt for him, the way her heart skipped a beat at the thought of seeing him every day. He was far too attractive for any woman under ninety to ignore, and she was afraid he knew it, afraid he knew that just looking at him made her feel good inside.

"No." She shook her head. "No, I can't . . ."

He took a step toward her, his eyes blazing with ebony fire, his mouth curved in a dazzling smile.

"Sure you can," he drawled softly.

She said yes before she realized she'd spoken the word aloud, afraid if she refused him, the fire that burned in the depths of his eyes would reduce her to ashes.

He had the good grace not to gloat. "You won't be sorry," he promised.

She was already sorry, but he was gone before she could say so.

It was near dawn when Kelly fell into a troubled sleep. She dreamed of her grandfather, and in her dreams he was a young man again, strong and vigorous. But then, gradually, his features began to change, his light brown hair darkening to the color of ebony, his freckled face turning to a copper hue, until the man in her dream was no longer her grandfather Frank, but the Indian who had accosted her in the street.

It's our land, Lee Roan Horse said, his voice ringing out with the strength of his conviction. *Our land!*

And suddenly it wasn't just a single voice clamoring at her, but the combined voices of every Lakota man, woman, and child who had ever lived.

Kelly pressed her hands over her ears, but she couldn't shut out the sound of their cries.

Helpless, she stared at the Indian, felt her heart constrict with fear as she saw not one man, but two—one of flesh and blood, and one of spirit—

two separate beings who stood face-to-face and then blended together until they became one and faded from her sight, leaving her standing alone in the darkness with only the pounding of a distant drum and the faint echoes of ancient voices.

Chapter Four

She woke with the sound of drumming still in her ears.

With a grimace, she buried her head under her pillow, hoping to shut out the noise and go back to sleep, and then she sat up.

Drumming? Cocking her head to the side, Kelly listened a moment and realized it wasn't the sound of a drum at all, but the sound of a hammer.

Muttering under her breath, she slid out of bed, pulled on a short terry cloth robe, and peered out the window.

What she saw took her breath away.

Lee Roan Horse was nailing a new fence post into place. It appeared he'd been hard at work long before she became aware of it. His shirt hung over the top rail of the corral, but it was the broad expanse of his back that drew her gaze.

She'd never seen such a magnificent sight in all her life and she couldn't help staring, her feminine eye pleased with the symmetry of broad shoulders that tapered to a firm, narrow waist. His muscles rippled beneath smooth copper-hued skin, skin sheened with a fine layer of perspiration. His hair was long and black and beautiful, surely the envy of every woman who'd ever seen it.

Her gaze drifted down, appreciating the way his faded jeans hugged his long, muscular legs.

She drew back from the window when, unexpectedly, he glanced over his shoulder. Had he seen her watching him? The thought brought a rush of heat to her cheeks. She wasn't in the habit of gawking at handsome men. She'd seen plenty of good-looking guys in Los Angeles. The place was crawling with gorgeous hunks who hoped to be actors or models. She'd even dated a few, but there had been something disconcerting about going out to spend an evening with a man who was prettier than she was.

But Lee Roan Horse . . . he wasn't pretty. He wasn't even handsome, at least not in the traditional sense of the word. But he had a rugged masculine appeal that she found attractive on some primal, earthy level she didn't care to examine too closely.

Kelly shook his image from her mind and headed for the bathroom. A nice cool shower was just what she needed.

Forty minutes later, she opened the back door and called Lee Roan Horse to breakfast.

He entered the kitchen whistling and tucking his shirt into his jeans. He nodded in her direction, then went to the sink to wash his hands. Big hands, Kelly thought. Capable hands that were scarred and callused. She wondered if they could be gentle.

Lee dried his hands on a dish towel, then stood beside the sink, his gaze moving around the kitchen. It was a large, square room. The walls were a pale yellow. Matching curtains fluttered at the open window. A badly scarred walnut table stood in the center of the room.

"Sit down," Kelly said. "Anyplace you like. I'm not used to having company at breakfast."

"Oh?" His look was curious.

"I live alone, remember?"

She filled a plate with hot cakes, eggs, and bacon and set it on the table in front of him, along with a cup of coffee, a tall glass of orange juice, and a plate of buttered toast.

"Eat it while it's hot," she said, and turned back to the stove to flip the hot cakes on the griddle.

Lee sat down, his nostrils filling with the aroma of bacon and coffee. He couldn't remember the last time a woman had cooked for him, or the last time he'd sat down to a breakfast that consisted of much more than black coffee. But all that would change when he had the gold.

Kelly joined him at the table a few moments later, surprised to find his plate nearly empty. She wasn't used to cooking for a man, but she'd felt certain that six hot cakes, three eggs, four slices of bacon, and toast would be enough. Apparently she'd been wrong. If he ate like this at every meal, she'd have to make a trip into town a lot sooner than she planned.

"Would you like some more?" she asked, a smile in her voice. She'd never considered herself much of a cook, but he obviously appreciated her culinary skills. Either that, or it had been a long time between meals.

He shook his head, not meeting her eyes. "No, thanks."

"Are you sure?" As soon as the words were out of her mouth, she knew she'd made a mistake. A muscle worked in his jaw and she had the very real impression that she'd somehow insulted him.

"It's just that . . . I mean, you must have worked up quite an appetite. I just thought . . ." Kelly shrugged. "It's just that I made too much and I hate to see it go to waste."

Lee stared at her from across the table, remembering the pitying looks he'd gotten from white women when he was a kid begging in the streets for food; food to feed his invalid grandmother, his little sister, his alcoholic mother.

Kelly frowned. Roan Horse was still hungry. She knew it as surely as she knew the color of her own hair. So she took a deep breath and said, "It's a long time till lunch, you know."

"I'm fine, thank you," he said, stiffly polite, and then he stood up and left the room, the rest of his food untouched.

Kelly stared after him, wondering why he was so touchy, wondering what she'd said to offend him.

Outside, Lee ripped the broken rails from the fence, attacking the corral as if it were every man or woman who had ever humiliated him. He'd hated begging for food, for money to buy medicine for his grandmother. He'd hated begging so badly he had turned to stealing instead.

In the old days, stealing from the enemy had been considered a great coup, and that was how he had looked at it. He'd been full of hate in his younger days, hate for the whites, hate for the poverty he lived in, for the ugly little house he shared with his family, hate for the father he barely remembered who had run off and left them all behind.

He was breathing hard by the time he'd removed the rails that needed to be replaced. He'd thought it was all behind him, the hatred, the anger, the bitterness he'd grown up with; he'd thought he'd buried it when he buried his mother.

Bracing one hand on a post, he rested his forehead on his arm and closed his eyes. They were all gone now. His grandmother had died peacefully in her sleep. His little sister had died of pneumonia when she was only eight years old. And his mother had finally drunk herself to death.

He swore softly. All his life, he'd wanted a vision. He'd gone alone to the mountains to fast and to pray; he'd offered tobacco to the four winds, to the earth and the sky, but always a vision had been denied him. And then, when he had given up all hope, his vision had come.

Even now, it was clear in his mind. He'd been

standing at his mother's grave, dry-eyed and alone, wondering what to do with his life, when the day had turned dark and cold. A heavy gray mist had fallen over the land, and then a man had materialized out of the mist. A tall man with long black hair and dark copper-colored skin. A warrior who wore a golden eagle on a thong around his neck.

You are not alone, the warrior had said. *Only believe, and all you desire will be yours.*

Who are you? Lee had asked. But the warrior hadn't answered and Lee had wondered if perhaps he had been seeing himself at some future time, but that didn't make sense. How could he foretell his own future?

The warrior had gone on to tell Lee of a cache of Lakota gold hidden in a cave in the mountains to the north.

Find the woman and you will find the treasure, the warrior had said, and then, like shadows running before a storm, he had disappeared.

Well, he had found the woman, Lee mused. His talk of buying the ranch had been just that, talk. He didn't have enough money to fill his gas tank, let alone buy the Triple M, but he'd done what he set out to do. Now all he had to do was find the gold.

A wry grin curved his lips as he recalled a sign he'd seen in an old grocery store in Virginia City:

THE GOLDEN RULE:
HE WHO HAS THE GOLD
MAKES THE RULES.

Well, he intended to have the gold, one way or another, he thought grimly. He hadn't spent a year in that damned jail for nothing.

"Lemonade?"

Lee's head jerked up at the sound of her voice. "What?"

He turned around to face her and she offered him a chilled glass of lemonade.

"I thought you might be thirsty," Kelly said with a shrug.

"Yeah, thanks," he replied, and taking the glass, he drained it in two long swallows.

"I guess I should have brought the whole pitcher," Kelly remarked, and then bit down on her lip, afraid she'd offended him again.

But he only grinned at her as he dragged the back of his hand across his mouth.

"You don't have to finish everything today," she said, indicating the corral.

Lee shrugged. "I like to keep busy."

"Oh. Well, I'd better let you get back to work then. I'll call you when lunch is ready."

He nodded, his conscience stabbing at him as he watched her walk away. He hadn't come here to work. He'd come here to steal. He tried to tell himself it wasn't stealing, not really; it was only taking back what was rightfully his. But he hadn't expected to like Kelly McBride. She seemed so open, so honest, not like Melinda . . .

Muttering an oath, he picked up his shirt and wiped the perspiration from his face and neck.

He'd fix the corral and patch up the roof, even paint the damn house. It was the least he could do for her, he thought, before he went looking for the gold.

Chapter Five

Harry Renford leaned forward in his chair, both hands flat on the desktop.

"I cannot believe you actually hired that man," he said, shaking his head.

Kelly frowned, baffled by the banker's obvious annoyance. "He needed a job. I needed some work done." She shrugged. "I don't understand why you're making such a fuss about it. A lot of the ranchers around here hire Indians."

"Don't you know who he is?"

"He said his name was Lee Roan Horse."

"Didn't your grandfather ever mention him?"

"Not that I recall. Why?"

"Your grandfather caught Roan Horse trespassing. He warned him not to come back, but the

45

Indian didn't listen. The next time your grandfather caught him sneaking around, he called the police and had Roan Horse arrested for breaking and entering."

"When was that?" Kelly stared at Renford, not wanting to believe him. And yet, hadn't she known, deep down, that Lee was hiding something? It was the gold, she thought. Lee knew about the gold. That was why he wanted to buy the ranch, why he had been so insistent that she hire him.

"It was quite a while ago, probably four or five years. Roan Horse did a year in the county jail. When he was released, he left town. He's only been back a few months, but he's already been in trouble. Bar fights and the like."

Harry picked up a thin gold pen and rolled it back and forth on the desktop. "Don't trust him, Miss McBride. Lee Roan Horse is bad clear through. Mean, too. I heard he broke Ronny Brogden's nose in a brawl just last week."

Kelly had a sudden mental image of Lee Roan Horse with his back against a wall, his hands curled into tight fists, his muscles taut as he took a swing at the aforementioned Ronny Brogden. She'd met Ronny years ago on one of her summer visits to Cedar Flats. He'd been a bully and a braggart, and she thought it likely that he'd probably only gotten what he deserved, but of course she couldn't tell the banker that.

"Please don't trouble yourself about it, Mr. Renford," Kelly said, forcing a smile. "Everything's under control. Now, is the deed ready?"

"Yes, the deed," Renford muttered, not meeting her eyes. "I'm afraid it's missing."

"Missing? How is that possible?"

Renford spread his hands in a gesture of appeal. "I'm not sure. All I know is that it's not in the vault. I'm sure it's simply been misplaced."

"I see."

"I'll call you just as soon as it turns up." Renford smiled. "Signing the deed is just a technicality. Even though your grandfather didn't leave a valid will, there's no question of who the ranch belongs to. Your grandfather had no other kin."

"I understand," Kelly replied. But she didn't, not really, nor could she shake the feeling that there was something Renford wasn't saying, something he wasn't telling her.

"I'll call you," Harry said. Rising, he extended his hand.

It was a curt dismissal.

Kelly was fuming when she reached home. It seemed as if everyone she met was conspiring against her. First she'd had to go into Coleville to exchange a few gold nuggets for cash. A trip that should have taken less than an hour took two because a truck had jackknifed on the road, bringing all traffic to a halt.

From Coleville, she'd driven back to town to settle her grandfather's hospital bill. No easy task. Her grandfather had spent three days in the hospital before he died. They had tried to charge her for six days, and then seemed annoyed because she had refused to pay them for the extra three days.

Renford hadn't been able to find the deed, and she was having second thoughts about the wisdom of paying off the loan and having nothing other than a receipt to show for it. And now it seemed that Lee Roan Horse had hired on under false pretenses.

Kelly blew out a long sigh. Maybe she should just take the gold out of the cave and sell the ranch to Lee Roan Horse. It would serve him right. And yet, even as she thought about taking the gold, more gold than she would ever need, she felt suddenly cold, as if the chill wind from the cave had blown into the car.

Switching off the ignition, she sat behind the wheel. From where she sat, she could see Lee sawing a new rail for one of the corrals. Of course he wanted to fix up the place, she thought bitterly. He intended to own it.

She let her eyes travel over his broad back. Didn't the man ever wear a shirt? Angry as she was, she couldn't seem to stop watching him. He moved with effortless grace, the muscles in his arms and back bunching and relaxing as he worked.

He'd been in jail for breaking and entering. She grunted softly, remembering the night he'd broken into the house. No wonder he knew what he'd be charged with when she had threatened to call the police. He'd already done time for breaking and entering. She supposed a year in jail could be considered a small price to pay in exchange for a fortune in gold.

Take only what you need. If you take one nugget more, my spirit will haunt you for as long as you live.

That had been the warning given to Charlie McBride when he first found the gold a hundred years ago. Thinking of it now sent a shiver down Kelly's spine. In the bright light of day, it was hard to believe in ghosts and curses, yet she knew she lacked the courage to enter the cave and remove all the gold.

So, what was she to do? Take as much as she needed and run back to L.A.?

She let her gaze sweep over the ranch. In the short time she'd been here, she'd come to love the place—the timeless beauty of the mountains, the quiet nights and peaceful days. She'd thought she'd miss the excitement of the city, but, to her surprise, she'd discovered that she preferred the soft pastoral sounds of tree frogs and crickets to the grinding of brakes and the shrill scream of sirens. She preferred blue skies and green trees to smog and tall, glass-fronted buildings. And she definitely preferred riding Dusty to braving the Los Angeles freeways!

She did miss shopping malls and TV, though, she thought, frowning, and then she smiled. She had money. She could buy one of those big-screen TVs she'd always wanted, and a satellite dish to go with it.

With a start, she realized that Lee was standing at the car door.

"You all right in there?" he asked, bending down so he could see her better.

"Fine." She pulled the key from the ignition, grabbed her handbag, and opened the car door.

"You look tired," he remarked.

"Yes."

Lee frowned. "Something wrong?"

"No."

With a shrug, he turned away and went back to the corral. If she wanted to tell him what was bothering her, she would. If not . . . he shrugged. It was none of his business. He'd vowed never to get tangled up with a white woman again, no matter how pretty she was, and it was a vow he meant to keep.

Picking up the new rail, he laid it in place, then reached for the hammer, cursing his weakness for smooth pale skin and soft blue eyes.

Melinda Kershaw's image danced across the misty corridors of his mind. Melinda, with her irresistible smile and honeyed words. Melinda, who had teased and tormented the hired help one summer. Lee's knuckles turned white around the hammer. That was a summer he'd never forget.

He'd been seventeen the year he'd gone to work for Melinda's father. Rich and spoiled, secure in her beauty, she had trailed after Lee while he cut the grass and trimmed the trees, flirting shamelessly, fascinated by the fact that he was an Indian and therefore forbidden to her. She had paraded around her family's swimming pool in a hot pink bikini that left almost nothing to the imagination. On more than one occasion, she had begged him to rub suntan lotion on her back and shoulders.

Nights, she had met him on the sly, vowing that she loved him, that it didn't matter that he was an Indian and dirt poor. She had kissed him and caressed him until he was on fire for her, and then, when her father had caught her in his arms, she had cried rape. And because Lee was just a dirty redskin, not fit to be in the same room as Frank Kershaw's virginal sixteen-year-old daughter, Melinda's father had believed her every word.

Melinda had spent the rest of the summer in the Bahamas, recovering from her dreadful ordeal.

Lee had spent eighteen months in a correctional institution.

He drove the last nail into place, then hurled the hammer across the corral. Chest heaving, he stared at his hands, remembering the nights he'd spent wishing he could wrap them around Melinda's pretty little neck.

But that was all behind him now. He'd find his ancestor's gold, get the hell out of Cedar Flats, and start a new life where nobody would know, or care, who he was.

And he'd never look at another white woman as long as he lived.

Chapter Six

He bent over the hand-drawn map spread on his desk. She wouldn't keep a fortune in gold in the house, he mused, that much was certain. Probably not in the barn, either. She might have buried it somewhere, say in the middle of one of the corrals or in the chicken coop. She might have hidden it in the well, but he didn't think so.

He frowned thoughtfully as his finger made an ever-widening circle around the drawing of the house. Under a rock, perhaps, or in a cave . . .

His gaze moved to the mountain that rose behind the house. A cave. What better place to hide a king's ransom?

He grunted softly as he lifted his head and stared out the window into the darkness. Roan Horse, a man who had avoided white women like the plague, had gone to work for Kelly McBride. Why?

A slow smile spread over his features. It was all so simple.

Roan Horse knew about the gold.

All he had to do was sit back and wait for the Indian to find it.

Whistling softly, he dialed the phone. "Trask? I need you."

Chapter Seven

She woke, knowing immediately that she wasn't alone. Her first thought was that it was Lee. But then she felt that familiar warmth, followed by a breath of cool air that sent a shiver down her spine.

"Who's there?" She sat up, the blanket clutched to her breast. "Lee?" Oh, please, she thought, let it be Lee.

Kelly swallowed hard as a corner of the room brightened, felt herself go cold all over when the light coalesced into the form of a man . . . a tall, dark-skinned man with long black hair. A man who was not a man at all.

"You!" She shook her head, refusing to believe what she was seeing. "No, it can't be."

The Indian stared at her through fathomless

black eyes. "You're him, aren't you?" Kelly asked. "The Indian from the cave?"

He nodded and then took a step forward.

Kelly's eyes widened as the Indian closed the distance between them. He looked even more impressive now than he had in the cave. There was no illumination in the room, yet he seemed to be surrounded by an aura of soft blue light. His skin was the color of dark copper, smooth and unblemished save for two faint scars on his chest. There were three white-tipped eagle feathers tied in his hair. A distant part of her mind wondered why he had removed his shirt and why she hadn't noticed the feathers before. His brows were thick and black and straight. Standing so near, he seemed taller, broader. Alive . . .

He's a ghost. Just a ghost. He can't hurt you.

She repeated the words in her mind as the specter reached the foot of the bed. Arms crossed over his chest, the phantom stared down at her.

Go away from here. He didn't speak, but she heard the words in her mind, as deep and dark as the night.

Kelly shook her head. "No. This is my home."

The Indian continued to stare at her, his expression blank. *This is my home.*

"Who are you?" Kelly demanded, though her voice quivered with trepidation.

The Indian smiled at her, silently applauding her courage. White people were always frightened by his appearance, probably because they had no ties to the world of spirits. They were a peculiar people. They had no bond with Mother

Earth, or with their four-footed brothers. They sought no vision to guide them through life. Not that he had known that many white people, he thought, amused. In the last hundred years, only a handful of *washicu* had found their way into the cave.

All had come to steal the gold.

All had left empty-handed.

All except this girl.

"I am Blue Crow of the Lakota."

Kelly blinked at him several times. "So you can talk," she muttered under her breath. "What do you want?"

"I want you to leave here. Like all *washicu*, you take what is not yours."

"This is my house," Kelly retorted indignantly. "It belonged to my grandfather and his father before him, and now it belongs to me."

The Indian made a sound of derision low in his throat. "You have taken gold that is not yours."

The eagle, Kelly thought.

"Give it to me."

She hesitated a moment, and then reached under her pillow, withdrawing the golden eagle. She couldn't keep her hand from shaking as she offered it to the Indian. His fingertips brushed hers as he took it from her hand. She felt the heat of his touch, the shock of it, sizzle through her like lightning.

Stunned, she stared up at him. Ghosts weren't supposed to have substance. She watched, unblinking, as he opened the small buckskin bag that hung around his neck and slid the eagle inside.

"How . . . why . . ." Kelly shook her head. He wasn't real. He couldn't be real.

"You want to know why my body was in the cave."

"Yes."

"I was killed by a *washicu* who wanted the gold. His companion buried me in the cave, and I have slept there ever since."

"But how . . . why? I mean, you're not alive, and yet . . ." Her words trailed off as he came around the bed to stand beside her.

"My spirit awakens whenever a *washicu* enters the cave."

"You've been there all this time to guard the gold?"

Blue Crow nodded.

"But why?"

"*He mitawa*," he said. "It is mine."

"But you don't need it!" Kelly exclaimed.

"Do you?"

Kelly opened her mouth, intending to say yes, of course she needed it. Who wouldn't need a fortune in gold? But the words died in her throat.

"You have taken enough for your needs," Blue Crow said. "You have paid your grandfather's debts, you have enough to live on, you have this house for shelter."

"But it's no good to you. You're . . ." She couldn't bring herself to say the word.

"Dead," Blue Crow said, supplying the word for her.

"Right. So why do you need a fortune in gold?"

57

"It is mine," Blue Crow said again. "I will decide who should have it."

"I don't believe any of this," Kelly muttered. "I don't believe you're real. I don't believe I'm sitting here at three o'clock in the morning arguing with something that doesn't exist."

"I am real, Kelly McBride," Blue Crow replied quietly. He held out his hand. "Look at me. Touch me."

She swallowed hard and then, feeling as if she had no control over what she was doing, she gazed deep into his eyes, felt her heart swell with compassion as she sensed the loneliness he had endured for over a century.

Of its own volition, Kelly's hand reached for his, but it was his fingers that closed over hers. For a moment she stared at their locked hands; his was large and scarred; hers was small and very white in comparison to his. But it was the heat of his touch that made her pulse race and her blood sing a new song.

When she tried to take her hand from his, he refused to let go, and for the first time since he'd entered the room, she was truly afraid. Afraid and confused. He couldn't be a ghost. Ghosts were vaporous, without mass or substance.

She blinked up at him, mesmerized by the heat in his gaze, by her sudden awareness that, ghost or no ghost, this was a man with all of a man's desires.

"I will not harm you," Blue Crow assured her, and though that had been his intent when he entered the house, he knew now that this woman was a part of his destiny. He would not harm her, and he would destroy anyone who tried. "I will not harm you," he repeated. "It is only that your skin is so soft, so warm and alive, and it has been so long since I have held a woman . . ."

His fingers tightened on hers and she felt him tremble, and then, without warning, he vanished from her sight.

In the morning, Kelly tried to convince herself it had all been a dream. There were no such things as ghosts.

But the eagle was gone.

And when she got up, she discovered a single eagle feather on the floor beside the bed.

Distracted, she dressed and went into the kitchen to prepare breakfast. A short time later, Lee entered the room and took a seat at the table.

Unable to help herself, Kelly stared at him all through breakfast. It was uncanny, his resemblance to Blue Crow.

"Something wrong?" Lee asked when she poured him a second cup of coffee.

"No, why?"

Lee shrugged. "I feel like a bug under a microscope."

With an effort, she drew her gaze from his face. "Sorry."

"You gonna tell me why you've been staring at me?"

"I . . . it's just . . . no reason."

"Can't be my good looks," he mused, locking his fingers around his coffee cup. "Did somebody say something to you in town the other day? Maybe warn you to stay away from me?"

She flushed guiltily, remembering Harry Renford's admonition. "No, of course not."

"Maybe you're having second thoughts about my working here?"

"No, it's not that."

"What then? Come on, Miss McBride, tell me what's bothering you."

Kelly shook her head. She couldn't tell him she'd been visited by a ghost. The ghost of Christmas past, she thought, smothering the urge to laugh. Oh, Lord, maybe she was losing her mind.

Lee frowned, wondering what was troubling her. She'd gone suddenly pale.

"Somebody told you I'd been arrested, didn't they?"

She started to deny it, then nodded. "Mr. Renford, at the bank, told me you'd been arrested for breaking into my grandfather's house."

A muscle tensed in Lee's jaw.

"He said you did a year in jail." Kelly took a deep breath. "That seems like a rather harsh sentence."

"I was carrying a gun at the time," Lee replied tersely.

"A gun! Why?" She stared at him in horror. "Surely you didn't mean to—"

"Of course not."

"Then why did you need a gun?"

Lee shrugged. He couldn't tell her about the gold, and yet . . . he swore under his breath, wondering if she knew about the treasure rumored to be hidden in the mountains, wondering if that was why she was so determined to stay.

Stalling for time, he lifted the cup to his lips. He wasn't the only one searching for the treasure. He'd seen tracks near the foot of the mountain, tracks that weren't his. Tracks that definitely weren't Kelly's. Somehow, he'd have to warn her she might be in danger without telling her why.

Kelly leaned forward, her elbows propped on the table, her chin resting on her folded hands. "Well?"

"It's dangerous out here after dark, Miss McBride. There are still wild animals prowling around, and not all of them are four-footed."

Kelly grimaced. Wild animals, indeed, she thought. And then she shivered. Not all of them are four-footed, he'd said. Did he know something he wasn't telling her?

Lee stood abruptly. "I'd better get to work," he said, and then paused, his hand on the door, one brow arched in question. "If I'm still working here, that is."

"You are."

His lips flattened into a thin line. And then, as if he'd made a difficult decision, he took a deep breath and blew it out in a long sigh.

"Then you might as well know the rest."

"The rest?" Kelly looked up at him, her fingernails digging into her palms as she waited for him to go on. His expression was bleak, his eyes as hard and black as obsidian. A muscle worked in his jaw.

"When I was seventeen, I was accused of raping a white girl. I did some time for that, too."

He stared down at her, waiting for her reaction.

Kelly's gaze was steady as it met his. "Were you guilty?"

"Only of being young and stupid."

She hesitated only a moment before she said, "I believe you."

Lee studied her for a long moment, wondering if she really believed him. And then he cursed himself for being such a cynical fool. Her face was as open and easy to read as print on a page. If she thought he was lying, it would be revealed in the depths of those amazing blue eyes.

"We're having hamburgers for lunch," Kelly said with a smile. "Don't be late."

With a nod in her direction, he left the house.

Kelly stared after Lee, her mind reeling with unanswered questions. Why had he really come here? What did he know that he wasn't telling her? Was she in danger? Why did he look so much like Blue Crow?

She grunted softly. The answer to that was obvious. They had to be related. If that was so, perhaps it answered her other questions, as well. He'd come to work here because he knew about the gold. And if he knew, perhaps there were others who also knew, or suspected.

If that was true, she would be wise not to trade any more of the nuggets for cash. Cedar Flats was a small town; so was Coleville. Anything out of the ordinary was likely to draw attention and be remembered.

Pushing away from the table, she gathered up the dirty dishes and filled the sink with hot water. The kitchen was on the west side of the house. There was a large window over the sink, affording her a view of the barn and the corrals.

Looking out, she saw Lee carrying a ladder and a can of paint out of the barn. He'd removed his shirt, and his skin glistened like fine bronze in the early morning sunlight. His muscles rippled as he placed the ladder against the side of the barn.

The dishes forgotten, she watched as he opened a can of red paint and then, with lithe assurance, made his way to the top of the ladder.

Using a brush pulled from the waistband of his pants, he began to paint the eaves.

She might have stood watching him all day, her hands immersed in a sink of water that was rapidly turning cold, if Harry Renford hadn't called.

After exchanging the usual pleasantries, he informed her that the deed was still missing, and that he had sent to the county seat for a copy.

Kelly thanked him for calling, assured him that Lee Roan Horse wasn't causing any trouble at all, and hung up.

Resisting the urge to spend the day watching Lee, she quickly finished up the dishes, made her bed, and dusted the living room furniture. She hadn't given the house a good cleaning since she arrived, and this seemed the perfect time to do it.

It wasn't a very big house. There were two bedrooms in the back of the house, a small but surprisingly modern bathroom, a good-sized living room, and a combination kitchen and dining room.

She stripped the sheets and blankets from the bed in the spare bedroom to air the mattress, scoured the bathroom fixtures, and mopped the floor.

She was ready for a break when lunchtime came.

The hamburgers were grilling when Lee entered the kitchen. She was relieved to see that he'd donned his shirt. For some reason, the sight of his bare chest aroused feelings she didn't wish to acknowledge or analyze.

Lee hesitated before he sat down, wondering if she'd had a change of heart about his staying on.

"Sit down," she said. "It's almost ready."

Nodding, he pulled out a chair and straddled it. He tried not to stare at her, tried to think of something else, but he couldn't keep his gaze from straying toward her, couldn't help noticing the way she filled out a pair of jeans, couldn't help wondering what it would be like to hold her in his arms . . .

He swore softly. She was a white woman, he reminded himself sternly, and he'd vowed never to get mixed up with a white woman again. It had been ten years since the incident with Melinda, but he hadn't forgotten what it had cost him the last time he'd let a pretty face override his better judgment, and as much as he longed to take Kelly in his arms and discover if she tasted as good as she looked, he had no intention of giving in to that particular temptation.

He ate quickly, thanked her for the meal, and left the house, determined to bury his lust under a coat of red paint and a lot of hard work.

By nightfall, Lee was bone weary. Feet dragging, he made his way to the house, convinced he'd managed to subdue his base feelings for a woman he hardly knew, but one look at Kelly's face and he knew he was kidding himself. What was there about this particular woman that drew his gaze again and again? Was it the pull of her soft golden skin, the sky-blue color of her eyes, or the simple fact that she was a challenge he was helpless to resist?

He shook his head imperceptibly. She didn't wear much makeup, only a bit of mascara and a touch of pale pink lipstick, and yet he knew he'd never seen anything as sexy as Kelly McBride clad in a pair of faded jeans and a white turtleneck sweater.

Get hold of yourself, Roan Horse, he chided. You're as randy as a young stud with his first mare.

They ate in silence. The lack of conversation made Kelly uncomfortable, and she was glad she'd turned the radio on until Vince Gill began singing a song called "Nobody Answers When I Call Your Name." The soft country ballad filled the kitchen, reminding Kelly of how lonely she was. All she'd ever wanted had been a home of her own and a man to share it with, yet she'd never found that one special man. Twice, she'd thought she'd been in love. The first time, she'd discovered that the man she adored was already married. The second time, she had simply lost interest in the relationship. She'd always been told that there was someone for everyone, but she was beginning to doubt it.

The song ended, only to be followed by another song about lost love and broken dreams.

Glancing up, she met Lee's gaze, felt her cheeks grow hot as she saw the barely concealed longing in his eyes. He was lonely, too, she thought.

Her heart seemed to climb into her throat as she watched Lee push away from the table. He rose to his feet with all the sleek, lazy grace of a tiger. He circled the table until he stood beside her chair, one hand outstretched.

Feeling foolish and giddy at the same time, Kelly put her hand in his, let him pull her to her feet, take her in his arms.

Kelly's heart was pounding so loudly she could scarcely hear the music as he waltzed her around the kitchen floor. She marveled at the way she fit into his arms. She had never been a particularly good dancer, yet she followed Lee as if they had danced together for years. She was acutely conscious of his long fingers folded over hers, of the pressure of his hand at her back. He had washed before coming to dinner, and she could smell the soap on his skin. Her left hand rested lightly on his shoulder and the flesh beneath her palm was warm and solid.

His leg brushed against hers, sending tremors of excitement through her whole body. His breath was warm against her cheek; his eyes were dark, intense, filled with unspoken dreams and secrets she was afraid to learn.

He didn't release her when the music ended. For a long moment they stood there, suspended in time. Kelly stared into his eyes, unable to look away. It was suddenly hard to breathe, impossible to think. She watched his gaze travel to her lips, felt her breath catch in her throat as she waited for him to kiss her. Shivers of anticipation skittered down her spine; she felt her knees go weak as heat spiraled through her.

He took a deep breath, as if gathering his strength, and then he let her go and took a step backward.

"Thanks for dinner," he said, not quite meeting her eyes.

"You're welcome." She glanced around the kitchen, wishing she could find a reason to make him stay. Her gaze settled on the pie she'd made that afternoon. The way to a man's heart, she thought, and blurted, "There's apple pie for dessert."

"No." He took another step away from her. "Maybe another time," he added, his voice thick.

"Good night, then."

Her voice moved over him, low and soft, and he knew he had to get out of there before it was too late.

Muttering a hurried good night, he opened the kitchen door and practically ran out of the room.

Chapter Eight

Outside, Lee paused in the shadows and drew in several long breaths. She probably thought he was crazy, running out of the house like that, but he had to get away. Away from the innocent enticement of sweet pink lips and the lure of summer-sky eyes. Away from the intoxicating female scent that clung to her.

He swore under his breath. She'd smelled of lilac soap and minty toothpaste and freshly baked biscuits, of woman and home, of kids and responsibility, and it scared the devil out of him.

He stared at his hand. He could still feel the warmth of her skin against his. His shoulder seemed to burn where her hand had rested. Hell, he was burning all over.

He sucked in another deep breath, blew it out

in a long sigh, then made his way to the corral behind the barn. The buckskin whickered softly as he approached. Bending over, he plucked a dandelion from a patch of scraggly grass and offered it to the horse. Then, one booted foot resting on the bottom rail of the corral, he stared into the distance, idly scratching the gelding between the ears.

Gradually, the quiet of the night settled around him, soothing him. He stared up at the stars, and from deep within a shadowed corridor of his mind he heard the echo of an ancient Lakota prayer.

He heard the words whisper in his mind and then, feeling awkward and a little foolish, he raised his arms overhead and spoke the words aloud.

"Wakan Tanka, whose voice whispers in the wind and the water, whose breath gives life to all the earth, hear my cry. I am small and weak, in need of Your strength and courage and wisdom. If You walk with me, all things are possible . . ."

After a moment, he lowered his arms and then, very slowly, he glanced over his shoulder.

The house, bathed in moonlight, looked like something out of a fairy tale. Light glowed behind the yellow-checked curtains, warm, inviting. He saw Kelly staring at him through the kitchen window. Lamplight cast soft red highlights in her hair.

His breath caught in his throat as he looked at her. *All things are possible . . .*

Feeling suddenly naked and vulnerable, he headed for the barn.

After putting the horse in a stall, he lit the lamp that hung from one of the rafters. He stood there for a long time, his heart racing as though he'd just run a marathon, his thoughts chaotic.

Kelly. One touch, and he wanted two. He held her hand, and wanted to smother her with kisses.

Damn! Gold or no gold, he had to get away from here. Away from her.

He dragged a hand through his hair, remembering the beating he'd gotten from Melinda's father. Of course, Frank Kershaw hadn't done it himself. Oh, no. He'd hollered for his two hired bodyguards and they'd beat the crap out of the boy who'd dared lay a hand on his little girl. They'd broken his nose and a couple of ribs before they were done. Lee had wondered how Melinda's old man would explain it all to the police, but no explanations had been necessary. The cops hadn't even blinked. They'd listened to Kershaw's story, readily accepting his word that Lee had raped his daughter without provocation, cuffed Lee's hands behind his back, read him his rights, and shoved him into the back of the police car.

Even now he could remember the humiliation of that night. Melinda's tears, her mournful sobs as she accused Lee of dragging her into the bungalow and raping her. He could remember the smiles of anticipation on the faces of the two bodyguards as they backed him into a corner, the sounds of their fists striking his face and body, the smell of his own blood and fear, the stench of their sweat as they worked him over, the look on Kershaw's face as he handed them each a crisp one hundred dollar bill for their trouble.

"It's over. Forget it." Lee muttered the words aloud, knowing he'd never forget it as long as he lived.

"Lee?"

He whirled around at the sound of her voice.

Kelly paused, her hand on the door. "I'm sorry, I didn't mean to bother you, but . . ." She shrugged, a faint smile flitting over her face. "I went for a walk and I seem to have locked myself out of the house, and I was wondering if you could . . ."

Her voice trailed off and she felt a rush of color flood her cheeks.

His eyes narrowed ominously. "And you knew I'd be able to pick the lock, since I'd done it before."

Kelly bit down on her lip. Of course, that was just what she'd thought, only it sounded awful when he said it aloud.

"I . . . never mind . . . I'll . . ."

"Forget it," he said brusquely. Hands clenched into tight fists, he swept past her.

"I'm sorry," she mumbled, but he didn't seem to hear her.

Needing time to compose herself, she spent a couple of minutes glancing around the barn. She hadn't been inside since Lee moved in. The floor had been swept clean. An assortment of tack hung from pegs on the far wall; there were several bales of hay and straw piled in a corner, along with a half-dozen bags of sweet feed. Her grandfather's saddle, cleaned and oiled, sat atop a wooden sawhorse. An old cardboard box held an assortment of curry combs and brushes

She walked down the aisle that separated the stalls. Dusty whickered softly and she paused to rub the gelding's nose. Glancing at the stall across the way, she saw that Lee had made a bed of sorts in the stall; the adjoining stall served as his closet. She saw a few shirts draped over the partition, an extra pair of boots, a couple pairs of blue jeans, a well-worn black hat. But what held her eye was the warbonnet hanging from a nail. Made of black-tipped eagle feathers that trailed to the ground, it was a thing of rare beauty, tempting her touch.

Giving Dusty a final pat, she crossed the floor and entered the stall, letting her fingertips glide over one of the feathers. And into her mind came an image of Blue Crow astride a black and white paint pony. He was dressed in a clout and moccasins, his face streaked with war paint, a feathered lance in his right hand. And a warbonnet on his head, a warbonnet that looked exactly like the one beneath her hand.

A shiver curled up Kelly's spine. Snatching her hand away, she left the barn and made her way to the house, anxious to ask Lee about the warbonnet.

Lee was waiting for her. The front door stood ajar. A stream of lamplight illuminated the porch.

"Thank you," Kelly said.

A corner of Lee's mouth curled up in a wry grin. "No problem."

Lifting her head and squaring her shoulders,

Kelly met his unblinking gaze. "I'm sorry if I offended you earlier."

"Forget it."

"I didn't mean anything, honestly. I . . . sometimes I say things without thinking. I really am sorry."

"Why should you be sorry? You didn't do anything wrong."

"But—"

"Listen, Kelly, I'm not a very nice guy. It's no secret that I've done time, and lots of it. Everybody in town knows it."

He paused, and then went on, deciding he might as well tell her everything and be done with it. "I got busted for stealing, for vandalism, for burglary." He shrugged. "You name it, I probably did it."

"Why are you telling me this?"

"Because you've got a right to know who's sleeping in your barn."

"It doesn't matter."

"Doesn't it?"

"It's all in the past. Isn't it?"

He couldn't meet her eyes. He couldn't lie to her, he couldn't make promises to those innocent blue eyes, promises he had no intention of keeping.

"Isn't it?" Kelly gazed at him intently, suddenly aware that she was shivering, and that it had nothing to do with the weather.

"I don't know, but if I were you, I'd keep my doors and windows locked."

Kelly glanced pointedly at the open front door and then at the piece of wire in his hand. "Would it do me any good?"

"Kelly—"

"I'm trusting you, Lee Roan Horse. I hope you won't let me down. Good night."

Only after she'd closed the door did she realize she'd forgotten to ask him about the warbonnet.

Lee stared at the closed front door, listening to her footsteps fade as she made her way toward her bedroom in the back of the house.

I'm trusting you . . .

Lee grunted softly. No one had ever trusted him before. He'd never realized what a burden it could be. He had to get out of here, he thought again, before it was too late.

But even as the thought crossed his mind, he knew he wouldn't go and he wondered which temptation was more enticing, the age-old lure of soft feminine curves and sweet pink lips, or the equally ancient lust for gold.

It was a question that kept him awake far into the night.

Chapter Nine

Kelly stared out the kitchen window, her mouth agape. Where had that horse come from? She was about to go outside to find Lee when she saw him walking toward the corral, a bridle in one hand. Mercy, he didn't mean to ride the beast! It was the biggest, blackest, wildest-looking horse she'd ever seen. The animal darted toward the far side of the corral when it saw Lee approaching. Nostrils flared, ears laid flat, the horse watched the man.

Whistling softly, Lee ducked into the corral. For a long while, he simply stood there, the bridle swinging from his hand. And then, moving without haste, he crossed the corral, his free hand outstretched.

Kelly held her breath, certain Lee was about to

be killed before her very eyes, but as soon as he got near the horse, the black bolted to the other side of the corral.

For the next half hour, she watched Lee stalk the horse, never able to get close enough to slip the bridle over its head.

Wild-eyed and wary, the black pranced around the corral, tossing its head, blowing loudly, until it had worked itself into a sweat.

Finally, muttering what Kelly assumed was an oath, Lee left the corral.

She was stirring eggs in a pan when he entered the kitchen.

"Morning," she said brightly.

"Morning."

"Where'd the horse come from?"

"I took it in payment for some work I did." A wry grin tugged at his lips. "I think I got taken."

"He's not broken to ride?"

"He's barely broken to a halter. I had to lead him here from the Montgomery place."

"That's five miles from here."

"I know." He accepted the cup of coffee she handed him and sipped it appreciatively.

"What kind of horse is it?"

"He's a mustang, and as wild as they come."

"Can I ask you something?"

"You can ask."

"Where'd you get the warbonnet in the barn?"

"From my grandfather."

"Do you . . . do you know who it belonged to?"

"My grandfather's grandfather, I think. Why?"

"No reason. It looks old. I was just curious."

* * *

It took four days before the stallion would accept the bridle without a fight, and another two days before the horse would stand still while Lee tightened the cinch. Even then, swinging into the saddle was like straddling a block of dynamite. And it wasn't because Lee didn't know what he was doing. He was a good rider, the best Kelly had ever seen, but the horse bucked like it was powered with TNT. Time and again, Lee went sailing through the air, only to regain his feet and try again.

After a while it was almost painful to watch, and Kelly wondered which stubborn creature would win—the man or the stallion.

It was late one night about two weeks later when something roused Kelly from sleep.

Rising, she went to the window and peered outside. A bright silver moon illuminated the yard. At first she didn't see anything, and then a bit of movement caught her eye. Leaning forward, she glanced to the left toward the corrals.

"Oh." The word whispered past her lips and then she grabbed her robe and left the house.

Moving silently through the shadows, she made her way to the corral, stopping out of sight behind a tall pine, her gaze focused on the man and the horse silhouetted in the moonlight.

She watched Lee walk toward the horse, speaking softly in a language Kelly did not understand, but assumed was Lakota. Slowly he closed the distance between himself and the black, a constant stream of words wrapping magically around the horse.

The stallion stood in the center of the corral, ears twitching, eyes watching the man's every move, until the man stood at its head and very slowly reached out to stroke its neck.

Kelly eased forward, listening to the soft words that seemed to have woven a fairy spell around the wild stallion.

She pressed a hand to her heart as Lee placed his hands on either side of the horse's head and blew softly into the animals nostrils.

And then, to her utter surprise, Lee vaulted onto the stallion's bare back. She held her breath, expecting to see the horse start to buck. Instead, the black craned its head around to look at the man on its back. Lee gave a gentle squeeze with his thighs and the horse began to walk around the corral as if it had been doing it every day of its life.

Speechless, Kelly left her hiding place and went to stand near the corral gate. Man and horse circled the corral, moving together as if they were one creature.

When they reached the gate, Lee spoke softly to the horse and the stallion came to a smooth halt. Lee slid off the horse, gave the animal a pat on the neck, and left the corral.

It was only then that Kelly realized it wasn't Lee at all. It was Blue Crow.

"How did you do that?" she asked. "Lee's been trying to break that stallion for days."

"Lee Roan Horse is a good man, but he has

wandered far from the true path. He has forgotten how to be one with his four-footed brothers."

"Oh. The warbonnet Lee has in the barn, it belonged to you, didn't it?"

"*Han.* How did you know?"

"I saw you wearing it."

"You saw me?"

"Yes. I don't know how to explain it, but I touched it the other day and I saw you riding a paint horse."

Blue Crow nodded. "At the Greasy Grass."

"You were at the Little Big Horn?"

"*Han.* It was a day to be remembered, *tekihila.* The Blue Coats fought bravely, but Wakan Tanka was on our side that day. It was a great victory for my people. I would have liked to share it with you."

Kelly took a step backward, suddenly aware that she was standing outside, clad in a nightgown and robe, alone with a ghost. A very sensual ghost.

A small smile flickered over Blue Crow's face. "You feel it, too."

"Feel what?"

"The magic between us."

"No," Kelly said, shaking her head for emphasis. "I don't feel anything."

"Do not lie to me, *tekihila.*"

"What did you call me?"

Blue Crow made a vague gesture of dismissal. "It is not important." My love, he thought to himself. How easily he had come to think of her as his. Day and night, he watched her, pleased because she had a good heart, a good soul.

"I'd better go inside," Kelly said. She wrapped her arms around her middle as a cool breeze stirred the air.

Blue Crow took a step forward. Before Kelly could object, he enfolded her in his arms and drew her close, his embrace gentle, nurturing.

"You shouldn't . . . I shouldn't . . ." All thought of protest fled her mind as his warmth infused her. She stared into his eyes, eyes as soft and dark as black velvet, as deep as a midnight sea. Eyes that glowed with a fierce desire, a barely suppressed hunger that created a wild fluttering in Kelly's stomach and made her heart beat faster.

"Tekihila."

The sound of his voice enveloped her like a silken web. Mesmerized by his nearness, by the strength of his arms, she could only stand there, her gaze trapped in his, waiting, hoping that he would lower his head and kiss her.

As if he'd read her mind, he did just that.

And there was magic between them, she thought, dazed. His lips were warm and firm, yielding and demanding. Desire seared through her, brighter than the tail of a comet, hotter than a thousand suns.

"Tekihila," he murmured. *"Skuya, skuya."*

"Skuya?"

"Sweet," he said. "So sweet."

"Tekihila?" It took an effort to form words when he was standing so close to her, the heat of his deep black eyes glowing like twin coals, warming her in places that had long been cold.

"My own love."

His love. It never occurred to her to argue. Standing on tiptoe, she touched her lips to his. This couldn't be happening, she mused. He wasn't real. Maybe he was only a figment of her imagination. But there was nothing imaginary about his mouth on hers, or the way her blood hummed in her veins. There was nothing imaginary about the rapid beat of her pulse, or the hard male thighs pressed against hers.

She was breathless, mindless when he took his mouth from hers.

Effortlessly he swung her into his arms and carried her into the house, moving confidently through the dark hall until he came to her bedroom. Removing her robe, he put her to bed, drew the covers up to her chin.

She stared up at him, wanting him as she'd never wanted anything in her life, but instead of crawling into bed beside her, he kissed her lightly on the forehead.

"Rest well, *tekihila*," he murmured, and then he was gone, leaving her alone, and lonely, in the dark.

Chapter Ten

She was still slightly dazed in the morning. Standing at the stove, she touched her lips again and again, remembering the touch and the taste of his mouth on hers, the sound of his voice calling her *tekihila*. My own love.

She might have stood there daydreaming until the bacon caught fire if Lee hadn't entered the kitchen, letting the door slam shut behind him.

"What the devil!" he exclaimed. "You trying to burn the house down!"

"What? Oh!"

Startled out of her reverie, Kelly jerked the frying pan off the fire and turned off the gas.

"From the smoke filling the room, I'd say breakfast is ready," Lee drawled. Pulling out a chair, he sat down, his brow furrowed in thought.

Kelly didn't bother to answer. Instead, she spooned some bacon and eggs on a plate and plopped it down in front of him. Filling a plate for herself, she took a seat across from Lee.

"Something wrong?" he asked.

"No."

He studied her face a moment, then sighed. "Okay, okay, I'm sorry about that crack about the smoke," Lee muttered.

"What?"

"Where are you this morning?" Lee waved his fork in the air. "First you practically set the bacon on fire, and now you look as if you're a million miles from here."

"I'm fine. I just have a lot on my mind."

"Anything I can help you with?"

"No."

He frowned, and then shrugged. "Funny thing," he remarked. "I threw a saddle on the black before I came up here. For the first time, he didn't fight me, so I climbed aboard."

"And?"

"Nothing happened. He just stood there like we were old friends." Lee shook his head. "It was the damnedest thing."

And that wasn't all of it, Lee thought, bemused. The black had whickered at him like he was glad to see him.

"Maybe he just got tired of fighting," Kelly suggested.

"Yeah, maybe, but . . ."

"But?"

"An outlaw like that doesn't just give up overnight."

"It hasn't been overnight," Kelly pointed out. "You've been trying to break him for the last two weeks."

"Yeah," Lee muttered in agreement, but he didn't sound convinced.

"More coffee?"

"Thanks." Lee watched Kelly cross the room, admiring the way she filled out her Levi's, the feminine sway of her hips. For a moment, he wondered if she'd been riding the black, but quickly dismissed the idea. The horse would have chewed her up and spit her out.

Kelly refilled Lee's cup and then her own before she sat down at the table again.

"So," Lee said, his hands folded around the mug, "now that we've got two horses, what do you say we take the day off and go for a ride?"

"A ride? Where?"

He shrugged. "Up in the foothills, maybe. Pretty country up there. Lots to see."

You don't know the half of it, Kelly thought.

"What do you say?" He lifted the cup to his lips and took a drink, watching her over the rim.

"It's gonna be hot again today. I'd rather ride along the creek bed, maybe take a dip."

A flicker of disappointment shadowed his eyes and then was gone. "Sounds good." Rising, he drained his cup. "I'll saddle the horses."

"And I'll pack a lunch. Ham sandwiches okay?"

"Fine."

Kelly stared after Lee as he picked up his hat

and left the room, shaken by the feeling that he knew about the gold.

She'd have to be careful, she thought, and then wondered if maybe she should just fire him and be done with it. She considered it for a moment, and then decided that if he was really looking for the gold, she'd be better off to let him stay where she could keep an eye on him.

An hour later, they were riding side by side along the narrow creek that flowed down the south side of the mountain and meandered, snakelike, across the southern portion of the Triple M.

Kelly had ample opportunity to observe Lee, since he had his hands full keeping the stallion under control. The horse might be saddle-broke, but he was still green. And young. He shied when a rabbit skittered across their path, bucked when a jay flew out of a tree, wings flapping loudly.

Kelly shook her head when the stallion bucked again, this time because he'd seen his shadow. Leaning forward, she patted Dusty on the neck, grateful she was mounted on a reliable old gelding instead of a high-spirited young stallion.

Lee was grinning when, a few miles later, he drew rein in the shade of a cottonwood tree.

"He's a great horse," he exclaimed.

Leaning forward, he stroked the black's neck affectionately, thinking that maybe he hadn't made such a bad bargain after all.

Dismounting, he turned to help Kelly from the saddle. It shouldn't have meant anything when his hands circled her waist. He was, after all, only helping her dismount, but she felt the heat of his hands penetrate her shirt, searing the skin beneath.

He felt it, too. She saw it in the brief flare of surprise in his eyes, heard it in the catch in his breath.

A muscle worked in his cheek, as if he were keeping himself in tight control, and then he swung her out of the saddle. Her hands rested on his shoulders, feeling the play of powerful muscles beneath her fingertips as he lifted her from Dusty's back.

As soon as her feet touched the ground, he released her and took a step backward.

Kelly stared up at him. They weren't touching anymore, but she was acutely aware of the male scent of him, of the remembered touch of rippling muscles beneath the thin cotton of his shirt. His eyes were black. Dark. Hypnotic. Somehow warning her away even as they burned with unspoken desire.

She was plagued by a fierce urge to caress his cheek and see if she could wipe the bitterness from his face; instead, she slipped her hands into her pockets. But, try as she might, she couldn't draw her gaze from his. It was like being caught in a whirlpool, being sucked deeper and deeper in black water until she was helplessly caught.

"Kelly . . ." Her name whispered past his lips, a prayer and a groan combined.

She blinked at him, unable to speak for the fierce pounding of her heart.

He shook his head, his face twisted with pain. "I don't want to hurt you."

"I don't understand."

"I'm no good, Kelly. Tell me to go, now, before it's too late for both of us."

"It's already too late."

She spoke without thinking, and knew that no truer words had ever been spoken. Right or wrong, she was drawn to this man in ways she could not fathom or explain.

Lee shook his head in denial. He didn't want to care for her. He couldn't care for her. She was a white woman, his enemy. He had come here to steal from her, to take what was rightfully his, not to become infatuated with sky-blue eyes and pretty pink lips.

He swore under his breath as he read the wanting in those same blue eyes. How could he steal from this woman? She was so innocent, so trusting. And yet that gold was his. His grandfather's grandfather had been killed on the mountain that rose behind Kelly's house, killed by a pair of greedy white men . . .

Lee frowned as a distant memory niggled at the corner of his mind. McBride . . .

"You don't happen to have an ancestor named Charlie McBride, do you?" he asked.

Kelly nodded, wondering at his sudden change of topic. "I saw his name on a genealogy sheet once. He was born back in 1854 or 1855, as I recall. Why?"

Lee shook his head. Charlie McBride had been one of the white men responsible for the death of his grandfather's grandfather, Blue Crow.

He felt a rush of adrenalin. He was on the

right track. The gold was here, in the mountains, as his great-grandfather had told him so many years ago.

"Lee, what's wrong?"

"Nothing."

He tried to ignore the hurt, the confusion, in her eyes. In the old days, she would have been his enemy. He would have thrown her across his horse and carried her off into the mountains. He would have made her his woman, willing or not. He would have buried himself in her pale flesh and exorcised the demons that haunted him.

He felt his blood heat at the mere thought of possessing her. For a moment, he was tempted to forget everything . . . the silent festering wound that Melinda's betrayal had left in his soul, his determination to have the gold, to forget everything but the woman standing before him.

He glanced at the black stallion. It would be so easy to grab Kelly, throw her on his horse, and run like the devil. But where would they go? In the old days, they could have lived off the land. He could have taken her far away, hidden her, kept her until he tired of her. But not now. Sooner or later they'd find him and he'd be back in jail, or dead.

A twinge of unease made Kelly take a step backward. A moment ago she had thought Lee was going to kiss her. Now he looked as if he were contemplating what it would be like to slit her throat, or worse. Unwanted came the memory that he had been accused of rape.

"Maybe we should go home," she suggested.

"No. Come on, let's take a walk."

She hesitated a moment, then nodded in agreement. "Okay."

Side by side, they walked along the winding creek. Willows and cottonwoods grew in scattered clumps. Wildflowers swayed in the breeze. Birds flitted from branch to branch, or dusted themselves in the sandy soil along the creek bank.

Once, Kelly's hand brushed Lee's. It was as if a spark of electricity arced between them. When it happened again, she came to an abrupt halt.

"Lee . . ."

He didn't say anything, only drew her into his arms and kissed her. His lips were firm and warm, asking but not demanding, entreating, hopeful.

Of their own accord, her arms twined around his neck and she pressed against him, hoping to ease the ache that was spreading through her, an ache made stronger by the probing fire of his tongue.

The strength seemed to be draining from her legs. She was aware of Lee's arms around her, slowly pulling her down until they were kneeling on the grass.

"Kelly . . ." He groaned softly. "Kelly, tell me to stop."

"I can't."

She leaned toward him, her breasts pressing against his chest as her lips sought his again.

His hands slid down her back, drawing her hips to his. Kelly's breath caught in her throat as she felt the evidence of his desire.

Her head fell back, giving Lee access to her

neck, and she shuddered with pleasure as she felt his mouth glide over the sensitive skin of her neck, behind her ear, at the pulse point in the hollow of her neck. She was tingling with delight, burning with need, as her restless hands explored his arms, his shoulders, his back. She pressed her hand to his chest and felt the rapid beating of his heart.

She'd never felt like this before. It was frightening, exhilarating.

He fell back on the grass and drew her down on top of him, his mouth covering hers. She felt the rumble of a groan in his chest and wondered if he was experiencing the same exquisite pain she was.

She wanted him, wanted him in a way she'd never wanted any other man. Wanted him in the most elemental, primal way that a woman could want a man. But, more than that, she wanted to hold him, to comfort him, to make a home for him . . .

She drew back so she could see his face, not knowing that her thoughts were as transparent as a pane of new glass.

With an oath, Lee sat up, and then stood up, carrying Kelly with him. Gently, but deliberately, he put her feet on the ground, removed her arms from his neck.

"We'd better head back, Miss McBride," he said, his voice as hard and cold as winter ice, "before one of us gets into trouble."

Without waiting for her reply, he turned on his heel and started walking back to where they had left the horses. How easily she broke through his resolve! How quickly she made him forget Melinda and all that happened afterward.

He shook his head ruefully. Some men had a weakness for firewater. He seemed to have an incurable weakness for women who were sure to cause him nothing but trouble.

Swinging into the saddle, he renewed his determination to find the gold and get the hell out of Cedar Flats.

Chapter Eleven

The man seated behind the desk drummed his fingers impatiently. "Well, Trask, what have you learned?"

"Nothing, boss. Roan Horse spends all his time working around the ranch, patching up the roof and fixin' the corrals. When he's not fixin' the place up, he's working with a black devil horse. If he's searching for the gold, he's doing it at night when we can't see him."

"And the woman?"

Trask's companion shook his head. "She rarely leaves the house. They went on a picnic." He shrugged. "Maybe all that talk about Indian gold is just that, talk."

"When I want your opinion, Bradford, I'll ask for it. In the meantime, I'm paying you two for information."

"Yessir."

"Next time I see you, you'd better have news. I'm getting damned tired of all this waiting around."

"Maybe we can stir something up," Trask mused.

"Do that. Now, go on, get out of here. And don't let anyone see you leave."

Chapter Twelve

Kelly stood at the kitchen window watching Lee put the last coat of paint on the barn. Two days had passed since their ill-fated ride. Two tension-filled days. Lee had avoided her except at mealtimes, and then he had been sullen and withdrawn.

She'd been tempted to take her meals in her bedroom, but had refused to let him chase her out of her own kitchen. If he didn't like her company, he could take his meals in the barn!

Dragging her gaze from his sweat-sheened back, and quietly cursing the fact that he rarely wore a shirt when he worked, she studied the barn. He'd done a good job, she couldn't fault him there. The freshly painted white trim made a vivid contrast to the dark brick-red paint. As soon as he finished the doors, the barn would be done and he'd start on the house.

Kelly wrapped her arms around her waist. She should let him go, she thought. He had warned her that there were wild animals prowling around, and that they weren't all four-footed. She wondered suddenly if he'd been warning her against himself.

She had no doubt that Lee Roan Horse could be a dangerous man. If she wasn't careful, he was going to steal her heart.

At five, he opened the back door and informed her that he was going into town.

Startled, Kelly had no time to do more than nod before he was gone.

The rest of the day seemed like a week. She hadn't realized how accustomed she'd become to Lee's company, how often she'd looked out the window to see what he was doing, until he wasn't around.

At loose ends, she wandered through the house, seeing things she hadn't really paid attention to before, like the old photograph of her grand-parents in the spare bedroom.

Sitting on the edge of the bed, she studied the couple in the picture. Her grandfather was sitting in a straight-backed chair, his expression solemn, a black bowler hat balanced on his knee, but it was her grandmother's image that drew Kelly's eye. Sally McBride stood slightly behind her husband, one hand on his shoulder.

Kelly stared at the photo, wondering why people in old photographs never smiled. Had life in the old days been that hard, or was it simply "not done"? What had it been like, living back then, when women were considered nothing more than property, like a man's horse, when they couldn't vote or wear pants or do any number of things that women did today?

Kelly stared out the window as darkness fell over the land. Would she have meekly obeyed the rules of the day, or would she have dared to speak out for what she believed in? Would she have defended a woman's right to own property, to have the vote, to smoke and drink in public?

Probably not, Kelly mused. She'd never been much of a fighter. And she wouldn't have wanted to live back then, either.

With a sigh, she fell back on the bed and closed her eyes.

A hand on her arm. A breath of warm air against her neck. The scent of sage and smoke.

Only half awake, Kelly opened her eyes and blinked into the darkness.

"Tekihila."

"Blue Crow."

She felt the mattress sag as he sat down beside her.

"Soft," he muttered. "How do you sleep on such a thing?"

Kelly shook her head. "What should I sleep on?"

"Mother Earth is the best bed."

She made a soft sound in her throat, neither agreeing nor disagreeing, mesmerized by the slash of his profile in the room's dim light, by the hypnotic touch of his fingertips slowly gliding up and down the inside of her forearm.

"Walk with me, *tekihila?*"

At her nod, he took her hand in his and helped her to her feet.

Outside, he turned north, walking toward the distant mountain.

"Where are we going?" Kelly asked.

"Does it matter, *skuya?*"

"No."

He smiled at her, his teeth gleaming whitely in the darkness.

"In the old days, we would have been enemies." He lifted his hand and let it slide through the thick fall of her hair. "Your scalp would have made a fine trophy."

Kelly shivered. "Did you . . . did you . . . do that?"

"Han!" he said, his voice ringing with pride. "I am a warrior." His hand slid down to her neck, resting lightly on her nape. "But I never took the scalp of a woman, *tekihila.*"

"I'm glad."

"I would not have wanted your hair, *skuya,*" he murmured, his voice washing over her like liquid sunshine.

"No?"

"No. I would have stolen you had I seen you then," he said fervently. "Had you been married, I would have killed your man and made you mine."

Kelly stared into his deep black eyes, not knowing if she should be flattered or afraid.

"I would take you now, *tekihila*, if I could."

"Would you?" It was an effort to speak past the thickness in her throat.

"*Han*. I would carry you high into the *Paha Sapa*, where all life was born. And there, in the shadow of the sacred mountains, I would give you laughter in the light of the day, and at night, in our lodge, I would give you sons."

No man had ever promised her anything as beautiful. Unable to speak, she took his hand in hers and cupped it to her cheek. His palm was hard and callused and warm.

For a time they stood there in the darkness, not speaking. Slowly his hand slid from her neck and he wrapped his arm around her shoulder, drawing her against him.

Wordlessly she moved into his embrace, placing her head against his chest. She could hear his heart beating strong and sure, and she wondered how that could be. He was a ghost, a spirit, yet he was the most solid thing in her life.

As though drawn by an invisible hand, she looked up, her eyelids fluttering down as his head lowered toward hers. His kiss was gentle, yet she felt as though she had been branded as his for all time.

Her lips felt bereft when he drew away. Gently he cradled her head to his chest again, his arms holding her close, making her feel as if nothing could ever hurt her again.

"Where is Roan Horse?" Blue Crow asked after
le.

"I don't know. He said he was going into town."

"Do you believe him?"

"Why shouldn't I?"

"He is a troubled young man, haunted by his past, afraid of his future."

"Afraid? Of what?"

"Who can say what another man fears? His life has not been easy. He does not trust others, or himself."

"Do you think he means to hurt me?"

"There are many kinds of hurt, *skuya*." His hand caressed her cheek. "Holding you brings me more pain than you will ever know."

"Does it? Why?"

"Because I have waited for you my whole life, and now that I have found you, I know you can never be mine."

Kelly gazed into his fathomless black eyes. There were no words to describe the emotion that his soft-spoken words aroused within her heart, no words to describe the tenderness that swelled in her soul.

She could only look at him, hoping he could read her feelings in her eyes, in the touch of her hand as she pressed it over his heart.

"You never married, did you?" she asked.

"No. I was waiting, searching, for you."

"And I was waiting for you," Kelly murmured, realizing only as she spoke the words that it was true.

She would never have been happy with the men she'd dated. She knew that now, knew it as surely as she knew the sun would rise in the morning, or that winter would follow the fall.

She loved Blue Crow.

"No, *skuya*," he said, his voice as deep and dark as the night that surrounded them. "You must not love me."

"It's too late," she said, her voice breaking. "Too late."

She buried her face against his chest, her eyes burning with unshed tears.

"Do not weep, *tekihila*," he murmured as he stroked her hair. "Your tears are like a knife in my heart."

"Kiss me," she begged, and threading her fingers through his long black hair, she drew his head down toward hers, losing herself in his touch, in his nearness.

She felt the instant response of his manhood as their lips met and she pressed herself against him, tears coursing down her cheeks because she'd fallen in love with the one man she couldn't have, a man who wasn't a man at all, but a ghost.

"Kelly! Kelly, are you out there?" Lee's voice ripped through the darkness. "Kelly?"

"Answer him," Blue Crow whispered.

"I'm over here." She clung to Blue Crow's hand when he started to pull away. "Don't go," she said, but he was already gone.

A moment later she saw Lee striding toward her.

"What the hell are you doing out here alone in the middle of the night?" he demanded, his voice laced with anger.

"I felt like taking a walk."

"You little idiot. Didn't I warn you it was dangerous to go prowling around alone out here?"

"It's no concern of yours what I do!" Kelly retorted.

Lee frowned at her. "Have you been crying?"

"No." She wiped her eyes with the backs of her hands. "Of course not."

"Have it your way. Come on, I'll walk you back to the house."

"I don't need a chaperon."

"Fine," he muttered crossly, "*You* can walk *me* back to the house. Does that soothe your feminine vanity?"

"I don't know what you mean!"

"You're probably one of those feminists, right?" He muttered an oath. "All that women's lib crap, it makes me sick."

"That's because you're not a woman."

"Damn right."

"Why are you so angry?"

"Why are you so stubborn?"

"I'm not."

"The devil you're not."

Kelly came to an abrupt halt, her hands fisted on her hips as she glared at him. "I hate you."

"Good. I hate you, too," he growled, and then, because he could no more resist the lure of her pouting pink lips than he could refuse to take his next breath, he yanked her into his arms and kissed her. Hard.

Kelly struggled against him, her fists pounding impotently on his back and shoulders.

"Quit that, you little hellcat!"

"Let me go!"

Ignoring her futile protests, Lee backed her against a tree, his hips grinding against hers, letting her feel the strength of his need. His lips slid to her neck, her ear.

"*Skuya*," he murmured, his tongue delving into her ear.

"Don't call me that!" Kelly exclaimed.

"What?" He drew back a little.

"*Skuya*. Don't call me that."

"Why not?" he asked, and then frowned. "You know what it means?"

"Yes . . . no . . . just don't call me that."

Lee studied her face closely. In the moonlight, her skin was like porcelain touched with star dust. Her tear-dampened eyes were luminous, her hair fell loose around her shoulders, a perfect frame for her beauty. A single tear hovered on the tip of her lashes.

His anger evaporated like smoke. "What is it, Kelly?" he asked quietly. "What were you doing out here alone? Why were you crying?"

She shook her head, refusing to meet his eyes.

With a muffled curse, he drew her into his arms and held her close.

"It's all right, Kelly," he murmured. "You don't have to tell me." He rocked her gently, his hands making lazy circles on her back. "It's all right, sweetheart, everything's gonna be all right."

And swinging her into his arms, he carried her home and tucked her into bed as if she were no more than a child.

"Lee? I . . . would you mind staying with me awhile?"

"No, I don't mind." And sitting on the bed beside her, he held her hand until she fell asleep.

The hand holding hers was strong yet gentle, telling her she was safe, telling her she was loved. She glanced up at the man walking beside her, the warmth of his smile washing over her like sunshine, heating her flesh with only a look, sending shivers of sensation running through her.

When they reached the river, he drew her into his arms, his lips covering hers in a kiss that made her blood flow like warm honey and drained all the strength from her limbs so that she swayed against him.

"Tekihila." His breath teased her neck.

"Kiss me," she murmured.

"Gladly, skuya."

Little soft sounds of pleasure rose in Kelly's throat as his mouth covered hers. His tongue was a flame of fire, threatening to engulf her until only cinders remained. She felt the need of his need and knew she longed for nothing more than to ease his ache, and her own.

Slowly they sank to the ground, surrendering to the soul-deep need between them.

She had never known a man.

He had not held a woman in more than a hundred years.

Their coming together was like an inferno, two fiery stars that collided in the night, coming togeth-

er in fury and exploding in a thousand bursts of flame until only ashes remained . . .

"Blue Crow?"

Kelly sat up, awakened by the cold and a sense of being alone. Glancing around, she saw that she was in her own bed, still dressed as she had been the night before.

Confused, she stared around the familiar room, her heart growing heavy with disappointment when she realized it had only been a dream.

She heard footsteps in the hallway, felt her heart give a little leap of anticipation as the door to her room swung open. The smile of welcome died on her lips.

It was Lee.

"I'm glad to see you, too," he muttered. "Here, I brought you a cup of coffee."

"Thank you." She took the blue flowered mug from his hand.

"You feeling any better today?"

"Better than what?"

Lee took a deep breath, striving for patience. She made him angrier quicker than any woman he'd ever known.

"Better than last night," he said brusquely. "You want to tell me why you were crying?"

Kelly stared into the cup to avoid his eyes. "I wasn't."

"Dammit, Kelly . . ."

"Let it go, Lee."

"Fine. I'm gonna start on the roof today. If you need to go into town, this might be a good time.

I'll be making quite a racket tearing off the old roof."

Kelly nodded. She did need to go to town. All week she'd been expecting Harry Renford to call about the deed. This might be a good time to find out just what was going on.

Putting the mug on the bedside table, she swung her legs over the edge of the bed. "I'll fix breakfast."

Lee nodded, wondering what was bothering her, wondering why she'd been crying last night.

"I'll go feed the stock," he muttered. On the way to the barn, he gave himself a stern reminder of what he was doing at the Triple M, a reason that had nothing to do with Kelly McBride.

Two hours later, Kelly was sitting in Renford's office, her hands clasped together in an effort to control her rising temper.

"How long does it take to get a copy of a deed?" she demanded. "It's been weeks!"

"I know, I know," Renford agreed with exaggerated patience. "But they're having some trouble in the records department at the county seat. Some nonsense about transferring the records to computers. You understand?"

"No, I don't. I have a good mind to drive up there and see what's going on for myself."

"Now, Kelly, I've told you before, there's no need to worry. The Triple M is yours, free and clear."

The smile that curved his lips didn't reach his narrowed eyes. "Free and clear, except for the balloon payment on the mortgage."

"What balloon payment? I thought I'd paid the mortgage in full. I have a receipt."

"Yes, well, I'm afraid I made a little mistake when I calculated the amount due. There was a rather stiff payoff penalty I neglected to allow for."

"How much?"

Renford made a vague gesture with his hand. "I believe it comes to just under six thousand dollars."

"I see."

Kelly looked out the window. Six thousand dollars wasn't a vast amount of money. She had a hundred times that much in gold, but she had very little cash in the bank. Well, she thought resolutely, there was no help for it. She'd just have to take a few of the larger nuggets and cash them in.

"How soon is the payment due?"

"It's . . . ah, past due now."

"Past due! Why didn't you let me know?"

"You're not the bank's only client, Kelly. I'm afraid I was unaware of the problem until my secretary brought it to my attention. The foreclosure papers have already been drawn."

"When's the money due?"

"Closing time tomorrow. Shall I expect you?"

"Damn right!"

Quivering with anger, Kelly stood up and slammed out of Renford's office. She had the feeling that the man was up to something, but what? He had nothing to gain from foreclosing on the ranch.

And what about Lee? She couldn't shake the feeling that he knew about the gold, that the only reason he had come to the ranch was to look for the treasure. And when he found it, he would leave without a backward glance.

Heavy-hearted, she slid behind the wheel of her car and headed for home.

Chapter Thirteen

"You look worried, *tekihila*," Blue Crow remarked. "Is something wrong?"

"I'm having trouble with the bank."

"What kind of trouble?"

"I owe them some money for the ranch. If I don't have it by tomorrow, the bank will foreclose."

"Foreclose? What does that mean?"

"It means I won't own the land anymore. It will belong to the bank, and they'll sell it to someone else."

Blue Crow traced the curve of her cheek with his fingertip. "Then you have no problem. The gold is there. Take what you need. Take it all, if you must."

"Not very long ago you told me quite emphatically that the gold was yours."

"I remember. And I also said I would decide who should have it."

"But you've spent an eternity guarding it. Somehow it doesn't seem right for me to take it."

"The gold is yours, *tekihila*," he murmured. "I want you to have it. You may do with it as you wish."

Kelly smiled at him, relief mingling with gratitude as she murmured her heartfelt thanks.

As always, Blue Crow had come to her in the dark of the night, and now they were sitting in the living room on the Navajo rug in front of the fireplace. Shadows danced over Blue Crow's bronzed chest and broad shoulders, sliding over his bare torso like a lover's caress.

The vast expanse of heavily muscled male flesh drew Kelly's hand. He shivered at her touch, a sensual shiver that bespoke his pleasure at her touch.

"Why don't I ever see you during the day?" she wondered aloud.

Blue Crow shrugged. "I guard the cave."

"What's it been like for you all these years?"

"I don't understand."

"You've been . . . you've been dead for over a hundred years. Have you been in the cave all that time?"

Blue Crow nodded.

"Do you ever get hungry?" Her gaze skimmed his bare chest. "Or cold?"

He smiled, his dark eyes bright with amusement. "No, *tekihila*, I don't get hungry or cold. Only lonely."

She covered his hand with hers. How had he stood it, staying in that cave, alone, for over a hundred years?

Blue Crow laced his fingers through hers. "Most of the time, I sleep," he said, answering her unspoken question. "And when I sleep, I dream, *tek-ihila*."

"Do you? Of what?"

His beautiful black eyes caressed her. "I dream of you, *skuya*. You have been my companion, the light in my darkness, my only weapon against the loneliness of a hundred years."

The man had the soul of a poet, Kelly thought.

"How could you have been dreaming of me all that time? I mean"—she grinned at him—"I'm only twenty-two."

"I cannot explain it to you. I only know that when I saw you, I knew you were the woman I had seen in my vision quest."

"You saw me in a vision?"

"*Han.* When I went to seek a medicine dream, I saw a woman with hair as brown and curly as a buffalo's and eyes as blue as the sky above. All my life, I searched for you. And now, too late, you are here."

His hand cupped her cheek. "You are in danger, *tekihila*. I have seen a man scouting the mountain. He has a bad heart."

"A man?"

"A *wasichu*. He has dark hair, and yellow eyes, like a coyote."

Her relief that he wasn't describing Lee was almost painful.

"You should leave this place, *skuya*. You are not safe here."

"But this is my home. I don't want to leave." Tears burned her eyes. "Will you go with me?" she asked, her voice thick.

"I cannot." He brushed his knuckles against her cheek. "I cannot leave this place."

"Then I'm not going, either."

"You must."

"No, I won't leave you."

"You are a young woman, *tekihila*. You deserve a man of flesh and blood, one who can share your life, give you children."

"I won't leave you," Kelly said.

"Ah, *tekihila*," he murmured, drawing her into his arms. "What a warrior's wife you would have made."

"I wish I had known you before," Kelly said, the tremor in her voice speaking of the pleasure his touch gave her. "Tell me, how did you come by the gold?"

"It was in the time of Long Hair," Blue Crow said. "The government had promised the *Paha Sapa* would belong to the Lakota for as long as the grass was green and the water was blue, but then Long Hair invaded the sacred hills and found the yellow iron that the white men crave as they crave firewater."

Kelly nodded. She'd never been a history buff, but she'd seen enough movies to know about Custer and the Black Hills and the Little Big Horn.

"The government tried to buy the *Paha Sapa*," Blue Crow went on, "but Tatanka Iyotaka, the one your people call Sitting Bull, said no. He was a man of vision and cunning, and he knew that if the white man could not buy the hills, he would steal them. Another of our chiefs who was wise in the ways of the whites decided we should gather as much gold as we could find. He, too, believed the whites would steal the hills, but he thought if we could gather enough gold, we might be able to buy them back.

"We picked up gold whenever we found it and hid it in the cave, along with whatever gold was taken in raids. But then Custer was killed at the Greasy Grass and the Army began to hunt our people. Those who were caught were sent to the reservation.

"I refused to surrender. I came here to guard the gold, hoping that one day I might be able to buy freedom for my people." He shook his head ruefully. "I never had the chance."

"And you've guarded it all these years. Has no one ever found the cave?"

"Some have come looking for the gold. None have lived to tell the tale."

Kelly bit down on her lower lip as she digested that bit of news.

"The yellow iron is mine," Blue Crow said. "I gave my life for it. Now I give it to you. Take it and leave this place. Find the happiness you deserve."

"You might as well stop trying to send me away," Kelly said, "because I'm not leaving."

"You are a stubborn woman, *skuya*."

"That's what Lee says."

Blue Crow grunted softly. "Roan Horse is blood of my blood, but he has strayed from the true path."

"That explains it, then," Kelly mused.

"Explains what?"

"Why you look so much alike. When I saw you riding the stallion, I thought it was Lee."

"He would have made a fine warrior in the old days. The blood of fighting chiefs runs hot in his veins."

"He has hot blood, that's for sure," Kelly muttered, remembering the two times when they had kissed. She had felt his hunger, the desire that arced between them whenever they were together. Kelly frowned in confusion. She loved Blue Crow, not Lee, yet she felt the same desire for both men. It was most disconcerting.

"Has he touched you?" Blue Crow asked.

"No."

"You would be good for him, *tekihila*."

Kelly stared at Blue Crow, too astonished to speak. Good for Lee!

"He needs a woman in his life, someone to believe in him, to reawaken the softness that he has buried beneath his anger and bitterness."

"You're talking about the girl that hurt him, aren't you? How do you know about her?"

Blue Crow shook his head. "I don't know how to explain it. When I am asleep in the cave, visions of my relatives sometimes come to me. Roan Horse was shamed and dishonored by the father of the white girl. I felt his frustration when he was locked in the white man's iron house. I felt his anger, his need for vengeance. It festers deep within him."

Blue Crow put his arm around Kelly and drew her close. "Think about it, *tekihila*. Perhaps Roan Horse would be good for you, as well."

"Are you trying to get rid of me?" Kelly asked. She tried to keep her voice light, but failed miserably.

"No, *tekihila*, never think that. I love you more than life, but it is a love that can never be." He smiled at her, his expression melancholy. "The thought of you in another man's arms is like a knife in my soul, but I cannot have you, *skuya*, and since I cannot have you, it would give me great joy to know that you are still a part of me, a part of my family."

Kelly shook her head. "I don't trust Lee."

"Why is that?"

"I think he knows about the gold. I think he came here to steal it from me."

Blue Crow grunted softly. "I fear you may be right," he remarked thoughtfully, "but clouds do not always mean rain, and rivers do not always run true."

"What do you mean?"

But he wasn't listening to her. He was staring at the front door through narrowed eyes. Kelly followed his gaze, wondering at his sudden wariness. When she turned to face him again, he was gone.

"I hate it when you do that," she muttered, and a moment later she heard a knock at the door.

"Kelly? You in there?" The knocking came again, louder and more insistent. "Kelly!"

It was Lee. Scrambling to her feet, she opened the door. "What's wrong?"

"Nothing now. I heard someone moving around behind the barn, but whoever it was was gone when I got there." He held out a small can of gasoline and an oily rag. "I found this."

Kelly frowned. "So?"

"So I think someone was planning to torch the barn."

"Why would anyone do that?"

"I don't know. You got any enemies around here?"

"No . . . well, not that I know of, anyway." She chewed the inside of her lip a moment. "What about you?" she asked. "Have *you* got any enemies around here?"

"What do you mean?"

"You're the one who sleeps in the barn." Kelly took a step backward, one hand holding the door open. "Come on in. I'll fix some coffee."

Leaving the can and the rag on the porch, Lee followed Kelly in and closed the door, then turned the key in the lock before making his way to the kitchen. He noticed she had to turn the lights on as she went. Apparently she'd been sitting in the dark.

He straddled a chair while Kelly brewed a pot of coffee. He'd assumed whoever had been prowling around was trying to drive Kelly away to get at the gold, but what if she was right, what if they'd been after him? But that was ridiculous. He didn't have any enemies around here, or friends, either, for that matter. His death wouldn't mean a thing

115

to anybody. He didn't own anything other than a beat-up truck, a wild stallion, an old saddle, and a moth-eaten warbonnet, certainly nothing worth killing for.

Lee shook his head. It had to be because of the gold. That was the only reason that made sense.

He lifted his gaze to Kelly. She was standing near the stove, her arms crossed over her breasts as she waited for the coffee to boil. Her hair, unbound, fell in a mass of unruly curls down her back and over her shoulders, a perfect frame for her tanned skin and sky-blue eyes.

He felt the first stirrings of desire as he let his gaze move over her, lingering on the swell of her breast, her narrow waist, her long shapely legs.

He cleared his throat, shifting uncomfortably on the hard wooden chair.

"What are you doing up so late?" he asked, hoping to take his mind off the enticing image of Kelly writhing beneath him.

"Nothing."

She took two mugs from the shelf over the sink and filled them with coffee. Lee took his black, but she added a generous amount of milk and sugar to her own before carrying the cups to the table. She set one down in front of Lee, then sat in the chair across from him.

"So," Lee said after taking a sip of his coffee, "you got any ideas about who might have been prowling around at this time of night, or why?"

"No." Her gaze met his, unblinking, unflinching, and slightly accusing. "Do you?"

He felt a sharp stab of guilt as he shook his head. "No."

Was he imagining things, or did she look disappointed?

"Maybe it was just some kids," Kelly suggested. "You know, a prank, or an initiation of some kind."

"Maybe. Do you sit alone in the dark often?"

"What if I do?"

Lee shrugged. "Hey, calm down. I didn't mean to ruffle your feathers."

"Sorry. I've got a lot on my mind, that's all. And that reminds me, I've got to go into Coleville tomorrow. I'll be gone most of the day."

"Want some company?"

"No," Kelly said quickly. Too quickly, but she couldn't have him with her when she cashed in the gold. "I mean, well, you are working for me, and I'd like to have the roof done as soon as possible. They're predicting a wet winter this year."

"Yes, ma'am, I'll get on it first thing in the morning."

"I didn't mean it that way, Lee."

"Didn't you?"

He laughed softly, bitterly, his dark eyes blazing with such anger she was surprised she hadn't been incinerated on the spot.

"Lee . . ." She held out her hand, palm up, in an ancient gesture of peace.

"Hey, I understand. I'm just the hired help, not somebody you'd want to be seen with in town."

"I told you I didn't mean it that way."

"Forget it," he said brusquely, and rising to his feet, he stormed out of the kitchen.

She heard the front door slam behind him, and then only a long, lonely silence.

Chapter Fourteen

He didn't come to breakfast the next morning, and when she went out on the back porch to call him, she saw that his battered old truck was gone.

Frowning, she went to the barn, certain she'd find his few belongings gone, too. She tried to tell herself it would be better if he was gone, that he was a complication she didn't need in her life, but even as she tried to convince herself of that fact, she was breathing a sigh of relief that he hadn't taken his things with him.

She gave Dusty a scoop of oats, then went back to the house and ate breakfast. Forty minutes later, she was riding toward the mountain.

Her heart was beating double time when she reached the cave. Dismounting, she hurried inside, wondering if she would see Blue Crow.

Lifting the lantern high, she stared at the shelf cut into the side of the cavern. The blanket was there, but he wasn't.

She was trying to fight her disappointment when she felt a warm breath whispering against the nape of her neck.

"Tekihila."

She whirled around, her heart fluttering with happiness even before she saw him standing in the shadows.

"Blue Crow!" She put the lantern on the ground, then went gratefully into his arms, resting her head on his shoulder. "I'm so glad to see you."

"My heart soars at your nearness." He drew her closer, delighting in her nearness, in her vitality, in the bright spark of life that glowed like a flame within her.

Lightly, he stroked her hair, thinking of all the years he had dreamed of her, waited for her. "Have you come for the gold?"

Kelly nodded, though it was hard to think of such earthly things as gold and foreclosures when Blue Crow was near, when his hands were moving in her hair, when his body was pressed intimately against her own.

"Be careful, *skuya*," he said, his arms tightening protectively around her. "I sense danger riding toward you."

"Danger? From whom?"

"The man with the yellow eyes. Be wary of strangers, *tekihila*. Trust no one."

"Not even Lee?"

"Not even Lee."

Kelly shivered, frightened by the warning in Blue Crow's voice, the concern in his eyes. "Lee left the ranch."

"I know." Blue Crow held her tight, wishing that he could go beyond the boundaries of the ranch, that he could be constantly at her side. "I will ask Wakan Tanka to watch over you."

"Thank you." She hugged him quickly, fiercely. "I have to go."

"Tekihila." There was a world of wanting in his voice as he cupped her face in his palms and slowly covered her mouth with his.

It was a kiss unlike any Kelly had ever known, filled with soul-deep yearnings and heartfelt dreams that could never come true. It was a kiss that spoke of caring and concern, of a love that could never be consummated.

Kelly's eyelids fluttered open and she gazed into the depths of his eyes, seeing hopelessness and the loneliness of eternity in their depths.

"Blue Crow." She could hardly speak past the lump in her throat.

"Go, *tekihila.*" Reluctantly he let her go and took a step backward. "Hurry. The sun is already high in the sky."

He was right, it was time to go, and yet leaving him there, alone in the darkness of the cave, was the hardest thing she'd ever done.

When she returned to the ranch, she saw that Lee's truck was still gone.

Hurrying into the house, she quickly changed

her clothes, brushed her hair, applied fresh lipstick.

Moments later she was on the road, heading
east toward Coleville. She switched on the radio,
only half listening as Jimmy Dean extolled the
value of his pure pork sausage.

She felt a sudden heartache as Vince Gill's voice
drifted over the speaker singing the same song that
had been playing that night in her kitchen when
Lee had almost kissed her.

Lee. Where had he gone? She hadn't meant
to hurt him, but she had. No wonder he had
such a low opinion of white women, she thought
ruefully. Either they were accusing him of rape,
or making him feel that he wasn't good enough
to be seen in their company.

Well, she couldn't worry about that now. She'd
apologize when she got home.

She finished her business in Coleville quickly,
adroitly sidestepping the questions that came her
way about where the gold had come from and
how she happened to have it.

Slipping the money into her purse, she left the
store and walked down the street toward her car.
With each step she took, she had the feeling she
was being followed. She was probably just being
paranoid, she thought, seeing muggers behind
every face because she had six thousand dollars
in her handbag.

Reaching her car, she slipped behind the wheel,
locked the door, looked over her shoulder, then
pulled away from the curb.

She breathed a little easier once she'd left

Coleville behind, certain she'd been imagining things.

"Good day, Miss McBride," Harry Renford said, shaking her hand. "Sit down, won't you?"

"Yes, thank you," Kelly said, unable to shake the feeling that he was surprised to see her.

"So, what can I do for you?"

"I came to settle the final payment on the ranch," Kelly said.

"Oh, yes, of course. That was six thousand dollars, I believe."

"Yes, I have it right here."

"I see." He took a deep breath. "Well, then, that settles that."

"I beg your pardon?"

"Nothing. I have your receipt right here."

"And the deed?"

"Yes, it's here, as well."

Kelly stared at him, wondering at his wan expression, at the way he tugged at his collar, as if it were suddenly too tight.

"Is something wrong?"

"No, no, nothing at all."

Kelly handed him the wad of bills, watched while he counted it, twice, then wrapped the bills with a thick rubber band and deposited it in his desk drawer.

"If you'll just sign here," Renford said, "and here. That's fine."

He handed her a hand-written receipt for the six thousand dollars, and the deed to the Triple M.

"I'm sure you'll find everything in order, Miss McBride, and if we can ever be of service again, please let me know."

Kelly stuffed the deed and the receipt in her purse, then stood up. "Thank you for everything."

Renford nodded. "Good-bye, Miss McBride."

His tone, and the look in his eyes, sent a shiver down her spine. Without a backward glance, she hurried out of his office and out of the bank.

Outside, she took a deep breath, welcoming the fresh air and the cool breeze on her face.

She was walking toward her car when she felt it again, that eerie sense of being followed, of being in danger.

Crossing the street, she stopped abruptly and whirled around, but there was no one there. Or was there? Was she imagining things again, or had she seen Lee Roan Horse duck around the corner? Or was it just that she wanted to see him?

She didn't breathe easily until she was sitting inside her car with the doors locked. For a moment, she clutched the steering wheel and then, releasing a deep sigh, she turned the key in the ignition and started for home.

It was almost dark when she pulled into the yard. The first thing she saw was Lee's truck parked near the barn. She was surprised at the relief she felt just knowing he was there, relief not only because he was back, but because it meant he couldn't have been following her in town.

He emerged from the barn as she stepped out of the car.

Kelly felt the pull between them vibrate like an electric wire. What was there about this man that attracted her so? It was more than his rugged good looks. Perhaps it was the air of vulnerability that he tried so hard to hide, perhaps it was the knowledge that he so badly needed someone to love, someone to love him. Whatever it was, it hummed between them, vital and alive and irresistible.

She watched him cross the yard toward her, felt her insides turn shivery as every step brought him closer.

"I'm sorry, Lee," she said. "I didn't mean to hurt you."

"It's all right."

"No, it's not. It's just that I needed to be alone today. I handled it badly, and I'm sorry."

"Forget it."

The hunger between them was almost palpable, as was the distrust that kept them apart. Invisible, unmentioned, it rose between them, shimmering like heat waves on the desert.

A muscle throbbed in Lee's cheek. "What did you do in town?"

"I went to the bank."

"Oh?"

"Yes. I needed to pick up the deed to the ranch."

He grunted softly, clearly not believing her.

"I thought I saw you there." The words were out before she could stop them.

He grunted again, neither affirming nor denying her suspicions.

"Have you eaten?" Kelly asked.

"No."

"Me either. I've got some steaks in the fridge."

"Sounds good."

"Dinner in half an hour then?"

"Fine," he replied, but he didn't move, and neither did she.

An awkward silence stretched between them.

"I wasn't in town today, Kelly. I drove out to the reservation."

"Really? Why? Do you have family out there?"

"No." He dragged a hand through his hair. "I don't know why I went out there."

He still didn't know. He'd driven around for hours before winding up at the cemetery. The graves of his family were untended, grown over with weeds. He'd spent an hour on his knees, clearing away the debris, trying not to remember how his little sister had followed him around, always wanting to be where he was, to do what he was doing. Why hadn't he spent more time with her when he'd had the chance?

Kneeling in the dirt, he'd begged for her forgiveness. For his mother, he felt nothing at all. Not love, not hate, not bitterness. She had courted death and it had found her.

He looked up, realizing Kelly was speaking to him.

"I've never been to the reservation," she was saying. "I'd like to see it."

"No," he said flatly, "you wouldn't."

"Oh."

Silence settled around them again. Kelly stared

down at her hands. She should go to the house, take a shower, fix dinner, but she couldn't seem to move. She slid a glance at Lee. He was standing so close, she could feel his heat, smell the perspiration and the scent of aftershave that clung to his skin. His hands were balled into tight fists, his eyes as dark as a winter night, his expression tormented.

"Kelly."

All he said was her name, but she heard more, so much more. He wanted her, wanted her in the most elemental way. He offered no promises, no words of love, nothing but a cry for help, a plea to be held while he battled the demons that were tormenting him.

She had never thought of herself as particularly maternal or nurturing; she'd never fussed over babies or felt any driving need to take on the hurts of the world. Being an only child, she tended to be selfish and self-centered. But now, gazing up into the haunted depths of Lee's eyes, she was overcome with the need to hold this man, to comfort him, to ease his loneliness.

Wordlessly she reached for his hand and led him to the house, down the narrow hall to her bedroom.

She didn't turn on any lights, didn't want him to see the indecision in her eyes.

"Kelly, maybe this isn't a good idea."

"Probably not."

"Then why . . . ?"

"Don't talk."

She put her arms around his neck and pressed her lips to his.

It was all the invitation he needed.

With a strangled cry, he crushed her in his arms, his lips grinding against hers. She tasted blood in her mouth, felt his hands roaming restlessly over her back. And then he swung her into his arms and carried her to bed.

Somehow their clothing disappeared and they were lying in each other's arms, his hard-muscled body surrounding hers, the curves of her body filling the hollows of his.

It was everything she had ever dreamed of, and more. All the fire and excitement that she'd only read about, all the wonder and magic she'd hoped for, she found in Lee's arms. His kiss gentled, his hands caressed her, aroused her, until all her doubts and fears were gone and she was aching for something she had never known.

She gasped with pain and pleasure when she felt the first sweet invasion by his body, but even as she was reaching for him, wanting to hold him closer, he was gone.

She opened her eyes to find Lee standing beside the bed staring down at her, a look of stunned disbelief on his face.

"Why didn't you tell me?"

"Tell you what?"

"That you've never done this before."

Kelly shrugged, confused by his anger. "It doesn't matter. What difference does it make?"

"It matters to me."

A vile oath escaped his lips as he pulled on

his jeans, remembering other slim legs that had wrapped around his waist, other blue eyes cloudy with passion, other pink lips, lips that had spoken only lies.

He closed his eyes, his hands shoved deep into the pockets of his jeans. He felt the bile rise in his throat as he recalled the horror of being accused of rape, of being locked up, of having his every minute watched and regimented. Even in jail, rapists were considered the scum of the earth.

"Lee? What is it? What's wrong?"

He yanked his shirt over his head, grabbed his boots, and headed for the door.

"Lee!"

"Leave me alone, Kelly. Please, just leave me alone."

She sat up, drawing the sheet over her breasts. "Won't you tell me what's wrong? I didn't mean to . . . to offend you."

He groaned low in his throat. "Kelly, it isn't you." He took a deep breath. He could feel her gaze on his back, feel her hurt and confusion. He wanted nothing more than to crawl back into bed and take her in his arms, but he couldn't.

Kelly McBride had been a virgin when he took her in his arms. She was still a virgin, at least technically, and he didn't intend to be the one to change that. He'd already ruined one girl. He didn't intend to make the same mistake twice. It had taken every ounce of self-control he possessed to let Kelly go, to back away when he felt the resistance of her maidenhead.

"Lee . . ."

"Good night, Kelly."

"Wait! You aren't leaving, are you?"

He closed his eyes. Leave, he thought, that was just what he should do. But he'd come here for the gold and he wasn't leaving without it. But that wasn't the only reason he had to stay. Someone else was prowling around out there, searching for the treasure, someone who might not be averse to killing Kelly to get what he wanted. Until he found the gold, or knew that it was gone, he'd stay and keep an eye on Kelly.

"No," he said hoarsely, "I'm not leaving."

And then, before she could ask any more of him, before his self-control shattered, he bolted from the room and shut the door behind him.

In the hallway, he braced one hand against the wall and pressed his forehead to the cool plaster. He was shaking all over, trembling from his need to protect Kelly and the startling, frightening realization that he was falling in love with Kelly McBride.

Chapter Fifteen

Kelly stood beside the front-room window, watching Lee wax her car. She had never known a man to work so hard. Lee was like a man driven by demons. He rose with the sun and didn't go to bed until long after dark. He had put a new roof on the house, repaired all the corral fences and the hole in the barn roof. Every day, he curried the horses, mucked the stalls. He tore down the old chicken coop and built a new one, then went into Cedar Flats and bought a dozen hens and a rooster.

Her grandfather had once kept a garden beside the house. Lee turned the soil under, fertilized it, raked it, and planted a variety of vegetables.

Tomorrow he was going to start painting the house. She'd already picked out the paint, a dark blue-gray for the walls and white for the trim.

She'd mentioned once, in passing, that she'd like a brick border along the walkway that led to the house. The next day, he'd come home with a truckload of bricks and she now had a nice winding red brick path leading to the porch.

With a sigh, Kelly left the window and went into the kitchen to fix lunch. The tension between them was almost unbearable. Lee no longer took his meals in the house but ate in the barn. He was careful to keep his distance from her, never getting close enough to touch, never saying or doing anything that could be considered personal.

She still didn't understand what had happened to cause the breach between them. It didn't make sense for him to be upset that she hadn't known a dozen men before him, yet she'd never seen such anger in a man's eyes, such a look of betrayal.

And then, like dawn bursting on the horizon, she knew, and wondered why it hadn't occurred to her before. He was remembering that other girl, the one who had accused him of rape.

Of course, that had to be it. Kelly grimaced. He was afraid that because one white girl had accused him of rape, it might happen again.

She experienced a moment of blinding anger that he would think her capable of such a reprehensible thing, and then, as quickly as it had risen, her anger was gone, deflated by an overwhelming sadness for all he'd been through.

She made Lee a couple of thick ham and cheese sandwiches, added some potato chips and pickles to the plate, got a cold beer out of the fridge, and then, taking a deep breath, she carried it outside.

He knew she was there even before he turned around. He could sense her presence, smell the faint scent of lilac soap that clung to her skin, the sweet womanly fragrance that was hers and hers alone.

"You've been working hard," Kelly said. "I thought you might be ready for a break."

"Thanks."

He tossed the rag on the hood of the car, wiped his hands on his Levi's.

"Looks good."

He lifted the sandwich from the plate, took the beer from her hands. His fingers brushed hers. That was all, just the merest touch of her fingers against his, but his body reacted instantly, warming, hardening with need.

He could mask the hunger in his eyes, but there was no way to hide the very visible evidence of his desire.

"Lee . . ."

"Let it go, Kelly."

"We need to talk."

"No, we don't."

"Yes, we do. I can't go on like this."

He took a long swallow of beer, wiped his mouth with the back of his wrist. "Do you want me go?"

"No, I want things to be the way they were before. I miss you. I don't like eating alone. I don't like having to watch every word I say."

"Do you think it's any easier for me?"

"No." Her gaze strayed to the telltale bulge in his jeans. "I know it isn't. I have needs, too, Lee."

"Then find someone else to satisfy them."

"I don't want anyone else."

He shook his head. *No more white women.* He drained the beer can, crushed it in his hand. *No more white women.* Kelly might think it didn't make any difference, and in a lot of places, it didn't. But here in Cedar Flats, decent white women didn't sleep with Indian men. It just wasn't done. And even if it had been, she deserved far better than he could give her.

He stared at the untouched sandwich in his hand. He was a man with a police record. If it weren't for Kelly, he'd be a man without a job. He'd almost stolen her virginity. And how did he intend to repay her? By stealing the gold.

"Here." He thrust the sandwich into her hands. "You eat it."

"You must be hungry," Kelly protested. "You haven't eaten since breakfast."

Lee shook his head, knowing he'd never be able to swallow past the lump of self-disgust that was threatening to choke him.

"Talk to me," Kelly urged. "Please. Let me help."

"You want to help? Then leave me alone, Kelly, just leave me the hell alone."

He watched the effect his words had on her, each one slicing into her like a knife until she stood bleeding before him, valiantly fighting the urge to cry.

"Kelly, I'm sorry."

He wanted to take her in his arms and beg her forgiveness, but he was afraid to touch her, afraid that it would be his undoing.

Kelly squared her shoulders and raised her chin. Pride drove the tears from her eyes. She looked at him for a long moment and then, very deliberately, she dropped the sandwich in the dirt at his feet, pivoted on her heel, and walked back to the house. Conscious of his gaze, she didn't run, and she didn't look back.

Lee watched her walk out of sight, knowing he had to get the hell away from the Triple M before it was too late. He had put off searching for the gold, telling himself that he owed it to Kelly to fix the place up as best he could before he robbed her. He'd convinced himself she didn't need the gold. She had a decent name, a good piece of land, a career to go back to. She'd be all right, and if worse came to worst, she could sell the Triple M for a good chunk of change. Anyway, she'd get married eventually and her husband would look after her.

Lee shook his head ruefully. He knew now he'd only been kidding himself. He'd been stalling because he didn't want to leave her, because he liked it here. It was the first real home he'd ever had. He'd left a part of himself on this land. His sweat and his labor were making a difference. The ranch didn't look neglected anymore. For the first time in his life, he felt a sense of pride in something he'd accomplished with his own two hands.

And as long as he was being honest with himself, he might as well admit that he'd kill any other man who dared lay a hand on her.

With an oath, he grabbed the rag and began removing the wax from the hood, hoping that the work would drive Kelly from his mind.

But it was no use. Kelly's image danced before his eyes, her curly brown hair the perfect halo for an angel's face, her lips as pink as a new rose, her eyes as blue as a midsummer sky.

He stared at his reflection in the hood of the Camaro, wondering if it was too late to start over. For too long he'd lived under the shadow of Melinda's accusation. It had followed him like a bad habit, turning up to haunt him again and again. Filled with anger and frustration, he had left home, determined never to return. But no matter how far he ran, he couldn't outrun who and what he was.

As far back as he could remember, people had been pasting labels on him. His teachers had called him a bad boy, incorrigible, wild. Time and again they'd warned him that he would come to a bad end. As he grew older, people called him a dirty Injun, a no-account redskin, and he'd proved every one of them right. Instead of trying to make something of himself when he got out of jail after he'd been arrested for breaking and entering, he'd left the state and headed west, the chip on his shoulder as big as the Grand Canyon. He had no family left, no one to give a damn if he lived or died, and he hadn't much cared, either.

He'd spent six years wandering from state to state, working at odd jobs just long enough to earn enough money to move on. He'd wasted his time and his money drinking, fighting, and gambling, never letting anyone get close to him until, finally, he'd gotten so disgusted with himself that he'd gone back home, back to the reservation, drinking himself into a stupor every night in an effort to forget how miserable he was. He'd spent six months feeling sorry for himself and then, from out of the blue, he had remembered something old Frank McBride had said while they were waiting for the police to arrive.

"It ain't for you, boy. You'll never get your hands on that treasure, not you, nor none of your kin."

Treasure. That one word had sobered Lee up. He had spent the next three weeks asking questions, gradually putting together bits and pieces of stories he had heard as a child, stories the old ones had told around the campfire, tales of an ancient warrior named Blue Crow who had died protecting a fortune in gold.

Lee glanced at the mountain that loomed behind the house. Somewhere in that mountain there was a cave, and in that cave was a fortune in gold. But to take what he wanted meant stealing from Kelly. When he had thought of her as the enemy, the thought of taking the gold hadn't bothered him at all. It was the Lakota way, to steal from the enemy.

But Kelly wasn't the enemy anymore.

And he didn't know how he could steal from her and live with himself afterward.

Chapter Sixteen

Lee stood in the doorway of the barn, his gaze on the house, the cigarette in his hand forgotten. Now and then he could see Kelly framed in the window as she moved around the kitchen fixing dinner.

He missed eating his meals with her, missed her nearness, the conversations they had shared. After his father left home, his family had rarely sat down to meals together. His grandmother had taken to her bed, heartbroken that her only son had shamed the family. His mother was usually barhopping at dinner time, or too drunk to eat. There had been only his little sister, Tanya, to keep him company, and more often than not, he had ignored her, too caught up in his own bitterness to think that she might be as lonely and unhappy as he was. He regretted the callous way he'd treated his sister more than he regretted anything else he'd done in his life. She'd adored him, and he'd repaid her love with indifference.

A light went on in the kitchen, shining like a beacon of welcome in the gathering dusk. He saw Kelly at the sink, felt the brush of her gaze over his face.

More than anything, he wanted to go up to the house, walk into the kitchen, fold his arms around her, and bury his face in her sweet-smelling hair. He wanted to tell her he was sorry for hurting her, beg for her forgiveness, and start over. But the lure of the gold, of the new life it promised, held him anchored to the ground.

He dropped the cigarette butt into the dirt and stubbed it out with his boot heel.

A few minutes later the back door opened and he saw Kelly walking toward him, a cloth-covered plate in her hands.

Kelly's heartbeat accelerated when she saw Lee silhouetted in the doorway. The black T-shirt he wore clung to his torso like a second skin, outlining his muscular chest and biceps. His jeans were so old and faded they were almost white.

"Fried chicken tonight," Kelly said, her voice deliberately cool. "Hope you like it."

"I'm sure it's fine," Lee murmured. He took the plate from her hands, but his mind wasn't on food, and when she turned to go, he caught her by the wrist. "Kelly . . ."

She kept her back to him, refusing to meet his eyes. "What?"

139

"I said I was sorry. I didn't mean to hurt you."

His voice poured over her, deep and dark and rich, as enticing as a chocolate sundae on a hot summer day. She wanted to forgive him, to trust him, but he'd hurt her once, hurt her more deeply than she had believed possible. She didn't want to be hurt again.

Resolutely she squared her shoulders. "My dinner's getting cold."

"Fine."

He dropped her arm as if it were something loathsome. He'd tried to apologize and she wasn't having any, and maybe it was just as well. If she didn't hate him now, she would soon, so maybe it was just as well.

But he couldn't ignore the grinding ache in his gut as he watched her walk back to the house.

Cussing under his breath, he tossed the chicken into the bushes for the coyotes.

It was time to remember why he'd come here, and what he hoped to gain, time to remember that Kelly McBride was just another white woman, the enemy. In the old days, her people had taken everything from his people—their land, their pride, their way of life.

Now it was time to get even.

Sitting on the sofa in the front room, Kelly stared into the darkness while her dinner grew cold. She'd reached a decision about Lee and it had killed her appetite. She stared at the food congealing on the plate. Tomorrow she would tell him she didn't need his help anymore.

140

A single tear rolled down her cheek. She started to wipe it away when a large, callused hand closed over hers.

"Why do you weep, *tekihila?*"

"Oh, Blue Crow!" she murmured, and fell sobbing into his arms.

He held her for a long time, rocking her as he would have rocked a child, whispering her name as he stroked her hair, her back. His lips grazed her cheek, tasting the salt of her tears.

Gradually her sobs subsided. When she would have pulled away, his arms tightened around her. "Stay, *tekihila.*"

And because it felt so good to be in his arms, so right, she relaxed against him, her head pillowed on his broad shoulder.

No words were needed. She knew somehow that Blue Crow was aware of what had happened between herself and Lee, that he knew and understood.

"Do you love Roan Horse?" Blue Crow asked after a long while.

"I don't know. I thought . . ."

"Tell me."

"Maybe I was trying to love him because he's so much like you. I guess I thought if I couldn't have you . . ." Kelly raised her head from his shoulder and gazed into his eyes. "Why can't I have you?"

A sad smile lifted one corner of Blue Crow's mouth. "I would think the answer to that would be obvious, *tekihila.*"

"But . . . what difference does it make if you're . . . if you're a ghost? I can see you, touch you, hold you. You're more real to me than anyone I've ever known."

"Tekihila . . ."

"You said you'd waited for me your whole life, that you saw me in a vision."

"Perhaps I misinterpreted the vision. Perhaps you were not meant to be mine. Perhaps I was only to keep you safe for someone else."

"Who?" Kelly asked suspiciously.

"Who do you think? He needs help, *tekihila*. He has lost his faith in himself and others. Maybe you were meant to give it back to him."

Kelly shook her head. "It's the gold. He came here for the gold. That's all that's important to him."

"He may think so now."

"I've decided to send him away."

"You must do what you think is best."

"But you think I'm wrong?"

"I think you cannot change what was meant to be, *tekihila*. You may fight it, you may run from it, but in the end you cannot change it."

"So it doesn't matter if Lee stays or goes, is that what you're trying to say? That whatever is meant to happen will happen?"

"Han."

She was suddenly too tired, too discouraged, to argue. Resting her head on his shoulder again, she closed her eyes, grateful for his arms around her, for his nearness.

She remembered the night that Lee had broken into her house. Just before she fainted, she had seen Lee's shadow on the wall, seen his shadow take on the shape of an eagle . . .

She should tell Blue Crow, she thought. Maybe he would know what it meant, but she tumbled over the abyss into sleep before she could form the words.

Blue Crow held her all through the night. In her sleep, she felt his nearness; when she hovered near consciousness, she was aware of his arms holding her close.

Once—she didn't know if she was awake or asleep—she let her hands wander over his broad chest, exploring the texture of his skin, the scars on his chest. She felt his lips on hers, felt her body sing a new song as his love enfolded her.

Dawn came too soon. When she woke, she was in bed alone, her cheeks damp with tears.

Staring out the window, she saw that it was raining. Lightning split the skies. Thunder rolled across the land, booming like the echo of distant drums.

Kelly turned onto her stomach and punched her pillow. On days like this, she liked nothing better than to curl up in front of the fireplace with a good book and a cup of hot chocolate. But that would have to wait. Rain or not, she had to go into Cedar Flats.

She groaned softly. She should have gone yesterday, but she'd put it off and now she was out of virtually everything.

She could send Lee, she thought, and then grimaced. No, she was going to fire him today. If it was fated for them to be together, then Fate could find a way to bring him back, but she wanted him gone, the sooner the better.

She'd tell him she wanted him to leave, and then she'd drive into town so she wouldn't have to watch him go.

Her decision made, she jumped out of bed, took a quick shower, then pulled on a heavy sweatshirt, jeans, sweat socks, and a pair of old boots.

Tying a scarf over her head, she paused with her hand on the door. She'd never fired anyone before. How, exactly, did one go about it? She puzzled over it for a moment, then shrugged. She was the boss here. She didn't have to explain her decision. She'd tell him to pack his gear, and then she'd go to Cedar Flats and pray Lee would be gone when she got home.

Resolutely, she opened the door and stepped out into the yard. She was picking her way through the mud toward the barn when a sharp report cut through the storm.

Kelly felt her heart skip a beat. She'd never heard thunder like that in her life.

She had almost reached the barn when another report rang out.

Only then did she realize it wasn't thunder, but gunfire.

Kelly's gaze followed the sound of the gunshot, wondering who would be out hunting on a day like this.

With a shrug, she started walking toward the barn again when Lee barreled into her, driving her down to the ground only seconds before another gunshot rang out.

Her breath whooshed out of her body as his weight landed on top of her. She felt Lee jerk as if he'd touched a live wire, and then he was firing wildly at a clump of mesquite near the barn.

There was a yelp, and a moment later, the sound of a truck roaring to life.

Lee scrambled to his feet, intent on following the truck.

Kelly screamed "No!" as a tan pickup emerged from the woods behind the barn, screamed "No!" again as she saw someone poke a rifle barrel out the window. It was aimed directly at Lee.

Suddenly, everything seemed to be happening in slow motion.

Flame spurted from the barrel of the rifle.

Lee staggered backward.

Kelly saw the blood then, a bright crimson stain blossoming near his left shoulder. Another splash of red was spreading down his right thigh.

And then the truck roared out of sight, leaving behind an appalling silence broken only by the gentle whisper of the rain.

Kelly stared at Lee. He was lying on his back on the ground, one arm flung out from his body. He didn't seem to be breathing.

"Lee . . ." Her legs seemed to be made of wood as she walked toward him. "Lee?"

His eyelids fluttered open. "Kelly?"

She murmured a quiet prayer of thanksgiving as she slid her arm under his shoulders. "Can you stand up?"

"I think so." He shoved the gun into the waistband of his pants, then put his arm around her waist.

"We need to get you to a doctor," Kelly said.

She pushed the terror of the last few moments into the back of her mind. She'd cry and fall to pieces later, but now she had to take care of Lee.

"No doctor." He hissed the words through clenched teeth.

"No? What do you mean, no? You're bleeding."

"No doctors, Kelly. Gunshot wounds have to be reported."

"Lee, those men tried to kill you!"

"Could we argue later?" he asked, grimacing as pain lanced through his side and down his thigh. "I don't think I can stand up much longer."

Exasperated, Kelly helped Lee into the house and down the hallway into the spare bedroom. She threw back the covers, then stood fidgeting while he pulled the gun from his waistband and placed it on the table beside the bed, then slowly sat down on the edge of the mattress.

"Can you . . . should I . . . ?" She took a deep breath. "You need to get out of those wet clothes," she said, not meeting his eyes. "Do you need help?"

"I'm afraid so."

With a curt nod, she knelt on the floor and pulled off his boots and socks. He obligingly unfastened his fly, stood up while she tugged on his jeans, exposing dark blue briefs and a pair of long, muscular legs.

Lee sank down on the edge of the bed while she unbuttoned his shirt and eased it off his shoulders. He didn't wear an undershirt.

She gathered up his blood-stained clothes while he crawled under the sheet.

"I'll be right back," she said, and hurried out of the room. She tossed his clothes in the hamper in her room, then went into the kitchen where she filled the teapot with water and put it on the stove. While she waited for the water to heat, she went into the bathroom to towel dry her hair and change out of her wet clothes, then she rummaged around in the medicine cabinet to see what kind of first aid supplies she could find.

Ten minutes later, fortified with a cup of strong black coffee, she went back into the bedroom. She drew the sheet away from Lee's injured thigh and shoulder, sucking in a deep breath when she saw the two bullet wounds. For all the bloody *Lethal Weapon* and *Rambo* movies she'd seen, she wasn't prepared for the real thing. Both wounds were red and ugly and dripping blood. Lee's face was pale and sheened with perspiration.

Kelly's hands were trembling as she placed squares of cloth over the wounds to stop the bleeding.

"Lee, I don't know what to do. Please let me take you to a doctor."

"No, Kelly. Just pour some iodine over it and bandage me up. I'll be okay."

When she started to argue, he jackknifed into a sitting position and grabbed her by the arm.

"Dammit, Kelly, just do as I say. I'll explain later." He took a deep breath, fighting against the blackness that was hovering all around him. "Please, *skuya*."

"All right."

"If I pass out, don't worry. Just do what I said. Did you lock the front door?"

"No."

"Do it now, before you do anything else. Check the back door, too, and the windows."

He was scaring her, he could see it in her face, gone suddenly pale, in the way her eyes widened.

"Trust me, Kelly, just this once. Do as I say. And don't go outside. I'll explain everything later."

Driven by a rising, all-encompassing fear, Kelly ran into the front room and locked the door. She checked all the windows, drew the curtains, then did the same in all the other rooms before returning to the back bedroom.

Lee's eyes were closed. His face was drawn and pale. The makeshift bandages on his shoulder and thigh looked very white against the dark bronze of his skin.

"You got any whiskey, *skuya?*"

"Yes."

"Think you could bring me some?"

"Sure." She didn't drink, but her grandfather had liked a snort every now and then.

She found a bottle in the cupboard in the kitchen, poured a good-sized amount in a glass, and added some water. She started back toward the bedroom, paused, and retrieved the bottle.

Lee's eyes were still closed when she returned to the guest room. If possible, he looked even more pale than before.

"Lee?"

He opened his eyes and she placed the bottle on the table, then slid one hand under his head while he took a drink.

"I think you could use a little fortifying yourself," Lee remarked. "Your hands are shaking."

"I'm scared."

"I know. Drink a little of the whiskey, Kelly; it'll calm your nerves."

She lowered his head to the pillow, then stared skeptically at the small amount of whiskey left in the glass. She'd never tasted anything stronger than wine, but she was game to try anything that would still the shaking in her hands. The whiskey was strong and burned a path all the way down her throat to her stomach. Amazingly, it did make her feel better.

"Thatta girl," Lee murmured.

For Kelly, the next forty minutes were the most nerve-wracking she'd ever spent. She swallowed the bile that rose in her throat as she washed the ugly wounds in his shoulder and thigh, trying not to notice the blood on her hands or the way the water in the bowl turned from clear to scarlet.

When that was done, she poured iodine over the bullet wounds, front and back, acutely aware of the pain she was causing Lee. He endured her amateurish doctoring in stony silence, his hands clenched into tight fists, while perspiration dripped from his face and neck, soaking the pillowcase. She breathed a sigh of relief as she taped the last bandage into place.

When she was finished, she stared at the bowl of blood-stained water on the bedside table. Never in her life had she treated anything more serious than a paper cut.

"You okay, Kelly? You look a little pale."

"I'll be all right."

"You sure?"

She wanted to say yes; instead, she shook her head, then bolted for the bathroom where she was violently ill.

Grabbing a towel from the side of the tub, Kelly wiped her mouth and face, then stood up. She rinsed her mouth, brushed the hair from her forehead, and went back into the bedroom.

Lee regarded her through eyes that were faintly amused. "I think you're in worse shape than I am."

"I doubt it. Can I get you anything?"

"Some more whiskey?"

"Is that a good idea?"

"At this point I don't much care."

She poured some whiskey into the glass. When she would have added water, he shook his head.

"I'll take it straight," he said, and drained the glass in two quick swallows.

"Lee, what's going on?"

"Later, Kelly," he murmured.

"You promised . . ."

"I know, but I'm . . . so . . . tired." His eyelids fluttered down. "The gun," he said, his voice growing faint. "Keep it close . . ."

Kelly stared at him. The whiskey and the pain and the loss of blood had caught up with him, she thought, and wished that she, too, could lose herself in oblivion, but she was too frazzled even to think of sleep.

She took the gun from the bedside table, its weight somehow reassuring as she walked through the house, rechecking the doors and windows.

She was surprised to see that it was still raining, a slow, steady drizzle.

Returning to the guest room, she sat down in the faded overstuffed chair in the corner, the gun in her lap. Drawing her legs up beneath her, she stared at Lee, watching the shallow rise and fall of his chest. He'd been shot. He could have been killed. Why? Who was after him, and what did they want?

She knew the answer, knew it as surely as she knew the rain would stop and the sun would shine.

They hadn't been after Lee at all.

They were after her.

They were after the gold.

Chapter Seventeen

"So, what have you learned?"

The two men standing in front of the desk exchanged glances. "Nothing."

"Nothing?" Renford leaned forward, his gaze intent on the face of the man with the odd-colored yellow eyes. "You assured me you'd be able to locate the gold within a week."

"I miscalculated."

"I'm not paying for miscalculations, Trask, I'm paying for information."

"Yeah, well . . ." Trask slid a glance at his partner.

The shorter man shrugged. "We . . . uh . . . changed our tactics a little."

"A little!" Trask exclaimed. "Bradford took a shot at the girl."

"You idiot! She's the only one who knows where to find the gold."

"He didn't hit the girl," Trask said brusquely.

Harry Renford squirmed in his chair. It had been a mistake, hiring these two thugs. Both were wanted men. He'd thought the promise of easy money would keep them in line; now he wasn't so sure.

He resisted the urge to wipe the perspiration beading on his brow. He was in too deep, and they knew too much, for him to turn back now. Secretly, he was afraid of Trask, afraid of the greed that burned in the man's cold yellow eyes.

"I don't want any more shooting," Harry said. "Is that clear? I only want to know if the gold exists, nothing else!"

"Sure, boss, don't worry." Trask fixed his partner with a hard stare. "This time we'll do it my way."

Chapter Eighteen

Kelly sat with Lee until he fell asleep, and then, after checking all the doors and windows one more time, she went to bed, only to toss and turn restlessly. Twice, nightmares woke her.

The third time she woke up, she found Blue Crow sitting on the foot of her bed.

"Go back to sleep, *tekihila*," he whispered. "I will keep watch."

"You know what happened?"

"*Han*. It was the man I warned you about, the one with the yellow eyes."

"I'm scared, Blue Crow."

"I know." He rose from the bed and padded quietly to her side. "I will keep you safe, *tekihila*, so long as I am able."

"Hold me?"

He murmured a soft sound of assent as he sank down on the bed beside her and drew her into his arms. The long blue sleeping gown she wore felt like dandelion fluff against his bare chest.

They fit together perfectly, Kelly thought as she snuggled against Blue Crow, like a hand in a glove, or two halves of the same whole.

She ran her fingertips over his broad back, amazed anew at the pleasure she found in touching him. He seemed so real, so alive, it was hard to remember that he was a ghost, a phantom who came to her in the dark of the night.

"Tekihila . . ."

His voice was low and husky, filled with the yearning of a hundred years. His hand played in her hair, caressed her nape, slid down her back, and everywhere he touched, she felt little frissons of sensual delight.

She gazed up into his eyes, eyes dark with passion, as Lee's had been dark the night she had almost lost her virginity. It was eerie, the resemblance between the two men. Sometimes she thought Lee and Blue Crow shared the same soul.

Blue Crow's gaze met hers. "You are thinking of Roan Horse," he remarked.

Kelly nodded. "You're so much alike, sometimes I forget you're not him."

"You have learned to care for him?"

"Yes."

Blue Crow nodded. It was what he wanted, what he hoped for, yet he couldn't suppress the sharp stab of jealousy that coursed through him when he thought of Kelly in another man's arms.

"Has he made you his woman?"

Kelly felt the heat flood her cheeks in bright red waves. Mute, she stared into Blue Crow's eyes, wondering what to say. Though they had been intimate, she wasn't sure if Lee considered her to be his woman. As far as that went, she didn't know if she wanted to be Lee's woman; she didn't even know if she trusted him.

"Do you love him?"

"I don't know."

"Does he love you?"

"I don't think so."

"Think again, *tekihila*. I have seen into his heart. He holds only good feelings for you, though he tries to fight them." Blue Crow smiled pensively. "He is afraid of you."

"Afraid? Of me?"

"*Han.*"

"Why?"

"You are white, *skuya*. Roan Horse has no good memories of anyone who is white."

Blue Crow's finger traced the line of her jaw, the curve of her cheek. "You did not answer my question, *tekihila*. Has he made you his woman?"

"Not exactly."

Blue Crow stared at her, one black brow arched in confusion. "I do not understand."

"He . . . we . . . that is, we started to . . ." Kelly shook her head. "He did and he didn't."

"Are you still a maiden?"

"Yes, but a very experienced one."

Blue Crow frowned. "You talk in riddles."

"We started to make love, but when he discovered I'd never been with a man that way before, he got angry and left."

"Ah, now I understand." Blue Crow smiled with pride. "He did not wish to defile you. Truly, he has the heart of a warrior."

"I guess so," Kelly said, and then yawned.

"Sleep, *tekihila*. I will stay with you until *anpetu wi* chases *hanhepi wi* from the sky."

"Lie with me."

With a sigh, he slid under the covers beside her, then drew her into his arms. It was torture of the sweetest kind, lying next to her, holding her close. The faint flowery scent of her perfume rose in his nostrils. Her hand rested against his chest, and he could feel the warm swell of her breast against his side.

"Good night, Blue Crow."

"Rest well, *tekihila*."

"You, too," she replied sleepily.

Blue Crow grunted softly. He would not rest this night, not with Kelly nestled against him, the heat and curves of her body playing havoc with his senses.

Holding her close, he stared into the darkness and prayed his self-control would last until dawn.

It was still raining when Kelly woke the following morning. She pulled on a pair of comfortable jeans and an oversize sweatshirt, stepped into a pair of furry bedroom slippers, then headed for the kitchen. There was just enough instant coffee left to make two cups.

While she waited for the water to heat, she called Brewer's Market and learned, to her dismay, that they didn't deliver except in rare cases of emergency.

Kelly hesitated, and then assured Tom Brewer that this was, indeed, an emergency and she was too ill to drive into town.

Brewer was sympathetic as he took her order, assuring her that his son would be out sometime before noon with her order.

Thanking him effusively, Kelly hung up the phone, made two cups of coffee, and carried them into the guest bedroom.

Lee was still asleep. After setting the mugs on the antique oak dresser, she laid her hand on Lee's brow. His skin was hotter than it should have been, she thought.

She watched him for a couple of minutes while she debated which he needed more: rest, or something to bring down his fever.

Frowning, she went into the bathroom and rummaged through the medicine cabinet for a bottle of aspirin. She filled a glass with water, then returned to the bedroom.

Lee was tossing restlessly, his hands clutching the covers, his knuckles white with the strain.

"Cowards! Turn me loose!"

Kelly bit down on her lip as she watched Lee's body go rigid. His lips drew back in a grimace, and then he began to swear, his voice harsh, raspy with pain.

She couldn't bear to watch. Bending over him, she placed her hand on his uninjured shoulder and shook it gently.

"Lee. Lee, wake up."

A vile oath hissed between his teeth and he sat up, thrashing wildly.

Kelly gasped as his fist slammed into her face just below her left eye. She reeled back, momentarily stunned, her hand automatically cupping her bruised cheek.

Lee fell back on the pillows, a low moan rumbling in his throat. "Don't hit me again," he whispered. "For the love of God, don't hit me again."

Cautiously, Kelly approached the bed again. "Lee, wake up."

A muscle worked in his jaw. "Damn you!" he roared. "If my hands were free, I'd beat the shit out of all of you!"

Where was he, who was he hiding from? Taking her courage in hand, she shook his shoulder again. "Lee, wake up. It's Kelly."

"Kelly?"

He opened his eyes, eyes that were dark and wild. For a moment he looked disoriented, and then his gaze focused on her face.

"Kelly?"

"I brought you a cup of coffee."

"Coffee?"

"Lee, are you all right?"

He stared past her, his gaze sweeping over the room. Gradually he released his death grip on the covers.

"Let me help you sit up." She reached behind

him, plumping the pillows, then helped him to a sitting position. "That better?"

"Yeah, thanks."

"Here." She handed him one of the mugs.

He drank it quickly, welcoming the warmth, the bitterness.

"Would you like some more?" Kelly asked, and when he nodded, she handed him her cup. "Go on, take it," she said when he started to refuse. "That's all there is until the Brewer kid shows up with the groceries I ordered. Go on, drink it. You need it more than I do."

For once, he didn't argue.

"Can I ask you something?"

"You can ask," he replied guardedly.

"What were you dreaming about?"

He stared up at her through eyes gone suddenly cold. "Why?"

"I . . . you were talking in your sleep, and I wondered . . . never mind, it doesn't matter."

"I'll tell you, if you'll tell me something?"

"What?"

"What happened to your eye?"

Kelly lifted a hand to her bruised cheek. "My eye?"

"It's turning black and blue."

"Is it?"

"What happened, Kelly?"

"Nothing."

"Did I do it?"

She turned her head to avoid his probing gaze.

"Did I?"

Kelly nodded. "You were having a nightmare,

160

and when I tried to wake you, you struck out. It was an accident."

"I'm sorry."

"It's all right. It doesn't hurt." She grinned at him. "Much." She folded her arms over her breasts and looked at him expectantly. "Now it's your turn."

"I'd rather not talk about it."

"That's not fair, Lee."

He stared into the empty coffee cup clutched in his hands. "I got sick while I was in juvenile hall. Ran a high fever for a couple of days. Sometimes when I get sick, it brings back memories I'd just as soon forget."

"Did someone beat you while you were there?"

His hands tightened around the mug until she thought it would shatter.

"Yeah."

"Who?"

A muscle worked in his jaw as the memories came flooding back, memories of constantly being teased and harassed because he was an Indian, memories of being cornered in the shower, of four white guys holding him down on the cold tile floor while a fifth beat him.

"Lee?"

He couldn't tell her. He couldn't tell her how bad it had been, how alone he had been. His sister had been too young to visit him. And his mother—she'd come once in eighteen months, so drunk she could hardly stand up. He'd never forget the humiliation he had felt when she walked into the rec room, her long black hair

161

stringy and unwashed, her steps uneven. He'd never forget the way she had cried and carried on about seeing "her boy" locked up because of what some *wasichu* girl had accused him of. That was the night the five white boys had ganged up on him, threatening to castrate him if he ever looked at another white girl.

"Don't ask me, Kelly."

"All right."

Teeth clenched, he put the mug on the nightstand, then swung his legs over the side of the bed.

"What are you doing?" Kelly asked, alarmed.

"I need to . . . dammit, I need to use the bathroom."

"I'll help you."

"No."

"Lee, you've been shot, remember? You've got a fever. Now stop being foolish and let me help you."

"I can do it."

"Let me get you a bedpan."

"No!"

Shaking her head, Kelly gathered up the mugs and stomped out of the bedroom. Men! Stupid macho jerks, all of them!

Standing up was a mistake. His legs felt like rubber and a wave of dizziness sent the room spinning out of focus. He knew he would have fallen if Kelly hadn't chosen that moment to return.

With a cry, she ran forward and wrapped her arm around his waist.

"Now will you let me help you?" she asked dryly.

Lee nodded. Draping one arm over her shoulders, he let her help him down the hall to the bathroom, thinking there was nothing like sickness to rob a man of his pride.

Kelly kept her head lowered as she helped Lee down the hallway. For all her bluster, she was as embarrassed as he was. Embarrassed, and acutely aware of the fact that he was wearing nothing but a pair of skimpy briefs. Why hadn't she thought to wrap a blanket around him, if not to keep him warm, then to cover up all that bronze male flesh? She tried not to remember the night they had almost made love, tried not to think of how warm and solid and intoxicating his touch had been.

Don't think about it, she chided herself. You were going to fire him, remember? If he hadn't gotten shot he'd be gone by now . . .

She glanced up, her cheeks flaming with the memory of that night, when he opened the door.

Wordlessly, she slipped her arm around his waist, trying not to notice the way his skin felt beneath her hand.

When he was settled back into bed, she poured him a glass of water, handed him a couple of aspirin, and fled the room.

She spent the next hour scrubbing the kitchen floor and scouring the old tin sink, and when that was done, she washed the stove inside and out.

She was about to start on the bathroom when there was a knock at the front door.

"Who's there?" she called.

"It's me, Jeff Brewer."

Kelly let out the breath she'd been holding, then opened the door. "Come on in, Jeff. I'm sorry you had to come in this weather."

"That's okay. Where do you want this?"

"In the kitchen on the table, please.

"There's another box and a bag in the truck."

"I was out of just about everything."

"My pa said you were sick."

"I'm feeling better, but I didn't want to go out in the rain."

"Yeah. I don't blame you." He put the box on the table, then went out to get the rest of her order.

Feeling safe with Jeff there, she ran out to the barn to feed and water the horses, then hurried back to the house.

Jeff was waiting for her on the front porch. "Anything else I can do for you, Miss McBride?" he asked politely.

"No, thanks, Jeff," Kelly said. "Tell your dad I really appreciate this."

"Sure 'nough. Take care of yourself, Miss Mc-Bride."

"Thank you, Jeff. Good-bye. And drive carefully."

He waved at her as he climbed behind the wheel of a bright green truck with the name BREWER'S FAMILY MARKET outlined in white letters on the side.

Kelly closed and locked the door, then went into the kitchen and began putting the groceries away. She'd emptied one box and was starting on another when she realized she was no longer alone. Glancing over her shoulder, she saw Lee standing in the doorway, a blanket draped around shoulders.

"You should be in bed," Kelly said.

"I got . . . lonely."

"You'd better sit down before you fall down. You look as pale as a ghost," she said, and then grinned. The only ghost she knew wasn't pale at all.

"Something funny?" Lee asked as he sank down on one of the kitchen chairs.

"No. Are you hungry? We have food again."

He shook his head. "Got any coffee in there?"

"Sure. But you need to eat. Some oatmeal, maybe?"

"Oatmeal!" He grimaced as though he were in pain.

"It's good for you." She sighed in exasperation. "How about some scrambled eggs and toast? And some orange juice?"

"Anything," he said, "just quit nagging me."

Kelly watched him out of the corner of her eye while she brewed a pot of coffee and scrambled a half-dozen eggs. He looked as though he were in pain, but she thought the hurt went far deeper than the two gunshot wounds.

With a weary sigh, he crossed his arms on the table and rested his head on his forearms. He looked terribly vulnerable.

The urge to comfort him rose up within her until it was all she could do not to reach out and stroke his head, to tell him that everything would be all right, that he wasn't alone any longer.

But she didn't. Fear of being rebuffed kept her from reaching out; the memory of his voice telling her to just leave him the hell alone made her turn away.

He was asleep by the time the eggs were cooked, and this time she let him sleep, deciding he needed rest more than anything else.

She stared at the eggs and then, with a shrug, tossed them into the garbage.

Leaving the kitchen, she went into the guest room and changed the sheets on the bed. She filled the pitcher at his bedside with fresh water, then went into her own room and made up the bed.

When she went back into the kitchen, Lee was awake.

"How do you feel?" she asked.

"Like hell."

She grunted softly as she placed her hand on his brow. "You're burning up. Come on, you need to get back into bed."

He didn't argue, and that worried her more than anything else.

Chapter Nineteen

His fever worsened during the night. Nothing she gave him seemed to help. Time and again she paced to the window and stared out into the darkness, wishing the rain would stop, wishing she hadn't promised not to call the doctor. If Lee wasn't better by morning, she'd call the hospital, promise or no promise.

She made him drink as much water as he could hold, applied more antiseptic to his wounds, noting that the one in his shoulder looked raw and red. She taped a fresh bandage in place, knowing she was wasting her time. Lee needed more help than she was capable of giving.

In despair, she went to the window and gazed out into the darkness. "Please, God, help me . . ."

"*Tekihila?*"

"Blue Crow!" She ran to his arms. "I've never been so glad to see anybody in my life."

"What is wrong?"

"Lee's got a fever and I can't bring it down. I think the wound in his shoulder is infected." She shook her head. "I don't know what to do."

"It will be all right, *skuya*," Blue Crow murmured.

And she believed him. Standing in his embrace, his arms warm and strong around her, she believed him.

Blue Crow smiled down at her and then, because she was so close, because her eyes were as blue as the wildflowers that grew along the Little Big Horn, because her skin was smooth and soft, because she glowed with life, he bent his head and kissed her.

It was only a gentle kiss, meant to reassure her, but it quickly built to something much more intense. He groaned as her arms went around his neck, felt his heart begin to pound like a Lakota war drum as she pressed her body to his. Her heat went through him like chain lightning, making him feel strong and vitally alive.

Holding her, knowing she could never be his, filled him with a soul-deep sadness, a hurt that went deeper than pain.

"*Tekihila*." Holding her close, he rested his chin on the top of her head, wishing that he had known her when he was alive, when he could have claimed her for his own. Why? he thought, his heart twisting with anguish, why had he found her now when she could never be his?

"Blue Crow?"

He drew back a little so he could look down into her eyes. "What is it, *tekihila*?"

"I don't know. You seem so sad."

"I am not sad, *skuya*."

"You wouldn't lie to me, would you?"

"No," he replied quietly. "I would not lie to you. I am not sad, *tekihila*. Only filled with regret that we did not meet a hundred years ago. I would have courted you as ardently as ever a warrior courted a maiden. I would have gone to one of the Buffalo Dreamers to obtain a love song, and then I would have played my flute outside your lodge. When the time was right, I would have taken horses to your father, as many as he required. And if he had refused to let you be my wife, I would have kidnapped you and taken you far away."

"Would you?"

"*Han.*"

"And then what?"

"I would have made a home for you and given you sons, *tekihila*, many sons."

"And daughters?" Kelly asked tremulously.

"Maybe one," Blue Crow allowed with a smile. "If she was as beautiful as you."

"I wish I had lived back then," Kelly said. "But wishing won't make it so."

"No."

"But you're here with me now." Her arms tightened around him and she buried her face against his chest. "Never leave me, Blue Crow," she murmured. "Promise me."

"I don't know if I can make a promise like that, *tekihila*. If Wakan Tanka calls me, I must go."

"No!"

He held her close, rocking her against him. "Let us not speak of parting," he said. And then, because it was painful to hold her close and not possess her, he drew away. "Come, let us look in on Roan Horse."

Lee! She'd forgotten all about him.

She followed Blue Crow into the guest room, stood on the opposite side of the bed while Blue Crow examined Lee's wounds, his face lined with concern.

"He'll be all right, won't he?" she asked.

"The wound in his shoulder is not healing."

"I wanted to take him to a doctor, but he wouldn't let me. Maybe . . ."

"There is no need for a *wasichu* medicine man," Blue Crow said.

"You mean it's too late, that nothing can be done?"

"No." Blue Crow drew the covers over Lee, then went to Kelly and took her in his arms. "There are plants nearby that will draw the poison from the wound. I will gather some."

He smiled down at her. "Do not worry, *tekihila*, all will be well." He pressed his lips to her brow. "I will be back soon."

"Hurry."

Blue Crow returned an hour later. Kelly watched as he built a small fire in an old tin bucket, then dropped a handful of sage and sweet grass onto the flames. Soon a plume of sweet-smelling smoke rose from the bucket.

Plucking an eagle feather from his hair, Blue Crow drew it over the bucket, drawing the smoke toward Lee. When that was done, he ground some leaves which Kelly thought looked like comfrey and marigold into a thick paste, then spread it over the wound in Lee's shoulder, and all the while he chanted softly.

The words, sung in a minor key, filled Kelly's mind with images of running buffalo, of tipis scattered over a grassy plain, of sun and wind and the sound of rushing water.

"I brought some herbs which you must brew," Blue Crow remarked, turning away from the bed. "When he wakes up, you must make him drink as much of it as he can hold."

"Okay."

"Okay?"

Kelly smiled. "I mean I will."

"*Han.*" Deftly he wrapped Lee's shoulder in a length of soft cloth. "He will recover, *tekihila*. He is young and strong." Blue Crow's gaze moved slowly over Kelly's face. "And he has much to live for."

The heat in his eyes burned through her, as warm and welcome as sunshine. The faint hint of jealousy in his voice filled her feminine heart with joy.

"Blue Crow . . ."

"You will be good for him, *skuya*. With you at his side, he will become the man he should be."

"What are you saying?"

"He cares for you," Blue Crow replied. His hands curled into tight fists. "You care for him. What else is there to say?"

Kelly shook her head. "No, it's not like that."

"*Tekihila*, did you not tell me that he made love to you?"

"Yes."

"You would not have let him do so if you did not care for him."

"That's true, but it's you I love, Blue Crow. Only you."

Her words were the sweetest pain he had ever known. But, as much as he loved her, desired her, yearned for her, she could never be his.

"Your love is wasted on me," he said, his voice harsh.

"No!"

The sight of her tears tore at his heart. Regret sliced through him, sharp as a Lakota skinning knife.

"*Tekihila*, forgive me," he implored. Tenderly he drew his thumbs across her cheeks to wipe away her tears, and then he drew her into his arms. "Do not weep, *wastelakapi*. I cannot bear your tears."

"My love is not wasted," she said, her voice muffled against his chest.

"I know. I was wrong to say such a thing."

Kelly sniffed. "What was that word you said?"

"*Wastelakapi?*"

She nodded. "Yes. What does it mean?"

"Beloved."

"Am I? Your beloved?"

Blue Crow placed his forefinger under her chin and tilted her head up. "Do you not know that you are? There has been no other woman for me, *tekihila*."

"You've never been in love?"

"No."

"But you've . . . you know?"

"I am a warrior," he replied, as if that explained everything.

"Of course," Kelly said, but inwardly she was seething with jealousy. She told herself she was being foolish. Any woman he might have had was long dead, but it didn't matter. He'd had other women.

Blue Crow looked past Kelly to the window. Outside, the rain had stopped. In the east, the sky was growing light. His arms tightened around Kelly's waist.

"I must go. Do not forget about the tea. Make it strong."

Kelly nodded. When he started to pull away, she held him close, pressing herself against him, drawing his warmth, his strength, into herself.

"*Tekihila* . . . "

"I know. It's just that I miss you so much when you're gone."

"No more than I miss you." He lowered his head to hers and kissed her then, savoring the sweet taste of her lips. She was light and life, banishing the darkness from his existence, and he loved her beyond words.

One last kiss, and then he was gone. Gone before his resolve disappeared, weakened by the tears that shimmered in her eyes and the silent invitation of moist pink lips.

Kelly stared after him for a moment, then sank into the chair beside the bed. Taking up the cloth from the bedside table, she dipped it in the bowl of water, wrung it out, and began to sponge Lee's fevered face, neck, and chest.

He stirred restlessly on the bed, muttering incoherently in a language she didn't understand. His hands worried the covers, clenching and unclenching. Once he cried out, as if in pain.

Dropping the cloth into the bowl, Kelly took one of Lee's hands in hers.

"Rest, Lee," she murmured soothingly. "You're safe here. No one will hurt you."

At the sound of her voice, his eyelids fluttered open. "Kelly?" His gaze darted around the room. "Where am I?"

"At the Triple M."

"The Triple M?"

She nodded. "Just rest, Lee, everything will be all right."

"I thought I saw an Indian."

"An Indian?"

He stared up at her. "I know it sounds crazy, but . . . never mind."

"Tell me."

"Not now. I'm cold, so cold."

Rising, she went into the linen closet and pulled out another blanket. After covering Lee, she went into the kitchen, filled the teapot with water, and put it on the stove to heat.

She thought about Blue Crow while she waited

174

for the water to boil. She was in love with a ghost, but a ghost unlike anything she had ever imagined. Ghosts were supposed to be invisible, weren't they? Able to walk through walls, to make things go bump in the night. But there was nothing spectral about Blue Crow. He was flesh and blood, as warm and real as any man she had ever seen. How was it possible?

The whistle of the teakettle scattered her thoughts. She dumped the herbs into the pot, let them steep until the water was dark green, then filled a mug with the bitter-looking brew.

Lee was staring out the window when she returned to his room.

"Here," she said, "I've brought you something to drink."

"What is it?"

"Herb tea. It'll do you good."

She piled the pillows behind his head so he could sit up, held the cup while he drank even though he insisted he didn't need her help.

He grimaced as he took a drink. "Tastes awful," he muttered.

"Drink it anyway."

"Where'd you get this stuff?"

"Just drink it, Lee."

He drained the cup, and then made a face, as if he were in pain.

"What's wrong?"

"I don't think that hot tea was such a good idea. I need to . . . you know."

"I'll get the bedpan," Kelly said. "I don't think you should get up."

"I don't want a bedpan."

"Lee Roan Horse, you are the worst patient I've ever had."

"I'm probably the only one you've ever had."

"That's beside the point."

She left the room in a huff, returning a moment later with an old slop jar she had found in her grandfather's closet. It was an antique. She had painted blue flowers on it and filled it with a bouquet of dried flowers, which she now removed. "Do you, uh, need help?"

"No." Lee ground the word out through clenched teeth. Damn, but it was humiliating, being waited on by a woman, especially a woman he wanted as much as he wanted Kelly McBride.

With a curt nod, Kelly left the room, grateful that he'd refused her help.

She gave him ten minutes, hoping it would be enough. When she returned to his room, the pan was on the floor. She emptied it, washed her hands, then went back to Lee's bedside.

"Can I get you anything else?"

"Would you lie down with me?"

"Why?"

"I'm still cold."

She hesitated a moment, then crawled under the covers and took him in her arms. She could feel him shivering against her, feel the length of a long bare leg pressing against hers. His arm was heavy across her waist, his breath warm against her neck.

Her emotions ran riot as she remembered lying naked in his arms, on the brink of discovery. She looked down at him, at the long black hair that fell over his shoulders and tickled her cheek.

She tried to think of something other than bare bronze skin, or the fact that they were pressed intimately together, that she had lost her innocence, if not her virginity, to this man.

She held him a long time, her fingertips gliding over his arm. Gradually his shivering ceased, his breathing grew even, and she knew that he was asleep.

She'd get up in a minute, she told herself. Just another minute. But he snuggled against her, his head resting on her breast, his arm holding her close. The minutes turned to hours, but she didn't get out of bed.

Lee woke to darkness, instantly aware that he was holding a woman in his arms, that their legs were entwined, that her head was pillowed on his shoulder.

Kelly! What was she doing in his bed?

He frowned. He'd been sick with a fever and she'd cared for him. He'd had one of his old nightmares, reliving the days he'd spent in that damned correctional facility. Funny, he always dreamed about getting the crap kicked out of him, but never about getting even. And he had gotten even. In spades. He'd found the five guys who'd beat him up. Found them alone, one by one. They'd never touched him again.

His frown deepened. Had he imagined it, or had he seen an Indian beside his bed? An Indian who wore a golden eagle on a leather thong around his neck. The same Indian he'd seen in his vision.

Lee shook his head. He must have been dreaming.

He looked down at Kelly, felt his heart turn over in his chest. She was so lovely. So young. So innocent. He felt his body harden as he remembered how she had felt in his arms, how close he had come to stealing something from her that was more precious than the gold he coveted.

She made a soft sleepy sound as she turned onto her side, her breasts pressing against his chest, igniting a fire in his body hotter than any fever.

He tore his gaze from her face and stared out the window. Someone had tried to kill Kelly. The reason seemed obvious. Someone besides himself knew about the gold and wanted it badly enough to kill for it. But who?

It had all happened so fast, he hadn't gotten a good look at the truck, or the two men inside. He remembered the rifle, though. He'd looked down the barrel and knew he was looking into the face of death, but his only thought had been to save Kelly.

He moved his injured shoulder tentatively. It was as stiff and sore as the very devil. His thigh, too. But his fever seemed to be gone. And he was hungry. Always a good sign.

He glanced down at Kelly to find her staring back at him, her cheeks rosy with embarrassment.

An awkward silence stretched between them.

Kelly wished she could think of something to

say, but she was all too aware of Lee's bare legs entangled with her own, of the solid wall of his chest against her breasts, of the very tangible evidence that he was feeling much better.

Lee broke the silence with a muttered, "Good morning."

"Morning," Kelly replied. She lifted a hand to his brow, pleased that his skin was cool to the touch.

There seemed to be no graceful or tactful way to extricate herself from his arms, so she simply rolled away from him and got up.

"I'll go fix breakfast," she said over her shoulder, and hurried out of the room.

She washed quickly, changed into a pair of dark blue sweats and a loose-fitting white sweater, socks, and her boots. After looking out the window, she opened the door and ran to the barn. The horses whinnied at her, obviously upset because she had neglected to feed them the night before. She tossed them each two flakes of hay, made sure they had water, threw a couple of handfuls of chicken feed to the hens, then ran back to the house.

In the kitchen, she made a pot of strong black coffee, fried up some bacon and eggs, poured two glasses of orange juice.

She'd spent the night in Lee's arms. Worse, she'd been glad to be there when she woke up.

She could hear him moving around in the bedroom. A moment later she saw him walk unsteadily down the hallway toward the bathroom, a blanket draped over his shoulders. Stubborn man. Why did he insist on doing everything the hard way?

She was placing his breakfast on a tray when he entered the kitchen.

"I'd rather eat in here," he said, sinking down on one of the chairs.

"You should be in bed."

"I've been in bed for two days."

"You ought to be in a hospital."

"Are you always such a nag in the morning?"

"Are you always this stubborn?"

"I'm not stubborn. I'm hungry."

"You are?" She smiled, pleased. Surely that meant he was getting better.

She handed him his breakfast, put her own plate on the table, and sat down across from him.

He was indeed hungry. He wolfed down everything on his plate before she'd made a dent in her own meal.

"There's more," she said, and before he could argue, she got up and refilled his plate. "More coffee?"

Lee nodded. "Thanks."

After breakfast, she insisted on checking on his wounds. Lee frowned when she took the bandage from his arm.

"Did you do this?" he asked, gesturing at the poultice on his shoulder.

"I . . ." Her gaze slid away from his. "Of course."

Lee looked at her suspiciously. "This is an old Indian remedy."

"Is it?"

Lee stared down at the table for a moment,

trying to remember what he'd seen, what he'd heard, but it was all so hazy.

Muttering an oath, he fixed his gaze on Kelly's face again. "He was here, wasn't he?"

"Who?"

"I don't know his name. Until now, I thought I'd dreamed it all, the chanting, the smoke, everything. But it was real, wasn't it."

Lee leaned across the table, his gaze holding hers. "Who is he, Kelly? What was he doing here?"

Chapter Twenty

Kelly put her hands on her hips and stuck out her chin. "I don't know what you're talking about."

"Dammit, Kelly, no city girl would know how to mix a poultice like this. There was an Indian here, and I want to know who he is."

"His name's Blue Crow."

"Blue Crow!" It couldn't be, Lee thought. It had to be someone else. Either that, or he was going slowly insane. "What does he look like?"

"He looks like you."

"Like me?" Lee dragged a hand through his hair. He had seen the resemblance between himself and the Indian during his vision, but he had thought it was part of his medicine dream, that he was seeing himself a few years down the road. "Does he wear a gold eagle on a thong around his neck?"

Kelly nodded, wondering at Lee's agitation.

Lee sat back in his chair. It couldn't be, but it was. Blue Crow had been the warrior in his vision, the man Charlie McBride had killed over a hundred years ago.

Kelly leaned forward, worried by Lee's sudden pallor. "Are you all right?"

Lee shook his head. He was going out of his mind, that was the only answer that made sense.

"Come on," Kelly said, rising to her feet. "I think you'd better go back to bed."

"Yeah," he muttered bleakly, "I think you're right."

Kelly helped Lee back to bed and when he insisted he wanted to be alone, she went back to the kitchen and washed the dishes.

The rain had finally stopped, leaving the world looking bright and clean.

Lee slept most of the day.

Left to herself, Kelly wandered through the house. She found her grandfather's photo album on a shelf in the hall closet and spent an hour looking at old pictures, remembering the balmy summer days at the ranch when her grandfather had taught her to rope and ride. They'd gone fishing together, too, though Kelly had never gotten over her queasiness at baiting a hook or gutting a trout.

She wished now that she had spent more time with her grandfather during the last few years, but instead of taking the time, she'd made excuses: she was busy at work, she was taking an accounting class, she couldn't afford the plane fare. Sorry excuses, she thought, and even the knowledge that she'd called often and sent cards on his birthdays and holidays didn't ease her conscience.

"I did love you, Grandpa," she murmured. "I hope you know that."

Lee woke up long enough to eat dinner and use the bathroom, and then he went back to bed, quickly falling asleep.

Kelly dashed out to feed the horses before it got dark, then ran back to the house and locked the door.

Once she was safe inside, she felt foolish for sprinting across the yard as if she were being pursued by demons, but she couldn't shake off the memory of those gunshots, or ignore the fact that those men had meant to kill her. Most frightening of all was the possibility that they might come back.

Unable to shake off her fears, she turned on all the lights in the house, then built a roaring fire in the fireplace.

Changing into her nightgown and robe, she curled up in the corner of the couch with her favorite author's latest romance, but, as good as the book was, Kelly couldn't concentrate on the printed page. Every night sound, every creak, every shadow made her jump.

Maybe, if Lee felt better tomorrow, she'd leave him long enough to go into town and buy a big dog and a couple of geese, she thought. She'd keep the dog inside, for company and protection, and let the geese patrol the yard. Their noisy honking would alert her to prowlers, and maybe the dog would make intruders think twice about trying to get into the house.

Her eyelids were getting heavy when she felt his presence, and then he was there beside her, gathering her into his arms, comforting her with his touch.

With a sigh, she rested her head against his shoulder and closed her eyes. She was safe now. Nothing and no one could hurt her while he was here.

Time lost all meaning as he held her. Her fragrance engulfed him, her nearness made him feel alive. He lifted a callused finger to her cheek, drawing lazy circles over her smooth skin, marveling at how lovely she was. He outlined the shape of her nose, her brows, the fullness of her lower lip. Fire shot through him when she took his finger into her mouth and caressed it with her tongue.

"*Tekihila* . . ." He murmured her name, then groaned softly as she wriggled against him.

Her eyelids fluttered open and she looked up at him, her beautiful blue eyes glinting with mischief. Her lips pressed butterfly kisses to his palm.

"*Tekihila*, I am not made of stone."

"Is something wrong?" she asked with mock innocence.

He stared at her, mute, afraid to move for fear he would come into contact with some tantalizing part of her anatomy that would shatter his hard-won self-control.

"Blue Crow?" She ran her hand through his hair, slid her fingers over his nape. And smiled when she felt him shiver.

"*Tekihila* . . . Kelly, you must stop."

"Why?"

"You are a maiden . . ."

"A maiden who wants you."

He groaned again, as if he were in pain, and Kelly drew back, frowning. Maybe he *couldn't* make love to her. He was a ghost, after all.

"Why aren't you invisible?" she asked, her passion momentarily swallowed up by curiosity.

"I do not know."

"Lee saw you last night."

Blue Crow grunted softly.

"Can anyone see you?"

"*Han.*"

Kelly shook her head. "I just don't understand. You're not like any ghost I've ever heard about. I mean, you've been, you know, gone, for over a hundred years. Why didn't your body . . . ?"

Kelly shook her head, unable to go on. The whole subject was just too gruesome.

Blue Crow shrugged. "I cannot explain it, *skuya*. Perhaps I walk between life and death because of you. Perhaps I was meant to guard the gold until you came to claim it." He gazed deep into her eyes, his soul touching hers. "Perhaps Wakan Tanka knew I would not be happy in the land of spirits until I had seen the woman of my vision, until I had held her in my arms."

He cupped her face in his hands and kissed her lightly. "The reason matters not. It only matters that you are here, that I can see you and hold you."

His words, soft-spoken and fervent, touched Kelly's heart. He was right. It didn't matter why he had been allowed to linger on the earth. She was only glad that he was here, able to hold her in his arms. He was a part of her, more necessary than her next breath.

And she wanted him, wanted him desperately, but she didn't say so again. Instead, she relaxed in his arms, content to be held.

"Ah, *tekihila*," Blue Crow murmured. "I wish . . ."

"What?" Kelly whispered. "What do you wish?"

"You do not know?"

"I can guess. It's what I want, too."

"I know, *wastelakapi*, I know, but it is not to be. Not now."

The words *not ever* hung in the air, but neither wanted to acknowledge them.

"You should leave this place, *tekihila*."

"Still trying to get rid of me?" she asked.

"I fear for your safety."

"I'm not leaving you. I told you that before."

"Ah, *tekihila*, you have the heart of a warrior."

"No, I don't. I'm scared to death, but I'm more afraid of losing you."

Blue Crow sighed heavily. If he couldn't convince her to leave, he would just have to watch over her more carefully, at least until Roan Horse was feeling stronger.

Lee woke with the dawn, feeling better than he had in days. He flexed his shoulder, pleased that the sharp pains had dulled to a mild ache.

He grimaced as he swung his legs over the side of the bed. His leg was still sore, but he could stand on it. Crossing the floor, he gazed out the window. In the east, the sun was rising, painting the sky with vivid hues of vermilion and ocher.

Pressing his head against the cool glass, he closed his eyes. When he'd been very young, he'd spent a summer with his grandparents. Even now he could remember how his grandfather had left the house at dawn each morning. Standing outside, his face lifted to the rising sun, he had prayed to Wakan Tanka, his voice rising in a song to the dawn. Sweeter than the trill of a meadowlark, his grandfather's words had climbed skyward.

"Hear me, Father of us all, maker of heaven and earth and all living things. Grant me the wisdom to listen to the wind, to remember that I am one with all Thy creatures—the two-footed, the four-footed, and those that ride on the wind. *Mitakuye oyasin*. We are all related."

"*Mitakuye oyasin,*" Lee murmured. "We are all related."

Opening his eyes, he gazed at the sunrise once again. Yesterday he had been certain it had all been a dream born of fever and loss of blood. Today he knew deep within himself that, incomprehensible as it seemed, impossible as it was to explain, it had indeed been Blue Crow who had treated his wounds.

Lee shook his head. Blue Crow hadn't looked like a ghost, nor felt like one. Weren't ghosts supposed to be made of spirit? But the hands that had treated Lee's wounds had been warm, callused. As tangible as his own.

A sound at the door drew his attention and he turned to see Kelly standing there. Belatedly, he realized he was wearing nothing but briefs.

Kelly flushed as Lee met her gaze, and then he shrugged, a glint of amusement dancing in the depths of his devil-dark eyes.

"No need to be embarrassed, Kelly," he said. "You've seen it all before."

But he'd been sick then, lying in bed with a fever. She'd been able to ignore the fact that he was too handsome by half, that he stirred feelings within her that she didn't want to acknowledge.

She tried to drag her gaze away, but she couldn't stop looking at him. The bandages on his shoulder and thigh were very white against his skin. Smooth, dark bronze skin that she yearned to touch.

She blinked and looked away. What was the matter with her? She loved Blue Crow, not Lee. But they were so much alike. Had the two men been the same age, she wondered if she'd be able to tell them apart.

"Kelly?"

With a start, she realized Lee was standing in front of her, apparently unconcerned with the fact that he was nearly naked.

"I want to thank you," he said.

He was close, so close. His heat, his maleness, seemed to encompass her. "Thank me?"

"For taking care of me. I owe you my life."

Kelly shook her head, wishing he'd get back into bed under the covers. "I didn't do anything. It was Blue Crow."

Lee grunted softly. "Blue Crow. Where is he now?"

"He's . . ." She caught herself in time. "I don't know."

"He isn't here?"

"No. He only comes at night."

"At night? Why?"

Kelly shrugged. "I don't know."

Lee's gaze held hers and she had the distinct impression that he knew she was lying, that he knew about the gold.

She saw him shift his weight from one leg to the other. "Is your leg hurting?" she asked, hoping to steer the subject away from Blue Crow. "Maybe you should sit down?"

"Yeah." He limped across the room and sat down on the edge of the bed.

"I'll fix breakfast," Kelly said.

"Maybe you could bring me something to wear?"

With a curt nod, Kelly left the room.

Lee stared out the window, his thoughts drifting like sparks in the wind. Blue Crow was here. And the Lakota gold was here, too, somewhere on the ranch. He wanted Kelly, wanted her in the most primal way. Wanted her as he wanted the gold, as he wanted the freedom it represented, as he wanted this land. An unwanted image of Melinda flashed across his mind. Melinda, with her sweet lying smile and her empty promises of love. He'd measured every woman he'd known since then by Melinda's treachery, refusing to trust any of them.

His hands curled into tight fists. He didn't trust Kelly McBride, either. She was a rotten liar. But he couldn't ignore the way his body hardened whenever she was near, couldn't deny that he wanted her. Just as she wanted him.

He swore under his breath. Hell would freeze over before he let himself get involved with another white woman, he thought grimly, and then he swore again. Whether he liked it or not, whether he wanted to admit it or not, he was already involved with Kelly McBride. He wanted her gold. And no matter how he tried to deny it, he wanted Kelly in his bed.

Filled with self-contempt, he called himself ten kinds of a fool, but the fact remained. He wanted her in his bed, in his arms, wanted her as he'd wanted no other woman he'd ever known.

Kelly stood in the doorway, watching the emotions that played across Lee's face as he stared out the window. He looked vulnerable sitting there, vulnerable and alone. She had a sudden urge to sit beside him, to draw him into her arms and cradle his head against her breast, to stroke his brow and tell him that everything would be all right, that he wasn't alone.

And then he glanced up, his eyes as hard and dark as obsidian, his jaw tense with anger, and the urge to comfort him was swallowed up in the urge to run away before it was too late.

"How long have you been standing there?" Lee asked, his voice harsh.

"Not long. I . . . here." Kelly thrust an armful of clothes at him. "Breakfast is ready when you are," she said, and hurried out of the room.

In the kitchen, she braced her hands against the sink and took a deep breath. His eyes, she thought; she had never seen eyes filled with such desire, or such hatred. His whole body had been tense, his hands curled into angry fists, every muscle taut.

She wished suddenly that it was dark, that Blue Crow were there beside her.

She heard the sound of Lee's footsteps in the hallway, and then he was there, his broad shoulders filling the doorway.

From the corner of her eye, she saw him limp toward the table and lower himself into a chair. The white T-shirt he wore made his skin seem darker, his hair blacker.

She took a deep breath, plastered a smile on her face, and poured him a cup of coffee.

"I fixed waffles," she said. "Do you want syrup or jelly?"

"Syrup."

She moved around the kitchen, getting the syrup and refilling his coffee cup before she sat down.

They ate in silence. Kelly was acutely aware of Lee's every move. She saw his grimace when he reached for his coffee cup with his right hand, inadvertently jarring his injured arm. She felt the heat of his gaze when his eyes met hers, felt the electricity that arced between them.

He wanted her.

And, heaven help her, in spite of everything, she wanted him.

Chapter Twenty-one

The silence stretched between them, awkward, uncomfortable, absolute.

Shaken by the intensity of his gaze and her own reaction to it, she dropped her fork. It clattered loudly as it hit the table.

And then that stark silence took over once again.

Kelly searched her mind for some safe topic of conversation, but it was as if she'd lost the power of thought, of speech.

She tried not to notice the way the thin white cotton molded itself to Lee's chest, tried to ignore the way her heart was slamming against her ribs.

And then he moved. She watched his length unfold from the chair. She noticed his limp, the way his faded jeans hugged his long legs.

He rounded the table and it was suddenly hard for her to breathe. Mesmerized, she stared up at him, her gaze trapped by his dark brooding one.

It was a mistake, Lee thought as he bent down and slanted his mouth over Kelly's. A big mistake. But he could no more keep himself from kissing her than he could refuse his next breath.

Her lips were soft, yielding. He ran his tongue over her lower lip, the tastes of coffee and syrup and woman mingling on his tongue as he boldly explored her mouth.

Heat shot through him, bright fingers of flame that burned away his resolve. His hands closed over her arms and he groaned low in his throat as he drew her to her feet, then wrapped his good arm around her, pressing her sweet feminine curves against his aching flesh.

And all the while, a part of him waited for her to reject him, to call him a dirty redskin and push him away.

But Kelly had no such thoughts. Rising on tiptoe, she wound her arms around Lee's neck and molded her body to his. Her eyelids fluttered down as the wonder of his touch spiraled through her. Like a leaf uncurling beneath the kiss of the sun, desire unfolded deep in the core of her being, growing, expanding, watered by the sound of her name on his lips, nurtured by their mutual need.

She pressed against him, wanting to be closer, closer, wanting to taste and touch every inch of his heated flesh.

She felt him take an unsteady step backward, heard him groan softly as he reached blindly for the table.

Her first thought was that he was rejecting her, repulsed by her boldness, and then she realized that he was in pain.

"Kelly, I've got to sit down."

She quickly drew away, her passion fading as concern took its place.

"Let me help you back to bed," she said, reaching for his hand.

To bed. He had a sudden image of Kelly lying beneath him, her lustrous brown hair spread across the pillow, her sky-blue eyes hazy with desire. Hard on the heels of that image came the memory of the beating he'd endured after Melinda's betrayal.

But this wasn't Melinda.

It was Kelly. Kelly holding his hand; Kelly looking up at him, her expressive eyes reflecting compassion and concern.

He grimaced as a twinge of pain ran the length of his leg.

"Come on," Kelly said, slipping her arm around his waist. "You should rest."

He let her help him down the hall to his room. He sat on the edge of the bed, his head bowed, as he waited for the pain in his thigh to subside. He was aware of Kelly waiting close by, and then she was standing in front of him, cradling his head against her breasts as she lightly stroked his hair.

Her touch was infinitely gentle, caring. He felt the sting of tears behind his eyes and knew if she didn't leave off mothering him, he'd make a complete fool of himself. But, try as he might, he couldn't bring himself to push her away. No woman had comforted him so tenderly since his grandmother died almost ten years ago.

Jaw clenched, his hands fisted at his sides, he closed his eyes and gave himself over to her touch. Just another minute or two, he thought, and he'd send her away.

But there was magic in the warmth of her hands as she stroked his hair, and then began to gently massage his neck and shoulders.

Hesitantly he lifted his hands to her waist, then let his palms slide over her buttocks and down the length of her thighs. Her hands stilled on his shoulders.

Immediately, Lee pulled away from her. And then he felt her hands on his head, drawing his face to her breasts once more.

"Kelly . . ."

"Hmmm?"

"Do you know what you're doing?"

"Yes."

"Are you sure?"

His breath penetrated her shirt, warm and inviting. She slid her fingers through his hair.

"Kelly?"

"I'm sure."

Afraid he was making the biggest mistake of his life, he tilted his head up so he could see her face.

"I won't stop this time," he warned. "Whatever starts between us, I'll finish."

"It's already started, Lee," she murmured, and knew there would be no turning back this time.

His eyes glowed like the burning embers of a fire as he drew her down on the bed beside him, his arms wrapping around her as he kissed her. And kissed her, his tongue delving deep into her mouth. It surprised her, that a kiss could arouse her so quickly.

He fell back on the bed, drawing her down on top of him, his hands tracing lazy circles over her back while his lips moved over her face and neck, slowly tantalizing her until she was on fire with need.

Her hands sought to know him, and he let her explore to her heart's content, learning the shape of him, the texture of his skin.

Somehow their clothing disappeared and she learned, to her delight, the sensual pleasure of bare skin against bare skin. She saw the admiration in Lee's eyes when he looked at her and was pleased that he found her desirable, that her untutored hands could bring him pleasure. She felt a keen, unreasoning jealousy because he had known other women, because she was not his first lover. Unbidden came the memory of Melinda. Had Melinda been his first love?

She fought down the bitterness that threatened to overwhelm her and began to kiss him hungrily, fiercely, determined to wipe the memory of every other woman from his mind.

She heard him groan low in his throat, and then he was tucking her beneath him, his legs parting hers.

He whispered her name, his hands tangled in her hair, as his body became one with hers.

And Kelly knew there would never be another man in her life. For as long as she lived, she would belong to Lee Roan Horse.

Kelly studied the face of the man lying beside her. He had fallen asleep soon after they made love, his arm wrapped around her shoulder. She would have gotten up, had she been able, but when she tried to slip out of bed, he had stirred, whispering, "Don't go," and all thought of getting up had left her mind.

A rumbling in her stomach told her it was well past noon. She should get up, take a shower, get dressed. Though she had enjoyed their love-making, she wasn't sure what was expected of her now. Would he expect to take her to bed at his whim, or was it something to be done once and forgotten?

She wished suddenly that she'd had more experience with this sort of thing. She gazed at Lee again, felt her heart stir at the beauty of the man. He had been a tender lover, making her feel beautiful, cherished, being certain he pleasured her before he sought his own release. And when it was over, he had held her close, stroking her hair, whispering endearments in her ear, holding her until she fell asleep in his arms, peacefully, blissfully, content.

His eyelashes were thick, like tiny black fans against his bronze cheeks. His lips were well-shaped, firm. She stifled the impulse to run her finger over his lower lip, afraid she would wake him. She let her gaze wander over his broad shoulders, over his heavily muscled arms.

She would have been happy to sit there staring at him for the rest of the day, she thought, but she felt him stir, stretch, and then he was awake, his dark eyes gazing into hers.

A slow flush crept into Kelly's cheeks as her eyes met his. Feeling suddenly awkward and more than a little shy, she looked away, only to feel his finger beneath her chin, turning her face to his again.

"It's all up to you, Kelly," he said quietly.

"What do you mean?"

"Where we go from here." He took a deep breath. "It can be the end, or it can be the beginning. It's up to you."

"What do you want?"

"I want you."

Kelly licked her lips. Her heart was beating wildly in her breast, her whole body was yearning to know him again. But before she could answer his question, there was something she had to know.

"Why did you come here, Lee?"

A shadow passed across his face. "What do you mean?"

"You know what I mean. Why are you really here?"

A hundred lies crowded his mind, but he couldn't utter a single one. Even knowing that the truth would bring her pain, he couldn't lie to her, not now.

A muscle twitched in his jaw. For a moment his gaze slid away from her face and then, slowly and deliberately, his eyes met hers.

"You know why."

Kelly sat up, clutching the sheet to her breasts. "I want to hear you say it."

"I came for the gold." The gold, he thought. It was the answer to every question. It was a way to escape from his past into a future where anything was possible. "The gold's here somewhere, and it's mine."

Kelly shook her head. "You're wrong. It's mine. Blue Crow gave it to me."

Lee's eyes narrowed ominously. "What do you mean?"

"Just what I said."

"Then you do know where it is?"

Kelly's heart seemed to stop. "He never told me."

It wasn't a lie, she thought. Blue Crow hadn't told her where the gold was, she'd found it with the help of her grandfather's map. She was glad now that she'd burned it.

She slid out of bed, taking the sheet with her, careful to keep her gaze averted. She didn't want to look at Lee, didn't want to remember how right it had felt to be in his arms. She'd been a fool to think he cared for her when all he cared about was the gold. But then, deep in her heart, hadn't she known that all along?

"Kelly."

His voice called to her, but she refused to look at him.

"I think you'd better leave," she said, and biting back the urge to cry, she swept out of the room, quietly but firmly closing the door behind her.

Chapter Twenty-two

Lee swore under his breath as he watched Kelly leave the room. He should have lied to her, he thought, and then, too late, he realized that he had lied to her. It wasn't the gold he wanted. It was Kelly.

He sat there for an hour, thinking of the brief interlude they had shared. He'd had his share of women, maybe more than his share, but except for Melinda, none of them had meant more than a means of physical relief. He'd made them no promises and expected none in return.

But Kelly was different. For the first time in his life, he'd known the difference between mere sexual gratification and love. She had offered herself to him freely, openly, soothing old hurts with the touch of her hand, vanquishing old ghosts with the gift of her love.

And he loved her.

Another oath escaped his lips. She'd never believe that now, not after what he'd said, never believe that she meant more to him than the gold.

The gold.

Lee stood up and began to pace the room as a niggling fear began to prey on his mind. Whoever else knew about the gold was getting tired of waiting. They'd tried to kill him once, and they would try again.

His hands clenched as a new thought occurred to him. He'd assumed the gunmen had been after him, but now that he thought about it, he realized it had been Kelly they were after. With her out of the way, the ranch would be sold to the highest bidder. He pondered the matter while he showered, then dressed in a pair of faded blue jeans and a black T-shirt.

Who else knew about the gold, he wondered as he stamped into his boots. Who else knew about it and wanted it bad enough to kill a woman for it?

Leaving the bedroom, he went into the kitchen in search of Kelly, but she wasn't there. The parlor, too, was empty. Turning back down the hall, he went to her bedroom and knocked on the door.

"Kelly? Kelly, you in there?"

Frowning, he put his hand on the knob. The door opened with a faint squeak, but the room was empty.

Where the hell was she?

He checked the bathroom, then went out to the barn. The horses whickered softly at his arrival, but there was no sign of Kelly.

He stood with his good shoulder braced against the barn door, wondering where she'd gone. He hadn't meant to hurt her, but then, he hadn't meant to fall in love with her, either.

Damn.

He was heading back to the house when something made him walk around to the back. He felt a sudden coldness in the area of his heart when he saw it, a faint scuff mark in the dirt beneath Kelly's window.

Squatting on his heels, Lee examined the print. It had been made by a man's hard-soled shoe.

Rising, he checked the ground for sign. Someone had tried to erase their tracks by using a leafy branch, but that, too, had left a trail of sorts.

Lee followed it until it disappeared at the edge of the woods beyond the pond.

He muttered an oath as he a single set of hoofprints heading away from the ranch.

Kelly struggled in her captor's grasp, but he had arms that felt as solid as steel and all her twisting and biting was in vain. All it earned her was a hard slap to the side of her face.

They'd been riding for almost two hours when her captor drew rein near the foot of the mountain.

He dismounted, then pulled Kelly roughly from the back of the horse. Pushing her to the ground, he tied her hands behind her back.

Kelly stared up at her captor, her stomach churning with fear. His eyes were pale, almost colorless. Lank, stringy brown hair fell over his forehead.

"What do you want?" she asked, her voice trembling uncontrollably.

"I want to know where the gold is," the man answered curtly. "You can make it easy on yourself and tell me now, or we can do it the hard way, and you can tell me later. Either way, you will tell me what I want to know."

"I don't know about any gold," Kelly said.

"The hard way, then," the man said with a smile, and Kelly had the awful feeling that he would have been disappointed if she'd told him what he wanted to know without an argument.

She started to plead with him, but before she could form the words, he hunkered down on his heels and slapped her, hard, twice.

Kelly's head reeled back, the salty taste of blood filling her mouth.

"The gold," the man said. "Where is it?"

"I don't—"

He slapped her again, harder this time, and then he sighed.

"We're wasting time," he muttered to himself, and rising to his feet, he gathered a handful of dry twigs and lit a small fire.

Kelly watched the flames lick at the dry tinder, her stomach muscles tightening with fear as the man pulled a jackknife from his pants pocket.

He looked at her, his pale eyes speculative as he

opened the knife and held the blade over the tiny dancing flames. When the metal was glowing, her abductor knelt beside her.

"Remember what your daddy always said when he was going to spank you?" he drawled. "Well, this is gonna hurt you a lot more than it hurts me."

Kelly stared in horror as he lifted the blade, holding it close to her left cheek. She could feel the heat radiating from the blade.

"Don't," she whimpered. "Please, don't."

"Just tell me what I want to know, and I'll let you go."

Tears welled in Kelly's eyes. He was lying. As soon as she told him what he wanted to know, he would kill her. She read the knowledge in his unblinking gaze.

He waggled the knife in front of her face. "Last chance, girl."

Kelly closed her eyes, her body shaking with fear. She could feel the heat drawing closer. She held her breath, waiting for the pain she could not begin to imagine. But it never came.

She gave a startled cry when she felt a hand on her arm.

"*Tekihila*."

"Blue Crow!" Tears of relief streamed down her cheeks as he cut her hands free and drew her into his arms.

"All is well, *tekihila*," he murmured soothingly.

"What . . . where? . . ." She glanced over his shoulder, shuddered as she saw the man's body lying face down a few feet away. "Is he . . . ?"

"*Han.* He will not hurt you again."

Trembling violently, she collapsed in Blue Crow's arms. He rocked her gently, his voice washing over her, soothing her while she cried, until nervous exhaustion overcame her and she tumbled into sleep's healing embrace.

And that was how Lee found them when he rode up a few minutes later.

He took in the scene at a glance: the body lying face down in the dirt, Kelly being rocked in the arms of a warrior clad in buckskin leggings and moccasins. A golden eagle hung from a leather thong around the Indian's neck.

Lee shivered as he met the warrior's gaze. Looking into the Indian's face was like looking in a mirror.

"Blue Crow," Lee murmured.

"*Han.*"

Lee shook his head. It wasn't possible. But he couldn't deny the proof of his own eyes. "Is she all right?"

Blue Crow nodded. Unconsciously, he tightened his hold on Kelly.

"What happened?"

"The *wasichu* threatened her life."

"And you killed him?"

"*Han.*"

"Good." Dismounting, Lee searched the dead man's pockets. There was no identification of any kind, only a set of car keys. "I'll get rid of the body."

Blue Crow nodded, his dark eyes thoughtful as he watched Lee place the dead man across the back of his horse, then swing up behind it.

Lee stared at Blue Crow, and knew he was looking at a man who embodied everything he himself had always yearned to be. Blue Crow was a warrior, indomitable, courageous, filled with a calm self-assurance that came from being at peace with one's self. Physically they looked very much alike, Lee thought ruefully, but that was where the comparison ended.

Blue Crow smiled under Lee's scrutiny. "Can you not believe the truth of your own eyes?"

"It's hard," Lee admitted. "Damn hard. Can you take Kelly home?"

"*Han.*" The smile faded from Blue Crow's face and his expression turned hard. "Be warned, Roan Horse. I will avenge any harm that comes to Kelly because of you."

"You think I'd hurt her?"

Blue Crow didn't answer, but his dark eyes continued to bore into Lee's.

"I thought you were here to guard the gold," Lee muttered.

"I will do that, as well. You have strayed far from the teachings of the People, Lee Roan Horse, far from the true path. You will not find the peace of mind you seek in a bag of gold."

"How do you know what I'm after?"

"I know your heart," Blue Crow replied confidently. "And I say again, you will live to regret it if you hurt Kelly in any way."

"I hear you," Lee said, his voice terse. He sent

a last look at Kelly, still sleeping in Blue Crow's arms, and then he reined his horse east, toward a deep chasm. He would dump the body there and cover it with rocks.

"Is he gone?"

"*Han.*"

Kelly sat up, her gaze seeking Blue Crow's face. "You don't think Lee would hurt me, do you?"

Blue Crow hesitated a moment, and then shook his head. "No, he will not hurt you, *tekihila.*" His arm tightened around her waist. "Not in the way you mean."

"I don't understand."

"I think you are destined to be together, though it will be hard for Roan Horse to admit that he needs you. He has spent his whole life alone, relying on no one but himself. He has not learned how to share his life, or his heart."

"You're wrong. He only wants the gold. He told me so."

"Sometimes a man does not know his own heart."

"It doesn't matter. I told him to leave, and I meant it." Kelly stared at Blue Crow. His silence made her uneasy. "You think I was wrong?"

"You must do what you think is right, *tekihila.* I cannot tell you how to live your life."

"But you think I'm wrong?" Kelly insisted.

"It may be right, for you."

Kelly sighed with exasperation. "Please, Blue Crow, just tell me what you think."

"I think you cannot fight your destiny."

"And you think Lee is my destiny?"

"I think you are his."

"I don't believe that."

"What do you believe in, *skuya?*"

"I don't know."

"Search your heart, *tekihila.*"

"I believe in you," Kelly murmured, laying her head on his shoulder. "I believe we were destined to be together."

"Ah, beloved, if only it could be so." His hand stroked her hair, the curve of her cheek and then, reluctantly, he stood up, drawing her up beside him. "Come, I will take you home."

"All right." Kelly looked at him, and then frowneded. "It's daytime."

He cocked an eyebrow in her direction.

"I thought you stayed in the cave during the day."

He nodded, comprehending her question. "I heard you call me, *tekihila.*"

"And you came."

"*Han.* As I will always come to you, *wastelakapi.*"

Blue Crow saw Kelly safely into the house. He took her into his arms and held her for a long moment. For a hundred years, he had waited for her. A hundred years of darkness and loneliness. Had he ignored the urging of his heart to go to her, had he arrived only a few moments later, she might have been badly hurt, perhaps killed. The thought was like a knife in his heart.

Closing his eyes, he pressed his cheek to the top of her head. Breathing deeply, he inhaled the fresh clean scent of her hair, her skin. Her breasts were warm and soft against his bare chest; the touch of her fingers gently kneading the muscles in his back aroused thoughts he should not have, desires he could not fulfill.

"I must go, *tekihila*," he murmured, his words thick with longing.

"You'll come back tonight, won't you?"

"If you need me."

"I'll always need you."

He looked at her through eyes filled with pain. "I think, if you look deep in your heart, you will find that it is Roan Horse you want."

A guilty flush heated Kelly's cheeks. He knew, she thought; he knew that Lee had made love to her.

A faint smile touched Blue Crow's lips. "It is all right, *tekihila*. I knew you could not be mine."

He placed his hand over her mouth, stilling her protest. "He is coming. Think carefully before you send him away," he said quietly, and then he was gone.

Lee knocked on the front door, then shoved his hands in his back pockets while he waited for Kelly to answer. Maybe she was right. Maybe it was time he got the hell out of here, or at least away from her. She could keep her damn gold. He'd leave Cedar Flats, go to California, see the ocean . . .

All his good intentions fled the instant she opened the door. "What do you want?"

"I came to get my things."

Kelly took a step back, allowing him entrance to the house.

"What did you do with . . . with that man?"

"You've got your secrets," Lee replied curtly. "I've got mine."

"If you buried him on my property, it is my business."

"You're better off not knowing anything about it, Kelly. If anybody comes around asking questions, you can honestly say you don't know."

She didn't like it, but she was in no mood to argue.

"Dammit, Kelly, I don't like leaving you here alone."

"You mean you don't like leaving the gold," Kelly retorted bitterly. "Besides, I'm not alone."

"You mean Blue Crow?"

"Yes."

"What's between you two, anyway?"

"That's none of your business."

"He's a ghost!"

"He loves me."

Lee cursed softly, hating the surge of jealousy that swept through him. Jealous! he thought irritably. He was jealous of a hundred-year-old ghost. It was ridiculous. But he couldn't forget how content Kelly had looked in Blue Crow's arms, or the trusting way she'd held onto the ancient warrior, even in her sleep.

"I'm sure you'll be very happy together," Lee muttered.

"What are you going to do now?"

"What the hell do you care?"

"I don't." But she did care. That was what hurt. She cared more than she wanted to admit.

Lee crossed the floor and went down the hallway to his room. He could hear Kelly's footsteps behind him.

"What's the matter?" he called over his shoulder, his tone caustic. "Afraid to leave me alone for fear I'll steal the family silver?"

"We don't have any silver."

He swore again, anger and jealousy and a deep sense of loss ripping through him, tearing at his insides like the claws of a mountain lion. He wouldn't have been surprised to see his life's blood spreading over the floor.

The first thing he saw when he walked into the guest room was the bed, the blankets thrown back, the sheets rumpled from their lovemaking earlier that day.

Lee shook his head ruefully. How had a day that started so good ended up so damn bad?

He turned to find Kelly staring at him from the doorway, a single tear glistening on her cheek.

"What's wrong?" he asked gruffly.

She shook her head, helpless to admit that she didn't want him to go, that, as much as she loved Blue Crow, she was also in love with Lee.

"Kelly, I . . . dammit, I'm . . ." He ran a hand through his hair. "I'm sorry, Kelly. I didn't want to hurt you."

With an effort, she gathered the shreds of her dignity around her. "You didn't."

"Liar."

His voice was soft, caressing. Another tear slid down her cheek.

"Kelly . . ."

"Go on, go if you're going."

Lee took a deep breath. Maybe it was time for truth, time to take a risk.

He took a step toward her, one hand outstretched in a silent plea. "I don't want to leave you."

Hope unfurled deep within Kelly, painful in its intensity. "I don't want you to go," she said, and placed her hand in his.

Slowly, Lee's long fingers closed over hers. "It's not because of the gold, Kelly," he said. "Maybe it was never the gold."

"I want to believe you. I do believe you, but . . ."

"But you don't trust me?"

"Trust has to be earned, Lee."

A smile turned up one corner of his mouth. "You're not gonna make this easy for me, are you?"

"Nothing worthwhile is ever easy."

"I wouldn't know," Lee said, a twinge of bitterness evident in his tone. "I've never had anything worthwhile. Until now."

"So," Kelly asked, her voice shaky. "Where do we go from here?"

"I don't know." Lee gazed into the blue tranquility of her eyes and felt as if he were drowning in sunshine. "I love you, Kelly," he whispered fervently. "I've never been in love before, and it scares the hell out of me."

"Lee . . ."

He pressed a finger to her lips to quiet her. "I love you, Kelly," he said again, surprised to discover how easily the words came to him now.

And then, very gently, he sealed his vow with a kiss.

For a moment they stood close in each other's arms, and then Lee drew back and gazed into Kelly's face.

"About the gold . . ."

She went rigid in his arms, the softness leaving her face, the dreamy expression melting from her eyes. "What about it?"

"Kelly, hear me out."

"I'm listening."

"You need to get rid of it."

"What do you mean?"

"I mean you need to cash it in and put the money in the bank."

"Why?"

"Because it's too dangerous to have it here on the ranch."

"How do you know it's here?"

"Because Blue Crow is here."

"The gold's been safe here for over a hundred years."

"It isn't just the gold, Kelly. You aren't safe here, either."

"What do you mean? That man who . . . who . . . he's dead, isn't he?"

"Maybe he wasn't alone."

Maybe you're working with him. The disloyal thought jumped to the forefront of Kelly's mind. Maybe all Lee's talk about loving her was just a ruse, a way to make her lower her guard and tell him where the gold was hidden.

As if reading her mind, Lee removed his arms

from her waist and took a step backward.

"Do whatever you want with the gold," he said tersely. "It's none of my business."

She flushed guiltily. "Lee . . ."

"This isn't gonna work, Kelly."

She stared up at him, not knowing what to say.

Lee drew in a deep breath and let it out in a soul-deep sigh. "You don't have to say anything. I can see the doubts in your eyes, Kelly. You're wondering if I'm lying about loving you, if it's just some kind of cheap trick to get my hands on the gold."

"No, I—"

"You're a terrible liar, Kelly. I can see the truth in your face, and I don't blame you. I haven't given you any reason to trust me."

She was too numb for tears. The joy she'd felt only moments before was gone, leaving the bitter taste of ashes in her mouth. But, oh, he was being so unfair! She'd only known him for a few weeks. And how could he blame her for being just a little suspicious when, only hours ago, he had boldly admitted that he'd come to the ranch to find the gold?

"You're being unfair!" she exclaimed, her anger rising.

"Unfair about what?"

"Everything. It's all happening so fast. One minute you tell me you want the gold, and the next you say you don't want the gold, that you love me. I don't know what to believe."

"Believe this," he murmured, and sweeping her

into his arms, he kissed her long and hard, kissed her until the world was spinning out of control, until her blood flowed like liquid honey, until she ached with a fierce need that made her sob his name.

Lee gazed deep into Kelly's eyes, and then, with a softly muttered oath, he tore his lips from hers, grabbed his gear, and left the house.

From the window, Kelly watched him bolt across the yard to the barn. Ten minutes later, he emerged carrying a gunny sack.

Heart numb, she watched him slide behind the wheel of his battered truck and roar out of the yard.

She had a terrible feeling that he wouldn't be back.

Chapter Twenty-three

Kelly took a long hot shower, scrubbed herself from head to foot twice, then pulled on a pair of jeans and an old sweater.

Sitting in front of the fireplace, she tried to sort out her feelings for Blue Crow, for Lee, but to no avail. She'd never believed it was possible to be in love with two men at the same time. Realistically, she supposed she wasn't in love with two men, since one of them was a ghost . . .

Right or wrong, flesh or fantasy, she was in love with Blue Crow. He was everything a man should be: kind, honest, loyal, trustworthy, gentle, tender. . . .

And then there was Lee. He wasn't honest or trustworthy. She doubted his loyalty. But he could be tender, so tender. Even now, she yearned to be in his arms again, to hear the husky rasp of his voice whispering her name, to feel his arms enfolding her, to know the touch of his lips on hers, trailing fire . . .

She had never dreamed that loving a man could be so fulfilling. Being in Lee's arms, his body united with hers, had been almost spiritual.

"And all he wanted was the gold."

She spoke the words aloud, hardly recognizing the sound of her own voice, she sounded so empty, so bitter.

Maybe he was telling the truth.

She tried not to listen to the little voice of her conscience. He had lied to her from the beginning. He never wanted to buy the ranch; he'd only wanted to steal the gold.

He said he loved you.

"Another lie!"

How do you know?

"Stop it! Just stop it!" She put her hands over her ears in a ridiculous effort to shut out the voice in her head. How would she ever know if he truly loved her, or if all he wanted was the gold? A lot of men married women they didn't love to obtain wealth, or power, or position. Lee'd been poor all his life. He believed the Triple M belonged to his people, that the gold should rightfully be his.

With a sigh, she buried her face in her hands. "What should I do?" she asked the empty room. "What should I do?"

"Follow your heart, *tekihila.*"

"Blue Crow." She sniffed back a tear as she lifted her head.

"Do not weep, *skuya*."

"I can't help it. I don't know what to do. Lee said he loved me, but I'm afraid to believe him. What if he only wants the gold? What if . . ." Kelly shrugged. "He hasn't asked me, but what if we got married and then he took the gold and left me?"

"What would you miss the most, *tekihila*? The man, or the yellow iron?"

"The man, of course."

"Then that is your answer."

"Lee thinks I should exchange the gold for cash and put it in the bank so no one else can touch it," Kelly remarked.

"Perhaps that would be wise."

"I guess so." Kelly gazed into Blue Crow's eyes. "What will happen to you when the gold is gone?"

Blue Crow shrugged. "I will follow *Wanagi Tacaku*, the spirit path, to *Wanagi Yata*, the place of souls."

"No!"

"Do you not think it is time?"

"But . . . what will I do without you?"

"You will no longer need me, *tekihila*."

With a wordless cry of protest, Kelly wrapped her arms around Blue Crow and hugged him close. She could not bear the thought of never seeing him again.

She felt his arms go around her, felt his lips move in her hair as he murmured her name over and over again.

"Please don't leave me," she whispered.

"Would you have my soul trapped forever in the cave, *wastelakapi*? Have I not wandered this part of the earth long enough?"

Kelly bit down on her lip. Selfishly, she had thought only of herself, of how much she would miss him when he was gone. Now, she thought how lonely he must have been all these years, caught between two worlds, belonging to neither. Kelly had always had a strong belief in an afterlife; now it occurred to her that he might have family waiting for him on the other side.

"Will you stay with me tonight?" she asked, her voice muffled against his chest.

"If you wish."

"I do."

Wordlessly, Kelly took him by the hand and led him to her room. After shutting the door, she drew him down beside her on the bed, sighed as his arms enfolded her.

She tried not to cry, but she couldn't stop the tears.

She clung to him all night long, memorizing the sight of his face, his touch and taste and smell. She whispered his name, vowing that she loved him, that even death would not dim her love.

He held her until she fell asleep in his arms, held her until dawn began to chase the stars from the sky.

Covering her, he placed a kiss on her cheek. "*Ohinniyan, tekihila,*" he murmured.

"Forever, my love."

* * *

Kelly rose early in the morning, her mind made up. She would take the gold from the cave, cash it in, deposit the money in the bank, and then take a long vacation.

A long sea cruise, she thought. Perhaps a few weeks away from the ranch, away from Lee, would help her to see things more clearly.

It was still dark outside when she went to the barn and saddled Dusty. The yard seemed empty without Lee's truck.

Dusty balked at being saddled before breakfast, but Kelly was too impatient to wait. It would take several trips to haul the gold down the mountain. It would be so much easier if she had someone to help her, someone to drive her car to the foot of the mountain so she wouldn't have to make the long ride from the cave to the Triple M on horseback. And where would she hide the first bags of gold while she went back for the rest?

Frowning, she urged Dusty into a lope. Having a fortune in gold was turning out to be more of a curse than a blessing. It had come between her and Lee; when it was gone, she would lose Blue Crow, as well. What good was money if you had no one to share it with?

Black clouds were gathering overhead when she reached the cave.

Taking a deep breath, she ducked inside, feeling for the lantern beside the entrance.

Holding the lantern high, she made her way toward the back of the cave. Toward Blue Crow's body.

It was there, on the shelf. Unable to help herself, she drew the blanket from his face and placed her fingertips on his cheek. The first time she had touched him, his skin had felt supple and warm. Now, it felt cool, hard.

Frightened without knowing why, she replaced the blanket, then began to fill a burlap bag with handfuls of gold nuggets.

She didn't realize she was crying until she felt the dampness on her hands.

She didn't look at Blue Crow's body as she dragged the heavy burlap bag out of the cave to where Dusty stood cropping a patch of yellow grass.

Grunting softly, she lifted the sack onto the gelding's back and secured it in place.

A faint sound from behind drew her attention and she whirled around, her heart hammering with anticipation.

But it wasn't Blue Crow.

"Lee!"

"Kelly."

Her gaze moved over him, her curiosity at his appearance quickly turning to fear when she saw the gun shoved in the waistband of his jeans. "What . . . what are you doing here?"

"What do you think?"

She didn't want to put it in words. He'd wanted the gold all the time, and now, it seemed, he'd come to take it.

Oddly enough, it no longer mattered. She thought of Blue Crow, and suddenly she wasn't afraid anymore. If she couldn't be with him in this life, perhaps they could be together in the next.

"Go on, take the gold," Kelly said. "I don't want it." A faint smile played over her lips. "I guess I won't need it where I'm going."

Lee frowned at her. "What the hell are you talking about?"

He took a step forward and then, to her astonishment, he staggered forward and fell face down at her feet.

She saw the other man then, and the sight of his cold yellow eyes sent shards of fear slicing through every fiber of her being.

Eyes like a coyote. In the back of her mind, she heard Blue Crow's voice warning her about a man with yellow eyes.

"Back off," the man said. "That's better. Now, turn around."

Kelly did as she was told. Behind her, she could hear muffled footsteps, the clink of metal, and then she felt a man's hand on her ankle, followed by the touch of cold steel. Looking down, she saw that he had shackled her feet.

"What are you doing?" The question escaped her lips before she could stop it.

The man looked at her as if she weren't very bright. "Just fixin' it so's you don't try to run off afore I'm through with ya."

Kelly glanced at Lee, still lying on the ground, and saw that his ankles were also shackled. While she watched, the man took Lee's gun and shoved it into the waistband of his trousers.

The man kicked Lee in the ribs, hard. "Come on, Injun, we're wasting time."

Lee groaned softly. He rolled over, one hand massaging the back of his neck. The chains around his ankle rattled, drawing his gaze.

"What the hell," he muttered. He looked at Kelly, and then, very slowly, glanced over his shoulder.

"Get up, Injun," the man said. "We've got a lot of gold to move, and we're wasting daylight."

"Who the hell are you?"

"Get up, Injun."

Keeping one eye on the pistol in the man's hand, Lee climbed to his feet and stood beside Kelly. "What now?"

"The two of you are gonna haul that gold down here." He jerked his head to the side. "My truck's waiting."

Lee glanced down the hill. A tan pickup was parked below.

The man grinned at the look of comprehension spreading over Lee's face. "My partner was a lousy shot," he remarked affably. "I'm not. Now, get movin'."

Lee followed Kelly into the cave, his mind racing. He had to distract the man long enough for Kelly to make a run for it. Run for it, he mused bleakly. She couldn't run with those damn shackles. Somehow, he'd have to overpower the man.

But their captor wasn't taking any chances. He kept well out of arm's reach. The gun in his hand never wavered.

It took a dozen trips down the hill to load the gold into the pickup. Kelly and Lee were both sweating profusely as they made their way up the hill the last time.

It was now or never, Lee thought. The last of the gold had been loaded into the truck. All that was left was for the man to shoot the two of them and leave their bodies in the cave.

Kelly tripped on a root and sprawled face down in the dirt. For a moment, she stayed as she was, too numb with fear to move or think.

She was going to die. Somehow, she hadn't felt any fear when she thought Lee was going to kill her, but now, facing death at the hands of this stranger, she was suddenly terrified.

She lifted her head to find Lee standing beside her. He was about to offer her a hand up when the yellow-eyed man struck him across the side of the face with the butt of his pistol.

Lee reeled backward, thrown off balance by the shackles on his feet.

Kelly scrambled to her knees, then gained her feet, her eyes widening as she saw the ugly gash on Lee's cheek. The blood trickling down his cheek seemed very red.

The gunman walked up behind Lee. "Put your hands behind your back," he said curtly, and when Lee hesitated, he hit him across the side of the head with the barrel of the pistol. "Come on, redskin," the man said impatiently, "I've got places to go and things to do."

Kelly felt a sudden overwhelming sense of hopelessness as she watched the yellow-eyed man lash Lee's hands together.

"Let's go," the man said, and gave Lee a shove toward the entrance to the cave.

Kelly followed Lee, the urge to scream rising in her throat. She was going to die. Where she had once counted her future in years, she now had only minutes.

She tried to pray, tried to force her thoughts away from the bloody images that were filling her mind: images of herself and Lee lying in pools of blood, their bodies left to rot, or to be torn apart by scavengers.

And then they were inside the cave, and she knew time had run out.

The man stood with his back to the entrance of the cave, the gun in his hand seeming to grow larger with every passing moment.

She wished she'd had time to tell Lee she loved him, that she could have seen Blue Crow one last time, and then there was no more time for thought.

The gun was pointed at her chest, the man's finger was curling around the trigger . . .

She screamed as Lee elbowed her aside, the shrill echo of her cry rising above the sound of the gunshot to echo off the walls of the cave.

And then everything happened in slow motion.

She saw Lee fall, his shirt front covered with blood.

She saw the gunman's face turn deathly pale as the body on the shelf rose to its feet and walked toward him. But it was not the body Kelly had seen when she lifted the blanket. This was a skeleton draped in hanging shreds of rotting flesh.

A wordless cry was torn from the gunman's throat as the walking corpse took the gun from his hand.

Was it only her imagination, or did the man look grateful when the skeleton put the gun to his chest and pulled the trigger?

She blinked in horror, and the corpse was gone.

A low moan drew her attention to Lee. With a wordless cry, she dropped to her knees beside him and cradled his head in her lap.

She pressed her hand over his chest in an effort to make the wound stop bleeding.

"Oh, God, Lee," she murmured as she freed his hands. "What can I do?"

"Nothing, Kelly." His voice was faint. "I didn't come here . . . to take the gold . . ."

"Don't talk. You've got to save your energy." She grabbed the scarf from her hair and pressed it over the wound in his chest. "I'll go get help. You'll be fine."

"No. Too late. I came . . . to help you . . . take . . . gold to town."

She nodded, the tears running down her cheeks. "I know, I know."

"Believe me."

"I do, I do." She stared at his chest, at the dark stain that was spreading ever wider. *Oh, God, please don't let him die, not now . . . please, I'll be so good . . .*

"Kelly . . ." He pressed his hand over hers. "Love . . . you . . ."

"I love you."

She whispered the words past her tears, but he didn't hear them.

With a sob, she kissed him, willing him to know with his last breath that she loved him.

She held tight to his hand, watching the shallow rise and fall of his chest. A moment later, a long shuddering sigh wracked his body, and then he lay still.

It was over, she thought, and then she felt a warm breath whisper past her cheek, felt a hand in her hair.

"Tekihila?"

Kelly opened her eyes, expecting to see Blue Crow kneeling beside her. Instead, she found herself gazing into Lee's deep black eyes.

She stared into his face, unable to speak.

"Tekihila, are you hurt?"

"Lee?"

"Roan Horse is gone."

"What do you mean?"

"Do you not know me, *wastelakapi?"*

"Blue Crow?"

"Han."

"No." She shook her head. "No, it can't be."

Taking her hands in his, he sat up, then slipped his arm around her shoulders.

"How?" Kelly asked.

Blue Crow shook his head. How could he explain what he, himself, did not understand? Still, he owed it to her to try.

"I watched his spirit leave his body," Blue Crow said, a note of awe in his voice, "and before I had time to think of what I was doing, I willed myself to take his place." He shook his head again, still unable to believe what had happened. "I cannot explain it, *tekihila*. My spirit lives in his body, and yet a part of Roan Horse remains."

"No." Kelly shook her head. "No, it can't be."

"It is true, *wastelakapi*."

Kelly stood up, needing a moment to be alone. It was all so incredible.

From the corner of her eye, she watched Lee . . . or was it Blue Crow? . . . stand up. He moved toward the stranger's body and searched the man's pockets until he found the key to the shackles. Removing the chains from his feet, Blue Crow turned toward her, a question in his eyes.

At her nod, he knelt to remove the shackles from her feet. Tossing the leg irons aside, he gazed up at her. His eyes were as black as ebony, soul-deep and filled with love.

"A hundred years I waited for you, *wastelakapi*. Will you now deny me?"

"It is you," Kelly murmured, her voice filled with wonder.

She glanced toward the shelf where Blue Crow's body had lain. Nothing remained but the faded Hudson's Bay blanket.

Blue Crow stood up and took her hands in his. "Will you be my woman, *tekihila?* Will you share your life with me here, and in the hereafter?"

"I will," Kelly replied breathlessly, and then he was kissing her, his lips warm with the promise of a thousand tomorrows.

Epilogue

Kelly sat on the top rail of the corral, watching Blue Crow put a young filly through its paces.

Three years had passed since the strange happenings in the cave. They had been the happiest three years of Kelly's life.

The first few days after the shooting, she hadn't known how to feel. She had been torn between the need to grieve for Lee and the need to rejoice that Blue Crow was alive, truly alive. And then she would remember that Blue Crow was alive only because Lee had sacrificed his life to save hers, and she wanted to cry all over again.

Most confusing of all had been watching Blue Crow. Sometimes, when she gazed into his fathomless black eyes, she saw Lee staring back at her, and she had come to believe that what Blue

Crow said was true, that a part of Lee's spirit had remained with them.

The morning after the shooting, they had gone back and buried the man in the cave. His driver's license identified him as Lucas Trask, age 31, unmarried. That same afternoon, they had taken the gold into Coleville and cashed it in.

A huge weight seemed to fall from Kelly's shoulders as they deposited the money in the bank. While they were opening the account, Kelly overheard one of the tellers remarking that Harry Renford had quit his job without giving notice and left town.

A week after the shooting, she had married Blue Crow in a simple ceremony, witnessed only by the minister and his wife.

For a time, she had worried about the two bodies buried on her property, but no one had come around asking after their whereabouts. Kelly couldn't help wondering if Harry Renford had been mixed up in the plot to steal the gold, if that wasn't why he had suddenly left town.

Kelly let her gaze wander over the ranch. The corrals were filled with horses now. Cattle grazed in the pasture behind the house. Chickens scratched in the dirt, a cat lay sprawled in the sun, a shaggy black dog slept in the shade under the porch.

In the last three years, they had remodeled the house, installing all new appliances, as well as wall-to-wall carpet in the living room and bedrooms. At the end of last year, they had added on a nursery for the baby that would be born in the summer.

And still they had more money than they could spend. At Blue Crow's suggestion, they had started a scholarship fund to help send underprivileged Lakota kids to college. It gave Kelly a deep sense of satisfaction, knowing that a large share of the treasure that Blue Crow had guarded for a hundred years was being used to help his people.

Kelly smiled as Blue Crow walked toward her. Reaching up, he lifted her gently to the ground. As always, whether they were apart an hour or a day, they could not keep from touching each other.

She went into his arms readily, her head resting against his chest, and knew she would ask no more of the future than to spend the rest of her life in this man's arms.

She felt Blue Crow's hand slide between them to rest on her stomach, now swollen with Blue Crow's child. It was a boy, of that she had no doubt, and his name would be Lee Roan Horse.

"Ohinniyan, wastelakapi," Blue Crow murmured.

"Forever, beloved," Kelly replied, and hand in hand they followed the path toward home.

Dear Reader:

I hope you enjoyed reading Heart Of The Hunter. I must admit, I do love writing stories with a paranormal/fantasy plot. There's a line in a song from *The Phantom of the Opera* that goes, "Open up your mind, let your fantasies unwind." And what fun that is!

Kim Buckles of Benton Harbor wrote me a letter and said she'd follow me to the Great Plains and the far reaches of other worlds and back again. I hope you all feel the same.

I love to hear from you. Please write me at P.O. Box 1703, Whittier, CA 90609-1703. Legal-size SASE appreciated.

Madeline

ANNE AVERY
DREAM SEEKER

Dream Seeker

For the first time since she'd become a dreamer, Calee hesitated at the entrance to her chamber, her body tense, her stomach tight with anxiety.

This assignment was a mistake, but none of her protests had rectified that error.

She raised her hand to the panel that would open the door in front of her. Her fingers trembled; her palm was damp. For an instant, she wondered if she even had the courage to open the door. But only for an instant. At her hesitant touch, the door slid silently open, revealing the chamber beyond.

The room was warm, but not too warm. It was small, slightly longer than it was wide, scarcely large enough to accommodate the massive couch draped with heavy silken throws that occupied the side farthest from the door. Lighting panels, hidden behind the rare, hand-carved wood trim along the ceiling, cast a subdued golden glow down walls covered with a richly textured fabric brought at great cost from a planet half the galaxy away.

Calee stood in the open doorway, letting her eyes wander over the familiar, precious space that was hers and hers alone. She had chosen the couch, the wall coverings, even the thick, soft carpet with its unusual jade green color.

If she'd wished, she might have had a larger room, one that opened onto the famed gardens of Dreamworld, or a room with a glass ceiling that gave her a view of the night sky and the stars she knew so well.

She hadn't wanted any of that. After years of living in the streets of Dantares, huddling in empty doorways to escape the constant rains, shivering in the winter cold with little protection besides the coarse, dirty rags that were her only clothing, Calee had wanted warmth, and softness, and a small, safe space that belonged only to her.

She'd achieved that when she'd completed her training as dreamer and gained the right to a room of her own. The right to this chamber where she could spend the hours and days and years of her existence listening to the songs of the stars. Those ancient songs, born in the internal fires of the stars themselves, were what she followed as she mentally guided the pilots of human spaceships through the dark of *within* and back to the physical world.

Without her, and other dreamers like her, interstellar travel would have been impossible. The only way for ships to travel faster than light was to go *within*. Unfortunately, human-made tracking devices didn't work in the amorphous nothingness that lay somewhere outside the bounds of normal space. Only a dreamer's ability to sense the tenuous connections that tied *within* to the physical universe made it possible for humans to travel with safety among the stars.

Dreaming was honored work, work Calee loved. That didn't mean she wanted this assignment.

She had even gone so far as to protest to the senior administrator, but Dame Kassta had simply looked at her calmly and assured her there was no mistake.

"But this pilot is a scout—and a male! I can't guide a male!" The words had burst from her before she could stop them, but Calee hadn't even tried to apologize.

Kassta hadn't blinked. She'd sat there, her wrinkled old hands calmly clasped in her lap, and nodded slowly. "Yes, you can."

"You've never made me guide a male before."

"This time we have to, regardless of your fears."

"But you always assign male dreamers to male scouts."

Kassta had sighed at the faint note of panic edging Calee's voice. "When we can. But this man's mission is urgent and cannot wait. The planet he seeks is on the far side of galaxy center, beyond the most distant star that humankind has yet reached. Right now he waits at the edge of the

Megelen sector, unable to go farther until there is a dreamer to guide him."

Kassta had grown silent for a moment, studying Calee. "There are few dreamers who can reach him, Calee; even fewer capable of taking him as far as he has to go. You are one of those few, and you are the only one available. You have no more choice in the matter than we did."

"But . . . I *can't* guide a male, Dame." Desperation had jostled with the fear inside her, driving Calee to plead with her superior. "It would be bad enough if all I had to do was touch his mind, help him guide his ship . . ."

The words had caught in Calee's throat, but before Kassta could stop her, she'd rushed on, heedless of the consequences. "*You* know what it's like to be a dreamer. You know what it means to share a pilot's mind, to see the ship with her eyes, touch it with her hands, to feel her body as if it were your own. You know what it's like to be *her* at the same time you are yourself."

Calee choked, then caught her breath, fighting for control. "Dreaming is hard enough with a woman, Dame, but with a man . . . ! Men are so . . . *big* . . . and rough and . . . I can't guide a male. I *can't!*"

Calee would have said more, but Kassta had held her hand up in a peremptory demand for silence. "You cannot hide from life forever, Calee," she'd said. "Not even here on Dreamworld."

Kassta had hesitated, then continued sadly, "We have tried to protect you from the memories of your past, Calee. We thought that, with time, you would come to accept the emotional costs of the work we do, that you would learn to venture out from behind the mental walls we taught you to build even if you never again left the safety of these physical walls that surround you."

Kassta's steady gaze had fixed on Calee. "Perhaps we were wrong. Right or wrong, however, we cannot protect you any longer. We have no choice but to assign you to this scout, Calee. No choice whatsoever."

Calee would have protested further, but something in the sad, stern set of her superior's face had deterred her. Without another word, she had risen and left the room.

Even here, standing at the entrance to her dreaming chamber, Calee wavered. She didn't want to guide a male. Males were dangerous, violent creatures given to physical excesses and passionate outbursts that threatened the peace of everyone around them. She especially didn't want to touch the mind of a male who was also a scout.

Calee drew in a deep, unsteady breath at the thought. She'd guided scouts before. They'd all been female, but they'd shared a bravado and a brash unawareness of their own mortality that she'd found both shocking and incomprehensible.

Even older, more seasoned dreamers had a hard time working with scouts. With their dangerous work of exploring the new worlds discovered by robot probes, the pilots of scout ships usually retired very young, or died even younger. Knowing that fact made guiding them emotionally draining for a dreamer.

It had always been even harder for Calee. She'd seen too much death when she was young to understand why anyone would face it so willingly. That's why she preferred guiding the pilots—the *female* pilots—of standard trade or transport ships. If they died, at least it was by accident and not because they'd deliberately put their lives at risk.

None of those considerations should matter, Calee told herself sternly. She had her duty, a duty she had never before failed to meet. She would not fail to meet it now.

Nervously, Calee tossed back her hair which fell in a heavy, dark blonde curtain around her shoulders and down to her waist. She adjusted the high collar of her gown, then smoothed the long, full sleeves as carefully as if she were checking invisible armor. The gown was like all her other gowns. She'd chosen it because it provided freedom of movement while allowing her to cover as much as possible of the physical side of her being. Her work—her *life*—was spent in her mind and Calee wanted no distractions, not even from her own body.

With deliberate resolution, Calee crossed to the couch. The train of her gown swished softly over the deep, thick carpet. She stood for a moment, forcing the calm she'd been trained to call up at will. When her heartbeat had slowed and some of the tension in her body had eased, she slid onto the couch and lay back against the soft cushions.

Lying still and quiet helped her concentrate on her dreaming. All her energies had to be focused inward as she mentally reached out to link with the mind of the pilot she'd been assigned to.

It didn't matter that he was on a ship half a galaxy away and she would never leave her chamber here on Dreamworld. Once they were linked, they would function as one entity. Through her dreaming, her listening to the stars, she would show him the path he had to follow. Though he could not hear the stars as she did, he would be able to share her awareness of them, then translate that awareness into a form his ship could understand and follow, even *within*.

In the two or three days it would require for Calee to guide the pilot to wherever he was going, she would match her activities to his as much as possible. She would eat when he ate, sleep when he slept, bathe and tend to her personal needs when he did. Mostly, however, she would lie here on her couch, more aware of his body than she was of hers while her mind soared free among the stars.

At a softly spoken command from her, the lights in the room dimmed to an even paler glow. Calee closed her eyes and breathed deep, then deeper still, opening her mind to the music that was never far from her conscious thoughts, the eternal, infinitely varied songs of the stars.

The first voice she heard was the low, grumbling chant of Dreamworld's own star, Rigeten. Then Rigonan, Rigeten's sister, added its soft lilt.

Slowly the chorus gained power as Calee reached farther. There was Abarakal and Kaispa and Tras and, farther still, Old Tom and Zacharius. From far away, pure and clear, came the ancient song of Sol, the song that all dreamers heard most clearly because it was that voice which had given humankind birth.

Free among the stars, Calee's fears of the assignment ahead eased. The pilot was just a man, after all. And what was one man, alone, compared to the vast majesty of the universe about her?

Reassured, Calee reached out to the distant Megelen sector, mentally searching for that spark of energy that told her another human was there, waiting for her.

The unknown scout wasn't hard to find. Even with the voices of the half dozen stars near him rising in chorus, his silent, human song rose stronger still, pushing against Calee's mind with a mental force that made her falter.

He was male. Definitely and inescapably male.

Although she had never even touched the mind of a male except in training, Calee had no doubt of that. There was something darker and wilder about his song, something far more intimidatingly potent than anything she had ever experienced with a female pilot.

Calee hesitated, groping for words to describe what she sensed. Words that could protect her against the contact, against his maleness.

Halfway across the galaxy, Calee shuddered, shaken by her doubts. The physical reaction brought a mental shock in its wake . . . and a sense of shame. She was a dreamer, and dreamers weren't supposed to allow their emotions to interfere with their dreaming. No matter how little she wanted this assignment, she could not turn back. Not now.

Once more Calee breathed deep, then willed her body to grow still. Cautiously, ignoring the doubts that pressed around her, she reached out to touch the edge of his mind.

At that first contact, she couldn't repress a small sigh of relief. His thoughts were focused on his ship and his mission, not on her. Perhaps he would never know that she was female, or that she was afraid.

"Pilot?" Calee let the word form in her mind, at the surface, where he would hear it.

"So you decided to stay." The words as they took shape in his mind were flat and uninflected. Beneath them, Calee sensed a doubt that was directed squarely at her.

"I beg your pardon?"

"You stayed with me. I wasn't sure you would."

He shouldn't have felt her first contact. *Couldn't* have felt her. "How . . . ?"

"And why are you female?"

"I—"

Calee wasn't sure what she would have said in response to a question like that. He didn't give her a chance to find out because the doubt that had shaped his thoughts suddenly disappeared in a surge of wry amusement.

"Sorry."

Even though her mental link with the scout was still the tenuous, surface connection of first touch, Calee could sense the slight smile forming on his lips.

"Let me rephrase that question. Why have they assigned a female dreamer to me?"

"They said your mission was urgent and that your destination was beyond the reach of most dreamers," she replied, unable to repress the note of asperity in her thoughts. It was one thing for her to question being assigned to guide a male, quite another for him to question her assignment to him.

"But not beyond yours, I take it. That still doesn't change the fact that you're female."

"Nor that you're male! And a scout!"

"You have something against scouts?"

"No, I . . ." His amusement was aimed directly at her. She could feel it, just as she could sense his words as they formed in her mind.

"I didn't ask for this assignment." Though she tried, Calee couldn't disguise her indignation. She didn't want to; indignation was so very much safer than fear. "But now that I have it, I will fulfill my duty and I expect you to fulfill yours. And that includes granting me a little respect."

For a moment, no words formed in his mind, but under the surface layer of his thoughts Calee caught a confusing jumble of emotions as his amusement died. Doubt, about her and her assignment to him. Concern for the unidentified mission that lay ahead of him. Eagerness to be started, despite the dangers that undoubtedly awaited him.

Deeper still were darker emotions that cast shadows across the surface of his mind without giving any hint of their nature, like vague reflections on the surface of an unstill pond.

Although it was forbidden for a dreamer to go too deep into a pilot's mind, Calee felt the tug of a curiosity that was growing stronger than her fear.

It wasn't just that he was male. And it wasn't that he was young. Well, relatively young, anyway. This man was around thirty, she'd guess, near her age and far older than any other scout she'd ever heard of. There was something else, as well, something she couldn't define that intrigued and attracted and repelled her, all at the same time.

To begin with, no one had ever laughed at her before.

Pilots would never dare laugh at the dreamers assigned to them. Calee thought she ought to be insulted by his amusement. Instead, despite the embarrassment he'd caused her, she wanted to laugh, too.

She should withdraw from the assignment, regardless of Dame Kassta's comments. Perhaps if she . . .

"Dreamer?"

The scout's mental query startled Calee. She'd almost forgotten they were still linked.

"If your assignment to me is a mistake, it has to be rectified now." His amusement was gone entirely and his thoughts were tinged with impatience. "I can't wait, and I can't risk you failing in your work because you're uncomfortable with me."

Jolted by his unexpected sternness, Calee protested, "I was told to reach the scout on the edge of the Megelen sector. You're the only scout I can find this far out."

"I'm the only one here. That's one of the reasons I got this assignment. But I hadn't expected . . ."

His surface comments trailed off into a jumble of thoughts too tangled and swift for Calee to follow without delving where she had no right to. Before she could respond, he was back, his thoughts forming into words that rang harshly in her mind.

"I'm headed to the far edge of the Sharack system and I can't afford to wait. If you were told to look for me here, then I assume you've the ability to take me where I'm going and that there's no other dreamer more suitable."

"Suitable! You mean male."

"Male. Or a female mature enough not to distract me from my work."

"I wouldn't . . ." Calee's protest died before she could finish it. It had never occurred to her that she might be a distraction to him.

All this time she had been thinking of herself and her own reservations. Never once had she thought of him or of what this urgent mission that Kassta spoke of might mean to him.

After all, it was his life that was at risk, not hers. She would never know what dangers he would have to face once he arrived at the unknown planet he sought. She wouldn't even know if he survived—once the journey was over and they'd crossed back into normal space, she would leave him to face what lay ahead, alone.

Such considerations were humbling. Her own fears and uncertainties about dealing with a male suddenly seemed embarrassingly insignificant.

"I'll take you where you are going, pilot." Even in her own mind the words sounded subdued.

For a moment, the scout said nothing. The mix of thoughts and emotions that Calee was accustomed to hearing behind a pilot's surface thoughts seemed oddly silent, as though all this man's energies were tuned to listening to her, testing her words for their truth.

Abruptly, he capitulated. "I believe you, dreamer. Shall we start, then?"

For a moment, Calee hesitated. But only for a moment. She had accepted her task, just as he had accepted his. She could not turn back now. .

She took a deep breath, then let her words form softly in his mind. "The stars have a voice, pilot. I would share their songs." The traditional greeting with which a dreamer offered her services soothed her.

"The future calls, dreamer. I would share the journey." He, too, spoke softly, caressing the words, drawing them out as if he found a meaning in them beyond that of custom.

With his invitation and the subtle relaxation of the mental barriers that protected him, Calee moved deeper into his mind. Not so deep that she could do more than sense the emotions at the very core of him, but deep enough to see with his eyes, feel with his hands, deep enough to make his small ship her own, as well as his.

Even that much was unsettling.

For a moment, Calee faltered, disoriented by suddenly seeing the small ship from his perspective.

She'd guided the pilots of scout ships before, but everything here was wrong. Too small, too close, too fragile-looking for the kind of ship she knew.

It took a minute for Calee to realize it wasn't the ship itself that was changed. It was her view of it. Or rather, her view of it as seen through his eyes.

There was the matter of height, for one thing. The pilot was tall. No, he was more than just tall. He was big. Broad-shouldered and heavy-boned, with huge hands and feet.

As she adapted to this changed perspective, Calee realized it wasn't just his size that was disorienting her. There was a power and a purpose to his movements that was totally unlike anything she'd known before. In comparison, the females she'd guided, especially the female scouts, had moved like the quick-flitting dragonflies of Dreamworld, first here, then there, never still.

Even if he lacked the female pilots' darting energy, the pilot possessed his own easy grace without ever being aware of it. As he set about the task of preparing his ship for the jump into *within,* he moved with an economy of motion that surprised Calee.

Even though she knew she should have been concentrating on following his preparations, meshing her perceptions of the stars with his ship's measurements, Calee found herself focusing instead on the way his body worked, the way it felt to her untutored senses.

As he stretched to reach a bank of controls set in the bulkhead at the end of the console, she could feel the pressure of his left elbow against the armrest of his chair, the smooth tug of the muscles along his right side.

When he cued the ship's systems linked to the command console, Calee could feel the way the muscles and sinews and bones of his hands worked together as he moved quickly over the lighted panel before him. The surface of the panel was smooth against his callused fingertips and pleasantly cool.

He shifted slightly in his chair, drawing her attention to the way his hips and thighs pressed against the soft leather, the way his long legs didn't quite fit in the space available under the console. The movement served as a potent reminder that his body was undeniably male.

Calee wavered, her discomfort with the situation rising again. She wasn't prepared for this. It would take too long, be too difficult to adapt to his very different physical reality.

"Dreamer?"

The pilot's query was sharp with impatience. His hand hovered over the controls. Even though he could not see her, his head was up and cocked slightly to one side, as though he were listening for her footsteps in the passages of his mind.

"Yes?"

"Are you ready?"

"I . . ." No, she definitely was not ready.

"If you're going to back out of this assignment, dreamer, back out now. I don't want to be left hanging *within* because you suddenly decide you can't go through with this."

"It's just—you're so tall!" The protest escaped her before Calee was even aware of it.

"I'm so—" Suddenly, the impatience disappeared, just as it had earlier. He grinned. Calee could feel it. As a grin, it was a little lopsided, higher on the left than the right, but it seemed to come remarkably easily. It felt comfortable on his face. "I can't make myself shorter for your benefit."

"No, it's just . . . Well, everything looks so much smaller. But it's not, is it? It just seems smaller because you're so big."

He glanced about the cabin, surprised. "Seems normal to me. Cramped, with everything too close together for my hands to handle sometimes."

He shrugged, but before he could respond, a beeping warning from one of the monitors reclaimed his attention. Without speaking, he turned back to the command console and the final details he had to attend to before crossover—checking the drive, the sensors that would be useless once they crossed *within,* the mechanical well-being of the ship itself. His actions were automatic, yet he missed nothing.

When all the panel lights at last glowed green, he spoke again. "The ship's ready, dreamer, and so am I. Are you?"

His gaze was fixed on the console before him, but Calee could feel his mental probing as he pushed at the edges of her awareness, testing her commitment. The sensation was new—and unwelcome.

"I'm ready, pilot," she snapped, fighting against her own uncertainty with a show of irritation. "Shall we proceed?"

He shifted for one last look out the viewscreen, where the stars shone bright in the encompassing night of space. Calee felt the tug of doubt in his mind, then a brief, sharp stab of regret. With the smooth, unhurried decisiveness that character- ized all his movements, he reached out and shut off the viewscreen, then dropped his gaze to the control panel.

"Let's go, then." An instant later he keyed in the final commands that would drive his ship out of normal space and into the shapeless dark of *within*.

Through his eyes, Calee saw the control panel lights flash and the monitors register the abrupt shift that signaled the ship was crossing over. With his senses, she felt the nauseating wrench as his body was subjected to the inevitable and disorienting forces created in the change from one reality to another. Despite the physical stresses assaulting him, the pilot was calm, totally in control, as though he had the same capacity as a dreamer to separate his mind from his body.

Calee had no more than an instant to let that brief thought register before it was swept away in her own joyous awareness of the abrupt crescendo in the stellar chorus about her. They were *within*.

Here the songs were stronger, more condensed. Just as physical space folded over in the unreality of *within*, so the stars' songs wrapped around themselves, forming a tangled, intricate web that human-made equipment could neither decipher nor follow.

Only she would hear the one song of all the millions ringing in her mind that was the voice of whatever star the pilot sought. Only she could track it, following the song through the intertwined voices to its source as she guided him across the convoluted, unreal space they now occupied to his destination on the very edge of the galaxy.

As always when she made the crossing, Calee felt a surge of wonder at the gift she had been given, and an equally potent regret that the pilot she guided would never hear the glory of the songs about them except through her.

The pilot gave no hint that he felt any lack. He was already checking his ship, his attention focused on running the equipment tests that would tell him how well his small craft had made the jump *within*.

"Where to now, pilot?" Calee asked when he completed his check at last.

His head came up in surprise, cocked to the side as he had before, as if he could see her. "Where to? They didn't tell you?"

"No. They don't always, you know."

"I know, but I would have thought in this case . . ." His thoughts trailed off in puzzlement and, Calee sensed, frustration. "And I thought I was the only one they weren't talking to," he muttered, more to himself than to Calee.

"All right, then. There isn't much, just the first reports that came in from a robot probe. An old probe, judging from the poor quality of the transmission." Even as the words formed in his mind, his hands were playing rapidly across the console, calling up the information he wanted from the ship's memory.

"Central Command sent this to me almost as soon as they received it. So far as I can tell, I was selected for the honor of this mission because I'm the only scout this far out. I suspect Dreamworld Admin was just as unprepared if they didn't tell you about this assignment—and just as desperate."

"But why?" Calee demanded. "There are still millions of those probes unaccounted for. How many report back every year? Thousands? What's so special about this planet?"

"You'll see." His thoughts were grim as he called up the information he wanted to the screen in front of him.

"That's impossible!" Calee exclaimed as the meaning of the information displayed on the screen sank in. "No planet has that much gallnite."

"At least, we've never found one. Until now," the pilot acknowledged. "If the probe is right, that one planet has more gallnite than we've encountered anywhere in the universe. Enough that if the Gromin ever find it, they can manufacture all the poison they need to kill every human on every inhabited planet in the galaxy. Easy."

"By the blessed stars!" Calee's mind reeled.

Humanity's greatest enemy, the vicious, alien Gromin, had devastated more than one world with their air-borne poison. Only human vigilance and the extraordinary scarcity of gallnite, the essential component for the poison, had prevented more deaths over the almost fifty years since the Gromin first appeared in the galaxy.

Unlike humans, the creatures all seemed to possess the capacity for finding their way *within*. They were irrationally violent and vicious by nature, savagely destroying any sentient life form they encountered in their push to gain control of the galaxy. The faster, better-armed ships of the United Forces had managed to destroy most of the Gromin ships they'd encountered. Most of them, but not all. The couple of Gromin ships that had managed to slip past the warning net and reach human-inhabited planets had been devastatingly successful in ridding those planets of all previous inhabitants, including humans.

So far, no antidote for the gallnite-based poison had been discovered. Humanity's only protection against the scourge was its own vigilance, and the elimination of every known source of gallnite. Up until now, the fighting had favored the United

Forces, but if the Gromin obtained even a portion of the essential mineral on this new planet . . . Calee shuddered. It didn't bear thinking about.

"You *have* to think about it," the pilot said harshly in her mind.

For a fleeting instant, Calee wondered how he had been so sure of what she'd been thinking; then the thought was buried under the flood of questions his news had raised.

"Why are they sending a single scout ship?" she demanded. "What can you possibly do to ensure the Gromin don't get their claws into that planet?"

"Absolutely nothing, of course. But I'm the only ship—the only official representative of the United Forces—out this far. They tell me they're sending a Forces cruiser with enough fire power to destroy the planet, but it will take them a while to reach us. All we can hope is that the Gromin didn't pick up that probe's transmission."

"What are the chances of that happening? There's no way to suppress a probe's signal. It's broadcast across the universe."

He sighed. "I know, and there's nothing I can do about it."

"But if the Gromin—"

"If the Gromin follow us, they follow us. My task is to assess the risk and report back. Probes have been wrong before. All we can do is hope this probe is wrong, too. But we have to know, and finding out is my job."

He sat up abruptly. "A job I need to get on with, dreamer." He cast a quick glance across the command console, adjusted a couple of controls, then asked, "Ready?"

"Ready," Calee replied, struggling to regain the calm that had been shattered by the pilot's unexpected news. Once more she let the stars' songs fill her mind, searching for the one song, the one star that was their destination.

Along with information on the planet, the probe's message had carried a recording of the electromagnetic emissions of the planet's star. The recording wasn't quite the same as the song a dreamer heard, but it was close enough to allow Calee to identify that particular star's voice among the millions. Once she found the star, finding the planet would be an easy task.

Calee paused for a moment, intrigued by the low, growling notes of the song. It was an old star by the sounds of it, its energy slowly fading after the long ages of its youth. When this star died, billions of years from now, it wouldn't end in the fiery heat of a super nova or collapse in the implosion that created a black hole. It would simply gutter to its death like a spent candle. Whatever planets surrounded it would die, too, as old and worn out as the sun that had once given them birth. None of that mattered right now.

"There, pilot." Calee opened her mind even further, blending her perceptions with his. "There's the star we seek."

The pilot paused, just for an instant, caught by the shared wonder of the song, savoring, as she did, the grumbling low notes and the slow, ponderous mid-ranges where the theme lay.

But only for an instant; then his attention fixed on aligning his ship to follow the invisible mental path that Calee had laid down for him. With an assurance born of countless passages *within*, he turned the hundreds of complex systems throughout the ship to his bidding, testing his ship's measurements against Calee's perceptions, balancing the man-made against her human senses, his knowledge and skills with hers. His concentration was intense, his relief at having the waiting come to an end almost overwhelming.

Slowly, carefully, they moved deeper into the nothingness where time and distance had no meaning except as they created it in their own, enclosed world of the small scout ship. In spite of her intention to maintain a wary mental distance, Calee relaxed. This was work she knew and loved. Work she was born to. And with each passing hour as measured by the ship-bound clock, the mental link between them strengthened and deepened, making her forget the physical differences between them in the shared demands of the journey.

At last, when both Calee's senses and his instruments told him the ship was set on its course for a while, the pilot straightened, then pushed back from the console. The action abruptly dragged Calee back to an intense awareness of the physical present, and of him.

"The planet's still a couple of days away, even traveling *within*," the pilot said, slowly circling one muscular shoulder, then the other, to relieve the tension of having sat still too long. "You're stuck with me until we get there, so how about if we make things a little more comfortable?"

"Uh . . . mmm . . . comfortable?" Calee stumbled over the query, too distracted by the slow, enticing sweep of his broad shoulders and the smooth interplay of masculine bone and muscle to form a coherent sentence.

"That's right." The pilot leaned back and negligently propped one booted foot on the edge of the console. "For instance, most pilots lead very circumspect lives while they're *within*. After all, you dreamers are always there, right? Seeing with our eyes, feeling with our hands. You're almost living in our bodies, but you aren't anything to us but a voice in our minds."

He raised his other foot off the floor, crossed his legs at the ankles, and stretched out, leaning back even farther. "Now, if you were a male, that wouldn't be much of a problem. But you're not. You're female. A rather enticing female, actually."

The retort that rose to Calee's mind went unexpressed. She was too disoriented by a sudden sense of vertigo as he tilted so far back in his chair that she feared he would tip over.

Stretched out this way, his body seemed to go on forever. Even though she couldn't see much, since he was staring at the curve where the wall of the cabin joined the ceiling, she could feel the way his body hung suspended, the only points of support at his shoulders, where he pressed against the back of the chair, his lean hips on the seat, and the narrow edge of the console where his feet were propped.

Between hips and ankles stretched a long, long expanse of legs. Calee could feel the way his pilot's suit hugged the length of bone and hard muscles, feel the pressure of his hips against the soft leather, and the way his suit stretched across his flat belly and strained over the bulge at his crotch. Even quiescent, his male flesh had a frightening sense of leashed power waiting to be released.

She shouldn't pay any attention. Was trained not to pay attention. But she had never guided a male before and his actions had forcefully reminded her that this body—*his* body—was most definitely not female.

His words suddenly interrupted her thoughts, wrenching her from her uncomfortable fascination with what shouldn't concern her anyway.

"The way I see it, if we're going to have to share my mind and my body for the next few days, we really ought to get to know each other a little better. Don't you agree?"

"There are rules that govern our work, pilot." Calee took cover behind a facade of indignation at his presumption. That way there was at least a chance he wouldn't notice her inability to keep her mind firmly focused on that same work. "Those rules are quite adequate for me."

"Is that why you seem so fascinated with just how long my . . . um . . . legs are, dreamer?"

"I . . . It's . . . I told you I'm still not comfortable with seeing the ship through your perceptions, pilot. Your body is so ridiculously large and cumbersome!"

"It is for this ship, at least. These damn scout ships were made for midgets, not for men my size. But that still doesn't explain your fascination with—"

"Don't you have work to do, pilot? Equipment that needs adjusting or something?"

"You know quite well there's nothing pressing. Haven't you been paying attention to what I've been doing all this time, dreamer? And by the way—"

"If I didn't have to follow you so you don't get off course, I'd—"

"No doubt. But you *do* have to follow me, so that's that. You can't abandon me now that we're *within* and you know it. But that's not what I was about to say."

"If it wasn't, why'd you say it then?" Calee demanded. It was a childish riposte and she knew it, but she was rapidly discovering that this pilot was capable of confusing her and rousing her ire at the same time. The combination didn't make for clear thinking.

"Just a polite reminder of your duties, in case you started considering the advisability of abandoning me here."

Although Calee would have declared it physically impossible, he leaned even farther back in his chair and put his hands behind his head with an air of casual confidence that Calee found totally infuriating. She couldn't have said why the action provoked her so much. It certainly couldn't have anything to do with the way his body shifted with the movement, or the disconcerting sensation as his muscles stretched with this motion, or the easy, powerful feel of his shoulders. It was just that—

"No, what I was about to say, dreamer, is that if we're going to spend the next few days so closely linked, it would be nice if we could get on a friendlier basis."

"A—What do you mean?" Calee demanded suspiciously.

"Well, names, for one thing. Don't you think it would be a lot more pleasant if we could refer to each other by name, rather than by title?"

"You know that's forbidden!"

"By whose rules? Yours, dreamer? Not by mine."

"By the rules that govern our work, pilot. You know that as well as I."

"And why should we care? We're beyond any human world. That means we're beyond the rules, as well. Who knows how much time we have?" He hesitated just for a second, then continued. "Doesn't it ever occur to you that dreamers and scouts spend most of their lives alone? That our time together is some of the only human contact we share? Don't you think it's foolish to make that time so damned impersonal that we can't even know each other's names?"

Even though he'd maintained his light, bantering tone, Calee thought she detected a note of anger behind his words. Anger and—was it loneliness? Longing? Or some combination of the two?

"Our minds are joined, pilot. We're sharing the journey. Isn't that enough?" Calee forced a note of calm rationality into her thoughts that she was far from feeling.

Never would she admit that his words had touched her own aching loneliness, a loneliness she seldom admitted to but that always lay there, safely hidden behind her facade of independent confidence. It was only when she was dreaming, listening to the stars themselves, that the core of loneliness ever eased.

For a moment, he didn't respond to her objection. Was it her imagination, or had he really pressed against her own awareness? Had he tried to sense her emotions, just as she could sense his?

Absurd. Pilots simply didn't have that ability. It was her brief self-indulgence, her admission of her loneliness, that had made her think he could sense her feelings. Calee pushed down the memory of her first contact with him.

When he finally spoke, the note of levity was gone. "My name is Bram Mason, dreamer. What's yours?"

Bram. She liked that. Calee let his name lie in her thoughts like a shell in her hand, something she could touch, something real.

"Dreamer?" He let the word form softly, but the question was clear. Would she venture out to meet him? Would she share some part of herself, just as he had? Would she risk making herself human in his mind, rather than remain a faceless, nameless dreamer?

For a moment, Calee was tempted. It wasn't so much to ask, after all. Just her name—a rather short name, at that. What was she risking? Nothing, really.

He could never touch her, harm her. She would never meet him and probably never again be assigned to guide him. What could it possibly matter if she broke the rules, just this once, and told him her name?

Bram Mason. Alone in her room on Dreamworld, Calee whispered it to herself. She liked the way the soft consonants caressed her ear. Would he like her name as well as she liked his? How would her name sound when he spoke it? Would he . . .

Calee jerked upright on her couch. Such thoughts were dangerous and they were strictly forbidden to a dreamer. "My name is not your concern, pilot."

Bram frowned. Calee could feel the mental pressure as he searched for the reasons behind her refusal, tried to gauge her resistance. Immediately, she retreated behind a protective mental wall of cold indifference. He shouldn't be able to do that. It was one thing for her to sense his emotions, quite another to have him sense hers.

"All right," he conceded at last. Anger made his words ring harshly in her mind. Abruptly, he dropped his feet to the floor and sat up. "It's your choice . . . and your loss."

Without another word, Bram stood and left the cabin.

Linked as she was to him, Calee had no choice but to go with him. "What about the ship?" she protested. "You're not supposed to leave the command until you've confirmed the ship is on course by a second verification check."

"It's on course. Didn't you just confirm that a few minutes ago?"

"But the rules—"

"Well, that's another rule I've broken, dreamer. It must be rather unpleasant, working with someone who breaks the rules so often. Besides, I guess I *do* have other work, even if it's not urgent. That ought to please you enormously."

Calee sensed more than mere irritation in his thoughts, but he was moving too swiftly for her to sort it out. He didn't seem to be rushing, but his long strides carried him quickly along the central passage that ran the length of the ship. Twice he had to duck to get through a hatch. To Calee, the motion was oddly disconcerting. She'd never been with a pilot who had to do that.

If Bram sensed her disorientation, he gave no sign of it, nor any hint that he was even aware of her continued presence. Her refusal to share her name had clearly irritated him, and he was retaliating in the only way open to him, by ignoring her.

From a rack set into the wall, he took down a bag of tools, then followed a short side passage to where it ended in a bank of equipment panels and blinking control lights. He tossed the bag on the floor, then knelt and carefully prized open a small panel near the floor to reveal a jumble of tubing and wires and controls. With a tool he'd picked from the bag, he gingerly proceeded to sort through the tangle, all his powers of concentration focused on the task before him.

He might as well have slammed a door in her face, so thoroughly had he shut her out of his thoughts.

She ought to be pleased by that, Calee knew. With the ship safely on course, she was free to let her mind wander so long as she maintained the minimum necessary connection with him. She had no obligation to keep him company.

Yet even as she let the stellar chorus swell louder in her thoughts, Calee found herself incapable of loosening her mental ties to Bram Mason. It was as though, among all the songs ringing in her mind, his voice alone possessed an inexorable power she could not resist.

No, that was a lie. She could break free if she wanted to.

She didn't want to.

At some point—Calee wasn't sure just when—the fear with which she'd first approached him had changed to fascination.

Now that he had withdrawn from her, it was . . . safer . . . for her to remain linked with him. For the first time since she'd established the mental link with him, she could explore those tantalizing differences between them without fear of discovery or risk of his mocking her.

The stars would wait; Bram Mason wouldn't.

Merging with Bram this time wasn't so easy, however. In shutting her out of his thoughts, he had shut her away from any shared awareness of his body, as well. Which meant Calee had to connect with that part of his mind that worked on the instinctive level, the part that controlled his body and made it respond to his demands without any conscious effort on his part.

Calee probed lightly, making sure he wasn't paying any attention to her, then moved deeper. It was as if she'd plunged into a churning sea of sensation.

Before, she'd sensed his body as he'd sensed it, moved with him when he moved, felt, seen, heard, and tasted as if his body were her own.

Now she was Calee and she was Bram, and for one terrifying moment Calee couldn't sort one from the other.

On Dreamworld, she lay on her couch, her small, slender body wrapped in a silken gown and surrounded by soft light.

On a scout ship half a galaxy away, she twisted uncomfortably, trying to fit her too-large hand and arm into a cramped space that wasn't designed for easy access. Her powerful arm muscles strained and bunched as she forced a fitting open, and her long, masculine body twisted uncomfortably, trying to find better leverage for the task.

Calee gasped, wildly groping for mental balance. There was nothing on Dreamworld to which she could anchor herself, and nothing on that small scout ship but one tormenting male who had willfully shut her out of his mind.

Her mind spun, then scrabbled madly to break the connection, regardless of the consequences.

Calee might have succeeded if Bram, trying to force a connector into its proper position, hadn't lost his grip on the wrench he was using. His hand slipped, the wrench twisted in his grip, and he banged his knuckles against the unforgiving rough metal of the panel opening.

With an angry curse, Bram flung away the offending wrench and jammed his bleeding knuckles in his mouth, trying to suck away both the pain and the welling blood.

The abrupt gesture caught Calee by surprise. Still too disoriented to sort out the sensations, she felt her mouth press against the injured knuckles and her tongue rasp over the broken skin. The stiff, dark hair on the back of Bram's hand and fingers brushed against her lips, and the muscles of her—his?—throat tightened as she sucked away the hot, coppery-tasting blood.

Or was it his mouth against her hand, his lips that pressed so hard and hot against her flesh? Had he somehow crossed the emptiness that divided them to take her, here in the sanctity of her room?

Where did the dividing line between them begin and end? Was the intense heat that suddenly flowed through her a part of her own hunger, or part of him, or of both?

The questions wheeled through Calee's thoughts like wildly spinning fireworks, blinding her. She was trapped in a disorienting universe whose borders had blurred until she could no longer sort out her sensations from his, herself from him.

And all the while the heat inside her—inside *them*—rose until it threatened to burst into a flame that would consume them utterly.

It was Bram who broke the spell. With another harsh oath, he stumbled to his feet, his scraped hand clutched tight against his chest.

"Stop it!" He shouted the words to the silence of his ship. They rang in Calee's mind as if he'd been in her room with her. "Just stop it!"

On Dreamworld, Calee jerked to a sitting position on her couch, trembling and wide-eyed. But it wasn't the walls of her room she saw. Instead, the hard, cold metal walls of the scout ship filled her vision. She was once more seeing the ship through his eyes, without the dangerous double perception that had so tempted—and so frightened—her a moment earlier.

Shame filled her. This wasn't the behavior appropriate to a dreamer, and it wasn't what she'd originally intended.

At least, she didn't think it was.

Or was it?

"I . . . I'm sorry," she offered at last. "I . . ."

"You what?" he demanded harshly when her apology trailed off into nothing. "You didn't think I'd know you were still there? You're sorry you . . ."

His thought trailed off in frustration. Calee waited, expecting his condemnation for her unwarranted and disastrously inappropriate intrusion.

Nothing came. He'd shut her out once more and this time Calee had no desire to push past the barrier he'd erected between them. She didn't dare.

Bram stooped to glare at the connector he'd

been working on. "It'll have to do," he muttered.

His body was taut with a tension that Calee knew had nothing to do with his uncompleted task and everything to do with her intrusion a moment earlier. He replaced the panel and tossed the tools he'd used into the bag, then grabbed up the bag and stormed back down the passageway, scarcely pausing to hang the tools in their appropriate place.

Calee could sense something more than irritation behind the wall he'd drawn up between them. The trouble was, she couldn't tell what that something was. She couldn't feel any anger or resentment. It was something else, something, she suspected, that caused him the pain she could barely feel, peeking out around the edge of his protective emotional wall.

The wall that shouldn't exist unless she created it.

The vague suspicions that had been floating at the back of Calee's consciousness began to solidify. "You can dream, can't you?"

He ignored her question as he ducked through a final, heavily plated security door into the passage leading to his personal living quarters. He turned and, with unexpected violence, shoved the door shut. He leaned his shoulder into the effort, and the muscles across his shoulders and back, through his hips and down his legs, strained with the effort.

"Why are you shutting the door, pilot?" she demanded, shaken by her intense awareness of the physical force behind his action. "And why don't you use the mechanical controls?"

"For a dreamer, you sure ask a lot of questions." He was panting a little, but the door swung shut with smooth precision.

"But why . . ."

"Because there's not enough to do on these little ships to keep me in shape, and the exercise equipment is a damned bore." The words were cut short and sharp by his irritation.

"Pilot, I—"

He froze, his hands still pressed against the now-closed door. "My name is Bram."

"I—"

"Bram. Say it." The words were fiercely sharp and hard.

Still Calee hesitated. She'd never called a pilot by name before. She'd never even known any other pilot's name. To say it now to this angry male was to risk an intimacy she neither wanted nor was sure she could manage, an intimacy that seemed, somehow, far more dangerous than the physical intimacy she had so unwittingly unleashed just a few minutes before.

"Say it." If he'd spoken the words instead of thinking them, they would have come out from between clenched teeth.

Calee flinched. Would it really matter so very much, after all? "Bram."

Once out, it wasn't so hard. In fact, his name flowed rather smoothly across her mind. "Bram?"

He remained still, his head slightly bowed, as though every particle of his being was focused on listening to her. "Yes?"

"You're a dreamer, aren't you?"

Now it was his turn to hesitate. "No. At least, not exactly."

"What do you mean, not exactly?"

"I can't hear the stars as you do. Not unless you share them with me. But . . ." He paused, as though searching for the right words. "I can *feel* you, feel some of your emotions when you aren't hiding behind that mental wall they teach you dreamers to build between yourselves and us pilots. Sometimes I can hear you even then."

He brought his hands up and gently rubbed the palm of his left hand across the lacerated knuckles of his right. "I could feel you, dreamer."

His words were like a whisper in Calee's mind: soft, intimate, tormenting.

"It was as if your lips were on my hand. I could feel them, feel the heat inside you . . . We could have made love, you and I, right there on the cold, hard floor."

Shock kept Calee silent.

She'd been prepared to believe he was a dreamer with limited, untrained skills. That happened, sometimes. Not often, but enough that it wasn't a total surprise. She'd almost been prepared to accept that he could sense at least some of her thoughts and emotions.

She hadn't been prepared for this.

"That bothers you, doesn't it, dreamer?" Bram demanded mockingly. "Knowing you can't hide from me quite as easily as you'd thought. That it's not going to be so easy to keep up your comfortable pretense of self-importance."

"I don't pretend—"

"You do, just like every other dreamer I've ever known." His words cut through her objections with ease. "You're even trained to protect yourself against such common, despicable human emotions as fear and pain and loneliness. You have your gift and you hide behind it, dreamer. Isn't that so?"

Stung by the biting truth in his words, Calee lashed out. "What would you know about it, pilot?" she demanded angrily, forgetting that strong emotion destroyed the mental barriers between them. "Don't you and your kind just go from day to day, no goal in sight but the next star, the next landing? What is it you keep running away from? At least Dreamworld is clean and safe. At least it's human. Can you say the same about those hell holes around every space port where everything—*everything*—is for sale to the highest bidder?"

"What do you know of such places? You've never seen—"

"Oh, yes, I have." Calee's thoughts vibrated with the intensity of the remembered terror that swept through her. As a child on Dantares, she'd feared being caught up in the depravity and despair around her far more than she'd ever feared death itself. "I've seen those places, seen what they do to people. It's ugly, pilot. Ugly and vicious. And you accuse me of hiding from reality?"

For a long moment he said nothing, just stood there, his body taut as he strained to sense what lay behind her impassioned outbreak. Too late Calee realized what he was doing. Desperately, she tried to rebuild the mental walls she had so effectively destroyed. She couldn't. He was there, pushing against her mind, feeling her raw emotions at a level no one else had ever touched.

"You really have seen those places, haven't you, dreamer?" he asked at last, very softly. "You really do know what fear is."

"I . . ."

"Who would have thought . . . ?" His words trailed off. The tension eased from his body. "I guess that explains why you find your assignment to me so distasteful."

"Females don't guide males." Her protest was weak and unconvincing, even to Calee, but any protest would serve so long as it helped keep Bram Mason at a safe emotional distance.

"No, not usually. But that's not why you're so disturbed by me, yet fascinated at the same time, is it?" His voice in her mind softened, gentled. "It would be so easy for you to make me into a monster. I live in the physical world, and you exist . . . somewhere else. But I'm not a monster, and I won't hurt you."

Calee could feel his compassion enfold her, wrapping around her mind like a soft blanket around a newborn babe. The sensation was as comforting as it was unexpected. It was also strangely unnerving.

She was a dreamer, Calee reminded herself sternly. She had her gift of dreaming, an honored position, a safe haven on Dreamworld. She had no need of compassion. What did she lack, after all? What could this pilot offer her that she did not already possess?

The answer was—*had* to be—absolutely nothing.

"I'm not afraid of you hurting me, pilot. I'm not disturbed by you, either. It's just . . . I wasn't prepared to find out you can read minds. That's all." Calee wished she were more convincing.

Bram shrugged, clearly irritated by her withdrawal from him. The simple, physical act immediately resurrected the mental barriers between them. "Of course not. How insufferably arrogant of me even to have suggested it."

He wheeled about and headed toward what appeared to be his kitchen and sitting room.

Calee had no choice but to go with him, the link between them once more the formal connection of pilot and dreamer. Which was as it should be.

So why did she suddenly feel so . . . bereft?

Bram busied himself with preparing a meal, then eating it while blatantly ignoring her. Even though she was free to eat, too, Calee could only pick at the simple fruit, bread, and cheese that had been left for her by attendants.

The fact that Bram could so easily cut her out of his thoughts disturbed Calee. The fact that it mattered to her disturbed her even more. Whatever her feelings, there was nothing she could do but remain in the background of his mind, aware of his surface thoughts and his every movement. Both her training and her fears barred her from trying to reopen direct communication until her work required it.

Always before, she had welcomed the emotional distance she was required to keep between herself and a pilot. It gave her a connection to another human being without making any demands on her, leaving her safe to dream without fear of becoming lost among the stars' songs.

That distance was now an irritant, and the stars, for the first time, provided no safe haven. Their songs were muted by her intense and totally inappropriate absorption in one irresistibly tempting male.

Calee could only be grateful when the ship inevitably began veering off course. It meant there was real work for her at last and a welcome respite from the dangerous trend of her thoughts. Surely she could suppress her physical awareness of Bram in the act of working with him to reorient the ship.

It only took a couple of minutes to demonstrate she couldn't.

Despite all the energy required to mesh her dreamer's perceptions with Bram's, some part of Calee still followed his hands as they played over the controls, the movements of his body as he adjusted to the narrow confines of his pilot's chair. She felt the tension in his shoulders, the frown that creased his forehead as he concentrated on bringing the ship about, the tightening of his lips as he studied an anomalous reading from a monitor.

Not once did Calee sense any special awareness

of her presence on Bram's part. She ought to be grateful, for that meant he knew nothing of her unwonted fascination with his body.

She wasn't grateful at all. She was . . . disappointed.

Which was absurd. After all, he was only maintaining the same emotional distance from her that she'd always maintained from other pilots. It made no sense whatsoever to feel such rejection.

Getting the ship back on course took a little less than an hour, far less time than they'd needed to set it on course originally. It was just long enough, however, to make Calee realize how tired she was. Bram clearly felt the same.

"I'm exhausted," he announced, pushing back from the control console after a final check to ensure that the ship was on track. He paused for a fraction of a second, as though waiting for a response from Calee, then stood and in one long, graceful motion stretched his hands over his head.

The simple action caught Calee unawares. Like an elastic band suddenly released, every part of her mind that wasn't still focused on the stars snapped back to Bram so abruptly it left her reeling.

Bram twisted, forcing his right hand higher. Calee could feel the pull of the muscles along his side and down his back. Her breath caught in her throat.

He twisted back in a smooth flow of bone and sinew and muscle that revealed the latent power that was so much a part of him and that denied the weariness Calee could feel dragging at him.

One by one he tensed the muscles of his shoulders and back and buttocks, bunching them until they trembled with repressed energy. He stretched, drawing himself up taller until she could feel the strain through his neck and along his spine, then hunched his shoulders and swung his hands forward, fingers laced together, until the muscles across his back drew hard and taut.

Calee was so caught up in her awareness of his body that when Bram suddenly straightened and marched out the door, she was left gasping, caught between her mental connection with him and her own disturbing physical response to his movements.

Bram's sleeping chamber was larger than any Calee had seen on other scout ships, but it held none of the cozy luxuries with which most pilots chose to assuage their loneliness. One small, faint light glowed from the baseboard at one side of the room, its dim glow ineffective against the encroaching black. The only piece of furniture was a single bed in the center of the room that seemed to float in the darkness like a shadow on the surface of the ocean.

Only gradually did it dawn on Calee that the chamber was neither so large nor so dark as she had at first supposed. The impression of black space was created by a viewscreen that occupied one entire wall of the room with its display of the endless, textured nothingness of *within*. The impression was one of overwhelming space, of being cast adrift with nothing but the bed and the meager light as a safety line.

Bram stood still for a moment, staring into the void, then slowly, without taking his eyes from the viewscreen, began to undress.

Calee tried to ignore his fingers as they fumbled at the fastenings of his clothes, tried not to feel the brush of cloth against bare skin as first one garment, then the next and the next slid off his body and onto the floor until he stood naked and unmoving, with nothing more than the silence and the darkness to cover him.

Only then did Calee become aware of the aching, physical weariness dragging at him, a weariness, she realized suddenly, that matched her own. How many hours had passed since she'd first joined with him? How long since he'd last slept?

Calee tried to remember just when she'd first learned of her assignment. She couldn't judge. The time spent dreaming always passed in a blur and the concept of night and day had little meaning except as it served to track their progress *within*. Such disconnection from the routines of planet-bound life had never mattered to her before. For some reason, she wasn't sure why, it mattered now.

Which was absurd. There was no special reason for her to cling to the minutes and hours she spent with this pilot. They should be no different than the time she spent with any other pilot.

Should be, but they weren't.

Instead of seeking his bed, as Calee had expected, Bram slowly moved toward the huge viewscreen as though drawn by the infinite darkness.

Something, some dark, unspoken emotion that Calee could give no name, vibrated inside him and found an echoing response in the room around him and the vast nothingness beyond. Although it was forbidden, Calee could not resist pushing against the mental wall he had erected between them, probing for the source of the darkness within him that matched the darkness without.

His defenses against her were too strong. Though she tried, she failed utterly to pierce the invisible wall between them. He might be able to sense her thoughts, but she could do no more than merely brush against the edges of his soul.

No matter how strongly he resisted her mental probe, however, he could not shut her out of an awareness of his body.

Naked as he was, his slightest movement was tormentingly vivid to her. She could feel the slight shift of his weight from side to side with each step he took, feel the swing of his arms and the alternate tensing and relaxing of the muscles in his buttocks and legs. She could feel the subtle interplay of muscle and bone in his feet and the soft lushness of the carpet against his soles.

Though she tried, Calee could not ignore the weight of his sex nor the almost imperceptible friction when it rubbed against the skin of his thighs as he moved.

Calee wished the faint stir of air in the room could whisper across her skin as softly as it did across his. She would welcome even the vaguest breeze if it could cool the sudden heat rising in her, the uncontrollable longing.

"I thought dreamers were supposed to respect our privacy."

Bram's harsh, biting words shocked Calee more than if he'd struck her, dragging her attention away from what she had no right even to notice.

"You deny me your name and then you indulge in a lascivious exploration of my body as if the rules of privacy and anonymity didn't even exist. Where is your sense of honor, dreamer? Tucked safely away on Dreamworld, just like you?"

Stunned by the hard mockery of his thoughts and shamed by their justice, Calee could think of nothing in response. He was right. By the blessed stars, he was right. She had trespassed, and in a way that would earn her the harshest censure.

"I am sorry, pilot."

"Bram! My name is Bram!"

He might as well have shouted, so loudly did his objection ring in Calee's mind. With an awkward jerk, he twisted around on his heel, his hands balled into fists at his side, his shoulders hunched, as though he expected to find her standing behind him. There was nothing but the bed and the dim glow of the hidden light.

For a long, long moment, silence hung between them, taut with his anger and her shame.

From somewhere deep inside her, Calee dredged up the courage to offer, "My name is Calee."

He remained still and tense, testing her intention, weighing the sound of her name in his mind. "That's it? Just Calee?"

"If I ever had another name, I forgot it long ago."

"Calee." Then, "How does one forget a name?"

"I . . ." How could she tell him? How could she risk the emotional pain of revealing what she had tried so hard for so long to put behind her? By the same token, what right did she have not to answer when she was guilty of an even greater intrusion on his privacy?

"I was a child on the streets of Dantares when a dreamer found me," Calee hesitantly ventured at last. "I have no idea who my parents were or why I was abandoned. If I ever had another name besides Calee, I don't remember it."

"Dantares." The tension eased from his body as Bram turned the word over in his mind.

"Dreaming has given me everything I ever wanted. I'm safe here. I don't have to worry about being hungry, or cold, or scared and I'll never have to leave the safety of these walls. I don't have to be afraid anymore." The words poured from Calee, a vehement protest against the criticism Bram hadn't even thought, let alone expressed.

Was she, Calee wondered, responding to his doubts, or to hers?

Clearly uncertain how to respond, Bram sat on the edge of his narrow bed and stared out at the dark on the viewscreen. " 'How vast the distance from one heart to another,' " he said at last, very softly. " 'How close the stars.' "

Calee recognized the passage from a famous poem by an ancient Rigellian bard. "Sh'aa Seyor."

"Yes." For a long while Bram remained silent, his thoughts a jumble Calee dared not sort out. "What do you look like, Calee?"

"Look like?"

"You've shared my mind and my body, but I have no idea what you look like. You're nothing but a presence in my mind, a . . . a *thing* that sometimes doesn't seem quite real." Bram's mind quivered with the rising intensity of his thoughts. His hands curved tightly over his knees; his back was stiff and his head up as though he could somehow see her across the vast emptiness in front of him. "I want to touch you, *feel* you. I want a real, living human being with me, Calee, not just a voice echoing 'round in my head."

"But . . . but how?" Calee demanded, confused, yet oddly stirred by his request. "You say you're not a dreamer, even if you can sense my thoughts. How can you possibly see me?"

"Show me who you are."

"Show you?"

"Surely you look in your mirror. Share with me what you see."

The suggestion made Calee's stomach tighten with a fear that was as new to her as it was unexpected.

What if he didn't like the way she looked? What if he was disappointed? Outward appearances didn't matter much on Dreamworld. After all, dreamers lived more in their minds than in their physical bodies. Even most of the communications between them were conducted through their thoughts, rather than in person. It was so much easier that way.

But Calee knew enough of life outside the protected world she lived in to know that physical appearance *did* make a difference, especially between male and female. She had no illusions about being beautiful. Whenever she bothered to look, her mirror told her she wasn't. She didn't bother to look very often.

On the other hand, what could it possibly matter if Bram knew she wasn't beautiful? They would never meet in person, probably never meet even as pilot and dreamer. Given her inexcusable invasion of his body, he certainly had a right to know at least something about hers.

With a trepidation almost as great as what she'd felt on her first contact with him, Calee opened her mind to Bram, letting him share her thoughts in a way she would never, ever, let anyone else share them.

Too thin. That's what she thought of herself. Plain, with an angular face, a long, sharp nose, and a mouth that was far too wide. Eyes that were too large under brows that arched too high. Thick, waist-length hair that was neither blonde nor brown, but some nondescript mix of the two. Her neck was too long and her breast bone too prominent. She liked her hands, which were small and delicate and very feminine.

Calee caught Bram's amusement at the thought and almost snapped at him before she remembered her own fascination with his hands, which were so large and strong and so very masculine.

A vision of her hand safely clasped in his suddenly formed in Calee's mind, startling her. She could almost feel the heat of his skin, the strength of his fingers as they wrapped around hers. The image was so vivid that she couldn't help curling her hand into a ball, as if she could capture the sensation and hold it in her palm.

Bram's soft "Thank you" intruded, dispelling the image. His words caressed Calee's mind like a benediction. Her mouth curved into a gentle smile of pleasure at his response.

The simple, physical expression caught Calee by surprise—not because she never smiled, but because she'd never before paid any attention to what happened when she did. She felt the way her lips stretched and the muscles at the side of her mouth tightened. Did her eyes always crinkle like that? she wondered. Did the tip of her nose always turn down, just that tiny bit?

Amazed, Calee scarcely noticed that Bram, too, was caught up in her childlike fascination with the subtleties of her smile. Through her, he was occupying her body as well as her mind, and he was no more capable of restraining his curiosity than she had been.

It was only when he withdrew from her, abruptly severing that strange and wonderful mental bond between them, that Calee realized just how vulnerable she had been.

She didn't have a chance to think about it, however, for Bram was stretching his long body out on the bed, pulling the covers up to his chin as he settled his head on the pillow.

"Sleep well, Calee," he said softly in her mind. "Sweet dreams."

An instant later, he was asleep.

*   *   *

Bram slept. Calee could not. Even the stars could not comfort her.

How was it that a male, and a stranger, could have led her to such an intense awareness of her own body and her own physical perceptions? Was there some special magic in him that he could so easily stir her to longings and desires she'd only vaguely sensed and never willingly acknowledged before now? By what secret sorcery had he tempted her from her fascination with the stars to wrap her in a new, disturbing, and intensely human fascination with him?

Awake while Bram slept, Calee felt adrift, as though somehow he'd provided an anchor she'd never had. She couldn't even divert her thoughts by exploring the ship because without him, the ship did not exist for her.

There remained only his body and his dreams to distract her, and neither one was safe.

Even sleeping, Bram's mind retained a dim awareness of his body. That awareness roused in Calee a tormenting desire to touch him, to explore his body with her own very human senses instead of with just her mind.

Even those closest to her on Dreamworld had never generated this aching need to touch and feel and taste. She wanted to press her palm to his, to have his breath warm against her skin and feel his body hard and strong against her.

If she could, she would run her hand across his shoulder as he lay there sleeping, a tiger temporarily tamed to her touch. She would trace the line of his arm as it lay against his side, then his forearm where it dropped across his belly until his hand lay curled like a child's between his body and the bed. She would trace the jutting angle of his hip, then the long, long sweep of his thigh. Somehow, Calee knew the hair on his legs would be coarser, springier to the touch than the hair that curled across his chest and arms. The muscles of his thighs and calves would be hard beneath her hand, his skin warm.

However vividly tormenting her thoughts, they were far safer than the temptation to dip into his dreaming mind, to move past the formless shapes that danced and spun at the edge of his unconscious until she reached the very center of his soul.

It was Bram's own dreaming that freed Calee from temptation. Still sleeping, he moaned, then muttered angrily and thumped the bed with his fist as though it were an enemy. He cried out, whimpered, cursed, and pleaded with the imaginary demons that chased him through his dreams, demons he couldn't escape although he writhed and twisted on his bed in a futile attempt at running.

Caught at the periphery of Bram's mind, Calee could feel the inchoate terrors that held him, feel the cold sweat on his body and the racking agony of his fear.

"No!" he cried. "Don't go! Don't leave me alone!"

Calee heard the words as clearly as if she'd been in the room beside him. She flinched and stretched out her hand into the silence of her room as if she could touch him and soothe his fears.

She couldn't touch him, couldn't even rouse him from his dreams. He was too deeply entangled in their terrors.

In the end, Bram came awake with a jerk, gulping in air in great, heaving gasps. His hand trembled as he wiped the icy sweat from his face, then pushed up into a sitting position, the bedclothes tangled around his legs.

"Are you all right?" Calee asked hesitantly.

"Yes, of course." He shook his head as though to shake out the last faint vestiges of the nightmare, then tossed back the bedclothes and swung his feet to the floor. Perched at the edge of his bed, he breathed in deep. "Just a dream."

Calee said nothing. What was there to say? Yet, somehow, she sensed that his tormented dreams had been no chance disturbance but something with which he was all too familiar.

"I was alone." He said the words aloud in a room where there was no one to hear. Calee knew he intended them for her. "Alone and dying on a world far from anyone, far from . . ." The words trailed off, and he shook his head again as if to physically rid himself of the memory.

"Do you dream of that often?" Calee asked, uncertain of her role yet unwilling to let the situation pass without acknowledging his pain.

Bram shoved to his feet, then paused, clearly torn between his need to put the nightmare behind him and the even greater need to share it with someone—with *her*—and thus rid himself of it, at least for the present.

"I . . . Not often, no. But it's always there, I think, at the back of my mind."

He shrugged, uncomfortable with the admission. His head came up and his gaze fixed on the darkness that showed on the massive viewscreen.

"I was glad of the chance to become a scout," he said at last, still speaking to the empty room—and to her. "It was a way to escape other people's emotions, the emotions I could never completely shut out no matter how much I tried. I liked the idea of doing something exciting and dangerous and important."

As though drawn, he rose to his feet and crossed to the viewscreen, then stretched out his hand to touch the cool, hard wall of darkness.

"After a while," he said, very low, "the silence out here presses against you like some huge, hungry beast. You can't escape it, and all the time you know that someday, somewhere, it will eat you alive."

He pressed his hand flat against the screen, his fingers spread wide as though he were measuring the vast emptiness beyond. "When you're gone, the administrators make a note in their log. Just a little note; then they send out someone else to finish up whatever you didn't."

Bram fell silent, staring at the nebulous dark in front of him. Calee said nothing. What was there to say?

"I tried settling on a planet once," Bram continued at last, as if he were remembering something from long, long ago. "Rom. It's a beautiful planet, one of the first I ever found as a scout. I used my settlement rights to start a farm near one of the new villages. Managed pretty well, too— for a while. But then I started thinking about the stars . . . and the silence."

He paused, as though listening to the stillness around him, then shrugged and turned from the screen. "I left the farm in the hands of a care-taker, reclaimed my ship, and here I am."

Calee could feel Bram's mouth twist into a wry smile as he added, "Out here, I have nightmares about dying alone. Back there, I couldn't sleep for all the voices in my head."

Bram's loneliness was soul-deep and aching-ly real, but Calee could sense no self-pity in his words, nor any hope of a solution to his dilem-ma.

"Surely someone could teach you how to shut out those emotions. On Dreamworld—"

"I tried," Bram interrupted, as abruptly as if she'd pricked him. "Whatever flaw keeps me from being a dreamer also prevents me from shutting you out. You or anyone else. I can build a wall between my mind and yours so you can't touch me, but that's all."

He turned back to stare into the darkness on the viewscreen—the measureless, infinite dark outside the fragile shell that was his ship. This time he didn't speak aloud and the words in his mind were so faint that Calee had to strain to hear them.

"You can't build walls forever, Calee," he said. "No one can, no matter how much they want to."

Calee had no answer for that, either. She could only be grateful when Bram, too restless to sleep, suddenly bent to gather up the clothes he'd abandoned earlier. Without speaking, he headed toward the shower, effectively ending further discussion on so dangerously personal a level.

Shaken by the intensity of his revelations, Calee didn't even think of trying to follow Bram. Right now, they both needed as much distance between them as their duty would allow. A bath, clean clothes, and a meal would help restore the mental balance they'd both need to deal with the difficult work still ahead of them.

While Bram showered and changed, Calee bathed in the small room attached to her dreaming chamber that was accessible through a hidden door in the chamber's wall. The attendants who brought her meals and clean clothes used another door leading out of the bathing room to come and go without disturbing her.

As she bathed, one part of Calee's mind was occupied with following the star they sought and, at the same time, resisting the temptation of sharing Bram's shower. The other part worried at the question of how to help him.

Not that he'd asked for help, or ever would. Bram was too fiercely independent for that.

"I tried," he'd said. Those two words spoke of a man determined to confront life squarely, to change what he could and to accept what he could not. Beneath the words Calee had sensed a hundred hurtful memories of all the times he'd tried—and failed—to silence the deafening chorus in his mind.

It wasn't hard for her to imagine what it must be like for him. As a child, she'd often wondered if she would go mad from the unintelligible but insistent songs ringing in her head. Only after she'd been taught how to sift through those songs, to shut out the ones she didn't want to hear and focus on the ones she did, had she realized what a marvelous gift she'd been given. Until then, it had been a curse, just as Bram's sensitivity must seem a curse to him.

How much more difficult to know, as he did, that there would never be any escape.

Only a man of rare courage could have accepted such a burden with such grace. Only a man of great dignity could have turned his pain to the service of others, as Bram had through his work as scout.

Calee did not doubt that Bram found surcease from the voices in his mind in the silence of empty space. At the same time, she didn't believe he'd sought such perilous work only to escape, or that he'd chosen it for the excitement it might bring, or the riches he might gain.

Through all the long hours they'd spent working together, far beneath his mockery and amusement and anger, beneath even the loneliness and pain he kept so deeply hidden, Calee had clearly sensed his resolve to do whatever was necessary to ensure the success of his mission.

A day ago, Calee would have scoffed at the idea of a scout being driven by anything other than a thirst for adventure and the possibility of wealth. But that was before she'd spent long hours working with a scout named Bram Mason.

It was humbling to realize how little of life and of others she truly understood.

She'd thought of scouts as arrogant, reckless care-for-nothings who would risk everything, including life itself, for a wild thrill and the chance of becoming rich. How many of them, Calee wondered now, had hidden fears and doubts and dreams beneath their brash behavior? How many had longed for the comforting voice of another human being, even if it was only in their minds?

And if she'd been wrong in her judgment of scouts, how much more mistaken had she been about men?

Calee knew she'd formed her fears and prejudices as a child in Dantares, where men were as rough and wild as the streets they walked. Even though the violence had never touched her directly, Calee was just beginning to realize it had shaped her in ways she'd never recognized . . . until now.

She should have put it behind her long ago, should have been able to venture out from behind the barriers she'd erected between herself and the rest of the world when she'd had no other defense. Instead, she'd chosen to hide in the safety of her chamber, closing the door and shutting out the rest of the world.

How long had it been since she'd first touched Bram's mind? A day and a half, perhaps? Not long, but more than long enough to learn that even a big, powerful man capable of dominating the world around him was vulnerable to pain and loss and loneliness. Bram knew what it was to yearn for something he couldn't have, what it meant to be afraid. When he was tired, he slept, and when he was hurt, he bled, just as she did.

At the thought, Calee flushed. An unmistakable heat rose inside her, rousing memories which were best left forgotten. Imagined memories of her lips against Bram's skin, devouring him in a fevered exploration that stirred him as much as it did her. Memories of his body, of the way he moved, of the inescapable maleness that had once frightened her so much and that now fascinated her even more.

With a clumsy haste that sent water spilling onto the polished stone floor, Calee rose from her bath. She shouldn't be indulging in such illicit thoughts, should never have permitted herself the indiscretions that had created the memories in the first place.

As she reached for a towel, Calee guiltily focused her thoughts on the ship, and on Bram. It required only a moment's concentration to determine that the ship had drifted off course—not enough to be a problem yet, but far more than was acceptable.

Bram was dressed and engaged in another of the seemingly interminable equipment checks that were so much a part of a pilot's life. He gave no sign he was aware of her presence, but Calee could clearly sense his growing impatience at the time their passage *within* was taking. Satisfied that Bram was safe and the ship at least not dangerously off course, she once more withdrew.

Calee knew the hours ahead would be punishingly intense. They were approaching the midpoint of the journey *within*, where the songs became even more confused and tangled and the possibility of becoming lost increased enormously. Once she renewed her close link with Bram, there would be no rest for either of them until they were well past midpoint and the ship was once again securely on course. For right now, she needed to take advantage of these last few minutes of relative privacy to tend to her own needs.

Roughly, Calee ran the towel she held over her shoulders and arms, then down her sides. Though the room was warm, the lingering dampness from her bath made it seem cooler. Her skin pricked into bumps and she shivered.

It was just a little shiver, but it was enough to rouse in Calee an unaccustomed and intensely disturbing awareness of her own slender body. Her hand that clutched the heavy towel froze in its path.

How delicate her bones were, she thought, staring down at herself in surprise. She'd never really noticed before.

Her skin was pale, not dark like Bram's, and the downy hair on the backs of her hands and along her arms was so light-colored it was almost invisible.

Slowly, wonderingly, she dragged the towel up her arm, across the ridge of her shoulder bone, then down the curving arc of her breast. She'd never paid attention before, but her breasts were lovely. Not too large, yet full and high and firm. Even Bram, with his large hands, would not be able to encompass one of them completely.

That didn't mean she wouldn't fit perfectly in his hand. If he tucked his hand under her breast just so, he could hold her in his palm and still run his thumb across the delicate nipple. He could touch that pale pink circle, caress it until it grew taut and pointed—just as it was hardening now under the stimulus of her hungry imaginings.

At sight of that blatant evidence of her physical response, Calee clutched the towel even tighter, pressing it against her breast as if it could wipe out the irresistible images in her mind.

It couldn't. No matter how hard she pressed, the vivid, startling pictures in her mind remained. A part of her she'd never known existed exulted in that fact.

Calee trembled, torn between the heated cravings of her traitorous body and the knowledge that she must somehow stop this madness. Yet even as her rational mind struggled for control, her woman's heart, so long denied, urged her on.

Without her willing it, Calee's hand dragged the towel away from her breast and down her body.

Bram would follow the same sweet path. He would slide his hand down across her belly, slowly, savoring the heat of her and the quivering tension in her muscles that was generated by his touch. His palm would be hot against her flesh as he first traced the inward-curve of her waist, then swept over her hips until—

Enough!

With a choking cry, Calee threw the towel against the far wall, then dropped to her knees, gasping for air.

From somewhere in her mind—some small, rational part of her mind that still clung to the last shreds of her pride—Calee watched her own agony. Watched, and was ashamed.

What had she done? She was a dreamer. She had her work, her room, her life. What madness had induced her to first betray her responsibilities as dreamer by intruding on Bram's privacy, then stoop so low that she could indulge her own lustful thoughts in such a contemptible way?

Helpless, Calee cowered under the lashings of her own conscience as the hungry need burning inside her raged hotter. The warring forces of shame and desire might have torn her very soul apart if madness hadn't claimed her first.

At least, Calee thought it must be madness. There was no one in the room with her, yet she could have sworn she felt the soft brush of a gentle hand across her cheek, comforting her.

She froze, willing her heart to stop pounding and her breathing to still so she could catch that caress when it came again.

A minute passed, then two. Nothing happened.

Calee drew a ragged breath, still fighting for calm, then slowly pushed to her feet.

It had been a faint and very fleeting touch, the kind a faint breath of air might have made. There was no way it could have been Bram. After all, he was half a galaxy away. He wasn't a dreamer.

He couldn't cross that vast distance as she could, couldn't link with her mind the way she could link with his.

There was absolutely no way it could have been Bram.

Calee wished with all her heart that it had been.

Her legs were weak and trembling, but they held her. Her hands shook, but she managed to pull on a clean gown and fasten it. For a moment, her fingers hesitated over the fastenings at her throat; then she hastily closed the collar all the way up to her chin.

With fumbling fingers, she undid the heavy coils of her hair that she'd pinned up before she'd bathed, slowly shaking them free until the strands fell around her shoulders like a veil.

She was ready. She had no further excuse for delay.

At the sight of her chamber and the dreaming couch, Calee faltered.

Somehow, despite her unforgivable self-absorption, she'd neither broken her connection with Bram nor lost the faint, fragile thread that would lead her to the star they sought. But Calee wasn't sure she could go on. Hadn't she just proven how unworthy she was?

You have no choice.

Calee sat down on the edge of the couch. Her fingers dug into the heavy silken throws that covered it, clinging to them as if they could anchor her in the safety of this quiet chamber.

You have no choice.

Kassta had spoken those words to her an eternity ago, it seemed. But this time it wasn't Kassta speaking. This time Calee knew she herself had voiced them. She was right, she had no choice.

She wouldn't leave Bram *within*, not even if there were another dreamer available to take her place. She'd promised him she would take him where he was going, and no matter what it cost her, that was what she would do.

If only it didn't cost so much!

Without intending it, Bram had shattered the safe, comfortable shell Calee had drawn about herself. He'd set free a woman Calee had never known existed inside her, a woman who felt and yearned and hungered in ways Calee had never dared, a woman who was a part of her, but who would never again be content with the sheltered existence of a dreamer.

Calee forced her hands to unclench, then lay back on the couch and shut her eyes, letting her breathing slow, her mind relax. She had her work. For now, that would have to be enough.

Bram was on the bridge of his ship, restlessly pacing back and forth.

"You certainly took your own sweet time." His words hit against her mind like stones flung at glass, shattering the fragile calm that Calee had struggled so hard to achieve.

"I'm sorry," she said. *More sorry than you will ever know.*

He didn't respond. Calee could feel the tension in him. Tension and a dark, hungry longing she could not identify and did not understand, even though it stirred an achingly responsive chord deep inside her.

Calee fiercely repressed a sudden urge to probe Bram's mind. There was no need to compound her sins by intruding further, no matter how badly she wanted to understand the source of the strange, tormenting emotion that drove him, and that found an answering resonance in her.

She could be grateful for one thing, at least: Bram couldn't possibly know what had happened in the privacy of her chamber. Just because he'd felt her . . . indiscretion when he'd scraped his hand didn't mean he could have shared her shameful fantasies on Dreamworld.

Calee pushed down the memory of a hand brushing softly against her cheek. Her imagination had conjured the sensation of that touch. Her imagination was no doubt tricking her into thinking there was something more than anger in his reception of her now.

"Are you ready, then?" he demanded as he took his seat in front of the command console.

"I'm ready." It was a lie, but there was nothing else she could say.

Bram reluctantly lowered the mental barriers he'd once more constructed against her. Calee just as reluctantly merged her perceptions with his.

Because of her inattention to her duty, the ship was now significantly off course. That, combined with the fact they were now so deep *within* meant the hours ahead would be long, hard, and exhausting. Both she and Bram would have to spend those hours totally focused on their work. There would be no opportunity for self-indulgence, no chance for any indiscretion.

It was small comfort, but it was the only comfort Calee could find.

According to the onboard clock, day passed into night and night once more passed into day before Calee was sure they could leave the ship on automatic pilot. Only her dreamer's perceptions told Calee how close they were to their journey's end. Despite the vast distance they'd covered, the dark outside the ship remained as formless and overwhelming as before.

Calee gratefully loosened the mental bonds she'd maintained with Bram for so long, letting an awareness of her own body seep into her mind once more. With a weary sigh, she curled into a tight ball, tensing her muscles to relieve the cramp of having lain still for so long.

She was exhausted. The hours she'd spent dreaming would have been grueling under any conditions. This time, coupled with her lack of sleep and the emotional tension between her and Bram, they'd ground her into near insensibility. She had to sleep, at least for a few hours, and Bram needed to rest just as much as she did.

Even though her work was done—for now, at least—Calee couldn't help letting her mind accompany Bram as he wearily trailed through the ship, running a last visual check on equipment before he allowed himself to stop.

Over the past hours he'd kept his thoughts and feelings carefully sealed away from her, as if he distrusted her ability to keep her distance. He had reason to doubt her, Calee sadly acknowledged, but his self-imposed isolation hurt, deeply.

She lingered despite the hurt, drifting at the edges of his mind, unwilling to let go. Only when Bram finally crawled into bed did she feel free to rest. As she slipped into oblivion, Calee couldn't help reaching out to reassure herself that Bram was still there, waiting for her in his sleep.

She awoke to the feel of a hand softly trailing down her cheek and along the line of her jaw. A thumb brushed across her lips, slowly tracing their outline.

It was a dream, of course. She squeezed her eyes shut, willing herself not to wake.

Once more the thumb swept across her lips. Calee's mouth opened in a sigh. She could feel the warmth as her breath reflected off that tormenting thumb and back onto her lips. She opened her mouth further, inviting the touch to deepen.

Instead, the thumb was replaced by a man's mouth—Bram's mouth. She'd never felt his lips before. Certainly never this way, pressing hard and hot and hungry against hers. She'd never imagined his tongue exploring her mouth like this—probing deep, as though he could reach the very core of her, demanding her surrender.

Calee surrendered willingly.

He didn't stay to savor the victory. His mouth abandoned hers as his tongue traced a line of fire down and around the curve of her chin, over the slight hollow on the inside of her jaw, then along her throat, just above where her pulse beat.

Calee gasped and rocked her head back against the cushions, opening her body to his tormenting exploration.

It was, after all, just a dream. Had to be a dream, because there were no barriers to protect her against Bram's questing mouth. There was no collar to be opened, no silken gown to be pushed aside when he placed a kiss at the base of her throat, then let his tongue once more lead him downward. Calee lay open to him, vulnerable, yet unafraid.

Gently, Bram brushed back a heavy lock of hair that had fallen across her breast. The silken strands slid over her skin in a tantalizingly light caress, preparing her for the even more tantalizing heat of his hand as he circled her breast, then cupped it in his hand.

"You wanted this." Bram's voice whispered in her mind, rich with promise. "And this."

Once more Calee gasped, shaken by the electrifying sensation of his thumb gently rubbing back and forth across the tip of her nipple, rousing it to a hard, hungry peak. She arched against him, into his touch.

"I know you wanted this." Bram's mouth claimed her nipple, surrounding it in a wet heat that magnified a dozen times over the electric energy surging through her.

Calee tangled her fingers in his hair so he couldn't abandon her. He was right. This was what she wanted, what she'd always wanted.

An inarticulate cry of exultation burst from her as he pressed his tongue against her breast, drawing her even deeper into his mouth.

Yes, this *was* what she'd wanted. This man, this moment. And if she could only have them in her dreams, then so be it. She was a dreamer, wasn't she?

"It's no dream, Calee. I'm here with you, as real as if I were here in the flesh."

The words were hard and insistent despite their breathless rasp. Calee froze, listening for some lingering echo in the room around her. When none came, she forced her eyes open, willing herself to waken.

She was alone.

"I *am* here, Calee. Here where it matters. In your mind . . . and your heart."

Calee could have sworn his fingers touched her breast, just above her heart. She brought her own hands up to cover the spot. They encountered nothing but the heavy silk of her gown. Her hand flew to her throat and found her collar, still fastened all the way up to her chin.

"You know I'm here, Calee. You can feel me, feel my touch."

"But how—?"

"Let yourself go, Calee," he pleaded. "All we have is the present, and that present is us. You and me. Right now."

"I can't—"

"You can. Remember?"

Bram kissed her again, on her hand this time, just as she had imagined he'd kissed her when he scraped his knuckles. She clenched her hand into a fist and held it tight against her chest.

"You can't be here," she protested. "Not like this."

"I am. Don't ask me how. Maybe you brought me here, or maybe, just for you, I can cross the universe. I don't know." His voice in her mind grew deeper, softer, infinitely sensual. "It doesn't matter, anyway. Nothing matters except the here and now. Nothing."

Once more Bram's hand caressed her cheek, then dropped to sweep across her breast and side in a touch that was feather light, yet searingly intense.

Calee desperately clutched at the fabric of her gown, trying to drive out the tingling, aching heat he'd left in his wake. It didn't help. The heavy silk only kept her locked inside herself. It couldn't keep Bram out, no mattered how much she wanted it to.

"Go away!" Calee shouted the words, fighting back tears.

"I can't." Bram's arms enfolded her, drawing her tight against his broad, bare chest. "I woke in the dark, Calee, but I wasn't alone because you were there in my mind. As much a part of me as my eyes or my hands or my heart. I can't explain it. I don't want to try. I only know I want you. I want to hold you like this and make love to you for as long as you're with me."

Calee gulped back the tears that threatened her, then shook her head fiercely, fighting off temptation. "We can't make love. Not really. What kind of lovemaking would it be?"

"It would be wonderful."

"But—"

"Don't you understand? Making love isn't just about sex, Calee. It's about mind and heart and soul. It's about imagination as much as physical desire."

"That's crazy!"

"Is it?" Bram's question was gentle with understanding.

He lightly brushed a finger along the outside of her arm, barely grazing her skin. Calee's body trembled, then tensed in automatic, involuntary response to the heat generated by his fleeting touch.

"You see?"

Calee could have sworn he'd whispered in her ear. His breath tickled, sending shivers along her spine.

"How many people have ever touched your arm?" Bram demanded. "A dozen? A hundred? More? Have you ever responded to their touch as you responded to mine, even once?"

"No." Calee drew the word out shakily. It was half protest, half plea. If he'd asked, she couldn't have said what she was protesting against, or what she was begging for. She was afraid he'd know without even asking.

"I love you, Calee. A few hours ago, I would have laughed at the idea. I wouldn't laugh now." His hands cupped her face, cradling it as if he could drink in the sight of her. When he spoke again, his words formed slowly, thoughtfully.

"It was strange. When I went to sleep, I was determined to keep you as far from me as possible. When I woke . . ." Bram hesitated, as though he still wasn't sure he hadn't been dreaming. "When I woke, I suddenly felt as if something that was missing had been found. I felt . . . whole. Because *you* were there, Calee. Because all the walls we've both worked so hard to keep between us were gone. Because you're a part of me, whether you realize it or not."

Calee's mind spun, wildly grasping for some stable point in a universe suddenly turned upside down.

He loved her. The words shone as bright as a sun gone nova, illuminating all the hidden recesses of her heart. Calee wasn't sure she could bear the brilliance.

What did it mean to love and be loved in return? Was she capable of loving? Could she give back even a small portion of what he offered her so freely?

Bram silenced the unspoken questions by claiming her mouth in a kiss that burned away her doubts and fears. "Just take the moment for what it is, Calee. I can't give you any more than that."

Bram's words hit her with the shock of ice against warm flesh. "What do you mean?" Calee could hear the sudden panic in her mind.

She reached for him, desperately wanting the reassurance of his touch even if he wasn't really there. His arms wrapped around her, as warmly comforting and reassuringly strong as if he really could reach across the vastness to hold her tight against him.

Unlike his touch, his words seemed to come from a great distance. "We have a few more hours until we cross back into normal space, Calee. That's all the future I can promise you. Beyond that . . ."

Bram's thought trailed off. It didn't matter. He didn't need to finish.

What lay beyond was an unknown planet and a deadly enemy he would have to face alone. Regardless of her protests or her prayers, there was nothing Calee could do to change it. Absolutely nothing.

Bram was right. They had this moment and each other. There was nothing more and never would be, no matter how many years might lie ahead.

With that admission, the last, crumbling bricks in Calee's mental wall collapsed and disappeared.

Tentatively at first, then with greater sureness, she reached toward Bram. She needed to touch him, just as he had touched her. Needed to feel his body move beneath her hands, feel the heat of him against her skin.

With their joining, a flash of white-hot sensation claimed Calee, bursting inside her with the coruscating fire of a solar flare. She gasped. Her eyes closed and her head dropped back as she arched to meet Bram and draw him closer still, close enough so she'd never have to let go. Not ever.

Yet even as she gave herself to Bram, Calee

could hear the stars singing somewhere deep in her mind. Their voices sounded weaker than before, as if the fire that burned inside her drew its heat from them, robbing them of their strength.

It was impossible, but it was a potent reminder that nothing endured forever, not even the stars.

They were approaching the point where they would cross over into normal space. Calee could *feel* the star they sought. Its voice rang in her mind with almost deafening clarity and power. The deep bass notes that had made it so distinctive reverberated inside her, infusing her with the strength she needed for these last few minutes, the most difficult of the entire journey.

Crossovers were always dangerous. Ships had to emerge at just the right point, close enough to the final destination so the pilots didn't waste days traveling in normal space to reach it, but far enough away that there was no risk of being drawn in to the nearest sun.

The difficulty was that the pilots were still running blind, their instruments useless, and the dreamers were struggling to thread their way among the stars' songs, which were even more tangled at the boundary with normal space than deeper *within*. To make matters worse, both pilots and dreamers were physically and mentally exhausted by the long hours and days of travel and the stress of the mental link that had bound them so closely for all that time.

This crossing would be the worst Calee had ever made. Not because of the crossover itself, but because she would have to sever her link with Bram once they were on the other side.

She didn't want to let him go. For the first time in her life, she was alive—vividly, achingly, humanly *alive*, and all because of a man who lived in the physical present and who had taught her, a woman who lived in her mind, what it was to dream.

Across the vastness that separated them, he had reached out and unlocked the woman inside her, shown her the infinite possibilities open to her if she were brave enough to take them. He'd taught her what passion was and the glorious promise of her own sexuality. Most of all, he had taught her how to love.

She couldn't let him go. Not now. Not ever.

And yet that was what she would do the moment his ship's systems confirmed he was where he was supposed to be. She had to. His assignment was too important to risk by interfering.

But once he was finished . . .

"You promise?"

Bram's words formed in Calee's mind with startling clarity, overlaid with an amusement that totally failed to disguise the yearning beneath.

A hot, bright flare of hope burst inside her, almost, but not quite, smothering the fear. The future lay ahead, if only she had the courage to take it.

The trouble was, in these last hours as they'd approached the crossover point, there'd been more than enough time for her fears to come creeping back in, pushing out the confidence that Calee had found in the heat of passion.

"Dreamers are forbidden to have any contact with pilots outside of the limits of their work." Defensive, cowardly words, but they rose in Calee's mind automatically before she had a chance to suppress them.

Given all that lay between them, all the wondrous dreams that she yearned to claim for her own, Calee knew her response was foolish—or worse. But dreaming of happiness was one thing, reaching out to grab it quite another.

Bram smiled. Calee could *feel* the sensuous, stirring memories that rose to the surface of his mind at her hedging response.

"Dreamers are forbidden quite a lot of things, Calee, most of which we've indulged in over the last few days," he reminded her gently.

"Where would we go? What would we do?" Even though she didn't speak out loud, her words sounded breathless, eager.

"Rom is beautiful. And if that doesn't suit . . ." Calee drew in a sharp breath at the feel of his hand softly caressing her cheek, tracing the line of her throat. "If that doesn't suit," Bram continued, "we'll find something else. There's a whole universe out here, Calee, and it belongs to us, you and me, if only we have the courage to take it."

It belongs to us. Calee grabbed his words and held them against her heart as if they were tangible things she could lock away, safe inside her, forever and ever.

"Do you promise there will be an afterward, Calee?" Bram prodded.

Calee couldn't help hearing the fear and hope that mingled in him, just as it did in her. Somehow, the knowledge that he shared her doubts, that he was as afraid as she was, reassured Calee in a way no words of encouragement could.

"I promise." Calee couldn't breathe. With two words she had committed herself to a future that carried no guarantees and offered no security. Those considerations didn't seem to matter very much right now. "Oh, yes, Bram. I promise!"

She refused to consider that he might be the one incapable of keeping that promise—not because he didn't want to, but because he couldn't. Whatever awaited him on the other side of the boundary they were so rapidly approaching would care nothing for mere human promises or human hopes.

"I'm coming back, Calee." His words were fierce and hard with determination.

"I'll be here, waiting for you." Calee would have said more, but there was no time. The crossover point was too near.

Working as one, Calee and Bram merged their perceptions to guide the scout ship across a deadly barrier they could neither see nor touch. After several long, anxious minutes of struggle, they burst into normal space with a gut-wrenching jolt.

For Calee, the crossover was far more unpleasant than the first. This time her senses were so closely linked with Bram's that she suffered his physical reaction to the transition more acutely.

She tried to share his jubilation at the successful crossing, but deep inside her, her heart was protesting the need to leave him. There was nothing more she could do, no help she could offer that would justify her staying. His mission was too important to allow her own wants and needs to interfere.

Already Bram was testing every system and monitor on his ship, assuring himself that everything was fully functional and that he was exactly where he ought to be. Her task was ended. In a few minutes, once Bram's equipment had confirmed what her senses already told her, Calee would have to break her link with him. She had no choice and neither did he. They both had to fulfill their individual responsibilities, regardless of their personal feelings.

It wouldn't be long, Calee told herself firmly. He'd scan the planet, determine if it really was as rich in gallnite as the robot probe had indicated, then report back to his superiors, one way or the other. At worst, Bram would have to wait a few hours, perhaps a few days until the United Forces cruiser that followed them showed up to destroy the planet, if that proved necessary. A straightforward assignment, really, with the only risk being that a Gromin ship would show up before the cruiser.

At the thought of the Gromin, Calee flinched. She'd almost forgotten them in her self-absorbed misery at having to leave Bram. She shouldn't have. They posed a far greater threat to his safety than anything else about this assignment.

With guilty haste, she scanned the nearby space, searching for any mental trace of the vicious aliens. Bram's sensors hadn't picked up anything, but that didn't mean much. The Gromin ships weren't easy to spot. She would probably feel the creatures' powerful if incomprehensible minds before his equipment could spot their ships.

Although she stretched her dreamer's sense to its limit, Calee could find no hint of the aliens' presence, either around the planet they sought or anywhere near the planet's sun. Calee relaxed. Thank the stars her inattention hadn't had more dangerous results.

Bram was still intent on his ship and its instruments, and his thoughts turned from her to the mission ahead of him. Calee longed to intrude, to grab a few more precious minutes with him. She didn't. The quicker he finished his work here, the sooner he could return to her. Until then, she would have to be content with the little time left until he officially dismissed her, releasing her from her assignment to him.

Calee tried to distract her thoughts by concentrating on the stars, but they had no more power to tempt her now than they'd had earlier. In just a few short days her universe had expanded to include a man who meant more to her than all the stars in the heavens. The songs that had for so long been her refuge from life had become nothing more than background music to the complex symphony of her love for Bram and of his for her.

Perhaps that was why Calee scarcely noticed when the first discordant notes intruded. It took a few minutes before the harsh, sharp notes registered on her conscious mind, a few seconds more before she could identify them.

"Gromin!" Calee's voice broke on the panic rising inside her. She ignored it, too intent on restoring her close mental link with Bram to heed her own fears.

"Where? My sensors don't show—"

"They're *within*. Two, no, three ships. Small ships like yours, but coming fast." Calee opened her mind further, desperately trying to connect what she sensed with what Bram's ship was telling him. It was impossible. So long as the ships remained *within*, his sensors could detect nothing.

"Break off, Calee!" Bram's voice in her mind was insistent, taut with urgency. His own mind raced as he considered, then discarded, a dozen courses of action. "I'll head toward the planet, use its mass to shield my presence. The Gromin won't know I'm here until it's too late. Break off, I tell you!"

"They'll know! So far as I can tell, they haven't picked up your presence yet, but they will. Have you forgotten they aren't blind when they're *within*, like you are? The minute they cross over they'll be scanning the planet, looking for the same thing that brought us here. Their scanners are going to pick you up, and you can't fight them, not all three of them. Let the cruiser deal with them. You have to run, Bram. You *have* to!"

Bram heard her fear, but he ignored it, just as he ignored the answering fear inside him that Calee could sense beneath the surface of his thoughts.

"The cruiser might be too late. I can't let the Gromin through, Calee. If there's any gallnite on the planet, even a little . . . Go back to Dream-world, Calee. Now! This isn't your fight, it's mine. Go back where you're safe."

This was the reality he was accustomed to, Calee realized with a shock, a reality where fear and the possibility of injury or death were always present and nothing was ever certain. It suddenly hit her just how much she was risking by choosing to accompany him.

If she remained linked with him, she would inevitably share whatever he experienced. His fears would become hers. If he were injured, she would suffer the same pain. If he died . . . Calee swallowed, fighting down her rising panic. If he died and they were still linked together, then she could very well die with him.

It wasn't too late to change her mind. She could still retreat, return to her safe life on Dreamworld and let Bram deal with the Gromin. They were a part of his world, not hers, and he was far better prepared to cope with the danger they represented than she was.

The thought brought a swift stab of pain, then anger. If Bram could be afraid and still function, so could she. She wasn't going to leave him, no matter what the price of her staying.

Ignoring his protests, Calee forced her way deeper into his thoughts, opening her mind so that they merged to become one, just as they had when they'd crossed back into normal space so short a time ago.

Bram's objections didn't last long. He knew as well as Calee that he needed the advantage her unique perceptions gave him. Alone, he stood little chance against the Gromin ships. With her help, the scales were a little more evenly balanced, even if they did still tip in favor of the approaching aliens.

"Show me where the nearest ship will cross over," he commanded her. "If I can eliminate that first one, before the other two suspect we're here . . ."

Even as he pushed his ship at top speed toward the point Calee showed him, Bram checked his weapons, weighed his options. They weren't many, but that didn't slow him. When the first Gromin ship dropped into normal space, Bram was ready. The ship flared once as its engines exploded under his deadly fire, then it was gone from the monitors, utterly destroyed.

One ship down and two to go, Calee thought, and the advantage of surprise was gone. The second ship was already crossing over and the third wasn't far behind.

"Take us *within*, Calee. Now!"

In the few seconds before the pilots of the remaining Gromin ships realized what had happened and turned toward them, Calee located a safe crossover point. Bram drove his ship over at a dangerously high speed, heedless of the risk.

"Can you still locate those two ships?" Bram demanded, ignoring the wrenching physical effects of the crossing. "Bring me between them, so they'll be in each other's line of fire when I emerge."

Calee had no time to admire his strategy or wonder at his ability to think at all under the circumstances. She simply obeyed his orders, as responsive to his commands as his ship, as much a part of him as his hands and eyes.

Bram's ploy worked long enough for him to fire on both ships, seriously damaging one. Then he was turning again, using his ship's greater speed and maneuverability to head toward the vessel that had been hit the hardest.

For a few brief seconds during the turn he was completely exposed. The other Gromin ship didn't miss the opportunity. Bram's craft rocked with the force of the blast that hit his ship. Warning lights lit up all across the control panel, but Bram didn't hesitate. He was already firing his own weapons, aiming for the heart of the crippled ship in front of him. Once more a bright, fiery star exploded on the viewscreen, then just as quickly faded into nothingness.

Two down and one to go.

If only it were that simple. The remaining Gromin ship was only slightly damaged and its weapons were far superior to their pitiful remaining stock. At the same time, the hit they'd taken on the starboard side had severely limited the maneuverability of their smaller ship.

Calee had to struggle to suppress the fear that threatened to swamp her. Up until now, the fighting had been so fast and furious, she hadn't had a chance to be scared. Now she was terrified.

"We'll get him, Calee. Hang in there!" Bram's voice in her mind was wildly, fiercely exultant.

Instead of reassuring her, Bram's excitement frightened Calee even more. Whatever fear he'd felt had burned away in the heat of battle, leaving a hot blood lust in its place that appalled her.

This raging warrior wasn't Bram. Not the Bram she knew, anyway. Here was raw power, a savage force that recognized no law, knew no pity, and would not pause until it had destroyed its opponents, or been destroyed by them.

"Give it up, Bram," Calee pleaded. On Dreamworld, her body shook with the fear that consumed her. Tears streamed down her face unchecked. She scarcely noticed. "You can't fight them, not now. I'll take you back *within*. They can't find you there. Give it up!"

He brushed her pleas aside. Almost by sheer will he dragged his ship around in a tight arc that would put him in position to fire on the remaining Gromin. The damaged hull screamed with the strain.

Bram fought against the enormous, invisible forces generated by the turn. His muscles bulged with the effort; the slightest movement sent wracking pain shooting through him—and through Calee.

"Bram! Give it up!"

"I can't, Calee! Don't you see? All they need is one ship and they can collect enough gallnite to kill millions of people. I can't run away. Not now!"

He was right. Bram wouldn't run away from this fight, not even if it meant his life.

Neither would she.

With grim resolution Calee tightened her mental link with Bram, then let her awareness expand until everything around them seemed magnified and sharpened. She ignored Bram's pain and the agony it generated in her, ignored the screaming alarms that sounded throughout the ship, ignored everything except the need to destroy the alien ship by whatever means possible.

Bram began firing the instant the Gromin came in range. His small ship rocked with the force of the recoil, then shuddered as another Gromin blast glanced off the hull.

The alien ship took two direct hits, none fatal. It fired again, and this time it struck home.

The blast ripped through the hull of Bram's ship, shredding it as easily as if it were made of paper and opening the outer passages and storage rooms to the raw vacuum of space. Even though the heavily shielded bridge area wasn't hit directly, its protective walls buckled, ripping loose half the equipment and control panels in the room.

One of the panels caught Bram in the chest, flinging him out of his chair and pinning him against the main console, mercilessly crushing him.

Calee screamed at the agony that ripped through Bram, then through her. An overwhelming, devouring darkness threatened to swallow her and drag her down. The pain was so great, Calee almost let go and let the darkness take her.

Almost. Then she remembered Bram. He was there, just at the edge of her mind, and he was alive.

Heedless of the risk, Calee fought to restore her link with Bram. He heard her, even through the pain.

"You can't stay. Not now." His thoughts were vague, unfocused, but he was struggling valiantly to regain control.

"I won't leave you. Not like this." Calee shuddered, horrified by the extent of his injuries. His left arm hung useless. Blood dripped from a dozen deep cuts on his face and chest. At least three and perhaps four of his ribs were broken.

It was the internal injuries that frightened her most. He was bleeding inside and there was nothing, absolutely nothing, she could do to help.

"Got to leave. Can't stay." The words cost Bram an effort. With a stifled groan, he used his right arm to pull himself up the edge of the console.

"Don't move!"

"Where's the Gromin ship?" Bram was on his feet, weaving unsteadily and clinging to the console for support as he tried to focus on the monitors and controls that were still working.

"You can't—"

"Got one good blast left."

"Bram—!"

"All it takes is one." Bram's words might be slurred, but the iron will inside him was still hard and strong.

Calee didn't try to protest. Despite her fear,

despite the pain that threatened to consume her, something in his determination roused an answering determination in her. They couldn't let the Gromin win. Especially not now.

"What are we going to do?" she asked.

Bram shook his head. Calee gasped at the sharp pain that shot through her. "Me. Not you," he insisted. "You can't stay."

"You *need* me."

Bram's right hand tightened around a torn metal edge of the console. Among all his injuries, he scarcely noticed the blood welling from this new cut on his palm. Calee winced and hugged her own aching hand tight against her chest.

This time Bram's words rang hard and clear in her mind. "You're already suffering what I am, Calee. If I die . . ." He faltered as a sudden wave of pain swept through him. "If I die, then you run the risk of dying, too."

"You're not going to die!" Calee protested hotly, taking refuge in anger because it was safer than confronting her fear.

"Calee, I—"

"The Gromin! They're coming up behind us!"

"Where?" Bram scanned the damaged control panel, then thumped it in frustration. "My sensors are gone! I can't see them!"

Calee opened her mind further, sharing her awareness of the approaching aliens. "There they are."

Bram could scarcely stand. His breathing was ragged and uneven. Every movement was pure torment and he was weakening rapidly. All that paled to insignificance compared to the necessity of destroying the remaining Gromin ship.

Using one hand and Calee's senses as his guide, Bram worked feverishly to get his remaining weapons working. "They think they got us, but they're not sure. That means we have a chance."

The Gromin ship crept closer.

"That's it," Bram crooned. "Just a little closer. I don't want to miss this time. Closer." He slammed his fist down on the weapons release.

The ship bucked beneath his feet. Bram staggered, then fell against the console. Pain ripped through him, shattering the remnants of his self-control.

This time Calee didn't scream as Bram's pain ripped through her, too. She was fighting too hard to maintain her link with him and track the Gromin ship at the same time.

An instant later, the enemy ship disappeared in a violent, fiery explosion.

"You got it!"

Bram heard her. Despite the pain, he managed a wobbly grin. "It'll do." The grin turned to a grimace as he sagged forward onto the console, too weak even to sink to the floor. "It'll have to."

Panic struck Calee. Bram was dying. She was half a galaxy away and his ship's limited medical facilities had been destroyed by the Gromin blast. He was going to bleed to death before the United Forces cruiser that was following them could arrive.

Bram knew it, too. He rested his forehead on the cold metal of the console, fighting for breath.

"Let go, Calee. Now, before it's too late." His eyes closed at the pain sweeping through him. "Farewell, dreamer," he whispered. "May the songs be ever sweet."

A sob tore at Calee's throat. His words were the traditional words from pilot to dreamer at the end of a journey. She didn't want to hear them now.

"No!" The fury of her denial astounded even herself. "You're not going to die! I won't let you!"

"Calee—"

"We still have work to do. We came to find out if there was any gallnite on this planet and that's what we're going to do." If he wouldn't fight for himself and he didn't have enough faith in her love for him to fight for the future, then maybe, Calee thought desperately, just maybe he might listen to the call of duty.

Bram groaned, but he was listening. "The planet?"

"That's right. We're going down to the planet."

From somewhere deep inside her, Calee found the strength to push past the pain and fear and doubts that threatened to overwhelm her. Bram wasn't going to die. She wouldn't let him. It was as simple as that.

Pleading and bullying by turns, she forced Bram into taking his ship down. If all else failed, she would keep him too occupied even to think of dying.

Her ploy seemed to work. At one point he grumbled weakly, "In case you forgot, *I'm* the pilot. You're not even supposed to be here."

"Well, I'm here and I'm staying," Calee retorted, encouraged by his display of spirit. She refused to think about what it might have cost him.

"That doesn't sound like someone who's spent most of her life playing it safe and following the rules."

His words brought Calee up short. She wasn't sure she could even remember what it felt like to be safe or secure or comfortable.

A few days ago she'd refused even to give Bram her name. Now her body burned with the shared torments of his injuries. Fear had become her constant companion, lying in wait ready to pounce on her whenever she allowed it out. Her future might soon be measured in minutes rather than years.

None of that mattered. Not when weighed against the precious gift that Bram had brought into her life. The love she'd won was worth any price. Of that Calee was certain.

They were sweeping down toward the planet in a low, unstable trajectory when Bram, prodded by an increasingly frightened and desperate Calee, set the remaining scanner to sweep the planet for traces of gallnite.

Her heart twisted at the effort such a simple task cost him. Even though she'd finally detected the United Forces cruiser that was rapidly approaching crossover, she wasn't sure Bram could last long enough for them to reach him.

Her own strength was dwindling just as fast, but she wasn't letting go. Not even if it cost her her life. If the cruiser arrived too late to save him, at least Bram would not die alone.

"It's there."

Calee jumped, startled by Bram's words in her mind. For what seemed like ages, he'd been far too weak to say anything at all.

"What are you talking about?"

"The gallnite. It's all there, just like the probe said."

He was right. They only had one scanner and it wasn't working very well, but it clearly revealed the presence of large amounts of gallnite beneath the planet's surface.

Calee couldn't help sharing Bram's relief. It would have been such a bitter irony to die because an ancient probe had malfunctioned and reported the presence of something that wasn't even there.

The landing was excruciatingly rough. With the ship so badly damaged and Bram so weak, they were lucky to land at all, but that last jostling was more than Bram's shattered body could bear. With a low moan, he crumpled into a heap on the floor.

"Bram!" Calee's sharp cry echoed in her small chamber, but she wasn't sure Bram had heard her—or if he even could. "You can't die! You can't!"

If only she could grab him and shake him! If only she could fight through the swirling mists that were pulling on him so insistently, and that were dragging her into the abyss with him.

"I love you, Bram!"

The mists retreated, just a little.

"You have to hang on, do you hear me? Help's

coming. You have to hang on till then."

The mists swirled back up, licking at her with the same hungry tongues as they licked at Bram.

"I love you!"

The mists rose higher still, wrapping around her and threatening to suck her under.

"Promise you'll *wait* for me, Bram," Calee cried, her voice choked with the tears streaming down her face. "Promise me!"

"I promise."

His words were faint, almost unintelligible, and they were the last thing Calee heard before the dark mists claimed her.

"Are you really sure this is what you want, Calee?" Dame Kassta asked, very quietly.

Calee glanced up at the older woman beside her, then turned her gaze back to the shuttle that sat waiting for her at the far edge of the lawn. When she was ready, the shuttle would take her to the ship now in orbit around Dreamworld, a ship that had been summoned specifically for her.

When she was ready. Calee's hands tightened around the handle of the small bag that held everything she was taking with her.

Even here, in front of the entrance to the vast labyrinth that was the heart of Dreamworld, she felt lost. She hadn't been outside the walls of the complex since she'd come to Dreamworld as a child. She'd never even considered leaving the safety and security those walls provided . . . until now.

"Perhaps you should wait until you're stronger," Kassta urged. "After all, it's only been a few days. This pilot you're seeking won't be able to leave the medical center for a while. Once he recovers, he could come here and—"

"No." Calee shook her head emphatically. "Bram needs me now."

Bram had almost died, and she'd almost died with him. Her attendants had found her unconscious in her chamber, her life force draining away as fast as his. Although they'd tried, not even the most skilled dreamers had been able to break her mental link with Bram until the United Forces cruiser had found him and she'd been sure he would survive.

Maintaining her mental link with Bram was one thing, however. Actually leaving Dreamworld and the safe, secure life she had known was quite another.

As she had so many times over the past few days, Calee mentally reached out to Bram, seeking reassurance.

"I'm waiting." His words formed gently in her mind, heavy with unspoken promises.

"I'm coming," she replied, comforted. "Soon."

Without relinquishing her link to Bram, Calee turned to face Kassta. "I have to go now."

Kassta hesitated for a moment, then nodded. In her eyes Calee read understanding . . . and acceptance.

"Yes," Kassta said. "It is time."

Her small bag firmly clasped in her hand, Calee started down the steps, then stopped abruptly as a sudden thought struck her. She was starting out on a voyage that would last for the rest of her life. It might be wise to begin it properly.

Shutting her eyes, Calee let her mind fly free across the vast, empty space that still separated her from Bram. "The stars have a voice, pilot," she offered softly, knowing he'd understand. "I would share their songs."

Calee could feel Bram's smile. He understood.

"The future calls, dreamer," he replied, his voice in her mind strong and sure. "I would share the journey."

For the first time in days, Calee smiled, too.

Head high, she walked on down the steps and across the lawn to the waiting shuttle.

Dear Reader:

I hope you enjoyed *Dream Seeker*. The story comes from my deeply held belief that love is as much a matter of the mind and imagination as of the heart and that the joy born when a man and a woman love each other springs from more than just the physical relationship.

The story also demonstrates the freedom that futuristic romance gives writers to explore this puzzling, marvelous thing we call love. Within a futuristic romance, the writer is able to wander the byways of dreams and fantasies as well as explore the broad highways of our romantic traditions; she is free to venture out to the stars as well as into the heart, and with that freedom she can create stories as rich and real and, above all, as romantic as any of the more traditional romances. More than anything else, I think futuristic romances are a vote for optimism in a world where pessimism often seems more appropriate. They affirm the belief that love will carry us through whatever darkness confronts us, both now and in the future.

In my last book, *All's Fair*, I dealt with the question of how love can handle issues of independence and individual freedom. In *Dream Seeker*, I explored the role of imagination in the romantic relationship. *Far Star*, my next book, delves into the kinds of courage and commitment it takes to build a home and raise a family. I believe that people in the years to come will find that challenge just as daunting and the goal just as important as we do today.

Dayra Smith dreams of building a new life for herself and her orphaned brother and sister on a raw, new world known as Far Star—no matter what the obstacles. Coll Larren is a drifter, a man whose dreams died so long ago, he's almost forgotten they existed. Together, they learn what it is to love and how high a price life can exact of lovers who dare to build a life together.

I enjoy hearing from readers who love futuristic romances as much as I do. My address is P.O. Box 62533, Colorado Springs, CO 80962-2533. A self-addressed, stamped envelope would be appreciated.

Sincerely,
Anne Avery

KATHLEEN MORGAN
THE LAST GATEKEEPER

Prologue

The Yengi woke from his long hibernating sleep, wending his way to full consciousness by slow, painfully frustrating degrees. The ice-rimed cave high in the mountains was cold, but the unseasonably warm summer had finally permeated even this most distant mountain fastness. Finally . . . after thirty long years.

The creature moved, chittered harshly. Blearily the Yengi scanned the cave. He yawned, his huge, scissorslike jaw opening to reveal needle-sharp teeth, a ragged black tongue, and a cavernous maw. The Yengi stretched his long arms, arms fitted with lethal, daggerlike extensions and joined from front elbows to the hocks of the back legs by immense, leathery, gliding membranes. Then he rose and, propelled by powerful hind legs, scrabbled awkwardly toward the light.

Thirty long, lonely years had he slept, forced into hiding when the last of his kind, his mother, had been set upon and killed. Thirty years to sleep, to grow to full maturity. And now the Yengi was hungry.

Clawing his way to the cave's opening, the creature paused, accommodating his eyes to the bright glare of light, then swung his thick, bony head about. His long, whiplike tail flicked in sudden excitement. Below, a lush, verdant valley spread before him, the simple huts of a small village and herds of domesticated plains striders dotting the land. The Yengi's chittering deepened, took on a more urgent tone.

He was *very* hungry, and this planet was rich with food. Rich, warm-blooded food to ease but never satiate a voracious, all-consuming hunger. With a roar the Yengi pushed off, his huge, pinkish gray body filling the sky, a fearsome creature of death and destruction. Soaring high into the air, he headed for the valley, his raucous, blood-chilling cry his only warning before he plunged to the earth below.

Chapter One

He didn't look at all the way she had imagined a Yengi Beastslayer. True, he was tall, broad-shouldered, and leanly muscled, his movements athletic and strong. But instead of shining battle armor, his garb was nothing more than tan leathern breeches, knee-high boots, and a simple, long, light brown shirt belted loosely at the waist. To add further insult to her expectations, he worked with some form of gentle herd animals, rather than in warrior's exercises with the impressive Yengi spearslayer.

The Voltaran was also far younger than she'd thought he'd be, if his wavy, shoulder-length black hair was any indication. The last Yengi Beastslayer who'd been called to her planet of Orcades had left over thirty years ago. This man looked *barely* thirty, if that old.

339

With a sigh of resignation, Karin de Cedrus wiped the perspiration from her brow and strode down the last few meters of steep mountain trail toward the animal pens and crude, hide-covered hut, her purpose determined, her heart resolute. This man, this Targe Marwyn, was the last hope for her people. After all these years, yet another fearsome Yengi was abroad in Orcadian lands, wreaking havoc, bringing death and destruction. The beast must be slayed, and, by tradition, only a Yengi Beastslayer, a *Voltaran* Yengi Beastslayer, could kill it.

As she approached the pen where Marwyn worked, fitting a rope halter about the head of one of the largest and shaggiest of the beasts, the pungent odor of animal manure filled her nostrils. Karin's nose wrinkled in distaste. By the fifth star of Orcades, these Voltarans lived in worse squalor and filth than even the poorest Orcadian! She didn't know how she'd endure the next several days with him, before he could be brought to the royal palace and sent out after the Yengi. Perhaps if he would just keep a respectful distance . . .

But then, when had a Voltaran ever been respectful or considerate of an Orcadian?

"Er, pardon, if you will," she called out as she halted before the rough wooden pen and peered over the top rail. "The villagers in the valley said you be Targe Marwyn, the Yengi Beastslayer. If that is true, I've come for you."

He turned slowly, a bemused look wrinkling his brow. Karin inhaled an admiring breath. He was the most strikingly attractive man she'd ever seen, Voltaran though he was. Rugged strength was carved into every feature of his sun-bronzed face, from his straight dark brows to the firm, sensually molded lips and arrogant jut of his chin and jaw. Piercing jade green eyes stared back at her, narrowing in speculation as his glance swept down her cloaked and gowned body and back up to her face. Then Marwyn grinned. The heart-stopping beauty the smile added to his features made Karin's pulse falter, then commence a rapid beating.

"A Yengi Beastslayer? Hardly," he said with a rich, throaty chuckle. "My name's Thorn Marwyn and I'm definitely no Yengi Beastslayer. That fool-hardy profession died out with my father, Targe Marwyn. But you're welcome to come for me." Something dark and heated flared in his eyes. "A pretty lass of your mettle is *more* than welcome. I get few visitors up here in these mountains, and none ever of your quality."

Marwyn led the herd beast to the nearest side of the pen and tied it to a support post. Then, after briefly rubbing his hands clean on his breeches, he strode over to stand before Karin. At close quarters his height, his intimidating male presence and rich, heady scent were too much to bear.

Though the wooden poles of the animal pen separated them from bodily contact, Karin couldn't help but take a few steps back to regain her perspective. She was on a mission of vital importance. She must not let him gain the upper hand, unnerving man though he was.

"I came not for a social visit," Karin forced herself to reply. "I am from the planet Orcades and was sent to seek out a Yengi Beastslayer. The villagers told me—"

"The villagers delight in making fools of sight-seers who come to gape and gossip." Marwyn leaned forward to grip the top rail with long-fingered, work-roughened hands. "I tell you again, no Yengi Beastslayer lives here."

"Then if you would be so kind as to direct me to where I might find—"

"No Yengi Beastslayer lives *anywhere* on Voltar," Marwyn cut her off. "If Orcades has further need of one, they'll have to find him from within their own kind from now on, distasteful as that consideration might be."

"But you be of the blood, be you not?" Karin's mind raced. No Beastslayer lived anywhere on Voltar? How could that be? It had only been thirty years. And it was said the gift was passed from father to son. "You still possess the ability whether you choose to use it or not!"

He shrugged. "Perhaps I do, perhaps I don't, but it matters not. I owe Orcades nothing and am quite content with my simple if unexciting life. And I've no wish to commit suicide."

"We will pay you well. *Very* well," Karin gritted, "as we have always done."

"To do your dirty work?" Marwyn gave a snort of disgust. "Though payment for a Yengi beastslaying always beggared your royal treasury, it's still not worth my life." He cocked his head in sudden interest. "Why did Orcades send a woman to seek out a Beastslayer? You hardly seem the sort capable of fulfilling such a task."

"I am more than capable of the 'task,'" Karin snapped, her patience with the man growing thin. "It is a sacred duty that has always fallen on the Chosen. No one else can open the gates between our worlds. No one else can bring others safely through. Who else would you have imagined it would be?"

For a fleeting instant Marwyn's eyes widened in surprise. Then he laughed. "So, you're a Gatekeeper, are you? And I'd thought they were as extinct as Beastslayers. Obviously, I was wrong."

"There be few of my kind left," Karin muttered, refusing to admit that she and her mother were all who remained of the famous race of Gatekeepers, "but enough to do the job. Now, I ask you again. Will you come with me or not?"

Marwyn chuckled. "You're a persistent one, that much I'll grant you. My answer, however, remains the same." He glanced over his shoulder toward his hut. "I'd still be pleased to invite you to stay awhile, though. I've a fine stew simmering over my cookfire. The meat's from an old damas buck and a bit tough and stringy but—"

She touched him then, her hand covering his upon the pole, soft, warm, and surprisingly stimulating. Thorn's gaze swung back to hers, startled, wary. Something shot through him, something hot, searing, and breath-grabbing. His body jerked; his head fell back. His mouth opened in a soundless cry.

Blackness engulfed him, swallowing him in a maw of swirling darkness. His knees buckled. He fell, unconscious before he even struck ground.

Karin stared down at him for a long, tumultuous moment. She hadn't meant ever to use that dark power, ever forcibly to compel another being to her will, but there was no other choice. Even now the Yengi pillaged the land, slaughtered her people. Time was of the essence. And Thorn Marwyn, despite his refusal to aid her, was of the blood. He would have to do.

She would fulfill her mission. She would bring a Voltaran Yengi Beastslayer back to Orcades as commanded. She just wished he hadn't fallen into the biggest pile of manure she'd ever seen.

Voices, angry and impatient, penetrated Thorn's consciousness. He groaned, stirred restlessly. His eyes fluttered open to a misty, distorted haze of moving figures. Pain shot through his skull. He clamped his eyes shut once more.

"You must waken, Thorn Marwyn." A familiar feminine voice rose from beside him. "We have a long journey ahead and little time. The Yengi waits for no man."

The Yengi. The woman from Orcades. It all came back in a nauseating rush of memory. Who would've thought such a small, delicate woman, a woman of lush pink lips, of beguiling blue eyes and luxurious dark brown hair could possess such painfully compelling powers? But she did, and she'd used them against him.

With an anguished grimace, Thorn levered himself to one elbow, the ropes binding his wrists behind him tugging awkwardly. He blinked, clearing his vision, and found himself in unfamiliar lands. Overhead, a red sun shimmered in a hazy blue sky. In the distance, hovering just above the horizon, sat two moons. He wasn't on Voltar anymore. That much was certain.

Thorn choked back a savage curse. She had drawn him through the Gate, through the invisible portal that lay between their two worlds. A portal only an Orcadian Gatekeeper could open.

He glanced up at her, kneeling beside him. "You took me through, didn't you? Against my will, despite my refusal to serve your people as a Beastslayer?"

Karin's gaze skittered away. "Yes, I did. There was no other choice. We be desperate and you possess the special powers."

"It'll do no good, you know." Thorn clenched his jaw against the relentless pounding in his head. "That myth about our powers was just that—a myth. One of my ancestors made it up to justify the extortionate sums all Beastslayers demanded each time a Yengi needed killing. The rest recognized a good deal and carried on the deception. But I tell you true. I possess no greater powers to kill a Yengi than any of your own men."

"That is not my affair." She met his furious glance with a calm one of her own. "You can convince our king of that or not. I have only to bring you to him."

Thorn shoved to his knees, wobbled an instant, then stood. Soldiers milled restlessly about him, sullen, hostile looks on their faces. There wasn't much chance of escape, he realized, unless he could lull them all into trusting him. "Then let's be off to see your king," Thorn growled, turning back to the woman. "The sooner I get this matter resolved, the sooner I can head back home."

Her lips tightened. "That is all I have ever wanted from you."

"The bonds won't be necessary. I know I can't return through the Gate without you."

"But remain they will," snarled a burly, red-haired soldier garbed in the bullion and buttons of an officer as he walked up to stand beside the woman. "Karin is far too valuable to be put at risk, especially by Voltaran vermin such as yourself. Your bonds remain until we reach the royal palace at Lacus Hedin. And, purported Beastslayer or not," he added, his gaze scornfully raking the length of Thorn's body, "any attempt to escape will be severely punished. Severely. Do I make myself clear?"

"Quite clear," Marwyn muttered. "So much for the joyous welcome and wild acclaim."

The officer's eyes narrowed dangerously. Karin hastily stepped between the two men. "He already said he will cause no difficulty. Let it be, I pray you, Captain Barth."

Barth smirked insolently. "That I will, for the time being. But you be wrong, Karin, if you think this Voltaran's to be trusted. It's obvious he came here unwillingly. What isn't so obvious is how you managed to 'coerce' him, you but a mere slip of a female and he the big brute that he is."

The man arched a speculative brow. "Have you, perhaps, additional powers? Powers you haven't yet shared with us, Karin? The king won't look favorably on such purposeful secretiveness."

"It is nothing like that," Karin immediately replied, not daring to let Barth put her on the defensive. If he should indeed discover her secret . . . "The issue here is fulfilling the king's command, and I but wish to bring the Beastslayer to him in fighting condition. No good is served if he is forced to go against the Yengi injured, is there?"

The officer scowled blackly. "No, I'd wager not. But, be that as it may, the fact remains his kind is greedy, grasping, and as eager to suck us dry as a spotted ictus is to drain the blood from a fatted jardma. Why, we be still recovering from the last Beastslayer's exorbitant demands. By the fifth star, how it sickens me to have to deal with the likes of him!"

"But we must," Karin soothed. "Our people be in the gravest danger." She motioned toward the trail winding down from the foothills where they all stood. "Now, please, Captain Barth, let us be gone. The morn is half fled already and we have a four-day journey to Lacus Hedin."

The red-haired man shot Thorn one final malevolent glance, then turned and strode away. With but a few terse commands, the rest of the soldiers were ready to leave, half going before, the other half falling in behind Thorn and Karin. In but an hour's time, their party had left the foothills and set out across the plains.

Tall, thick grass swayed in the brisk morning breeze, the green vegetation undulating like waves upon the Quiran Sea. The Quiran Sea . . . back home on Voltar, Thorn thought glumly. He wondered if he'd ever see his own planet again. Though the Orcadian soldiers were armed with the most primitive of weapons—short, stout clubs, long-bladed war knives, and a strange form of multi-pronged spear—Thorn knew that even if he managed to free himself and escape, there was still the issue of the Gate to deal with. The Gate, and a certain puzzling little Gatekeeper.

She definitely had some special powers, strange, frightening abilities in one seemingly so young and innocent, powers that, heretofore, she'd apparently revealed to few. That presented yet another question—why did this Gatekeeper hide some of her powers from her own kind? And could he possibly use his knowledge of them to his own advantage?

Thorn knew he needed Karin to get him back to Voltar. He also knew he couldn't force her to help him. She would just touch him and render him unconscious again. But how to win her over? His desires would hold little weight against the plight of an entire planet.

Though Thorn had only heard tales of the terrible havoc wrought by the Yengi, they were tales told by a firsthand witness—his father. And they were tales that would chill the heart of the bravest man. If this Yengi was allowed free run of Orcades, the consequences, in just a few years, would be catastrophic.

Not only did the beast possess the ability to fly, swooping down from the skies with the barest of warnings, but it was equally lethal on the ground. Its daggerlike arms could move with blinding speed, the lethal tips spearing hapless people and animals like so much meat on a skewer. Its long tail could whip around with the swiftness of a Rurian slime snake, entangling its victim in a strangling vise. And its appetite was insatiable. Save for a few days every month when it sought refuge to digest its weeks of meals, the Yengi was constantly on the move.

No, the planet of Orcades was in the greatest danger. He'd have little if any influence with the Gatekeeper Karin, even if he *had* possessed any talent for charming a female. Years of living in virtual isolation, high up in his mountain hideaway, had done little to sharpen his skills of seduction. His monthly visits to the village in the valley and its solitary pleasure woman hadn't required much more of him than the coin to buy her favors.

Frustration filled Thorn. He was going to die, and all because of some spurious heritage of his forefathers. To be a Yengi Beastslayer had been their free choice; to accept money for superhuman battle powers they didn't possess, their decision. It was not—and never would be—his. He must find some way to escape, even if it meant remaining trapped on Orcades the rest of his days. Even *that* was preferable to being eaten alive by a Yengi.

With a shudder of revulsion, Thorn banished further contemplation of such a gruesome fate from his mind and turned his attention back to the matter at hand: escape . . . at all costs . . . before they reached the royal city of Lacus Hedin.

They traveled all day, pausing only for infrequent stops to quench their thirst with swallows from leathern bags of a watered-down Orcadian beer. Thorn was forced to choke down a few gulps of the bitter brew from the bag Karin held to his mouth, for Captain Barth refused to untie him even then. Only when they made camp for the night in a grove of ancient trees beside a burbling brook did the Orcadian officer allow Thorn a moment of freedom to relieve himself. And even that freedom was under the scrutiny of four armed guards.

Karin awaited him at the campfire. She shot one glance at his scowling face when he lowered himself to sit beside her, and flushed. Grasping a platter of bread and cheese, she scooted close. "I-I am sorry you must be treated so," she haltingly began, "but we dare not risk losing you. The king commanded I bring back a Yengi Beastslayer, and . . . and innocent people will suffer if I fail."

"Yes, I know." Thorn shifted off a stone he'd sat on and folded one leg beneath the other. With an exasperated toss of his head, he flung a dark lock from his eyes. "No one deserves a death such as a Yengi gives."

"No, you do not understand." Karin paused to glance about her. The soldiers, Captain Barth included, were all busily engrossed in preparing their own meals or eating them. None, for the moment, paid Karin or her prisoner any attention. She turned back to Thorn. "My mother. She is ill, needs medicines. Medicines that be rare and costly. The king vowed to provide her with all she needed if I brought back a Yengi Beastslayer."

Karin sighed ruefully. "As if the welfare of my people was not enough." Her hands clenched about the wooden platter. "I know it is of little comfort to know this, considering that your life may well be forfeit, but I did not take you without cause. If there had been any other choice . . ."

He lifted his gaze to hers, a gaze deep and dark and disturbingly sensual. "Part of me doesn't care that this was difficult for you. That part of me hates you. But another part understands, as well." He grimaced. "A sorry dilemma, accepting there's a reason for my death—a very noble and glorious reason, mind you—yet still finding no comfort in it whatsoever."

"You may not die, you know. You be of the blood. Surely your father told you how he slew the Yengi, of the creature's weaknesses as well as its strengths. He used the Yengi spearslayer," she said, gesturing to the strange-looking multi-pronged spears propped against a nearby tree. "They be deadly weapons. Once a spearslayer is stabbed into a Yengi, it cannot be removed. If one can just hold on and twist it deeply enough—"

"I've heard tales aplenty of the killing techniques," Thorn interrupted angrily. "I don't want for knowledge, you can be sure. But aside from my lack of any special powers against the beast, the fact remains I just don't possess the killing instinct. My inclination is to care for animals, not slaughter them."

Karin recalled the gentle herd beasts she'd seen him tending. "The animals you were working with," she asked softly. "What be they called?"

"Damas. They're called damas." A pained look clouded his eyes. "I must get back to them before they starve. They've no one to care for them now, alone, penned up in the mountains. They'll die if I don't return."

"And my people, my mother, will die if you do."

Their glances locked, green eyes slamming into those of blue, and, for a splintering moment in time, something arced between them. Then Karin sighed, breaking the unnerving and strangely stimulating visual contact. She picked up the bread and tore it into bite-sized pieces. The cheese she cut into small chunks with a little paring knife she pulled from a pouch hanging at her waist. Once more she glanced up at him, her expression now distant and determined.

"Come, allow me to feed you, Thorn Marwyn," she said. "The night grows on and we both need our rest for the days to come. As you need this food to sustain your body."

Karin reached out and offered him a bit of bread. Thorn's keen eyes knifed into hers, piercing through to her very soul. Then he opened his mouth and accepted the bread from her hands.

Chapter Two

Thorn's first chance to escape came late the next morning. As they wended their way upstream through a narrow gorge slashed by a turbulent river, he made his decision. The river ran downstream for several kilometers before emptying over some minor falls into a vast lake. It was a desperate plan, but if he could break free and fling himself into the water, there was a good chance its force and speed would quickly carry him out of range of the spearslayers and away from the soldiers.

True, he'd have to battle the river with his arms tied behind him, but he'd always been a strong swimmer. And, considering the horrible fate most certainly awaiting him at the end of the journey, it was well worth the risk.

For an instant, as Karin drew up alongside him and shot him a quick smile, Thorn's resolve faltered. He truly felt sorry for her plight and that of her people. In the end, though, it changed nothing. He wasn't the man for the job. Let some of her own kind, some of these brave soldiers who kept such a wide berth around him, fight the Yengi instead. It was *their* home, their planet, after all. He owed them nothing.

She'd brought him through the Gate. She'd done her job. Her king should credit her with holding up her end of the bargain and give her mother the medicines she needed. Now, if he escaped, the fault would be the soldiers', not Karin's.

He felt frustrated and resentful. The realization that he even cared what happened to Karin only added to Thorn's confusing swirl of emotion. Despite her admission of regret for forcing him through the Gate, there remained one inescapable fact. She was willing to sacrifice his life, to send him up against a savage, man-eating Yengi. And he, beguiled by a pretty face, soft words, and a lush woman's body, was the sorriest of fools if he worried about her!

She would turn on him in an instant, use her hands on him as she had before, if she'd even the faintest inkling of what he planned. He must remember that. Remember that, in the end, she was like the rest of her kind. Too proud to sully her hands in the defense of her planet, when she thought some greedy fool could be procured to do it for her. Some Voltaran vermin, as Captain Barth had so succinctly put it.

Anger welled within him, blotting out further thought of the beauteous Gatekeeper. Thorn turned, instead, to watch and wait for his best opportunity. It finally came as the path beside the river narrowed around the thick trunk of a large tree. With a sudden sideways leap, Thorn threw himself into the river.

A surprised shout, then a feminine cry reached him just before he plunged into the water. The river churned wildly, sucking him down. Thorn fought against the treacherous pull, kicking with all his strength to turn and fight his way to the surface. All the while, though, he let the current drag him downstream, away from where the soldiers stood and, hopefully, far out of range of the spearslayers.

His lungs burned. He thought he'd lose his breath before he reached the surface. At last, his head broke water. Thorn gulped in great lungfuls of air, flailing his legs wildly to stay afloat. He whirled around toward the shore, just in time to see that he hadn't gained as much distance downstream as he'd planned—and too late to avoid the spearslayer flying toward him.

A woman's scream—Karin's—pierced the air. Then there was nothing but blinding, burning pain as the spearslayer plunged into and through his shoulder. With a strangled cry Thorn jerked back in the water, the impact slamming him into the river's surging depths.

Water filled his mouth, gushed down his throat and into his lungs. He choked. He gagged. He strangled.

Over. It was all over.

Then, with an excruciating tug, he was wrenched upward. By slow, agonizing degrees, Thorn felt himself pulled to shore. The spearslayer imbedded in his right upper chest was attached, at its end, to a strong cord. He was caught, helpless to tear the multi-pronged blade from him.

Waves of nauseating dizziness washed over him. He saw Karin standing on the shore a short distance from the soldiers reeling him in, her face white, her eyes huge and horrified. Then she blurred, went dark. Everything—sight, sound, sensation—was swallowed up by the unrelenting, fiery torment in his right shoulder.

Thorn awoke to a vague sensation of movement, of a swaying from side to side. Then something lurched. His body was jostled about roughly. White-hot pain shot through him. He gasped, caught his breath, choking back a groan.

"By the five stars!" a rough male voice grumbled to the right of his head. "This cursed Voltaran goes and gets himself wounded and now we be forced to carry him the rest of the way to Lacus Hedin. He's rapidly becoming more trouble than he's worth."

"That he is," another male voice to Thorn's left agreed. "And all our efforts may be for naught, if the man is not willing or able to slay the Yengi for us. Perhaps it would be better to stuff him full of poison and set him out as Yengi bait. Then he'd at least serve some purpose in slaying the creature."

He was on a litter, Thorn thought, being carried by four soldiers. Somehow, when he was unconscious, they'd removed the spear from his shoulder. He lifted his left hand to touch his right shoulder gingerly. Someone had cared for his wound and bandaged it. That someone, Thorn wagered, had most likely been Karin.

The memory of her expression when he'd seen her standing on the shore after he'd been speared came back to him. She'd stared at him with a sick, haunted look. Yet there'd also been a concern, a surprising caring. The realization both moved and startled Thorn.

Frustration flooded him. He didn't need some female distracting him from what he must do. He was a desperate man. And she was Orcadian. Orcadian, a people who, thanks to centuries of exploitation and deceit by his avaricious ancestors, despised the planet Voltar and all its inhabitants. In the end, there'd be no help from her any more than from the rest of her kind. He must never forget that, not if he wished to live.

The hours dragged on, the swaying movement of the litter intermittently lulling him into a semiconscious state until he was once more jerked awake by a soldier's stumble or some shouted command. His shoulder throbbed fiercely but, save for the occasional lurches of the litter, he found he could tolerate the pain. Karin must have applied some form of pain-killer to his wound. It was the only explanation.

Though his thoughts and dreaming were filled with her, he didn't see her until dusk when the party halted for the night. His litter was lowered, none too gently, to the ground, and suddenly, out of the deepening twilight, Karin appeared. He turned to her, strangely hungry for her presence, before his shoulder reminded him of his limitations.

Thorn swallowed a groan and eased his way back onto the litter.

"How do you feel?" Karin knelt beside him. "Would you like some water?"

Water. Thorn realized he hadn't had a drop to drink all day. He swallowed, and found his throat was as parched as the deserts of Morava. He nodded.

She rose, walked away, and soon returned with a leathern flask. "Can you lift your head to drink?"

He tried and fell back weakly, debilitated by yet another surge of pain. "N-no. C-can you h-help me?" he croaked.

Karin hesitated. The Orcadian revulsion of all things Voltaran had evolved to the point that to touch a Voltaran was tantamount to soiling oneself for life. Captain Barth, the soldiers, would shun her if she did. Even now, though Barth had his suspicions, he had no proof she'd placed her hand on Thorn Marwyn to coerce him into coming with her. And if he ever did . . .

But there was no help for it now. No one had been willing to touch the Voltaran. Even the removal of the spearslayer had been managed without anyone actually touching any part of his body. Captain Barth had put a booted foot on

Thorn's chest and pushed the spearslayer clear through his shoulder, where the barbed point was cut off and the spear then pulled out. But now, now there seemed no other choice.

Marwyn needed water desperately. Already his cheeks had a hectic flush, the first sign of fever. He needed far more than water to keep his wound from festering, but until she reached her mother's home, there was nothing more she could do. Nothing more than keep his wound clean and give him water.

Karin stared down at the man, torn by indecision. It wasn't just the social taboos holding her back. It was also the memory of the shocking pleasure she'd experienced when she'd touched him that first time to force his compliance. The admission frightened her, for she found she wanted to feel it again. Wanted *intensely* to feel it again.

"K-Karin?" Thorn's voice, halting and weak, beckoned her back to the moment at hand. Her gaze refocused, seeing him once more.

He stared up at her, a puzzled look in his deep green eyes. "Please. I-I'm so thirsty."

At his entreaty, something in Karin shattered. She leaned down, slid one hand beneath his long, silky hair to grasp his neck and upper back, and lifted him slightly. As her fingers touched Thorn's flesh, the same startling surge of pleasure coursed through her. With a forceful, frightened effort, she tamped it down. Concentrating on the task of helping him instead, Karin raised the water flask to Thorn's lips.

His gaze locked with hers. A sudden comprehension flared in his eyes. Then he drank.

She finally had to pull the flask from him. "Not so much so soon," Karin chided gently. "You will only make yourself ill." She lowered him back to the litter. "Rest now. I will make you a nourishing broth for your supper, then, cleanse your wound again and redress it. It is all I can do until the morrow."

"The morrow?" Thorn mumbled, already sliding back into the torpor of his rising fever.

"We will reach my village, two days' journey from Lacus Hedin. My mother has herbal potions and salves that will heal your wound. She will help you."

"Is she . . . forbidden to touch me, too?" he whispered, his eyes closing in spite of his best efforts to keep them open.

Karin flushed, knowing he'd correctly interpreted her hesitation to touch him. It was pointless to hide the truth, now that the subject had been broached. "All be forbidden to touch a Voltaran."

"So, I may well manage to irreparably soil two Orcadian females, will I?" Thorn shifted restlessly, grimaced, then stilled. "I'm sorry for that, little one . . ."

His voice faded and Karin knew he slept once more. She picked up the water flask and rose, turning to face the disgust and loathing of her own countrymen. Surprisingly, she found herself unconcerned with what she had wrought, though a lifelong stigma would now be hers.

She must have always been beyond redemption, Karin mused wonderingly, to toss the years of Orcadian tradition aside so easily. So very easily . . . since the moment she'd first met the darkly handsome Voltaran named Thorn Marwyn.

The Yengi sighted them as they left the Ardallian Forest the next afternoon and set out once more across the plains. With only a warning shadow passing suddenly before the Orcadian red sun, the creature was upon them. Roaring his dreaded death cry, he plunged from the sky, swooping down to cut a bloody swath through the line of soldiers.

The men carrying Thorn dropped him to the ground and ran screaming in four directions. For an instant Thorn lay there, gasping in pain, overwhelmed by the cacophony of shrieks and moans of dying Orcadians. Then, with a superhuman effort, he rolled off his litter.

Not twenty meters away, the Yengi sat, consuming the still writhing bodies of two soldiers. A stench reached Thorn, foul, choking, reeking of fresh blood and filth. The gorge rose in his throat and he fought back an urge to vomit. Even as he watched, the Yengi's thick, bony head swung in his direction. Small red eyes focused on him.

Fear gripped Thorn. He must get away. Now, or he'd be the Yengi's next meal.

Inhaling a fortifying breath, Thorn pushed to his knees. Pain shot through him. A dizzying mist clouded his vision. He swayed, groaning in despair. He hadn't the strength to get away.

Then Karin was beside him. Her arm encircled his waist, pulling him to his feet. "Come," she whispered hoarsely, her voice taut with terror. "Let us be away from here."

Thorn nodded. There was little strength left to spare on words. He followed her, his gait stumbling and unsteady. Behind him, the Yengi crunched bones and slurped, still engrossed in his human meal.

Now, Thorn thought. Now would be the time and opportunity to attack the creature while it was momentarily distracted. The Orcadians possessed the feared Yengi spearslayers. There were enough of them, as well, if that arrogant Captain Barth was capable of rallying his men.

But it wasn't his concern, he reminded himself, whatever they chose to do. If the Orcadian men were such cowards, they condemned not only themselves but their entire planet to the marauding Yengi. His goal was to survive. He must always remember that.

"There," Karin said, pointing toward a small overhang of rock sheltering a deep-set cave in a nearby hillock of land. "If we can make it there, the Yengi won't be able to reach us."

Thorn glanced over his shoulder. The creature had just swallowed his last morsel, belched, and risen to his daggerlike front legs. He looked around, his long tail whipping about him. The only movement it saw was that of Thorn and Karin hurrying toward the cave.

The Yengi's mouth opened, exposing his needle-sharp teeth. He belched again, this time quite loudly. His gaze focused on them.

"Go, Karin!" Thorn cried, twisting free of her clasp and shoving her forward. "Get to the cave. Now!"

He fell then and began to crawl after her, knowing, even as he did, there was no chance of his reaching the cave in time. Then Karin was back at his side, grasping him under both arms, pulling, dragging him along.

The pain in his injured shoulder was excruciating. Thorn groaned. "Karin . . . don't. You can't save—"

"Enough, Thorn Marwyn!" she screamed back at him. "Help me or you will kill us both!"

Thorn knew she meant it. Knew she wouldn't leave him no matter the cost. Freshened blood pumped through his veins. Energy he didn't know he possessed flooded him. He jerked free of Karin's hands and scrambled to his feet.

"Run!" he cried.

Behind him, the death roar of the Yengi filled the air. Then they were at the rock overhang and Thorn was knocking Karin down and pushing her beneath it.

Once more the stench engulfed him. The darkness of a big body looming overhead encompassed him. All Thorn knew was a total, soul-grabbing terror. He glanced above him and nearly passed out.

He flung himself down, striking his wounded shoulder hard on the ground, and rolled beneath the overhang. The earth shook as the Yengi landed just millimeters from where Thorn had stood.

Then Karin's hands were on him, dragging him back into the dark recesses of the cave.

Outside, the enraged creature attacked the hillock wherein they lay. Chunks of dirt and rock fell, showering Thorn and Karin until he feared for the stability of their underground shelter.

At last, though, the Yengi seemed to lose patience. His roars abated and he began to chitter agitatedly. He moved away. For a time, the sound of flesh tearing and bones crunching filled the air. Then a heavy silence settled over the land.

Thorn lay there, panting in the darkness, as much from the pain of his now badly bruised as well as wounded shoulder, as from the terror. Try as he might, he couldn't seem to wipe from his mind that last horrifying sight of the Yengi, jaws wide and slavering, bearing down on him. He shuddered, his body wracked by his physical response to the fearful memories.

"Calm yourself," Karin soothed, scooting close to stroke his sweat-sheened face. "The danger is past. The Yengi is gone."

"Is-is it?" he demanded unsteadily. "Perhaps for you, but my fate's to meet the beast in battle—or have you so quickly forgotten?" He jerked away, suddenly and unaccountably angry. "That's why you risked your life to help me, isn't it? Because you feared losing the only man who might save your people?"

"Think what you like." Karin's voice, taut with pain, rose from the darkness. "But that fails to explain why you tried to save me at the expense of your own life." She gave a strident laugh. "Ah, yes, I too had forgotten. You need me to open the Gate back to Voltar, don't you?"

"Something like that," Thorn growled. "I see we understand each other at last."

"You understand nothing, Beastslayer," Karin shot back. "But it does not matter in the end. We be both pawns to a higher purpose and power. The sooner you accept that, the sooner you will return home."

And the sooner I will be free of you and the needs you stir in my heart, she silently finished, fearing above all the admission of feelings, of desires she'd never experienced for any other man.

Chapter Three

Of the twenty soldiers of their original party, only eight survived. Captain Barth was one of the dead. As Karin re-dressed Thorn's freshly bleeding shoulder, the remaining soldiers discussed their options. After hearing much debate that decided nothing, Karin finally rose and walked over to them.

"The solution is simple," she began with as much authority as she could muster. "My village is but another three hours away and our mission has not changed. We must bring the Voltaran to the king."

"We risk much with the Yengi in the area," the now senior ranking soldier grumbled, "if we continue to be slowed by carrying the man. I say we march on to Lacus Hedin as swiftly as possible without him."

"And leave behind our only hope for finally destroying the Yengi?" Karin gave a disparaging laugh. "Then go, all of you, and give your explanations to the king when you return not only without the Beastslayer, but without me."

The men exchanged uncertain glances. All knew of their king's infamous anger—and the consequences of driving him to that anger. "Three hours isn't all that long, I suppose," the new leader admitted. "And we do owe our king the utmost loyalty."

"A wise decision," Karin murmured. "One of a true leader."

The man brightened at her praise, squaring his shoulders self-importantly. "Quite true. Quite true." He motioned toward where Thorn lay. "Is the Voltaran ready to travel? We must be on our way."

Karin nodded. "Yes. If you would just assign four of your men to carry him . . ."

"He'll have to climb onto the litter under his own power. None of us will touch him."

"He is strong enough to do that much, but we must hurry. His wound has begun to fester."

The leader made an impatient gesture. "Then all the more reason to hurry, wouldn't you say?"

"Indeed," Karin agreed and, without another word, turned and walked back to Thorn. Kneeling beside him, she touched him gently on the shoulder. "We will be at my mother's in but a few hours."

He turned to her. His eyes were fever-bright,

his breathing rapid and ragged. "A consolation, to be sure."

She frowned. "Despite what you may think of my motives, I do not wish to see you suffer. And my most intense desire is for you to kill the Yengi and return safely to your world. I only wish you would believe that and not hate me so."

His brows lifted mockingly. "Hate you? I think it would be far easier if I did." Thorn's glance softened for a fleeting moment. "But then, I suppose I've been a fool too long to change now."

The arrival of the four soldiers with the litter squelched Karin's attempt at a reply. A troubled tumult in her heart, she watched them lower the litter to the ground and Thorn painfully roll onto it. Then the soldiers lifted him and they set out once more.

The rest of the journey to Karin's village was uneventful. As they moved along, it became rapidly apparent the Yengi had recently cut a wide swath of destruction through the area. Thorn felt his resolve to distance himself from the Orcadians' plight slip a little as they passed devastated farmers' huts, the bloated remains of slaughtered plains striders and other domesticated animals, and the people with their hollow, haunted expressions.

For the soldiers and their king, on the other hand, Thorn felt no compassion. They had the power and skills to fight the Yengi. But the common people, the peasants who worked the land and raised the herd beasts, were truly helpless against such a fearsome and deadly creature.

Yengis were fabled to have unusually long life spans. If their own king and army refused to aid them, the peasants were the ones who would pay the greatest price, over and over again.

"*They* be the ones I brought you through the Gate for," Karin said, drawing up to walk beside his litter. "Not for the king or his royal palace, not for the nobles or rich landowners, but for these good, simple people. They, above all, have no way to protect themselves from the Yengi. The king and his court have strong stone walls and buildings to hide within. And the Yengi prefers easier prey."

"Like a lone man sent out to fight it?"

Karin's gaze jerked to his. She flushed. "Bringing a Beastslayer back from Voltar always worked in the past. How was I to know you would stubbornly persist in refusing to help us?"

"Perhaps when I first told you, in no uncertain terms, no?"

"And perhaps you have just not been offered the right incentive," Karin muttered in rising exasperation. "An incentive that has never before failed to buy the services of your kind."

"There's always a first time." He sighed and closed his eyes, suddenly too weary to continue the conversation.

Thorn slept the rest of the journey, exhausted by the pain and fever that drained his remaining strength, not awakening until they entered Karin's village and drew up before her hut. The joyous exclamation of her mother finally roused him from his fitful slumber. He turned, just in time to see Karin run up to a gray-haired woman and hug her.

The familial resemblance was strong, in the pert nose and full lips, the blue eyes only a shade darker than her daughter's, and the proud cast to her shoulders. But the debilitating effects of the woman's illness were just as evident. The hands that clasped her daughter shook, and her skin was almost translucent. As with everything Karin had told him, her words about her mother were true.

"Mother," she said, finally disengaging herself and stepping back, "I have brought the Yengi Beastslayer to you. He is sorely wounded. Will you help to heal him?"

The older woman's gaze lifted to where Thorn lay on the litter. "You know I will, child. He is the salvation of our people."

Karin bit back the remark that Thorn Marwyn had no intention of saving anyone, then thought better of it. There was no point in upsetting her mother unnecessarily, or the villagers who'd gathered around them, for that matter. What the Voltaran and her king ultimately decided was their decision. She had only to deliver him alive and well and her part of the mission was over. After that, she would be free of him.

The thought was strangely unsettling, Karin realized as she followed the soldiers who carried Thorn into her home. Somehow, she knew she would never truly be free of him. In the short time since she'd met Thorn Marwyn, he'd already managed to touch her on so many levels: in a physical sense, with the surprising stimulation of his flesh upon her hands; in a moral sense, in the guilt and rising regret for having forced him into such dire circumstances; and in an emotional sense, in the forbidden feelings she had for him.

The emotions were the most difficult of all to deal with. She cared about him, wished to know more about him, his desires, his dreams, his deepest secrets. She wished to touch him the way a woman touched a man, to meld lips and bodies and hearts. And, above all, she wanted him to care for and desire her as she did him.

Shameful. Those secret cravings were shameful. He was alien to her, of a race of people different and beneath her own kind. Yet she didn't care. All that mattered was Thorn.

With an angry shake of her head, Karin flung the forbidden thoughts aside. She had matters of greater import to deal with than her feelings for a stranger. Matters such as seeing to his healing so she could complete her mission for the king.

The soldiers laid the litter on the bed. Taking the greatest care not to soil themselves by touching him, they then assisted Karin to remove Thorn from the litter. At last he made it onto the bed, damp-skinned and white-faced from the painful exertions. Karin pulled off his boots and quickly covered him with a blanket, then turned to the soldiers. "We have no further need of your services. There is a small inn at the end of the village where you can find room until the Voltaran is again ready to travel."

"And how long will that take?" the leader

demanded. "We can't remain here long. The king expects us."

"He also expects a Beastslayer well enough to go out after the Yengi," Karin snapped, at the limits of her patience and stamina. "It will be several days, one way or another. *If* my mother's healing potions and salves work with their usual swiftness."

The man scowled. "Well, I suggest you make certain they do. We've wasted enough time and effort on the Voltaran as it is."

"I will see what I can arrange." Karin firmly escorted the soldiers from the hut.

Upon her return, she pulled up a chair close to Thorn's bedside and assisted her mother over to it. "Mother, this is Thorn Marwyn," she said after she'd seated her in the chair. "Thorn, this is my mother, Arda."

His lids lifted. "I'm pleased to make your acquaintance, lady."

Arda smiled. "As am I, Voltaran. I only wish this meeting had found you in better health." She hesitated over him but an instant, then, with strong, efficient movements removed the bandages. An inflamed wound, oozing yellow pus, spanned the length of his right shoulder. She glanced back at her daughter. "How came he to such a grievous wound?"

Karin paled. Here it comes now, she thought. "He tried to escape and the soldiers used a spearslayer on him."

"Tried to escape?" Arda arched a graying brow. "And came he not to us willingly?"

"No, Mother."

"Then how were you able to bring him through the Gate?"

Karin averted her gaze. "It is best if you do not know."

"But I ask, nonetheless."

"I have powers to compel," Karin explained, forcing herself to meet her mother's questioning glance. "I laid my hand upon him and made him follow me."

Arda frowned. "I had hoped you would be spared those particular abilities. They be naught but a danger and a curse."

"I did not realize I possessed such powers until of late."

"And you were wise to keep them secret. Somehow, I think whatever use our king would decide to put them to would not have been for a good cause."

Karin's hands tightened on the back of her mother's chair. "Captain Barth suspected, I am afraid. But the Yengi killed him. Hopefully the other soldiers have not the sense to wonder how I brought Thorn through the Gate without his cooperation."

Her mother turned back to Thorn. "But the king will, once he discovers the Voltaran came here unwillingly. Then what will you do, Daughter?"

"I-I don't know. Help me, Mother."

Arda's blue eyes locked with Thorn's. "There is no help for it, unless this man will aid us."

"How?" Thorn asked warily.

"You must agree to tell the king you came willingly enough through the Gate, and then changed your mind. It is Karin's only hope."

"And why should I help her?"

The woman smiled thinly and leaned forward. "Think on it, Voltaran. Our king is a man of few morals and even less conscience. If he learns his Gatekeeper also has the ability to coerce others against their will, he can use her to pass through to any planet in the galaxy and force the inhabitants to his will. And, after all the centuries of animosity between our planets, I would wager Voltar would be his first target."

"Your daughter would also become a target. Many would seek her death to prevent that from happening."

Arda eased back in her chair, her body slumping in despair. "Yes, that I know as well. Why do you think I have kept my own powers hidden all these years, as have all our kind? But I failed in not warning Karin before it was too late. She should never have forced you, no matter how great our need."

Karin laid a hand on her mother's shoulder. "I am sorry. If it had been anything other than your health and the Yengi threatening us once again . . ."

"I know, Daughter." Arda covered Karin's hand with one of her own. "You did the best you could. You just never expected a Yengi Beastslayer to refuse to slay a Yengi, did you?"

Both women's gazes turned back to Thorn. Guilt surged through him, then anger. "Ah, so that's how it is, is it?" he growled. "Because of my refusal to risk my life for you and your planet, it now becomes my fault that Karin's secret is in danger of discovery. How selfish of me to expect some choice in the matter!"

"We be desperate, Beastslayer."

He glared up at the older woman. "I don't care! I owe you nothing!"

"You be of the blood. You cannot turn from our need."

"Can't I?" Thorn shifted, attempting to roll over onto his side and turn his back to them. His efforts failed in the weakness of fever-sapped muscles. "I cannot help what my ancestors—even my father—chose to do, but that doesn't mean I must choose the same path. I'm my own man, have the right to make my own way in life."

"Yes, you have the right," Karin's mother softly agreed, "but you must also follow where your destiny leads. And who is to say your destiny was not always meant to bring you to Orcades?"

He scowled blackly. "That would certainly suit your purposes, wouldn't it? But I refuse to accept that. It's too easy an answer."

"Perhaps it is. And then, perhaps it *is* so easy because it is the way it must be, and you just choose not to accept it." She paused. "Now, enough talk. Your wounds need tending." Arda turned back to Karin, shot her a quick smile, and patted her hand. "Will you bring my box of supplies, some clean cloths, and a basin of water, Daughter?"

Karin nodded and did as requested. Together, the two women stripped away Thorn's tattered shirt. Then, as her mother busied herself steeping a joya bark decoction, Karin washed his face and upper torso.

It was like touching fire and ice, Karin mused as she drew the soapy cloth over Thorn's body. He was hot and hard, all smooth, sculpted muscle and corded sinew. His broad shoulders tapered from a powerful chest to trim waist and narrow hips before the line of his leathern breeches met flesh. The feel of him sent a tremor of excitement through her, prickling down her spine, chilling her flesh, tightening her nipples into firm little buds. Never had Karin been so stimulated simply by the act of washing a man's body.

But it wasn't just any man—it was Thorn. Thorn of the long black hair as soft and silky as the finest Orcadian luster cloth. Thorn of the sun-bronzed skin rippling smoothly over hardened swells of muscles, from his bulging chest to his tautly undulating abdomen. Thorn of the seductive lips and mesmerizing eyes, so beautiful, so alluring, and so daunting.

And then there was no more of him to wash, and Karin finally realized she had scrubbed the same spot for the past few minutes. With an embarrassed motion, she tossed the bath cloth into the basin and turned to the care of his wound. Taught well by her mother, she flushed and packed the huge gash with a mixture of herbs and healing molds and rebandaged it.

Arda next poured the foul-tasting brew she'd

been preparing down Thorn's throat, assuring him it was a potent painkiller and fever-soother. The issue of his leathern breeches came next. "You need those washed and a complete bath," she commented with a jaundiced look at the lower half of his body.

It was Thorn's turn to blush. "I haven't been washed by a woman since I was a babe, and have no intention to begin now."

Arda shrugged. "Have it your way. We can pull your breeches out from beneath the blanket and then hand you the washcloth to cleanse yourself. But that is the best I will allow. No dirty man will remain under my roof."

Thorn eyed her narrowly, then nodded. "Fine. That'll be fine. I don't care for filth myself, at least not under normal circumstances."

"Good. It is comforting to know you can be reasonable if you wish to." She turned to Karin. "I grow weary, Daughter. Please help me to my bed."

"But Thorn's bath . . ." Karin glanced from her mother to Thorn and back.

"And be you not capable of assisting him? He said he would wash himself. All you must do is help him with his breeches."

Karin stared at her mother, saw the exhaustion furrowing her features, flattening her expression, and knew she teetered at the limits of her strength. She rose, moving around to stand before her mother and help her to her feet. "As you say. I am quite capable of assisting Thorn myself."

She guided Arda to her alcove bed, swept aside the curtains, and lowered her gently to the straw-filled mattress. Pulling the blanket up over her, Karin stepped back and grasped the bed curtains to close them. She paused, gazing down at her mother for an instant more. "I am glad to be home, Mother. More than I can say."

"He frightens you, does he not?" Arda whispered softly. "Yet he calls to you, too."

Karin paled. Her fingers clenched in the bed curtains. "I-I do not know what you—"

"No more secrets, Daughter," her mother said. "I saw how you looked at the Beastslayer as the soldiers brought him in."

"Mother, I was just concerned about him. I do feel some responsibility for his welfare."

Arda smiled up at her. "And perhaps you, too, seek an easier path than your destiny calls you to. You be the last of us, Daughter, the last Gatekeeper. When I am gone, it will fall to you to carry on our proud tradition. But perhaps it is not meant for you to do so in the same way as of old."

Puzzlement darkened Karin's eyes. "I do not understand."

"Why do you think our kind has died out, until only you and I be all who remain? Everything has a reason, a purpose. Why do you think the Beastslayer's kind has dwindled, as well?" She shrugged. "Perhaps it is time for Orcades to take a different path, to seek its own way in the galaxy without aid of other planets. Perhaps then, we will regain the humanity, the self-respect, the appreciation for each other that we left behind, and, in that search, also regain an understanding of others different from ourselves."

"And what does any of that have to do with Thorn or me?"

Arda sighed and closed her eyes. "That is the question, is it not, Daughter? And something not easily answered this day." Her lids lifted. "In the meanwhile, do you not have a man waiting for the rest of his bath?"

Karin's mouth tightened in exasperation. "Mother, do you know how vexing you can be at times?"

"Yes, Daughter, I do." Once more Arda's eyes closed. "But you still love me, do you not?"

"Yes, Mother, you know I do." Karin let the curtains fall closed. Like a woman going to her execution, she turned and headed back across the small, dirt-floored hut, back to where Thorn lay, still awake, staring up at the ceiling.

As she approached, his glance moved to her. "Solve the problems of the universe over there, did you?"

"Hardly." She walked around to his feet and, lifting the blanket, grabbed hold of his breeches. "If you would be so kind as to untie them, I will pull these off you."

A smile glimmered on his lips, then was gone. Thorn reached below the blanket, fumbled with the laces fastening his breeches closed, then, grasping hold of the blanket, lifted his hips slightly. "Have at it, little one."

Karin arched a slender brow, then tugged. In a

few quick jerks, the breeches were off. She folded them and placed them on the table, then took a clean cloth, dipped it in the basin of fresh water, soaped it, and lifted the blanket to expose Thorn's feet and legs to his knees. Without a moment's hesitation, Karin scrubbed his lower limbs, rinsed them, and patted them dry.

She paused. "Can you finish the rest of your bath?"

His brow furrowed as if in intense consideration. "I'm afraid I haven't the strength."

"Indeed?"

Thorn nodded solemnly. "Indeed."

Karin scowled. Was he playing some game? Well, if he thought to fluster or embarrass her, he thought wrong. She'd helped her mother nurse nearly every villager at some time or another. "Have it your way then." With a quick flip of the blanket, Karin folded the covering back until it protected only his groin.

She could feel his gaze upon her as she slowly washed his leanly muscled thighs, sensing rather than seeing his eyes boring into her, his rising excitement and arousal. A prudent woman would have finished the bath in record time, but, suddenly, Karin didn't want to be prudent. All she wanted was to savor the feel of his hair-roughened flesh beneath her hands, the smooth slide of his skin over hard muscle and bone. To feel his heat, to probe his essence, to discern the man he truly was.

It was madness to desire such physical contact with a man—an otherworlder no less—to want, no, need it as badly as she did. The realization frightened Karin. She'd touched other men before but none had affected her as Thorn did. That excitement, that need, had been hers from the first moment she'd seen him.

"Are you enjoying touching me as much as I'm enjoying being touched?"

The huskily couched question startled Karin from her preoccupation with Thorn's body. "Wh-what?" She jerked her hand away.

"Don't. I didn't mean for you to stop."

Heat flooded her face. "You be very forward, you know."

He cocked his head and smiled. "I'd call it honest. And I asked you an honest question. Aren't you woman enough to give me an honest answer?"

Karin turned and busied herself rinsing the bath cloth. "I do not know what you be talking about."

"You certainly looked as if you were enjoying washing me."

She wheeled around, the cloth in her hand. She shoved it at him. "Here. One way or another, I am finished with your bath. The rest is up to you." Karin left him and stalked over to the hearth, her chagrin churning to anger and self-disgust the longer she stood there.

Thorn was right. She'd all but groped his entire body, if not physically, at least mentally. It was ridiculous now to deny it, to play the offended maiden. Ridiculous and dishonest.

Her fists clenched as she squatted before the hearth to poke the dying embers back into some semblance of a fire. By the five stars, she cursed the day she'd met him! Her mission was rapidly losing its focus. In spite of everything that was prudent, she found herself becoming more and more attracted to a man forbidden by law and tradition—a man who could never be anything more than an instrument to serve her people.

Chapter Four

To Thorn's surprise, his fever quickly subsided and his wound began to heal within the next two days. By the third day he was walking, by the fourth, he was feeling almost back to his old self. Once he was up and about, thanks to Karin, he was permitted to move around without being bound, as long as he remained within the confines of the closely guarded hut. Yet all the while she avoided him whenever possible, her mother caring for his wound and seeing to his other needs as if by unspoken agreement between the two women.

Karin's purposeful avoidance irked Thorn. He'd done nothing but state the truth about her response to him, that evening she'd bathed him. He'd revealed his own arousal as well. Yet Karin had acted as if he'd insulted her.

It all came down to the fact that he was an awkward oaf when it came to women. Too many years of self-imposed exile in the mountains had dulled his ability to interact with others. Too many years of attempting to avoid his "proud" heritage, to carve out an existence that was uniquely his own.

Yet, in the end, what had it gained him? His heritage as a Beastslayer had still brought him to the same fate as the rest of his ancestors. He'd still ended up on Orcades, most likely soon to face a Yengi in battle. And, for his efforts, all he'd accomplished was to mire himself in a hopeless situation with a woman.

The realization that he desired Karin, that he wished to hold her, to kiss her, to mate with her, startled Thorn. His blood must be very hot indeed to ignore all she'd done to him and still see her only as a beautiful, desirable woman. He was a fool, a cursed, desperate, doomed fool.

That night as they all shared the evening meal, Karin broached the subject of their impending journey. The leader of the soldiers had informed her earlier that day that the Voltaran looked well enough to travel and they'd depart on the morrow. Though she was loath to leave her mother and begin the last leg of the journey that would deliver Thorn into the king's hands and force him to go up against the Yengi, Karin knew there was no other choice. She had brought him through the Gate for that reason and that reason alone. She must not let emotions, or an unexpected and unsettling physical attraction, sway her.

The Last Gatekeeper

"We leave on the morrow," she began without preamble when all had finished their meal. "You be well enough to travel."

Thorn set down his cup of Orcadian beer. "I cannot deny it, though I never would've believed such a rapid recovery was possible." His expression turned coolly speculative. "Can't wait to be rid of me, can you?"

Karin's head jerked up from her own cup, which she'd been swirling distractedly. "What?" She glowered over at him. "It is not that. It . . . it . . ." She set down her cup and rose. "What do my reasons matter anyway? The responsibility for you will soon be out of my hands whether I wish it or not."

With that, Karin turned and strode out of the hut. Thorn frowned. He made a motion to rise when Arda stopped him with a gentle hand upon his arm.

"Why do you care what my daughter feels about you?" she softly demanded. "I would think, after what she did to you, you would hate her. Yet you watch her with hungry eyes when you think she's not looking, and you prick at her as if you wish far more from her than such casual acquaintance permits."

He jerked his arm away. "My thoughts and desires are my own. I'll not lay them out for you to mock and laugh over. It matters not, at any rate. Though Karin has soiled herself in the eyes of her people by touching me, she did so out of pity, out of a sense of duty, not because of any true feelings for me."

"Perhaps, but perhaps not." Arda smiled. "I only wonder what you would do if she did care for you. You seem as unskilled in the art of courtship as is she."

A deep flush crept up Thorn's neck and face. "This isn't seemly, you speaking of such things to me."

"And did your mother ever teach you of the way it is with women?"

"No. She died when I was but six. My father raised me."

Arda cocked her head in amusement. "Then perhaps you might allow me to take your mother's place for a short time? To teach you a bit about women. If you care enough to learn?"

He studied her for a long moment, then sighed and adamantly shook his head. "There's no time to woo Karin, even if she were of a mind to consider me. I refuse to go out after the Yengi, and there are few other options left me but death or escape. For Karin's sake, it's best I leave things as they are."

"You cannot turn from your destiny, Thorn Marwyn," Arda solemnly said. "And, as difficult, as frightening as it may be to face, my daughter is part of that destiny." She offered her hand to him. "Now, since you seem not of a mind to talk further, it is past time I find my rest. Would you help me to my bed?"

Thorn did as she requested, then returned to sit before the hearth fire. Karin remained outside for a long while, and Thorn, though sorely tempted to go out to her, didn't. Arda's words, claiming that her daughter was part of his destiny, roiled like a raging whirlpool in his mind. Try as he might, he couldn't seem to sort through it all to find the easing he so desperately needed. Not the easing nor the acceptance.

His life had changed far too rapidly to deal with. Once again, he felt out of control. Thorn found that the most frightening thing he'd ever known.

The nearer they drew to the capital city of Lacus Hedin, the greater the crowds grew. Farmers and herders, their woolly little ovis milling about them, mothers holding their babes at breast, craftsmen with their tools in hand, all came to stand beside the road leading up to the royal city. As Thorn passed and he was identified as the Yengi Beastslayer, looks of relief, then cheers, rose from the people.

He bit back an urge to deny his willing part in the whole matter, to tell them to find their beastslayer from among their own kind, but didn't. It wasn't their fault he was here. It was their king's—and Karin's.

The breach between them had widened even further since his accusations the night before last at the evening meal. Karin had barely spoken to him the next morning. She despised him, Thorn had finally decided. She regretted her former friendliness and foolishness in touching him, caring for him.

Arda had glanced worriedly at her daughter, who refused to meet her gaze. Then, as Thorn's hands were once more retied and his own expression set in a stony mask, Arda made her way over to him.

"This cannot go on," she softly chided him, her voice pitched low so the others wouldn't overhear. "You and Karin must make peace between you, begin to work together before it is too late."

"And what would you have me do?" Thorn gritted, wheeling about to glare down at her. "The only thing Karin wishes is to send me to be the Yengi's next meal. And I find that wish a bit hard to stomach, much less cooperate with."

"It is your destiny, as it is hers."

He gave a disbelieving laugh. "What? That Karin should fall victim to the Yengi, too? No wonder she shies from me like a damas does a wild canus!"

"Will you tell the king how you came to Orcades? That Karin forced you?"

"I hardly think he'll imagine me a willing participant, once I tell him what he can do with his plans for me."

Arda sighed. "Then you will destroy my daughter."

Thorn's gaze narrowed. He stepped closer. "Why? She'll have fulfilled her mission. She'll have brought me to him."

"But it was *how* she brought me to him that will interest the king most," the old woman patiently explained. "And Karin will not allow him to use her secret powers for evil purposes. Even now, her heart sorrows for what she has done to you. She will never do such a thing again, no matter if you survive and return home, or die. No matter if it costs her own life."

"How do you know this?" Thorn's mouth went grim. Apprehension rose within him. "Did she tell you?"

"No, Karin did not tell me, but I saw it in her eyes nonetheless. And I know my daughter. You will kill her, Thorn Marwyn, if you don't bind her to you."

He studied her long and impassively. "So, this, too, is now placed on me. Not only am I responsible for the lives of her people, but for Karin's life as well. Why do you think I'd care?"

Arda smiled. "I trust my daughter's judgment in all things. And she would not feel for you as she does if you were not a very special man."

Thorn's eyes widened in incredulity, but Arda said no more. She simply turned and limped away, her cane supporting her halting steps. There was no opportunity to go after her and question her further. The soldiers were there, pulling him away to join them. The journey had begun.

The royal city of Lacus Hedin was one of the largest and most impressive Thorn had ever seen. Its outer walls were almost twenty meters high and at least five meters thick. Constructed from some of the hardest rock known in the galaxy and found in abundance on Orcades, the hazy gray-blue mordax stone provided a virtually impregnable fortress.

As they climbed the wide road leading up to the main gates, the crowds grew until the thoroughfare was lined with what seemed the entire populace of the surrounding countryside. Though none would allow even their garments to brush against Thorn, lunging over backward into the others milling around him if he drew too near, he could tell, nonetheless, that they were glad to see him. Or maybe just relieved, he thought sourly. Relieved they now wouldn't have to risk their lives or lower themselves to fight a Yengi.

They passed through heavy, metal-banded wooden doors spanning the huge entrance to the fortified city and walked through the city to the palace at its center. Entering the long, pillared hall, Thorn, Karin, and the soldiers headed toward jewel-encrusted, golden doors opening into an even larger and more ornately furnished room. There, sitting upon a gilded dais and beneath a shimmering canopy of crimson luster cloth, was the King of Orcades. Without hesitation, Thorn strode forward to meet him, wishing to have this ordeal over and done with at last.

His guards pulled him back before he could mount the dais and confront the king man-to-man. Thorn was forced to halt and stare up at him from below. The king, a robust man with pale hair and eyes, studied Thorn speculatively.

"Strange," the ruler of Orcades murmured. "You don't look at all like what one would expect a Yengi Beastslayer to be."

Karin, who had followed closely behind, drew up beside Thorn and his guards. Momentarily, she was startled at how closely the king's initial observation of Thorn mimicked hers. The memory of that day she'd first seen him rushed back with a bittersweet pang. How long ago it now seemed. He'd been so beautiful, standing there tall and proud, caring for his damas. So content, so happy.

And now . . . now he was a prisoner, facing certain death if he defied the king—and an almost just as certain death if he didn't and went out to fight the Yengi.

"He is the son of the last Beastslayer to come to Orcades, sire," Karin said, lifting her voice to carry to the king. "I searched long and hard for him. He is all who remains of his kind."

The king smiled. "Then we be doubly fortunate to find him. It seems only fitting that the last Yengi on Orcades be killed by the last Voltaran Beastslayer. And afterward, we'll have no need of one ever again."

"You have no need of one now," Thorn growled. "Send out your own soldiers to fight the Yengi. It's your battle, not mine. And this Beastslayer isn't fighting any Yengi."

"Indeed? An unwilling Beastslayer?" The king's glance swung to Karin. "Didn't you inform this man of the riches he'll earn by serving us? For shame, Karin."

"My freedom is riches enough for me!" Thorn cried. "I want nothing from you but to be permitted to return to Voltar. Do you hear me? Nothing!"

A pale head dipped. A bejeweled hand stroked a regal chin. Then the king looked up. "And how came you to Orcades if you were so unwilling? I sent but a woman to fetch you. How could she have brought you here against your will?"

Thorn froze. His head turned; his glance met Karin's. Terror and a look of wild entreaty burned in her eyes.

This was the moment he could finally avenge himself on her, Thorn thought, perhaps even divert all the attention to Karin and save himself. Yet, even as he considered the act, he knew he could never betray her secret. Too much hung in the balance if he did—the welfare of an entire galaxy if the king subverted Karin's powers, not to mention her very life. But it wasn't the galaxy he saw when he gazed down into her deep blue eyes. It was Karin. Only Karin.

"What can I say?" Thorn tore himself from the beguiling woman who stood beside him and looked back up at the king. He forced a disinterested smile onto his face. "At first, I thought her offer very attractive and willingly followed through the Gate. But then, when I'd a chance to reconsider, it was too late. She banged me up alongside the head with a big rock when I made to turn back. The next thing I knew, the soldiers had me."

"And now you be here," the king prodded. "Be you quite certain you will not reconsider?"

"After the encounter we had several days back with the Yengi?" Thorn laughed. "I think not."

The Orcadian ruler sighed with mock regret. "Then perhaps a short stay in our royal dungeons will help you find a change of heart."

"I think not."

An elegantly garbed shoulder lifted negligently. "Well, there be worse ways to die than fighting a Yengi." He eyed Thorn with a speculative, almost anticipatory light. "And I think you would die quite slowly and very, very painfully.

"I am a fair man, though. I give you a choice." The king arched a pale brow, a thin smile upon his lips. "What do you think, Beastslayer? Which one would you choose?"

Chapter Five

It was so wet, so cold, so filthy. Thorn didn't think he'd ever feel warm or dry or clean again. He'd been here a week, seven long days and nights since the Orcadian king had condemned him to imprisonment. Not that he'd been able to discern one day from the other in the black depths of the royal dungeons. Thorn only wondered when the king would finally lose patience and begin the torture he'd promised—torture that could only end in his death.

A faint light flickered somewhere on the stairs leading down to the deepest cells. Thorn shifted awkwardly on the hard dirt floor. It must be time for another meal. Meals were the only opportunity he had for human contact and a bit of light, however brief. Even now, the king wished to keep him well fed. Even now, there was still hope that Thorn might change his mind and submit at last to Orcadian will.

His cell door swung open with a nerve-grating creak, piercing the heavy, stone-muffled silence. Torchlight flooded his cell, blinding him. Chains clanked as Thorn lifted his manacled hands to shield his eyes. There was a rough rasp of a food tray sliding across the floor, then the sound of the door slamming shut once more. Strangely, though, this time the light remained.

Thorn lowered his hands and blinked to focus. Eyes too long bereft of light watered painfully. Then a form, backlit by the torch left flaming in its wall bracket, moved toward him. He lurched back and shoved himself to a squatting position. His hands clenched into protective fists.

"Wh-who is it?" he hoarsely demanded. "Don't come a step closer!"

"Thorn?" Like a soothing caress, a soft voice washed over him. "It is I, Karin."

He squinted hard. A feminine form, garbed in a dark cloak and long gown, stood no more than a few meters away. Inexplicably, joy filled him.

"Karin?" He uttered the word as if it were some prayer. "What are you doing . . . ? Why did you come? I thought you'd gone back to your home."

"I did," she whispered achingly. "I could not stay, though, knowing you were here in this terrible place. I had to see you, talk with you one last time."

"But how . . . how did you get down here?"

"Not all Orcadians be mindlessly loyal to the

king. My mother and I once cared for the dungeon master's wife."

She moved forward. In a whisper of fabric and a flurry of delicate woman's fragrance, Karin knelt before him. Thorn inhaled deeply, savoring her scent, willing himself never to forget it. Her visit here would be the only consolation and comfort in the long days to come.

"Be you all right?" she asked after a long moment. "Has the king harmed you in any way?"

"Not yet," he muttered dryly, "if you discount the total darkness and sorry state of my cell."

"Ah, Thorn, I am so very sorry. I never thought it would come to this." Karin reached out to stroke his cheek.

He jerked away before she could touch him. "Don't. I haven't had a bath in over a week. I'm filthy."

"I do not care."

At her words, irrational anger surged through him. "And I don't need your pity."

Karin lowered her hand back to her side. "Is that why you think I came to visit you? Because I pity you?"

"Why else?" He laughed harshly. "I can't think of anyone in a more pitiable situation."

"Well, neither of us can spare the time for pity." She rose, walked across the cell, and returned with his supper tray. Lowering herself to the ground before him, Karin settled the tray across her lap and began lifting the metal lids covering the food. "Hmm. You have quite a generous serving of roast ovis meat, fresh bread with butter, a large wedge of Thesarian herder's cheese, beer, and some ripened ruga fruit for your supper."

"All the better to fatten me up for the Yengi's next meal, perhaps?"

She smiled. "I am certain that is the king's reasoning. Is it working?"

"No." Thorn reached out toward the tray. "But I intend to make the most of the food while I may. Would you please hand me a slice of bread and a chunk of cheese?"

Karin did as requested. Thorn paused with the bread and cheese at his lips. "You can help yourself to the food as well. There's always more than enough for my needs."

"I am not hungry." She paused, forming her next words carefully. "Have you come to any decision in the past week?"

"About whether I should obey your king or not?" he asked between bites of bread and cheese.

"Yes."

"I'm hoping to wear him down until he finally develops a conscience and decides to send me home."

Karin exhaled an exasperated breath. "Thorn, this is no time to joke. The king means to send you to his torture master on the morrow." She couldn't help a small shudder. "He is a most cruelly inventive man."

"Most torturers are." Thorn swallowed the last of his bread and motioned back toward the tray. "How about some of that ovis meat? It looks quite tasty."

"How can you be so casual about this?" Karin grasped his wrist as he reached toward the tray. "We be talking about your torture . . . torture unto death!"

Jade green eyes locked with hers. "And what would you have me do? Lie here in this stinking darkness and weep and wail over the unfairness of it all? Little good that would do. I'll die soon enough, whether I'm finally forced to choose a battle to the death against the Yengi over a slower one by torture. But until then, I mean to enjoy what few pleasures are left me."

She refused to release him. "Come with me then, this very night. I will help you escape and take you back to the Gate."

"And then what, Karin?"

"I will open the Gate to Voltar. You can go home."

Thorn sat there, his mind racing. Was this but another Orcadian trick? Had the king once again convinced Karin to coerce him to his needs?

The possibility angered Thorn. He didn't want her in the middle of this anymore. He didn't think he could bear any more conflict between them. Not now, not after all he'd been through of late. And not with all the unrequited emotions for her still roiling through him . . .

Twisting his arm in her clasp, Thorn grabbed Karin by the wrist. With a quick jerk, he pulled her to him. The tray clattered to the floor, the sudden, forward movement of her body spilling the dishes and food.

A soft, woman's body slammed into his, full

breasts, a flat belly, and slender thighs. At the feel of her, the most overwhelming sense of rage and primal hunger gripped Thorn.

Honor battled ferociously with need. It would be so easy to throw Karin down, to muffle her cries for help with his mouth, to tear aside her clothing and mate with her. It might well be the last time he'd have a woman, and who else but she owed him the sweet pleasures of her body? She'd taken everything else from him, still sought to, for all he knew. She should give him something in return.

His hand snaked behind her head. He pulled her face down to his. "Let's talk about escape later," Thorn urged huskily. "Right now I want you."

"No, you fool!" Karin hissed. "There is no time for such madness. I have come to take you away from here, to send you back through the Gate. There may never be another chance."

"Fool, am I?" Thorn released her with a jerk. "The only fool here, I think, is you, if you think I believe your offer of escape." His gaze narrowed. His lip curled. "What's your real game, Karin?"

Puzzlement wrinkled her brow. "What be you talking about? I came to help . . ." Her voice faded. "You think I still work for the king. That I mean to betray you."

"That would seem a logical assumption, considering the circumstances."

"No, Thorn." Karin sighed. "That might have been a logical assumption in the beginning, but not now. I could not live with myself if I let you die."

"Your attack of conscience comes a bit late, wouldn't you say, Karin?"

"Perhaps so, but it is not just my conscience compelling me finally to help you." She hesitated, as if considering her next words, then squared her shoulders and forged on. "I-I care about you, Thorn Marwyn. And, more than anything, I wish for you to be happy once again."

His dark brows lowered. Suspicion gleamed in his eyes. "*Care* about me? But how could that be? I'm a loathsome Voltaran. I stand too far below your high and mighty Orcadian breeding ever to be worthy of one such as you. Whatever could you find in me to care about?"

Tears filled Karin's eyes. Her hands clenched into fists. "Do not mock me, Thorn Marwyn. Not me nor my honest sharing of my feelings for you! If you do not wish to accept my explanation, that is your right. But you wished to know the real reason I want to help you return to Voltar, and I told you." She wiped away the tears spilling down her cheeks. "Curse you. Ah, curse you!"

His mouth went grim and a decidedly uncomfortable look flared in his eyes. "I didn't mean to mock you, Karin. I'm just not very good at this sort of thing, and I can't understand how you could possibly care for a man like me."

She pulled a small cloth from the pouch she wore about her waist and noisily blew her nose. "Be you mad? You be the kindest, the gentlest man I have ever met."

"Kind? Gentle? Me?"

"Yes, kind and gentle. I saw you with your

damas. Somehow, I knew you would be just as gentle with a woman. And you be the most handsome man, too. If you had not chosen to hibernate up there on that mountain of yours, you would have discovered that quickly enough, with all the women swooning over you." Karin paused, a considering look in her eyes. "I never asked you this before, but why *did* you choose to live in such isolation?"

Thorn grimaced. "Rebellion, perhaps. From the moment I was born to the instant he died, I was not only forced to endure my father's endless tales of our proud and glorious heritage, but his rigid control of my life. He never doubted that my fate was to be a warrior, if no longer by slaying Yengis—since he thought he'd killed the last of them—then in hiring myself out as a soldier of fortune when I came to manhood." A bitter light gleamed in his eyes. "Our kind wasn't suited for much else, my father always said. *He* certainly wasn't . . . after his battle with the Yengi."

When Thorn paused to drag in a shuddering breath, Karin scooted close and took his hand in hers. "What happened to him, Thorn?"

He met her questioning gaze with a furious one of his own. "The Yengi left him blind in one eye, horribly scarred, and paralyzed from the waist down. When my mother died shortly thereafter, even the riches my father had acquired weren't enough to give him pleasure. There wasn't much else left him, save in making plans to relive his life through me.

"I turned my back on him two years ago, when

I had finally had enough. I left my father and what remained of the money he'd squandered in his loss and unhappiness. He died alone, without anyone close who truly loved him, and the hangers-on, the human scavengers who'd called themselves friends, took whatever was left."

His mouth went grim. "In the end, what did the great wealth of a Yengi Beastslayer bring him? Nothing. Absolutely nothing that truly mattered."

With infinite tenderness, Karin lifted Thorn's hand against her cheek. "I am sorry, Thorn. I understand now why you feel the way you do. You meant to make your own way, to build a life to meet your own expectations rather than that of others, and then I came along and once again tried to force you into some preconceived mold. Not to mention attempted to force you to risk life and limb for some promise of riches you already knew held little value for you."

"Well, at least now you know me for the man I truly am, which is not at all the man you make me out to be."

"You be all the man I ever imagined and more, you stubborn son of a Beastslayer," Karin softly protested. "And despite everything you have told me, I know you feel for the plight of my people, and the terrible destruction the Yengi has wrought."

He shrugged. "I still won't fight the beast for them. I refuse to be told what to do ever again, to have my life controlled or planned by another. It's your king's responsibility to protect his people—with his own army, not at my expense!"

"Yes, it is our responsibility. And we need to face that, and many more responsibilities to the land and the people, at long last. But I fear it may never arise from the king and his kind. Though I have begged him to reconsider his punishment of you, to send his own soldiers out against the Yengi, he will not be swayed. The responsibility *and* the action will have to come from the people themselves. People like me."

There was a note of resignation, of finality in Karin's voice that gave Thorn pause. Suspicion gnawed at him like the unrequited hunger of a starving man. "And what exactly do you have in mind? If you help me escape and send me back through the Gate, your king will know you betrayed him. Your life could be in jeopardy."

"It does not matter. By the time the king determines what has happened, I will have either won his favor again—or be dead." She turned and kissed Thorn on his palm, then released him. "Now, time draws short. Will you come with me or not?" She grinned wryly. "Or, should I say, do you trust me and my motives enough now to come with me?"

He smiled. "Yes, I suppose I do trust you, as difficult as that is for a man like me. But I'll leave here tonight only if you vow to pass through the Gate with me. Once you help me escape from Lacus Hedin, your life may well be forfeit. It'll be safer for you on Voltar. You can stay with me and, perhaps in time . . ."

Thorn caught himself before he said more. His own feelings for Karin could well be clouding his judgment. Despite all her kind words and evident concern for him, she was still Orcadian and he, Voltaran. Though they'd spanned much in the course of a few weeks, the centuries-old inter-planetary animosity and revulsion still ran deep. And he'd revealed more than enough of himself this night.

"You can stay with me," he forced himself to continue, "until you've time to make some decisions about your life."

"My thanks for your generous offer, but I cannot leave Orcades." Karin lowered her gaze. "My mother, my people, still need me."

"Then we'll take your mother with us. And your people will go on as they have before. Whether you leave or stay will matter little in the total scheme of things."

She shook her head. "I-I cannot. The Yengi. The creature must be destroyed."

"And what would you do against it?" Thorn's grip on her arms tightened and, when she didn't answer, he gave her a quick shake. "What would you do, Karin?"

At the rising apprehension in his voice, Karin's head snapped up. "You said the responsibility for the Yengi was ours. And I have special powers to stun and compel that might work against the Yengi long enough to take it by surprise. I am stronger than I might look. I can wield a spearslayer against the beast."

Horror widened his eyes. "So that's how you hope to regain the king's favor, or die in the effort. You'll let me go back to Voltar and then take my place against the Yengi. Is that it, Karin?"

"Yes," she cried, "and do not sound so outraged by my plan. You owe us nothing. You have no right to determine how we solve our problems."

"I didn't mean for a lone woman to go after the Yengi, either. Especially not you!"

"You cannot stop me, Thorn."

He held her, frantically considering all the threats, all the ways he could prevent her from carrying out her plan, and knew she was right. Though Karin would never compel him to her command again, she also wouldn't hesitate to use her powers against him if he should try to stop her. And she meant to go after the Yengi. He could see it in her eyes, feel it in the set of her slender body.

Destiny. Karin's mother had spoken of a shared destiny between him and Karin. Thorn had scoffed at it then. He no longer did. It must be destiny. Why else would he be making the decision he now was? Why else, indeed?

"No." He sighed his acquiescence, admitting to himself the truth at last. "I can't stop you. I can't make you do anything you don't wish to do, and I wouldn't even if I could. But I can't let you go alone to fight the Yengi, either." Thorn pulled Karin to him, cradling her in the protective clasp of his arms. "Curse you, little gatekeeper. You've finally discovered the one and only reason that could ever compel me to attempt what I've turned from all my life."

He gave a husky, self-deprecating laugh. "Why, I didn't even know what the reason was myself until just now."

"And that is?" Karin whispered from the warm, hard-muscled haven of his chest, dreading what his answer might be yet still needing to know with all her heart.

"I care for you, too, Karin de Cedrus. We are bound now, not only by destiny, but by that affection. Bound . . . in life as in death. And not even the fearsome powers of a Yengi can ever separate us again."

Chapter Six

Taking only the pack of food Karin had secreted outside the city and the two spearslayers and Orcadian war knives she'd stolen from the armory, they journeyed all night and through the next day, reaching Karin's village near midnight. No one save a few dogs that barked, then quickly quieted when they recognized her, noticed their passage to Karin's hut. Arda received them, apparently not at all surprised that her daughter had returned with Thorn. After feeding them a hot meal and providing them with warm water to bathe, she sent Thorn off to sleep in her curtained bed and Karin off to hers. Not a word was uttered or a question asked as to why they were there.

Thorn woke first, late that afternoon. A surreptitious peek outside confirmed that the day was spent as the setting sun bathed the land in a soft, golden glow. He dropped the leather window covering and turned back to Arda.

"We need to be off as soon as the darkness covers our leaving," he said, his voice pitched low to avoid waking Karin. "The king's soldiers will soon be hot on our trail and I don't want you implicated in aiding us."

Karin's mother shrugged. "It matters not. I have not much longer to live, despite the medicines Karin received from the king." She eyed him closely. "My passing would free Karin as well. Free her to go with you back to Voltar, if you wish it of her."

He strode across the hut to stand before her. "It may all soon be a moot point, no matter what either of us wishes. Karin might not want you to know, but I feel you have the right." Thorn paused for the space of an inhaled breath. "We mean to go after the Yengi."

Arda paled. "I feared as much. Karin holds the plight of her people too close to her heart ever to turn her back on them. Though she refuses to allow you to be used or mistreated further, she will not leave her people in such distress. I just never imagined your destinies would lead to this."

"If it's any comfort, when the time comes, I'll try to convince her to let me fight the Yengi alone."

"I know my daughter too well to find much comfort in that." The old woman smiled. "You will not stop her from aiding you."

He shoved a hand through his hair in exasperation, setting the long strands awry. "Perhaps not,
but I'm determined to try, nonetheless. She's so
young. She deserves more than just a few days
left of life."

"Hush." Arda placed a gentle finger upon his
lips. "None of us can know how long our living
will be. Make the most of what you have. There
is much that can be experienced, much that can
be shared, in even so short a time."

A soft, wondering smile curved his lips. "Yes,
I'm beginning to see that."

"Come now." Arda guided Thorn to the table
and pressed him into a chair. "You need a good
hot meal in your belly before you leave." She
filled a pottery bowl with a generous helping of
stew and placed it before him, then shoved over
a platter of sliced bread still warm from the bake
oven and a small crock of sweet butter. "Eat,
and while you do, I will prepare two packs of
trail food and supplies for you and Karin to take
along."

Thorn paused with a spoonful of stew halfway
to his mouth. "Is there any way to talk with the
villagers in the meanwhile as well? To ascertain if
they've heard anything about what direction the
Yengi was last seen headed?"

"I already know. The Yengi's whereabouts is
the constant talk nowadays. The creature's lair is
three days' travel into the mountains. Rumor has
it the time is near for the Yengi to return there
to rest awhile." She smiled grimly. "To rest and
digest all its meals of late."

"Good." Thorn picked up a slice of bread and slathered it with butter. "The Yengi's dormant phase is the best time to attack it. The beast will be sluggish and sleepy. If I can take him by surprise, the chances of success will be strong. My father, as well as his father before him, killed their Yengis in just such a manner."

Arda nodded approvingly. "Already you begin to think like a Yengi Beastslayer. One cannot escape one's heritage, can one?"

Thorn glanced up in surprise. "No," he agreed, his expression turning thoughtful, "perhaps one can't."

Karin woke a short time later, ate the stew her mother placed before her, then helped with the packing. Their farewells were long and heart-wrenching, for both women knew they might never see each other again.

"Be happy, child," Arda whispered as she clasped Karin to her. "Be happy with Thorn as I was with your father. It is all I could wish for you."

"I will, Mother, if he will have me," Karin whispered in a tear-choked voice. "I-I will return when this is over."

"No." Arda leaned back. "It will be too dangerous for you. The king is unpredictable in his favor as well as anger. Though you slay the Yengi for him, he may turn on you still."

"I do not care." Karin's jaw set in implacable determination. "I will not leave you, no matter the danger."

"You must. Your fate lies with Thorn now, not with me. It is the way of things, part of the continuum of life and death." Arda added emphasis to her words with a solemn nod of her head. "Head straight for the Gate and Voltar. And one thing more, sweet child." Tenderly she wiped away the tears streaming down Karin's face.

"What is that, Mother?"

"Once you pass through the Gate, close it behind you forever. You be the last of our kind. When you be gone, the king can never again use us to pass through to other worlds. Orcades will finally be forced to depend upon itself to solve its own problems."

"But what of you?" Karin protested. "You, too, can open Gates. He can still use you."

"Not for long, even if he were able." Arda released her daughter and stepped back. "Do not worry about me. It is your life that matters now." Thorn walked over, a pack and spearslayer clasped in his hand, an Orcadian war knife strapped to his thigh. Arda smiled. She handed Karin the other pack and her spearslayer. "Go now, child. The night draws on. Go out to meet your destiny . . ."

Tears welled once more in Karin's eyes, but she bravely nodded and turned toward the door. Pausing there, she wheeled around one last time. "I love you, Mother," she whispered achingly. "Always and forever."

"I know, child," her mother replied. "I know."

Then, without looking back, Karin stepped into the night and slipped from the village, Thorn at her side. They journeyed for a long while in silence,

Karin overcome with emotion, Thorn not knowing what to say or do to comfort her. Finally, he took her by the arm and halted her.

"Karin," he began uncertainly, "I'm sorry about your mother. If . . . if we succeed against the Yengi, I'll come back for her and bring her to you. Then we'll all head for Voltar."

"No." She shook her head firmly. "It would be too dangerous for you. Besides, Mother knows her days be numbered. I think she would rather live out the time left her on Orcades and be buried close to my father. I would not take her from here." And I will not leave her, either, as long as she still lives, Karin silently added.

She chose to withhold that admission from Thorn, however. Enough lay ahead of them without the complications of emotional issues, promises of committment, questions about the future. There would be time enough later, when the Yengi was dead. *If* Thorn wanted her . . .

She forced a wan little smile. "I appreciate your offer, though. It is most kind."

Thorn gave an awkward shrug. "I didn't know what else to say, but I couldn't bear for you to be so unhappy."

Karin gazed up at him for a long moment. A wild impulse flared within her. Why not? she asked herself. There was so little time remaining and so much living left to do. Her long, dark lashes lowered. "You could hold me for a moment, perhaps even kiss me. That would help."

"Would it really?"

He pulled her close, encircling her in the muscled clasp of his arms. Karin's heart began a frantic staccato beat. He was so strong, so warm, so male, and she wanted him with every fiber of her being. By the five stars, but it frightened her how much she wanted him!

She lifted her face to his. "Yes, Thorn, a kiss would help very much."

"Then it is yours, little one," he rasped, lowering his mouth to hers.

Before Karin could even think, much less reply, Thorn's lips settled over hers, surprisingly soft, warm, and oh, so gentle. His mouth opened, searching, hungry. He pressed her against him until she felt every muscle and sinew of his suddenly taut and straining body.

For an instant, Karin was taken aback by the change in him, the surprising intensity of his need. Then Thorn groaned.

"Kiss me back, Karin. Please, little one."

She whimpered softly. She clasped his face in her hands and leaned up to him. Hesitantly, Karin kissed Thorn, reveling in the feel of him, his scent, his passion, his need. His tongue flicked over her lips, lightly at first, then more urgently, insisting she part them. The strange, unfamiliar feel of him there, at the opening of her mouth, startled her, yet excited her all the same. A heat flared deep within Karin's belly. Excitement thrummed through her.

On a whispering sigh, she opened her mouth to him. The moment she did, Thorn plunged his tongue inside to intimately and most thoroughly join with hers. Teasingly, tormentingly, he advanced, then withdrew until Karin was wild with the need to hold him deep within. She arched against him, flattening her breasts against the hard, flat planes of his torso, grinding her hips against him in a rising agony of desire.

Her response surprised him. Though Thorn hadn't meant for his efforts at comforting her to go this far, the blood nonetheless pounded through his body, pooled in his groin. He swelled, thick and hard.

"Karin," he groaned. "We must stop. Stop before I take you right here and now."

She didn't seem to hear him, so crazed was her need. Thorn's grasp upon her tightened. Just a moment longer, he thought. Just a moment more of this hot, ardent ecstasy. Then, with all the strength still left in him, Thorn shoved her away and stepped back.

Karin stood there, panting, still passion-driven, aching with an unrequited yearning. Gradually her excitement eased. She stared up at Thorn, confused and suddenly so bereft she wanted to cry.

"Why . . . why did you push me away?" She wrapped her arms tightly about her as if to regain some of the heat and closeness of him.

"Why else?" he hoarsely replied. "You made me so hot with wanting you I feared for my control. And this is neither the time nor the place for lovemaking. There are soldiers behind us."

Wonderingly, Karin touched her kiss-swollen lips. "I did not know . . ." She flushed. "I was so caught up in the pleasure of it all . . ."

"As was I." Thorn grinned down at her. "If it pleases you, though, I'd like very much to continue this at a later date." He took her by the arm. "In the meanwhile, however, we need to put as much distance as possible between us and the king's men."

He'd been as excited as she, Karin realized, feeling the tremors shaking his hand as he held her, sensing the desire he held so tenuously in check. Exhilaration flooded her. By just her kiss and touch alone she had stirred this big, beautiful man. Her woman's powers, powers she'd only heard tales of but never experienced until now, must indeed be great.

She smiled. "Yes, I too would like to continue what we began here. Promise it will not be long in coming."

Something hot and primal flared in Thorn's eyes. "I promise, little one. It won't be long. I promise."

As dawn's first light drowned the land in rosy splendor and they began their climb into the foothills, the movement of a large force across the plains could be seen in the distance. Thorn muttered a few choice curses and urged Karin to a quicker pace.

"There won't be any rest for us this day," he growled as he grasped her arm to steady her ascent. "We won't be safe from the king's soldiers until we're near the Yengi's lair. Once they've ascertained where we're headed, though, I'd wager they'll pull back and await the outcome."

"H-how much longer?" Karin panted, already near the limits of her endurance after an all-night march. "How long before we reach the Yengi's lair?"

Thorn scanned the peaks rising before them. "It's hard to tell, but from the looks of it, I'd say at least another two days' travel. The old trader we met earlier said the Yengi lives in the highest part of the mountains. Luckily for us, he also claimed the trail would get easier and easier to follow the closer we drew to its lair."

"A consolation of sorts, to be sure," Karin gritted and forged on.

By mid morn, Thorn was forced to call a halt and allow the exhausted Karin a short rest. As they took their fill of bread and fruit, washed down by a skin of watered-down beer, he worriedly studied her.

She looked haggard. Dark smudges bruised the skin beneath her eyes. Her shoulders slumped, her lids sagged, and it appeared as if she'd fall asleep at any second.

Thorn's heart went out to her. He touched Karin gently on the arm. "Rest here and let me go on without you. I'll be back, if I'm coming back, before the soldiers can make it here. Then we can continue on to the Gate."

"And if you do not come back?" Karin demanded, her head snapping up, anger flashing in her eyes. "What then?"

"You head to the Gate alone. You know where my hut in the mountains is. You can live there in safety and seclusion until you choose otherwise."

"And why would I wish to live alone on Voltar?" Karin unsteadily shoved to her feet. "I would just come back to take on the Yengi at any rate." She firmly shook her head. "No, we go on together or not at all. It seems your choice is to go on, so let us be on our way."

With that, Karin grabbed her pack and spearslayer and set out up the mountainside. Thorn watched her for an instant more, awestruck at her stubborn pride and determination. Then, shoving the food supplies back into his pack, he slung his own spearslayer over his shoulder and scrambled after her.

Karin's resolve, however, could only fuel her weary body so far. By midday, Thorn was forced to take an extended break to allow her to rest. They set out once again in mid afternoon and traveled until it became too dark to traverse the increasingly steep and rocky terrain, then made camp inside a deep cave. Working together, they quickly started a fire for warmth against the cool mountain air and laid out their bedding.

"We should near the Yengi's lair tomorrow," Thorn said a short while later as he cut into a round of herder's cheese and offered Karin a few slices. "I don't know how long we'll have to wait if the beast isn't there yet, but if it already is, time is of the essence. Once its dormant phase has passed, our advantage is lost."

Karin placed the cheese on her bread. "Then we attack as soon as we reach the lair?"

"We'll wait until sunset, but no later. The Yengis tend to have poor vision, and the twilight darkness will grant us another advantage." Thorn laid down his knife, his expression solemn. "I would ask you again to reconsider your decision to join in the fight. It may be selfish of me, but I'd like to know that one of us will survive, no matter what happens. If I die, I could at least die in peace if I thought you were safe."

Karin set aside her bread and scooted close to him. With the most exquisitely tender of touches, she stroked his cheek. "And I wish nothing more than to give you peace and happiness. But I could not live with myself if I were not there in your most desperate of times, at your side, fighting the Yengi. Please do not ask me to stand back and watch you do battle alone. If our destinies be joined, let them be joined in this as well."

He took Karin's hand and placed it over his heart. "Let our destinies be joined then in all things, for the rest of our days." Thorn lifted her hand to his mouth and kissed it. "Will you lie with me tonight, little one?"

Karin nodded, her eyes aglow, her body vibrantly alive with anticipation and yearning. "Yes."

His hands moved to the laces of her tunic and he began to untie them, then paused, suddenly uncertain. "Will you permit me the liberty of undressing you?"

Karin swallowed hard. She had never exposed her body to a man. "Yes, if that is what you wish," she forced out the words. "Anything, if it will please you."

He smiled, a sudden wolfish twist to his mouth. In a swift movement, Thorn pulled the tunic over Karin's head.

Instinctively, as her bare flesh met the chill of the mountain air, Karin covered herself with her arms. She glanced up apprehensively at Thorn.

"Uncover yourself, little one."

The rough rasp of his voice shivered down Karin's spine. His eyes, glittering with a hot, almost feral light, seared her skin. A tremor of excitement rippled through her. Slowly she lowered her arms.

The sight of her, of slender shoulders and delicate arms, of full, jutting breasts tipped with rosy, cold-hardened buds, stirred an answering response in Thorn's body. He wasn't sure why she'd agreed to mate with him—it could be anything, affection, lust, or just a need to reward him in some way for what they would attempt on the morrow.

The possibility that gratitude was motivating Karin's response sent a sharp pang knifing through him. Thorn shoved it aside. The morrow was soon enough to delve into motives. Tonight was his to savor, to experience to the fullest.

His shaft filled, thickened, throbbing hot and hard against his inner thigh. His breath quickened; his heart pounded in his chest. A fine sheen of sweat broke out on his brow.

He reached out to stroke the curve of one breast, his touch hesitant, almost reverent. At the feel of his fingers on her skin, Karin gasped.

Thorn smiled. "There's nothing to fear in my touch, little one. It's but the way of a man loving a woman."

"It is not so much fear as . . ." Karin paused for an instant, unsure of what she truly was feeling, " . . . as it is surprise."

"Surprise?"

She nodded. "Yes. I was surprised at how good it felt."

Thorn moved closer until he knelt before her. He grasped her by the arms. "Then let me make you feel that way again." His head dipped and he took her nipple into his mouth, suckling gently.

"Th-Thorn!" Karin breathed. "Ah, Thorn!" She gripped his arms, digging her nails into the cloth of his tunic. As wave after wave of exquisite sensation coursed through her, Karin's head fell back in ecstatic abandon. Never had she felt so wild, so aroused, so—so yielding!

Suddenly a need to see Thorn naked, to stroke every bit of his hard male body, filled her. Her fingers clutched at his tunic, jerking on it. "Your clothes," she whispered, her voice ragged. "Take off your clothes."

Thorn lifted his head. "Have a care, little one. I teeter close to losing control as it is. If I take off my clothes—"

"I do not care!" Karin cried. "I want you, Thorn. I need the feel of your flesh against mine, your warmth and strength. I want to be with you, to be as close to you as I can get. And I want our joining. It . . ." Her voice broke on a sob. "It may well be the one and only night we have. And I want it all, over and over again!"

"Then you shall have it, to your heart's desire." Thorn swiftly divested himself of his tunic and boots, then unlaced the front of his breeches. With one final glance up at Karin to assure himself of her resolve, he spread his breeches apart and tugged them down.

A long, thick organ jutted forth, its tip engorged and flaring. Karin eagerly reached out for it but Thorn stayed her hand. "No, not yet," he cautioned hoarsely. He completed the task of removing his breeches, then leaned over to push Karin down onto their bedding. His hands quickly worked the fastenings of her own breeches free and began to pull them down.

She watched him as he worked, stretched over her, all whipcord muscle and sinew, a virile, magnificent, masculine man. She reached up to circle a dark, flat male nipple with inquisitive fingers, to stroke his smooth-skinned chest, reveling in his warm, sun-bronzed flesh. Tracing a sinuous line down between his taut abdominal muscles, Karin followed the dark river of hair from his navel to his hot, thrusting sex.

Caught unawares as he twisted to lay aside her breeches, Thorn gasped in surprise when her fingers entwined around his shaft. He turned back to her, his excitement swelling to ungovernable heights. He covered her hand with his where it lay clasped about him, staying her intoxicating stroking movements.

"Karin." He could barely force out the words. "Let me go. Now!"

She shook her head, a pleased, knowing woman's smile upon her lips. With gentle but insistent tugs, she pulled him down to her. "No, Thorn. I want you and mean to have you—and I do not intend to wait a moment longer."

"Then have me you will," he growled, coming to her at last.

His questing fingers parted her, exploring her secret, silken depths, gauging her readiness. She was hot and wet. Thorn shifted his weight atop her, wedging his knee between her legs. Without a moment's hesitation, Karin spread herself for him. He leaned down onto her, his lips claiming hers even as their bodies met and melded.

He touched his tongue to her lips, coaxing them to part. When they did, his tongue slid gently between them. In the instant that Karin accepted him into her mouth, Thorn grasped his shaft and guided it equally as gently into her. When it finally met the resistance of her maidenhead, he paused for the space of an inhaled breath.

"Now," he whispered, darkly, passionately. "Now we'll at last be one." As he plunged his tongue into Karin's mouth in a wildly frantic kiss, Thorn arched his hips, thrusting past her maiden's barrier.

She stiffened, cried out, but the sound was buried in the torrid depths of their mouths. Then nothing mattered. Nothing but the thick, searing, sensual haze engulfing her. Instinct took over where experience was lacking. Her hips lifted to meet his, thrusting, writhing, drawing him in to her fullest depths.

The rhythm of their straining bodies increased in tempo and force. They panted, they groaned, they twisted against each other, crazed by the wild, rioting mass of sensations. And then, in that last instant when the pleasure grew to unbearable, agonizing heights, they came as one. Ecstasy—white-hot and violent—engulfed them.

His mouth joined with hers, Thorn cried out his release. His body shook with desperate, pulsating pleasure. Never had he known such joy. Never would he again . . . save in Karin's arms and buried deep within her sweet woman's body. But it was enough, though he lived but one more day. He'd known love, devotion, and fulfillment at last.

Clasping Karin to him, Thorn pulled the blanket up to cover them, holding her close until they both nodded off to sleep.

Chapter Seven

As the sun slowly sank behind the distant peaks, Thorn and Karin crouched behind some boulders on a rocky mountainside over the Yengi's lair. Shadowy fingers stroked the land, bathing the rock-strewn terrain in twilight. The time to attack was upon them.

"Remember, Karin," Thorn whispered beside her. "I take the Yengi from the front. Once I engage his attention, you sneak up and try to stun him. Don't take any chances, though. If the beast catches wind of you and turns in your direction, you run back to the rocks until it's safe to try again."

"There is nothing safe about this, Thorn Marwyn," Karin replied disgustedly. "And, if you think to bear all the danger, you be sadly mistaken."

He shot her a narrow look. "There's danger enough for all, but you're worse than no help if you don't obey me in this. You're a dangerous distraction. I can't concentrate all my efforts on the Yengi if I'm worrying about you, can I? And you know I will, if I can't count on you following my directions."

Karin hesitated, a fiery protest on her lips, then sighed. "Yes, I know you will worry and I do not want my efforts to be cause for harm to you. I will do as you ask."

"Good." Thorn wrapped his arm about her shoulders and gave her a quick squeeze. Then, gazing down at her, his expression softened. "Thank you for last night. It meant a lot to me."

"As it did to me." She smiled wanly, wishing for more from him than that meager admission. But his simple statement was for the best, she told herself. So much had happened in such a short span of days. There hadn't been time to allow things to develop any more deeply between them. And a commitment as special as love couldn't be hastened or forced. Yet, if she didn't already love Thorn, Karin realized with a small start of surprise, her emotion was certainly something very close to it. Something very close indeed . . .

Reluctantly, Thorn released her. His glance swung to the sun, its final burst of radiance extinguished at last. He gripped his spearslayer in his hand, checked the long Orcadian war knife strapped to his right thigh, then rose. Climbing swiftly and silently, he made his way along the upper edge of the Yengi's lair and then down its side.

The Yengi slept deep within, its sonorous snores filling the air. It wouldn't sleep for long, Thorn thought grimly. A battle within its cave might seem the best strategy, as the beast was sure to have difficulty moving about in the confined space, but the darkness would hamper him as much as the Yengi, in the end giving the beast the advantage. That was why the battles had always been fought in the open. He would follow tradition.

Thorn tossed some pebbles into the lair, shouted the hoarsely strident Beastslayer battle cry, then hurriedly hid behind a boulder. The Yengi was nearsighted and engorged, but he wasn't deaf.

A harsh chittering and scrabbling sound heralded his approach to the mouth of the cave. A thick, bony head, covered with pinkish gray skin peeked out and swung slowly to and fro. Small red eyes blinked blearily, attempting to focus. The beast's nostrils flared, sniffing the air.

Thorn knew the instant the Yengi caught his scent. The creature froze. His scissorslike jaw opened, needle-sharp teeth glowing dully in the dim light. Then, with a mighty shove, the Yengi slid out of his lair. Twisting his huge body in a surprisingly agile move, he sprang at Thorn with a raucous, blood-chilling cry. Thorn leaped from behind the boulder, his spearslayer held high. As the creature momentarily flew over him, he plunged it upward at the Yengi's soft underbelly.

A daggerlike arm, joined to the creature's back leg by an immense gliding membrane, lowered at just that moment, deflecting the spearslayer from its intended target. The multi-pronged spear caught in the leathery wing, ripping a long, jagged hole nearly its entire length. The Yengi screamed, changed direction in midair, and flung itself at Thorn.

There was no time for Thorn to do anything but drop the spearslayer and dive aside. The Yengi's body caught him nonetheless. Its ravaged wing and belly dragged Thorn down by his legs. A horrid odor engulfed him. Terror rocketed through him.

He writhed, his fingers digging into the earth. Frantically, Thorn tried to claw his way out from beneath the Yengi's crippling weight, to no avail.

Thorn grabbed for his dagger, wrenched it free, and twisted onto his back. Above him, the Yengi rose, its cavernous maw wide. The stench of death encompassed him. He saw it in the Yengi's eyes, in its slavering jaws and dagger-tipped arms as they slowly closed around him. Thorn gripped his dagger with both hands and stabbed upward, hoping, praying he'd wound the Yengi badly enough so he could break free.

Then, in a lightning-swift move, the Yengi darted down, engulfing Thorn's dagger and hands in its mouth. Thorn's torso was lifted in the air, though his legs remained pinned beneath the beast's body. He felt as if he were being torn in half. Tiny, pointed teeth bit into his flesh, piercing to the bone.

Crazed by pain, Thorn shoved his left shoulder into the Yengi's mouth, twisted and levered the creature's jaws open. With an agonizing wrench, he jerked his right arm free. Somehow, he still clasped the dagger in his hand.

Again and again he stabbed at the Yengi's head, puncturing one eye, slicing deep into its face, frantically going for the throat. Nothing seemed to faze the creature. Its grip on Thorn's left arm tightened, grinding down through flesh and muscle and bone.

Excruciating pain engulfed him. A blinding kaleidoscope of colors whirled before Thorn's eyes. He arched back in the Yengi's grip, every muscle in his body going rigid. He screamed, over and over and over.

"Karin!"

Suddenly Thorn felt himself flung to the ground. A heavy, smothering weight settled over him. Everything went dark and he couldn't breathe, couldn't even exhale deeply enough to drag in air. Was this what it felt like to die?

"Thorn! Ah, Thorn!" came a muffled cry from somewhere far away.

There was a tug on his legs. He felt his body slide along the ground—his hips, his belly, his chest. He dragged in a lungful of air. Then his head and arms were free.

"Thorn, be you all right?"

Hands pulled at him, turning him over. He blinked in the deepening twilight. Karin leaned over him.

Pain seared through Thorn. His left arm felt on fire. He tried to move it, but it lay limp and unmoving above his head. "My arm," he groaned. "I can't move my left arm."

She grabbed for it and pulled it down to his side. Karin bit back a cry of horror. Blood drenched his arm, spurted from several jagged tears on his forearm. The skin was ripped apart, exposing muscle and bone. She pulled out her knife, cut off what remained of Thorn's lower tunic sleeve, and wrapped it around his arm just above his elbow. With several quick twists of the cloth, she deftly fashioned it into a tourniquet.

"Th-the Yengi," Thorn groaned. "What happened to the Yengi?"

"I stunned it. I crept up on the Yengi while he had you and placed my hands on him." She moved to his side and slid her arm beneath his shoulders. "He will not stay stunned long, though. I need to get you out of danger. Can you stand?"

He struggled to sit and nearly blacked out. "N-no," Thorn whispered. "G-get your spearslayer. Kill the Yengi before it awakens. It-it's our only hope."

"I left it by the lair. Let me first—"

"No!" With a painful effort, Thorn emphatically cut her off. "Leave me and get . . . the . . . spearslayer. Now!"

She lowered him to the ground, rose, and sprinted off. Behind him, the Yengi stirred. Thorn levered himself up with his good arm and turned. A single red eye stared back at him, its expression malevolently furious. Desperately, Thorn cast about for a weapon, and saw his dagger, lying but a meter away.

The Yengi rose, pushing up with its daggered arms. It advanced on him. Thorn flipped over, ignoring the sharp stab of pain in his left arm, and grasped frantically for the dagger. He heard Karin's terrified scream, but had no time to warn her away.

His fingers glanced off the dagger. With a desperate grunt, he lurched forward, stretching with all his might. This time, his hand closed around the dagger's hilt.

Then the Yengi was upon him. Darkness and the breath-grabbing stench once more engulfed him. Thorn stabbed up blindly, again and again. Repeatedly the blade made contact, plunged deep and hard. Hot, sticky wet blood began to trickle, then pour down onto Thorn. The Yengi shuddered, gave a startled, chittering cry, and finally pulled away. The ground shook as it fell, the dagger, imbedded in its neck, jerked out of Thorn's hand.

Thorn rolled over onto his side. The world spun dizzily before him, but through the gray mists slowly encompassing him, he saw the Yengi writhing in its death throes. A grim satisfaction filled Thorn. He'd killed the last Yengi. He was finally a Beastslayer, like all his kind before him.

With that thought to comfort him, Thorn fell back, surrendering to the horrible pain at last.

"Now, Thorn. Walk through now," Karin urged, fiercely fighting back the tears. The Gate shimmered before them, an opalescent force that filled the air with a skin-prickling static charge. "The king's soldiers are right behind us. There's no time for talk. Not anymore."

"There's time enough to hear your real reason why you won't go back with me. And hear it I will!" Thorn shot Karin an angry look as he readjusted the sling holding what remained of his left arm more comfortably about his neck. Though they'd barely had the luxury of one day since the battle with the Yengi to rest and recover, it had almost been the death of them. The king's soldiers had come upon them and they'd been forced to flee into the night.

"And what other reason could there be, save I will not leave my mother as long as she still lives?" Karin's gaze caught on the sling. Fresh guilt surged through her. She couldn't help it. Though the Yengi was finally dead and her people safe forever from the horror of the creature's destructive rampages, the cost had been almost too high to bear.

She'd fought as hard as she could to save Thorn's terribly savaged arm, but it had still been impossible to salvage the lower half. All that remained was a useless stump ending at the elbow.

Thorn was deformed, a man all but crippled with the use of only one arm. Crippled . . . just like his father . . . and it was her fault. *She* had been the one to bring him to Orcades. *She* had been the one who forced him into the position of finally choosing to go against the Yengi, even though he'd never wanted to.

True, his decision had been based on his loyalty and concern for her, but it didn't ease Karin's guilt—her guilt *and* fear that someday Thorn would come to hate her for what he'd lost. And

that he'd always imagine, if she went with him
now, that she did so out of pity.

"I think you don't need me anymore," Thorn
snarled, finally answering her question. "I think
you find my mangled arm disgusting. And I think
there was never anything of real value between
us."

It was his pain, his anguish over the loss of
his arm speaking, Karin well knew. But she also
knew that her protests, at a time like this, would
solve nothing. They needed time to work things
through—and they didn't have it.

"And what would you have me say?" she asked,
controlling her sorrow, her bitter sense of frustration and futility with the greatest of efforts. The
sounds of heavy-booted feet, of weapons clanging,
rose to her ears on the early morning breeze. "That
I love you, Thorn? That I will come to you, but not
just now? Well, I do and I will. I swear it."

For a fleeting instant something softened in
Thorn's gaze. Hope flared; the first flickerings
of the old passion smoldered once more to life.
Then, as if by some conscious effort, they were
snuffed out. Something dark and final shuttered
Thorn's thoughts from her.

"Fine. In the end, you'll either come or not.
There's nothing more I can do about it, one way
or another." His glance shifted toward the trail
where the soldiers would soon appear. "It's farewell then, is it?"

"Yes," she whispered achingly. "It is."

He eyed her narrowly, hesitating as if to say
more, then turned and strode through the Gate.

Karin watched him disappear, the tears streaming freely down her cheeks.

Behind her, the soldiers crested the trail. When they saw Karin, they gave a cry of triumph.

"I *will* come, Thorn," she breathed in fervent resolve. "I swear it." Then, with a quick mental effort, Karin closed the Gate—and turned to face the men rushing, even then, down to her.

A freshened breeze blew through the mountains, bringing with it the first glimmerings of spring. Birds flew overhead, bearing twigs and bits of grass to build their nests. Melting snow dripped from the sun-warmed rocks, carving little rivulets into the rich, damp earth, coursing ever downward to join with others until they formed streams and then rivers.

The tang of wood smoke wafted by. Karin quickened her pace, excitement and a rising apprehension filling her. Soon, just over the next elevation in the trail, she would look down on Thorn's hut.

It had been eight months since she'd last seen him. Eight long months since she'd bade Thorn farewell and sent him through the Gate back to Voltar. Thanks to the king's medicines, her mother had lingered longer than Karin would ever have imagined, but the time spent with her had been precious. It was time Karin would cherish for the rest of her days.

But that same time had perhaps convinced Thorn she'd never intended to come to him. What thoughts had passed through his mind in the past eight months? Had he felt pain at what he envisioned as her betrayal? Had he vowed never to forgive her? She wouldn't blame him if he did. Yet his rejection would tear her heart out just the same.

Karin paused as she reached the top of the trail. There, down below, lay Thorn's crude, hide-covered hut and animal pens. Strange, but the first time she'd seen it, it had all seemed so primitive, so foreign to her. Now, it looked like heaven, for only there in those simple surroundings would she find what she'd dreamed of, craved every day and night of the past eight months.

She'd find Thorn . . . if he would still have her.

He was working in the largest of the pens, struggling to get a newborn damas calf to nurse from a hide bag he'd fashioned to feed it. The fuzzy, tan-colored calf was obviously orphaned. Even more obviously, he wasn't taking well to his first meal.

"This isn't the best of ways to begin our relationship," Thorn gritted as he struggled to hold the squirming calf to him with the stump of his left arm and shove the milk bag into its mouth with the other. "I'm your new mama whether you like it or not, and you're not cooperating at all."

In apparent reply, the damas calf threw up its head, slamming its bony skull into Thorn's chin. At the same time, it reared up, long, spindly legs flailing wildly in the air. The sudden movement threw Thorn off balance. He toppled over backward and went sprawling in the dirt, the damas calf atop him.

The baby animal promptly leaped off him, turned to give him a chagrined look, then trotted across the pen.

Karin couldn't help a small giggle.

At the soft sound, Thorn froze. Ever so slowly, he turned to look over his shoulder. When he saw Karin standing there, peering through the slats of the pen, his eyes widened and his face went pale. Thorn's mouth opened, then clamped shut. An expression of fleeting anguish, then shuttering coldness swept over him.

"What are you doing here, Karin?" he ground out hoarsely. "Has Orcades perhaps managed to dredge up another Yengi needing slaying?" He gave a harsh laugh and held up the stump of his left arm. "No able-bodied Beastslayer here, as you can well see. You'll have to search elsewhere this time."

"The King does not need another Beastslayer, and even if he did, he would not find help again from me." Karin leaned down to climb into the pen. "I came because you asked me to, as I promised I would."

As she approached, Thorn rose and hastily brushed off the dirt from his leathern breeches. Though the day was cool, he wore no tunic and he followed Karin's gaze as it snared on his scarred stump. "It doesn't look any better after eight months, does it? The wound healed well, thanks to your skills, but it's still ugly. Any way you look at it, I'm deformed."

Karin jerked her gaze back to his. "And I should find you disgusting because of it. Is that what you

435

mean to imply, Thorn? That I am incapable of loving a man because he lacks part of an arm?"

He shrugged, the expression in his eyes flat and unreadable. "You didn't hasten to follow me through the Gate. I'm no fool, Karin. Your action, or should I say, lack of it, told me all I needed to know."

"My mother lived for eight months." She stepped up to stand before him. "I told you I would come when she died. I am here now. I love and want you still. There is nothing more I can say or do to convince you of that. Nothing, save this."

Before he could respond, Karin took Thorn's face and pulled it down to hers. She kissed him, full and long and passionately until, with a low groan, Thorn wrapped his good arm about her and jerked her to him. For a moment slowed in time they stood there, clinging to each other, content just to be together.

Then Karin's hands slid down to rest upon his smooth, strong, sun-bronzed chest. She pushed back to stare up at him. "The Gate is closed. I can never return to Orcades."

"As well it should be," Thorn growled, his face clouding with bitter memories. "It's past time the Orcadians stop using Voltarans to do their dirty work, whether the pay was good or not."

"Yes," Karin murmured, smiling shyly and still a bit uncertainly up at him. "There be far more pleasurable tasks that Voltarans can be put to use for. And I have something particularly pleasurable in mind for a particular Voltaran, if he still wants me."

"Oh, I want you all right, little one." He stared down at Karin, searching her face for confirmation of what he imagined he heard in her words. The love he saw shining there took his breath away. "I've never stopped wanting or loving you, even when I lost all hope of ever seeing you again."

"And that hope, that love, called me at last through the Gate."

Thorn grinned, and the heart-stopping beauty it added to his features took Karin's breath away. There was no need for further words anyway. She flung her arms about his neck and kissed him again. She had found her happiness, her destiny. It was all she would ever need.

As if to add its own particular emphasis to their moment of joy, the damas calf ambled back over, butted Thorn in the leg, and squalled for its milk.

Dear Reader:

Enchanted Crossings is an eclectic anthology, both from the standpoint of combining a contemporary romance ghost story with two novella-length futuristic romances and in the wide diversity of style and plot line between its futuristic romances. For those of you who already read futuristic romance, I think you'll find the shorter length a fun change of pace. And, for those of you just venturing into your first love stories set in some distant future galaxy, I can't think of two more creative approaches than those that lie between the covers of this book. But that's what makes futuristic romance such an exciting and rapidly growing romance subgenre. The sky, so to speak, is the limit. The creative freedom, the wondrous wealth of stories and conflicts, the promise of love still to be found far out in the vast reaches of space, have only begun to be touched. There's so much more to come. . . .

If you'd like a personal letter and excerpted flyer of my next book, please write me at P.O. Box 62365, Colorado Springs, CO 80962. Be sure to enclose a legal-sized self-addressed, stamped envelope. I'd love to hear what you thought of "The Last Gatekeeper." For those of you interested in my backlist, the following books can be ordered either through your bookstore or directly from Leisure Books: *The Knowing Crystal, Heart's Lair, Crystal Fire* (all futuristic romances/Leisure), *Child Of The Mist* (historical romance/Leisure), *Firestar* (futuristic romance/Lovespell), and *Demon Prince* (fantasy romance/Love Spell). Meanwhile, happy reading!

Kathleen Morgan

TIMESWEPT ROMANCE
TIME REMEMBERED
Elizabeth Crane
Bestselling Author of *Reflections in Time*

A voodoo doll and an ancient spell whisk thoroughly modern Jody Farnell from a decaying antebellum mansion to the Old South and a true Southern gentleman who shows her the magic of love.

_0-505-51904-6 $4.99 US/$5.99 CAN

FUTURISTIC ROMANCE
A DISTANT STAR
Anne Avery

Jerrel is enchanted by the courageous messenger who saves his life. But he cannot permit anyone to turn him from the mission that has brought him to the distant world—not even the proud and passionate woman who offers him a love capable of bridging the stars.

_0-505-51905-4 $4.99 US/$5.99 CAN

Futuristic Romance

Love in Another Time, Another Place...

Heart's Lair

KATHLEEN MORGAN

Although Karic is the finest male specimen Liane has ever seen, her job is not to admire his nude body, but to discover the lair where his rebellious followers hide. Never does Liane imagine that when the Cat Man escapes he will take her as his hostage—or that she will fulfill her wildest desires in his arms.

_3549-9 $4.50 US/$5.50 CAN

FUTURISTIC ROMANCE
FIRESTAR
Kathleen Morgan
Bestselling Author of *The Knowing Crystal*

From the moment Meriel lays eyes on the virile slave chosen to breed with her, the heir to the Tenuan throne is loath to perform her imperial duty and produce a child. Yet despite her resolve, Meriel soon succumbs to Gage Bardwin—the one man who can save her planet.

_0-505-51908-9 $4.99 US/$5.99 CAN

TIMESWEPT ROMANCE
ALL THE TIME WE NEED
Megan Daniel

Nearly drowned after trying to save a client, musical agent Charli Stewart wakes up in New Orleans's finest brothel—run by the mother of the city's most virile man—on the eve of the Civil War. Unsure if she'll ever return to her own era, Charli gambles her heart on a love that might end as quickly as it began.

_0-505-51909-7 $4.99 US/$5.99 CAN

Futuristic Romance

Love in another time, another place.

CIRCLE OF LIGHT

NANCY CANE

"Nancy Cane sparks your imagination and melts your heart!"
—Marilyn Campbell, author of *Stardust Dreams*

Attorney Sarina Bretton deals with hard, cold facts, not fantasies of faraway planets and spaceships. Then a daring stranger whisks her to worlds—and desires—she's never imagined possible. Despite her yearning to boldly explore new realms with Teir Reylock, destiny appears to decree that Sarina shall fulfill an ancient prophecy in the arms of another man. Besieged by enemies, and bedeviled by her love for Teir, Sarina vows that before a vapor cannon puts her asunder she will surrender to the seasoned warrior and his promise of throbbing ecstasy.

_51949-6 $4.99 US/$5.99 CAN

$\mathcal{F}uturistic\ Romance$

Love in another time, another place.

New York Times Bestselling Author
Phoebe Conn writing as Cinnamon Burke!

Lady Rogue. Sent to infiltrate Spider Diamond's pirate operation, Drew Jordan finds himself in an impossible situation. Handpicked by Spider as a suitable "pet" for his daughter, Drew has to win Ivory Diamond's love or lose his life. But once he's initiated Ivory into the delights of lovemaking, he knows he can never turn her over to the authorities. For he has found a vulnerable woman's heart within the formidable lady rogue.

_3558-8 $5.99 US/$6.99 CAN

Rapture's Mist. Dedicated to preserving the old ways, Tynan Thorn has led the austere life of a recluse. He has never even laid eyes on a woman until the ravishing Amara sweeps into his bedroom to change his life forever. Daring and uninhabited, Amara sets out to broaden Tynan's viewpoint, but she never expects that the area he will be most interested in exploring is her own sensitive body. As their bodies unite in explosive ecstasy, Tynan and Amara discover a whole new world, where together they can soar among the stars.

_3470-0 $5.99 US/$6.99 CAN

LEISURE BOOKS
ATTN: Order Department
276 5th Avenue, New York, NY 10001

Please add $1.50 for shipping and handling for the first book and $.35 for each book thereafter. PA., N.Y.S. and N.Y.C. residents, please add appropriate sales tax. No cash, stamps, or C.O.D.s. All orders shipped within 6 weeks via postal service book rate. Canadian orders require $2.00 extra postage and must be paid in U.S. dollars through a U.S. banking facility.

Name_____

Address_____

City _____ State_____Zip_____

I have enclosed $_____in payment for the checked book(s).
Payment <u>must</u> accompany all orders.☐ Please send a free catalog.

TIMESWEPT ROMANCE
A TIME TO LOVE AGAIN
Flora Speer
Bestselling Author of *Viking Passion*

While updating her computer files, India Baldwin accidentally backdates herself to the time of Charlemagne—and into the arms of a rugged warrior. Although there is no way a modern-day career woman can adjust to life in the barbaric eighth century, a passionate night of Theuderic's masterful caresses leaves India wondering if she'll ever want to return to the twentieth century.

_0-505-51900-3 $4.99 US/$5.99 CAN

FUTURISTIC ROMANCE
HEART OF THE WOLF
Saranne Dawson
Bestselling Author of *The Enchanted Land*

Long has Jocelyn heard of Daken's people and their magical power to assume the shape of wolves. If the legends prove true, the Kassid will be all the help the young princess needs to preserve her empire—unless Daken has designs on her kingdom as well as her love.

_0-505-51901-1 $4.99 US/$5.99 CAN

A Vampire Romance In The Immortal Tradition Of *Interview with the Vampire*.

For years, Cailie has been haunted by strange, recurring visions of fierce desire and an enigmatic lover who excites her like no other. Obsessed with the overpowering passion of her fantasies, she will do anything, go anywhere to make them real—before it is too late.

Mysterious, romantic, and sophisticated, Tresand is the man of Cailie's dreams. Yet behind the stranger's cultured facade lurk dark secrets that threaten Cailie even as he seduces her very soul.

__3593-6 $4.50 US/$5.50 CAN